AFRICAN BALL

AFRICAN BALL

HARRY PETERSON

Order this book online at www.trafford.com
or email orders@trafford.com

Most Trafford titles are also available at major online book retailers.

Printed in Victoria, BC, Canada.

ISBN: 978-1-4269-2475-0 (sc)
ISBN: 978-1-4269-2476-7 (dj)

Library of Congress Control Number: 2010900407

*Our mission is to efficiently provide the world's finest, most comprehensive
book publishing service, enabling every author to experience success.
To find out how to publish your book, your way, and have it available
worldwide, visit us online at www.trafford.com*

Trafford rev. 04/12/2010

 www.trafford.com

North America & international
toll-free: 1 888 232 4444 (USA & Canada)
phone: 250 383 6864 ♦ fax: 812 355 4082 ♦ email: info@trafford.com

To Samantha, who read the half-finished work and said she could not put it down.

I could tell the clinic, 'Remove the pain, but leave the swelling'.

Chapter 1

The morning sun shone weakly through the darkly tinted double-glazing. Phil Jones Junior, a special investigator for the FBI, stared at his computer screen. He was part of a new task force, which had been formed after the Nine-Eleven attacks on the Trade Centre.

The function of the department, which occupied one complete floor of the building, was to search for possible terrorist funds hidden within the American financial structure. His particular field of expertises was company investment. Stocks and shares. The people with prior knowledge of the Trade Centre attacks had made a killing on the stock market. Any abnormal trading before and after September eleventh had been quite easy to detect, and the funds had been frozen until each investigation had reached a conclusion. The task allocated to Phil was more difficult. He was searching for any long-term investments where the ownership of such funds was not clear.

The work was tedious, time consuming and boring. When each avenue of computer investigations reached a dead end, the case was handed over to field investigators to continue the paper case. Phil was in a kind of limbo. He started every investigation, but never saw the end results. A fly buzzed frantically in the bottom corner of the window in its quest to escape the building.

Phil shook his head. "There's no way outta here, old buddy."

Job satisfaction was something he had heard about, but never really experienced. After his formal FBI training, he had been allocated to the fact-finding side of the law enforcement agency because of his outstanding computer ability and his photographic memory. He regarded it as more of a curse. Instead of arresting the bad guys after a shootout, he had ended up with eye strain and haemorrhoids. *Well, someone's got to do it,* he thought to himself as he slowly polished his thick bifocals.

His father, PJ Sr., had worked his way up from being a rooky Negro cop to station commander by shear hard work and guts. Even here in Washington, the old days had been difficult for any ambitious Negro. In a close-knit society like the police force was, there had always been some redneck wise guy to instigate some sort of racist undercurrent. His father's advice had been to keep a low profile, but make yourself indispensable. That way you were guaranteed a steady climb up the ladder without stepping on too many toes. It seemed to be working for him. He was quite highly placed, as computer jockeys go, and also well thought of by John Collins, the head of department.

The main fly in the ointment was his immediate boss, Joe Lozano. An asshole of the first degree, with no real talent for doing anything well. He was the kind of guy who survived by his wits. Unintelligent, but very clever. Lozano was probably one of the longest-serving agents in the whole building who had never managed to reach a senior position.

Phil had instantly disliked him on their first meeting because of his overbearing manner, but had later found out this was merely a smoke screen to hide his inaptitude. Feeling sorry for him, he attempted to make friends, but eventually gave this up as a lost cause. Lozano was completely oblivious to the fact that he was his own worst enemy, and just blindly continued annoying everyone he came into contact with.

Phil reflected on some of the good times before he had been transferred to this sole-destroying place. His proudest moment had been to see his father's smiling face at graduation day. A substantial amount of family savings had been used in Phil's education. After receiving his badge and pistol, he felt ten feet tall. Being six four, he was pretty close to that anyway.

Agent Jones. Just the sound of it made him feel good. Five years later, his official title was now 'Special Agent Jones'. Special, because he had never fired his gun in anger, or special because he was handcuffed to a computer. He couldn't decide which.

Formation of this new section had breathed some interest into him. Like any war situation, it gave everybody a sense of purpose. He wasn't just chasing bad guys now, but enemies of America. Over the last few months, his enthusiasm had turned to disillusion.

He replaced his glasses and noticed Joe Lozano walking in his direction through the open-plan office. Phil had wised up to Lozano. He used information from Phil to make himself look good.

"Anything interesting today?" Lozano enquired.

"Yeah, according to this print out, your wife's having it off with the window cleaner."

Joe's face darkened. "Very funny."

He glanced around and raised his voice. "Why don't you cut the crap and start producing some results?"

Everyone in earshot looked in their direction, then quickly back to their consol. Joe strode away importantly towards his own desk at the other end of the office.

"Asshole," Phil muttered.

He knew if it came to the crunch, Collins would fire Lozano before himself.

Joe reached his desk, sat down and picked up a pencil.

"Godamn Nigger," he whispered.

There was a sharp crack as his pencil snapped in half. One of these days he would fire that upstart's black ass. Collins wouldn't be around forever to protect him.

He thought for a while, then decided to phone his wife. *That window cleaner was around a bit too often for his liking.*

Chapter 2

A third of the way round the world, in central Africa, it was late afternoon. This day was almost like any other at the crushing site. Hot, noisy and dusty.

Most of the noise came from the primary jaw crusher. It broke down blasted rock to a uniform zero, to one hundred and fifty millimetre size. Today there was less noise than normal, because they were crushing overburden for a road foundation. The primary jaw sounded like a heavily-laden steam train pulling smartly up a steep incline. Usually there was the occasional explosive crack of the harder pieces of granite, but not today. Overburden was softer. No good for concrete stone or road chippings, but ideal for the foundation material.

Other sounds joined the chorus of noise. The secondary crusher, although of a completely different principle to a jaw crusher, also sounded like a steam train, but running at top speed. This was accompanied by the heavy, undulating growl of crown and pinion gears meshing at high pressure.

All this noise joined to form a picture in the mind of the expat supervisor, Bill Parker. It was the regular and pleasing sound of good production. To the experienced crusher man's ear, any unusual noise indicated a problem that was starting to materialise. A prompt shut down usually saved the company a lot of time and money. The formula for success was: good maintenance equals good production at low cost.

Unfortunately, not every contractor adopted this way of thinking, resulting in some construction projects making a loss. Bill's predecessor had been a man of this type, and had run the crusher into the ground. Needless to say, men like these moved around from one unsuspecting contract to another. Eventually, their past catches up with them. In the international contracting community, word gets around.

Over the years, Bill had established a good reputation and was quite sought after. Let's face it; crushing stone in the middle of Africa was not everyone's cup of tea. Contracts usually lasted one to four years, depending on the size of the construction project involved. Bill had been doing this kind of work in Africa for the past twenty years, so had purchased a house in Johannesburg as a base of operations. He only returned to England on holiday to visit relatives every two or three years, but made sure it was midsummer. An English winter would be too much of a shock for him now.

His wife had passed away and his children were married and had flown the nest. So for all intents and purposes, he was single again. A fellow expat had once said that the difference between a married contractor and a normal person was that the contractor had dumb kids and broken furniture.

Bill regretted the time he had lost by being away from the family, but his wife had married a contractor. It had been her choice. When the children were young, it had been possible to move the family from one contract to another. At high school age, they had needed a permanent home or they would have fallen into the dumb kid category. That is when had Bill purchased the house in Johannesburg and worked away on single status.

Walking round the plant, but keeping upwind, out of the dust, Bill had noticed—just by the machine's sounds—some adjustments and repairs that needed doing. There was a slight thumping noise from low down in the primary. The drawback spring needed to be tightened. An unusual whirring sound came from the screen. He would instruct the night shift to grease the bearings before starting again. There were a few conveyor rollers squeaking, and one speed reducer was noisy.

Bill made a metal note for these things to be checked during the next morning's maintenance period.

His senses were suddenly bombarded with a hammering from the secondary, which shook the ground. *Bang, bang, bang.* He spun round in time to see the top half of the crusher jumping on its springs. Some un-crushable object had just passed through it. Joseph, the day shift foreman, ran over to the discharge conveyor to remove the object before it could go round the system back into the crusher again.

In the trade, this was called tramp metal, and usually hitch hiked with the stone from the quarry. A large object, like an excavator tooth or the head of a sledge hammer, could cause the crusher to be jammed and the V-belts to burn on the motor pulley. These objects would have to be cut with an oxy-acetylene torch to remove them, unless it was a modern machine, which could be opened hydraulically. This offending object was small enough to pass through without jamming. Probably a drill bit head.

Joseph quickly snatched something off the moving belt and raised his hand, smiling. Bill waved back and gave him a thumbs-up sign, then pointed towards the workshop container.

He was teaching his men not to leave any pieces of metal lying around the site. When they cleaned the area with a loader on Sunday, he wanted to recycle the spillage through the crusher again, into product.

Production and cost. That was the name of the game. The only thing more important was safety. He had spent many hours arguing with the contracts manager about dust suppression and safety boots. Eventually, the boots had been supplied, along with some new hard hats. The dust suppression, he was still pushing for. In the meantime, all the men wore white dusk masks over their mouths and noses. Four men had turned up for work in the morning with no boots. Bill had lost his temper and sent them home again. Bare feet or flip flop type sandals were not acceptable. The boots had either been sold or were highly polished, ready for church on Sunday.

Bill preferred working with Africans. Once they had understood that the expatriate knew what he was doing and was genuinely concerned about their well being, then the expat had gained their respect. After that, they would move Heaven and Earth for their boss. Having grey hair also helped in this regard. In the African culture, it is normal to follow instructions from an older person. Bill pitied some of the young expatriates he had come in contact with. It was extremely difficult for them to control African labour. Sometimes the frustration ended up with harsh words. Most Africans regarded a verbal insult on the same level as being physically attacked, and the situation could easily escalate out of control.

Bill raised his hand and smiled as one of the men waved. Every time he went on 'walk about' round the plant he was greeted with a cheery wave from each of the men. Bill was starting to sweat and his arm was getting tired, so he changed direction and turned towards the workshop containers. He wondered, *does the queen end up with an aching arm and face from all the waving and smiling?*

A hundred metres upwind from the crusher, there were three six-metre containers. One was for tools and lubricants, and the other for storage of spare parts. These two were positioned parallel to each other, with a five-metre gap between them. The third one was the office container, and was placed over the other two like a bridge. This container had a normal door fitted at one end, and windows that faced the crushing plant and stock piles of crushed material. The most important additions were the insulated walls and an air conditioner that managed to keep the inside temperature at a steady twenty-five degrees Celsius. On hot days, the office attracted Bill like a magnet. Underneath, in the shade of the office, was the workshop area, complete with steel table and vice.

Joseph was standing at the table with a puzzled expression on his face. Bill neared the containers and called out, "What went through the crusher this time?"

"I do not know, Mr. Bill. I do not know what this is."

Bill arrived in the shade. "What do you mean you don't know what is it? Show me."

Joseph's gloved hand held up a silver ball about the size of a small tomato. Bill had been expecting to see a broken drill bit, so was very surprised to see a silver ball.

"What the hell is that?" he demanded.

"I do not know, sir. I do not know what…."

"Okay, okay," Bill cut him off sharply. "Put it in my lunch bag up in the office. I may have to take it to the main workshop to see if they know what it is. I'm going to check in the quarry. It could be from the excavator."

Bill was on edge. This ball could indicate the start of a major break down. Things don't just turn up in the stone from the quarry by themselves. They either fall off the machines or are left there by some idiot.

He strode over to his 4x4, parked under the one and only tree on site, and climbed in. Inside the cab, the heat was stifling, so he left the door open and started the engine. It would take about half a minute before the air conditioner started cooling down the interior.

Closing the door, he drove off towards the quarry, which was about a kilometre away, on the river bank. The dump trucks were still arriving regularly, fully loaded with blasted rock, so everything was still working down there. He hoped the rainy season would start soon. At least the dust problem would be solved and there would be a reasonable temperature drop. The only new problem would be the humidity and, of course, the fucking mosquitoes. They still managed to kill about one million people a year in Africa. The first world countries did not care. It didn't affect them. They were more interested in the price of beer and the football results than worrying about Africa. Bill couldn't really blame them. Half of them didn't know what the hell was going on in the rest of the world anyway.

*   *   *

The normal life cycle in Bill's home town involved getting some girl pregnant, having a shotgun wedding, and then moving into a house one street away from the girl's mother. You clocked in and out of the same factory door for the next forty years, and sat at the same table in the local pub—presuming your wife would let you go out. They, the wives, would spend most of their lives gossiping over the garden fence or nagging at their husbands. After a few years, they didn't care if the husbands ducked out to the pub or not. No other woman in their right mind could ever fancy a man like hers, and besides, she could sit all night in front of the television in full control of the channel selection. The gossiping would eventually progress into house calls. All the women in the same street, or surrounding streets, would take turns visiting each other. A new story or bit of information would spread like wildfire and end up nothing like the original. Bill discovered there was a third stage to this process, called talking but not listening. One day, as a teenager, he had sat at the same table where his mother and the women from across street were having a two-hour session. Normally, he would have left the room and found something to do out of earshot, but he had been curious to see what these women found so exciting.

Step one was to make a pot of tea and generally discuss the weather. This was a warming up period.

Step two involved one of them taking a deep breath and embarking into the latest scandal. When she had eventually paused, breathless, to take a sip of tea, the field was wide open for the next one to start. This continued for some time before Bill realised that each one was talking about something completely different from the other. In a state of shock, he left the room, utterly mystified. Communication between these two persons was zero. The voices in the other room rose in volume. Bill was able to hear them both speaking at the same time. This must be step four.

Step five could only be the 'loony bin,' as far as he was concerned.

He sat down in the parlour and scanned the front page of the Sunday paper. He presumed the reason they made these newspapers so small was so that you didn't bang your knuckles on the shithouse walls when you opened them. There had been a huge picture of a half-dressed woman splashed across the front page.

The headlines had read: **Boss Tries to Seduce Secretary.**

Good grief, he didn't even get to fuck her and he made the headlines.

The voices droned on through the wall. At that point in time, Bill made a decision. He would finish his apprenticeship, get some experience and then travel the world.

The Bell dump truck roared towards him up the hill, carrying a full load of rock from the quarry. He slowed down and drove on, completely blind for five seconds in its following dust cloud. Bill picked up his radio. "Crusher to workshop, crusher to workshop; come in."

"Workshop receiving," came the crackled reply.

"Send me a water tanker for the quarry road. You can see fuckall, and all this dust will block the air filters."

"We have one under repair. Will send it when it is finished."

Bill cursed. "Okay, as soon as possible. I have been trying to get one since this morning."

Towards the bottom of the hill, he could see the river glinting in the afternoon sun. There was a water tanker busy refilling from the pump stand pipe. Bill pulled up alongside and greeted the driver.

"Spray the road on your way up," he requested.

"Sorry, sir; they tell me to do the road near the office."

Bill knew it was useless to argue and lit a cigarette while watching the river swirl passed the rounded rocks.

He didn't want to spend too much time on the river bank, because there was a certain black fly that bit you and caused you to swell up. Once bitten, twice shy, so they say. It usually took a few days for the swelling to go down. *Maybe I should hang my dick out. I could go to the clinic and tell them to remove the pain, but leave the swelling.*

The driver switched off the diesel water pump and climbed into the truck. Bill waved as the driver pulled away, while the tankers exhaust blew dust up from the road. Undercover from this dust, Bill ran to the back of the truck and opened the valve. Water sprayed out from a horizontal pipe that had a line of small holes in it. The exhaust still kicked the dust up in front of the spray, so the driver unknowingly trundled up the hill wetting one side of the road. Bill grinned in satisfaction. Sometimes you had to help these guys do their job. Some Africans followed orders without any discretion, which could be a bit frustrating at times. *That office road was watered at least twice a day, so fuck them, too. They are all sitting in air conditioned offices shuffling paper.*

One trainee engineer had bothered Bill in the beginning about the increase in drilling and blasting costs. Bill had explained that the extra cost in the quarry was recovered five times over by high crushing production and less wearing parts. The trainee had agreed that the cost per ton of crushed stone had reduced dramatically, but he was still worried about the quarry costs. Some admin idiot had told him to solve the problem. Eventually, Bill had told the embarrassed trainee to fuck off.

The sky was dark and heavy. Something should happen in the next few days. He climbed back into the pick-up and drove towards the excavator, which was working further upstream. While driving the short distance, he visualised all the working parts of the machine. *Possible ball from the turntable. Jesus Christ, I hope not. That would be a major fuck up.*

The excavator was busy scooping up the sandy-coloured, over burden rocks, depositing them in the back of a truck. He signalled the operator to finish loading the truck, and then to stop. Together, they checked the machine, examining the turntable all the way round. Finding nothing wrong, Bill instructed the operator to start loading the next dump truck. For one of the turntable balls to fall out, the housing would have to be broken. Everything looked normal. For Bill, this was a relief, but it did not solve the puzzle. He sat on a nearby rock listening, and watching the fluid movements of the machine and operator working as one.

The trucks don't have any big silver balls, he thought as he lit a local cigarette. *Anyway, all machines are female.* He grinned. Taking a pull on the cigarette, he coughed, spitting amongst the rocks. *With the dust and smoking this shit, I'm busy killing myself.* He absentmindedly scratched his leg and elbow. There were white patches of skin on top of red lumps. Those bloody flies had managed to zap him. He was going to suffer for the next three or four days.

That night, at his park home in the camp, Bill removed his empty water bottle from his lunch bag and out rolled the silver ball.

"Oh, it's you again," he said, picking it up. *Jesus, this thing is light. It's definitely not a ball bearing. No wonder Joseph was puzzled. It's not natural.*

Taking it over to the bedside light, Bill had a good look at it. Not a scratch on it. He stared at his own distorted reflection in the polished surface.

The usual piece of metal that makes the secondary jump ends up distorted and flat. This thing is perfect. The same weight as aluminium or it's hollow. Joseph must have picked this up somewhere else. It's not possible for this to have passed through the plant. Maybe it's his idea of a joke to mess up the white man's brain.

Placing the ball in the ashtray on the night table, he refilled his water bottle and put it in the fridge. Bill undressed, throwing his clothes into the wash basket, then turned on the shower. The hot water made the insect bites burn. Sometimes he would come home to find no water, and had to try to sleep without washing the days' dust from his body.

It was a regular occurrence in the local town to suffer from no water and power cuts. The camp was more reliable, with its own generator and water storage tank. No water was more of an inconvenience than no power. Without water, you could not drink, cook, wash or shit. When the rains started, the power in the town would be a real problem and the sewerage system would overflow. At least the camp had its own septic tanks and soak away. He sat naked on the bed and pulled his portable radio out of its charger.

"Ammed, Ammed, crushing plant, come in."

The Egyptian night shift foreman eventually answered, telling Bill the screen had been greased and the plant was running. Bill could hear the noise of the plant in the background.

"Good. I will see you in the morning."

He switched off and replaced the radio in the charger. Exhaling a sigh of relief, he swung his legs up onto the bed and lay back, switching off the light. There was semi-darkness in the room because of the camp flood lights filtering through the curtained windows. Listening to the steady hum of the air con and the distant growl of the generator, Bill told himself, *I need two more years. Just two more years, then I can retire. At fifty, I am too old for this shit. Seven days a week of noise and dust. Battling against the environment. Lack of spare parts, which are coming but never seem to arrive.*

Sometimes you get a project manager that is a genius on paper, but an imbecile in practice. This hydroelectric project should be finished in two year's time. One thing about this Italian company is that they are very good at building dams.

At least I am saving most of my salary now. There is only me left.

Bill turned over onto his side. The ball in the ashtray seemed to have a slight glow radiating from its surface. He picked it up, thinking about his past mistakes. The things he should have said and done when his wife was alive. Bill felt a tingling sensation as he held the cool, smooth surface, which was somehow soothing. He relaxed into a deep, peaceful sleep.

Chapter 3

Phil was pleased to enter the glass doors of the building, which slid closed behind him, shutting out the cold wind. The white folk standing in queues, waiting to pass the security checks, all had red noses and ears. *How the heck can they call us black people coloured?*

He smiled back at a blue-eyed, blond girl. She worked on the same floor. Something to do with records. A hot cup of coffee would sure hit the spot this morning. Even the crap from the machine would taste good.

Five minutes later, he sat at his desk waiting for his hands to warm up. Lozano's system of working back from Nine Eleven was soul destroying. If he did not know any better, he could swear Lozano was slowing everything down on purpose. He wouldn't be in for another half an hour, so Phil decided to try something different. He rubbed his hands together and flexed them before typing rapidly on the keyboard. The best way of disguising the identity of share ownership would be to register in someone else's name. To do this legally without any risk, one would have to have an iron-clad agreement drafted by a lawyer, stating who the actual owner was.

Phil's theory was that if you used a lawyer to organise this, then why not use the same firm of attorneys as the front to register? He had asked the computer to list all share holdings in America registered under law firms. Screens and screens of information flashed by on the consol.

"Shit!" *Another needle in the haystack.*

He would have to narrow the field down somehow. The obvious way would be to use Lozano's method of working back

14

from Nine Eleven, but he was darned if he was going to do that. *Okay, let's hook into the firm that has the most registrations.*

He typed in the instruction and activated the search.

There were no people around the coffee machine, so now was a good time to grab a cup. He pushed himself away from the desk and stood, stretching, nearly touching the ceiling.

Phil was an introvert and didn't mix with people very well. The other kids at school used to make fun of him because of his obsession about polishing his glasses. He did it without thinking, especially when he was nervous.

Lozano hadn't arrived yet. *He's probably sitting in his car waiting for the window cleaner to come around.*

The machine peed the coffee into a plastic cup. Phil used a double cup so as not to burn his fingers, and carefully carried it back to his desk.

Okay, let's see if old Sheila has got the job done.

He placed the coffee on the work top and wheeled himself back in front of the consol. The name at the top of the screen was: Birkett and Sanderson.

Phil sipped his coffee. *Never heard of them.*

There were about thirty company names below, with the percentage of share holding. Two percent; four percent—nothing above five percent. Phil ran his gaze over the company names and choked on the coffee in his mouth. *These are not companies. They are corporations. Who the heck are Birkett and Sanderson?*

He wiped the coffee from his chin with a serviette, then absentmindedly polished his glasses. Replacing them, he saw a blurred screen. It took him a second to realise his glasses were smeared with coffee. He pressed a few more keys and moved the mouse. *Total stock value.*

Phil was not used to so many digits, so he had to count from left to right. He whistled; seven thousand million. *Okay, need this on paper.*

A printout emerged from the printer. *Now, who the heck are these mothers?*

Search Birkett and Sanderson. Eighth avenue, Chicago. Founded eighteen ninety-two as Birkett, and then son. Sanderson came along later and must have joined the son. No; much later. He must have joined the son of the son. Family business with one partner who had joined in nineteen seventy-four. Their annual dividends must run into millions.

Phil thought for a while. *I wonder what the IRS has to say about these guys.* He started typing again.

Joe Lozano came in, removed some papers from his briefcase, then left the office. Phil watched him over the top of his glasses. *Must be on his way to John Collins to do some ass creeping.* Surprisingly, the IRS had no complaints. Burkett and Sanderson were paying quite a hefty amount in tax every year. *I wonder what happens to the rest of the dividend.*

Phil decided to phone Lozano. He didn't have authority to access company bank accounts without written permission, and he couldn't bypass Lozano and go directly to Collins. Lozano would squash Phil's line of enquiry if he didn't follow procedure. Phoning him while he was in Collins office could mean Collins would get in on the act.

Phil picked up the phone and dialled Lozano's mobile. Joe had spread a lot of papers out on top of John Collins' desk and was trying to explain the function of his new work schedule. Collins looked unimpressed. He couldn't see any advantages of this system over the old one, and even for him it seemed very confusing. Joe's phone interrupted him while he was trying to prove how brilliant his new system was.

"Lozano," he barked. "Oh, hello PJ," he managed to say in a controlled voice. He raised his eyes to the ceiling for effect.

"No, it's not possible to see you now. I am in a meeting with the departmental head. Urgent? Well it will have to wait until I am finished here with Mr. Collins. If I regarded everything as urgent, I wouldn't complete my own work programme, now would I?"

John Collins wore a tired expression. "Give me the phone," he commanded, holding out his hand. "Phil's properly got a handle on something."

Collins had an abrupt but straight forward manner, and impatiently moved his hand up and down, waiting for the phone. Joe's bubble had burst. His self-important speech to Phil had backfired.

"Hold on for Mr. Collins," he managed to croak.

"Hi Phil, give me what you got… Hmm, a big value share holding controlled by one attorney in Chicago. Yes, could be something; bring your figures to my office now."

Collins handed the phone back to Joe. "Don't underestimate Phil; he is a good man. He wouldn't have called you unless it was urgent."

Joe looked physically smaller in his chair, as if he had shrunk. He cleared his throat. "This is probably going to turn out to be a wild goose chase. The share holders are normally legitimate in these cases."

Collins looked at him sharply. "Yes, but our function is to check them out, right."

"Yes, sir." Joe started to fiddle with his pen.

There was a knock on the door and Phil entered with some papers. Collins scooped up all Joe's papers and pushed them to one side.

"Okay let's see what's cooking."

Phil laid the print outs down in front of Collins. Joe thought it was time he took over the situation. After all, he was PJ's boss.

"So, what is the value of these shares controlled by this law firm?" he asked.

"It looks like about seven and a half," Phil answered.

Joe gestured with one hand. "That is not so big. It's certainly not what I would call urgent."

Collins grunted. "They took out the Trade Centre with peanuts."

Phil interrupted, "I am not talking millions here."

Joe looked puzzled. He was thinking thousands.

Collins stared at Phil. "Holy Mother of Mary. You mean to tell me one attorney is controlling seven-and-a-half billion dollars of stock and we didn't even know about it?" He switched his stony gaze to Lozano.

Joe's pen slipped out of his fingers and rattled onto the desk.

Phil intervened. "It's all very small holdings in huge corporations. Draws less attention that way. Not so easy to hook onto."

"All the more reason to suspect things are not kosher with this bunch of shysters. Their clients could be a whole army of Arabs for all we know."

Joe was busy going through Phil's print outs. His lips slowly curled into a smile. "Mr. Jones, I see you have not been following our procedure."

"What do you mean?" demanded Collins.

"Jones has completely ignored one crucial fact. Our whole system is to work our way back from Nine Eleven by using the purchasing dates of stock. The last date for buying original stock here, was twenty years ago in a computer company. Everything else, after buying original stock, has been reinvestment of dividends. Ninety percent of this stock was purchased a hundred years ago."

Joe clasped his hands in front of him and smiled broadly at Phil. "We are searching for funds belonging to the people who had a hand in destroying the Trade Centre, not for someone who may have sunk the Titanic or blown up the Hindenburg."

Collins picked up the printouts and carefully examined each one. "There is a pattern here," he exclaimed. "Some of these corporations have changed their names over the years. If you match their original names with the first buying of stock."

He picked up Joe's pen and listed all the original names with the initial buying dates, then threw the list over to Lozano. "What does that tell yeh, Joe?"

Lozano glanced down the list. "All this tells me is that we are wasting our time."

"And you, Phil, take a peek at that and tell me what you see. I hope your knowledge of company history is one up on Joe's."

Lozano scowled as he reluctantly handed the list to Phil, who stared at it, not seeing any sort of sequence. "Its just names and dates," he said.

"Exactly, names and dates. Presume these names and dates were on gravestones. There would be one date missing."

Phil's eyes widened. "Holy shit, now I see. The date of death is missing. All these dates are when these companies started. When they were born," he added.

Collins smiled. "Yup, quite a coincidence, I reckon."

He rubbed his chin while making a decision. "Okay, Phil, you started this so you can finish it. Get your ass on the next flight to Chicago." He checked his watch. "Take the rest of the day off and catch the nine o' clock in the morning. Be at the airport at eight and collect your ticket from the desk. Joe will organise everything."

He switched his attention to Lozano. "Have him met by the local police, who are to assist him while he's there and book him into a good hotel."

Collins stood and shook Phil's hand. "Okay, go to it, Phil; about time you got out the office for a change. Kick some butt and don't take any crap. Keep me informed. This is gonna be interesting, if nothing else."

*   *   *

Thousands of miles away, an old man stirred in his sleep, then suddenly awoke.

Something had happened. The premonition was strong. There had been an occurrence that could not be reversed.

He could feel it. The beginning of the end had finally started.

Chapter 4

Mornings were Bill's worst times. The alarm clock would start beeping at a quarter to six. Then he would immediately switch it off and lay there until the last minute, before forcing himself out of bed at ten past six. This morning he only lay for about five minutes, with the silver ball in one hand and his own two balls in the other. He swung himself out of bed and placed the silver ball in the bedside cabinet draw.

During a quick shower to freshen up, Bill noticed something strange. The insect bites were gone. There was no trace of them. After dressing in his working shorts, shirt, ankle socks and boots, he drove round to the canteen for his usual bowl of cornflakes.

In the beginning, the other expatriates had stared at him for going to work in shorts. The normal working dress for Italians was a chequered shirt and jeans. If you worked in an office, then you wore a white shirt. The younger Italians only wore shorts in their leisure hours. They displayed their white legs in the evening and were normally feasted upon by the mosquitoes. That was the time Bill wore his jeans.

Malaria was a serious problem in this part of the world. It was usual to have ten percent of the labour force out of action due to the activities of this parasite.

The old school Italian sitting at the next table smoked a minimum of sixty Rothman a day, and was about to light up his first cigarette. The idle chatter of half a dozen foreign nationals gradually faded as everyone turned to watch the performance about to unfold.

He stuck the cigarette in his mouth, lit it and took his first puff. Quickly taking the cigarette from his mouth, his face contorted into an agonised mask with bulging eyes. Then the coughing started to reach a point where he was unable to breathe. If he could pass this point without falling off the chair, the fit of coughing would recede, enabling him to finish the cigarette without too much of a problem.

The smokers in the room stubbed their cigarettes out with worried expressions, and finished their coffee. Bill finished his cornflakes and walked outside, taking deep breathes in the cool morning air. Today he was feeling quite fit. *Must have had a good night's sleep for a change.*

Driving to the crushing site along the dirt road from the camp, the doors ratted and jumped in their frames. This was due to the corrugations in the road's surface, which are formed by vehicles accelerating. When the road reached the stage of trying to dismantle your car, the grader was overdue to smooth out the surface again. Because the tyres were only making contact with the tops of the bumps, it felt like driving on ice when cornering.

He approached a group of school children in the distance. Children in Africa had a habit of darting across the road when you least expected it. He slowed down and tooted his horn, trying to reduce the amount of dust he was kicking up behind him. Children were normally dressed in rags and cast-offs, but for school they were turned out as smartly as possible. Some of the blue uniforms were faded and mended, and many did not fit properly, but all were clean. As he passed, the younger ones jumped up and down, pointing and crying, "Mzungu, Mzungu." *White man, white man.*

Bill always gave them a smile and cheery wave, and laughed when the smallest beamed back at him gleefully.

"Mzungu, Mzungu," they cried in delight.

This had become a morning ritual for him and the children. It made him think of the lost time with his own family. He wondered what future was in store for these happy African children.

"Mzungu, Mzungu." The cry faded in the distance.

At the plant, Bill waved at the gate guard and parked under the tree. Ammed's battered pick-up was standing near the office steps ready for a quick getaway after his long, twelve-hour shift. They had the usual cigarette together in the office as they discussed the night's production and problems. There were some small repairs to do, and the servicing, before being able to start-up at 9 am.

After Ammed had gone, Bill glanced through the night shift report book again, and smiled to himself at the Egyptian's English. He had written 'fun belt' instead of 'fan belt'. *Sounds highly erotic*, thought Bill. *Still, must be bloody difficult for the poor little bugger. Their normal writing is a bunch of scribble going from right to left. Strange how every Englishman thinks that everybody else should be able to speak, read and write English perfectly. Any other language is foreign, old chap. Must be a left-over impression from the empire days.*

After the plant was started and was running smoothly, Bill called Joseph to one side. "Now tell me truthfully, Joseph, where did you get that silver ball yesterday?"

He looked at Bill, not understanding his line of questioning. "I picked it from C6, the return belt from secondary."

Bill narrowed his eyes and set his jaw. "But that is not possible. It is not damaged."

Joseph frowned. His boss did not believe him. "But, sir, it still had some stone on it that I knocked off at the workbench."

"Show me," said Bill quietly. He could feel one of his headaches coming on.

From under the steel table, Joseph picked up a piece of yellow stone and gave it to Bill. The one side had a smooth indentation where it had once joined the ball. Bill stared at the stone for sometime before realising the implications. "Jesus Christ, I don't believe this."

His headache flared. Joseph shrugged, seeing Bill had no more questions, and went back to his duties. Bill was actually speechless and just stared at the stone.

Yes, if everyone around panics while you stay cool and calm, may be you don't understand the situation.

"Joseph," he called. "Are you sure about this?"

Joseph turned with a hurt expression on his face. "Yes, sir, I picked it from C6."

Bill felt the indentation with his finger. It was as smooth as glass. Sweat ran down the side of his face.

He called to Joseph again, "If anybody wants me, I will be at the lab."

"Okay, sir," Joseph replied, still pondering what all the fuss was about. After all, the ball had not broken anything.

It was a very thoughtful man who drove to the camp laboratory. After a near collision with a truck, he forced himself to concentrate on his driving.

*   *   *

Roberto Dimodica smiled as Bill entered his office at the prefabricated laboratory. The young geologist and Bill worked together well and had struck up quiet a friendship.

"You are too early; we have not finished this morning's sample; no result yet."

Bill sat in front of the air conditioner and removed his cap, running his fingers through his short grey hair. The palm of his hand came away wet with sweat.

Roberto pushed himself away from the computer with his long legs, and swung round in his chair to study the older man. "You do not look so good today. I think you need a coffee and a Chesterfield."

He stuck one in his own mouth and offered the pack to Bill, who took one without thinking.

"Two coffees," Roberto bellowed through the open door. "What seems to be the problem? You are a looking broken."

Bill lit his cigarette and blew out a plume of smoke. He was deciding whether he should tell Roberto about the ball or just keep quiet. "What do you make of this?" he asked as he placed the piece of stone on Roberto's desk.

Roberto picked it up and rotated it round and round with his long fingers. He peered at it through narrowed eyes and examined the indentation on one side. "This looks like what you are crushing now. It is from the quarry, between the quarry and the river. I tested this stone last week. It is good for sub base. I told you before it is good. What is the problem?"

Bill cleared his throat. "The problem, my friend, is this." He pointed at the indentation. Roberto ran his finger over the smooth cavity.

"Yes, I was wondering about this. How did you make it so smooth?"

Bill passed his hand through his hair again and rubbed one eyebrow with his fingers. "Now why would I spend my time making hollows in lumps of stone?"

Roberto gestured with his hands. "I do not know. I thought you like to make a small ashtray."

A lab assistant entered with two tiny cups of black coffee.

"*Gratzie.*" Roberto smiled and handed Bill a cup.

Bill found the Italian coffee too strong, but would not say so. Roberto was very proud of anything Italian, and waited for Bill's reaction after taking a sip. Bill forced a smile and nodded, thinking that he probably wouldn't sleep that night. *This stuff could resurrect a dead elephant.*

Roberto drank his coffee quickly and sighed with pleasure.

"I think what you need, Bill, is to come with Sara and I to the gas station tomorrow night."

The gas station was a bar-come-restaurant in Malenga, the nearest town. Bill nodded his approval. The local beer was first class, but last time he had sat at one of the tables in the forecourt, a chicken had shat on his foot.

"Yes, I think you are right; getting drunk is a good idea."

Roberto picked up the stone again. "So, you did not make this hollow?"

"No, we found it like that."

"Hmmm, sometimes you get round lumps of bog iron in quartzite, but not in this area. I have seen it before in Tanzania. This could have formed over a hard, round pebble from the river."

Bill blew out another plume of smoke. "How long would that have taken?"

"Oh, not long; anything from one-and-a-half to two million years."

Bill placed his head in his hands. "That is what I was afraid of," he groaned.

Roberto was puzzled. "I do not understand the problem."

Bill stood and closed the door, then sat down again. He finished his coffee in one gulp, then looked at Roberto intently. "This stone had a silver ball stuck in it until it went through the crusher."

Roberto's brows knitted together, then a big smile spread across his face. "Vafanculo." He laughed.

"I have the ball in my park home," countered Bill defensively.

Roberto's laughing faltered. "But that would make the ball the same age as the stone. Now stop pulling my pisser, as you English say. It is not the fool of April day."

Bill now understood how Joseph had felt, and his anger rose as Roberto continued laughing.

"I came here to share this problem, not to make it twice as big."

Bill picked up the stone and walked out, slamming the door behind him.

Roberto sat for long time, thinking. The sound of the concrete batching plant nearby did not help his concentration. Trucks full of concrete passed by every five minutes, on their way to the dam wall downstream. Maybe the Englishman was a getting too old. He worked unceasing from early morning to late evening. Was it possible Bill had cracked up? Everybody was under stress in this type of work. What Bill had suggested about the stone and a silver ball was crazy. Some local man had probably given him the wrong information. It happened all the time, especially there at the lab. *I will see him tomorrow night at the gas station. He will have calmed down by then. Better tell my girl, Sara, to bring a friend. He needs a woman to get some of that tension out of him.*

That evening, after work, at seven, Bill arrived at the company bar and drank a couple of stiff whiskies while watching two men play pool. He usually drank beer, but the whisky went down well.

Next stop was the canteen for a plate of food, then to his park home to shower. It was pointless going over to the television room. There was normally a Chinese man there who changed channels every three minutes.

He lay in bed examining the ball, trying to make some sense out of everything. The ball shone back at him in defiance as he rolled it between his fingers. *One-and-a-half to two million years. Joseph must have been mistaken.*

Roberto's laughter echoed in his head. He had made a fool of himself, but would apologise tomorrow night.

Holding the ball made him feel relaxed and content, like he felt after good sex. *I must try that whisky again*, he thought as he drifted off into a deep sleep.

Chapter 5

The two uniforms walked up to the middle-aged detective sergeant at the airport arrival area.

"So who is this guy who is flying in?" one of them enquired.

"Some computer whiz from the FBI. We have the job of nursemaid until he is finished here. Probably doesn't know his ass from his elbow on the street."

"So what is he doing here in Chicago?" the other one asked.

The detective spat the toothpick out of his mouth and replaced it with a new one. "He is part of the anti-terrorist crack down. We have to give him some back-up at this law firm on eighth."

"Strange place to look for terrorists. A downtown law firm," the uniform laughed.

"We are not looking for terrorists, dumb dumb; we are looking for their money. You take away the greenbacks and they are up the creek. Everybody knows that."

The sergeant had had this explained to him half an hour previously, so he was quite an expert on the subject.

"If there are any bags, you two assholes get to carry them. My back is giving me hell and besides, I 'ain't no porter for the goddamn FBI."

Ten minutes later, people started to emerge from the arrival gate, pushing trolleys. A tall Negro walked directly towards the policemen.

"Looks more like the NBA than the FBI," said the detective said through the corner of his mouth. He forced a smile and held out his hand. "Agent Jones, I presume. I am Sergeant Baxter; have a good flight?"

Phil showed his ID and also forced a smile. "This is the first time I have flown. I prefer my feet on the ground."

Phil had a fear of flying, but did not want to admit it. Could be flying was becoming part of the job.

"I see you travel light," remarked Baxter, noting only one overnight bag and a laptop.

"Yep; I have everything I need. Now let's get started, shall we?"

"Okay, you ride with me and we will follow these assholes in their black and white."

The uniforms nodded and led the way to the exit. Baxter walked alongside Phil, with a bored expression on his face. *Still wet behind the ears and as keen as mustard. Probably won't have chance for coffee and doughnuts with this one.*

He checked his watch. *Soon be lunch time.* His stomach rumbled.

*   *   *

It was easy for them to push their way through the traffic by following the police car.

Halfway down Eighth Avenue, they stopped in front of an old office building in a no parking zone. At the entrance, they read the information board, and saw that Birkett and Sanderson were in room 309 on the third floor.

They rode up to the third floor in the elevator, while Baxter whistled an unrecognisable tune.

Entering 309, the receptionist asked if Phil had an appointment. Baxter stepped forward and flashed his badge. "Police; we don't need one."

She looked quite startled, not used to being suddenly confronted by a burly policeman. Phil stepped in front of Baxter and showed his FBI identification. "We would like to see Mr. Birkett or Mr. Sanderson, please."

The detective turned away, shaking his head.

"Mr. Sanderson is out for lunch, and Mr. Birkett is on a call. If you can wait a moment, I will show you in to see Mr. Birkett."

Phil nodded. "Yes, that would be fine."

The two uniforms felt uncomfortable in the plush office, and stared at the pictures on the wall.

"Would you gentlemen like some coffee and cookies?"

Baxter warmed immediately to this suggestion, and removed his overcoat. "Yep, that would be great."

He made himself comfortable on the couch, and waved impatiently for the other two to sit down. The secretary returned with four mugs of coffee and a large plate of biscuits. Phil drank his coffee and nibbled on a biscuit while standing at the reception counter.

"So how are things here for you, working for Birkett and Sanderson?"

She smiled. "This is the best job I have ever had, and Linda says the same."

"Linda?" Phil enquired.

"She is the assistant accountant for Mr. Sanderson. Both partners are real gentlemen."

"So there are only the two of you. Don't you find you're overworked?"

"Oh no, not at all; it's very relaxed here. There is not much to do and we never see the clients."

A green light went out behind the counter.

"He has finished his call. I will tell him you are here."

Phil waved Baxter over to the reception. "I don't think we will need your men; they can stay here until we know a bit more."

"Okay; you're the Boss."

Still chewing, Baxter brushed the crumbs from his tie.

"Something is very wrong here," Phil continued. "This firm is too small to handle a vast amount of money on the stock market."

Baxter raised his eyebrows. "Well, we can't arrest them for that, now can we?"

The secretary returned. "Go right through; it's the second office on the left."

Birkett came out to meet them and shook their hands warmly. Phil estimated him to be in his late sixties.

"This is interesting." Birkett smiled. "We have never been visited by the FBI, or the police, for that matter." His blue eyes twinkled. "Take a seat."

He waved them into his comfortable office. Baxter stared at the oil paintings mounted on the wood-panelled walls.

"Wow, I hope you have got insurance on this lot."

Birkett beamed. "They are not by the old masters, but I find them quite pleasing. We have had them on this wall for the past forty years, but I haven't finished looking at them yet. At my age, it's important to surround yourself by beautiful things. How can I help you gentlemen?"

Phil explained that he was part of a special task force searching for terrorist funds. Due to the large amount of stock controlled by this firm, it had to be checked out.

"How exciting. I was wondering when someone would notice our total stock. If you are interested in our records, Mr. Sanderson would be more helpful than I."

He glanced at the ornate clock on the antique book case and pressed the intercom. "He is very punctual and should be in by now." The old man smiled. "Paul, please come to my office; we have some visitors."

A short, bald man, slightly younger than Birkett, entered the office and Birkett made the introductions. After Phil had explained the reason for his visit, Sanderson nodded. "There is a computer in my assistant's office; we have nothing to hide. Please help yourself, Agent Jones; if you have any questions, don't hesitate to call me."

He showed them through to his secretary's office, and instructed Linda to help Phil with the records before he left. Baxter shook his head. "If these two guys are criminals, then I'm Jack Frost. I'm gonna leave one officer in reception. He will call me when you are through. I will go and do some real police work. See ya later."

He walked out, deciding which doughnut store to visit first.

Phil settled himself in front of the computer and got to work. The computer gave him a sense of security, of being on familiar ground. Two hours later, the ground he was on was far from familiar. He asked Linda to buzz Sanderson.

"Agent Jones would like to see you," She nodded back at him.

Phil entered Sanderson's office armed with a handful of printouts, and sat down in front of his desk.

"Mr. Sanderson, I have never seen any share holding, big or small, handled in such a way before. I have never seen any law firm, big or small, run in the same manner as this one. There is no income from clients; why is that?"

"We don't have any."

"Why is that?"

"We are not allowed to have any."

"Why is that?"

"Because of the instructions and the agreement we have signed with the owners of the shares."

"But the shares are in your name. What's to stop you from running off with them?"

"The agreement states that all stock registered by this firm belongs to them."

"Who are them?"

"I don't know. I have not seen the agreement. I have only seen the standing instructions."

"Who are the instructions from?"

"The stockholders. They tell us what we can and cannot do. It is only signed by us, and not the owners."

"How do you vote at share holders meetings?"

"We vote with the majority."

Phil was starting to feel out of his depth.

"I see the annual dividends have grown over the years into millions of dollars. After tax, you pay ten percent into your account and sixty percent is reinvested into the share holding that generated the dividend. What happens to the other thirty percent?"

"It is paid to the owners."

"How do you pay them if you don't know who they are?"

"It's paid into Swiss Bank account numbers. A different number for each share holding."

Phil thought for a moment. "How do you receive new instructions? You purchased stock in a new company twenty years ago."

"Instructions are sent by the bank with a special code number on them."

Phil removed his glasses and gave them a quick polish. "Who signed the original agreement and instructions?"

"Mr. Birkett's great-grandfather."

"Where are the instructions and the agreement?"

Sanderson shrugged. "In Mr. Birkett's safe, I presume."

Phil stood up. "I need to see Mr. Birkett. I have never heard of a firm dealing with people they don't know. If these people, the owners, are so keen on remaining anonymous, what's to stop you from taking over the share certificates and risking a legal battle? They obviously don't want any publicity."

"We wouldn't do that. We make a good living from the ten percent dividend. Another reason is that we don't have the certificates. After purchase, they were sent to the same Swiss Bank safety deposit. We have no access to them. The only wrong doing we could do is run off with the dividend. Ten percent is ours anyway, and sixty percent is reinvested to make more dividends, so the only loss to us is the thirty percent the owners receive. This is small price to pay considering none of our funds were used on the initial purchase. The other benefit to us is that there is no risk. It's not our money and all the stock ever purchased by the owners always makes a profit. We are riding on the crest of their wave, so to speak."

Phil tugged on the lobe of one ear. "That is quite something. They either have insider information or a crystal ball."

Sanderson looked uncomfortable. "It's strange that you should say that. There is one thing that troubles me."

"And what is that, Mr. Sanderson?"

"Did you notice what happened in the thirties?"

"No, I haven't got that far back yet."

"The owners instructed us to sell everything except a token amount of stock in each company, and then, a year later, to buy everything back again."

"So, what is so special about that?"

Sanderson shifted in his chair. "Surely you know about the stock market crash. Most of the shares became worthless overnight. The owners made a killing when they reinvested. It was as if they knew what would happen."

Phil paused with his hand on the doorknob. "Could have been a lucky guess. Charley Chaplin also sold before the crash. Can you buzz Birkett for me? I need to know who these people are. Thanks for your help. At least I know why this firm is so small."

Phil found Birkett practicing his putting on the thick office carpet. He was tapping golf balls over a six yard length of carpet towards an upturned glass.

"Come in, come in. As you can see, I'm not exactly overworked. I normally go home after Paul returns from lunch. He does most of the work. My head is no good for figures. I stayed on because I was expecting you. I have been expecting someone like you for a long time. Sit down. I suppose you want to ask me some questions."

Phil sat in a leather armchair and stretched his legs in front of him. "Mr. Birkett, I need to know who the owners are of the stock that is in your firm's name. You can prove this to me by showing me the agreement."

Birkett finished putting the last ball and looked sadly at Phil. "I'm afraid I'm going to disappoint you, Agent Jones."

He walked over to the safe and started to dial the combination. "The agreement I have is an unsigned copy. It's just for reference purposes. The signed agreement was taken away and signed by the owners before they purchased the first lot of shares."

Birkett handed Phil a roll of parchment, on which an agreement was written by nibbed pen and ink. The particulars for the share owners were blank.

Phil was speechless for a moment. "But if both signings were not witnessed by a justice of the peace, it would not be legal."

Birkett smiled and shook his head. "Believe me, it was legal and binding. The witnesses are long dead and we don't even know who they were."

Phil slowly removed his glasses and polished them. "Also, the owners must be dead. This is an agreement between dead people."

"No, don't you see. Birkett Attorneys at Law is still alive. Different name, but still alive. Birkett and Sanderson have the same registration number. If the owners were a syndicate, company or family, they will also still be alive. Legally, that is. The only way for you to find out who they are would be to fight with the Zurich National Bank."

Phil replaced his glasses. "Tell me everything you know about these so-called owners."

Birkett replaced the agreement in the safe and seated himself opposite Phil. "When I joined the firm and was still young and curious, I asked my father a lot of questions. Many of which he would not or could not answer. He told me that just after his grandfather opened the business in 1887, he was approached by a man with a bag full of diamonds."

Phil raised his eyebrows. Birkett nodded and rested his hand on Phil's forearm.

"Yes, it's true. This man was very well educated and had already written out the agreement. There was also a list of companies with dates. My great-grandfather was instructed to buy shares in these companies when the date next to the company name became due. The amount of shares was also stipulated. Some of the companies, like the railroad, he was to buy shares immediately with the money from the diamonds. For the others, the man said he would return with more diamonds just before the purchasing dates. They both went to the diamond dealers in the city and eventually turned them all into cash. The shares were purchased and this man took the certificates away with him. My great-grandfather was paid a very handsome fee, with which he purchased these office premises."

Phil leant forward in the armchair. "So what about the agreement?"

"The original agreement was signed by both parties at another lawyer's office, and was also taken away by this man."

"So when did the Swiss Bank get involved in all this?"

Birkett thought for a moment. "It was in the nineteen-twenties. That is when the new instructions were issued, and this man never returned after that."

"So this man kept coming and going for about thirty-five years?"

"That is if it was the same man. According to my father, he saw this man once when he was still a boy in this very office. He says the man he saw was too young to be the same man. The man he saw was about thirty years old."

"Did your father describe this person?"

"He didn't like to talk about him, but he did mention the little finger of his left hand was missing. The strange thing was that both these men had their little fingers missing. That is what my great-grandfather wrote in his journal about the first man."

The eagerness showed on Phil's face. "Show me that journal. I would sure like to read it."

"I'm afraid I'm going to disappoint you again. It used to be in the safe. I read half of it until my father saw me. That is the only time he ever struck me. He said it was the ravings of a madman and threw it into the fire. You see, both my great-grandfather and my grandfather had a history of mental illness that was almost identical. It started late in life and they both raved about the same thing. Something about selling their souls to the Devil. It must have been hereditary. Lucky my father and I didn't share the same fate. My father suffered greatly from insomnia, but he was quite sane and, as you can see, I seem to be alright. There is one thing that doesn't add up. According to the journal, my grandfather says the companies on the list, from which shares were purchased later, did not exist when the list was handed to him."

Birkett smiled, shaking his head. "The story about the list has to be false. Even in our records, the shares were purchased just after the companies were formed. There was no time for a list to be previously made out."

Phil scratched his head. "Well, these stories are very interesting, but not what anybody could call evidence. They are contradictory. Was there anything else that seemed out of place over the years?"

Birkett looked uneasy. "Well, this has probably got nothing to do with anything, but I know it worried my father. During the period when this man used to come and go, or should we say men, there were three or four horrible murders. In that time, the city was full of gangsters and robbers due to an influx of immigrants, so murder was quite common place. The thing that worried my father was that these particular murders happened on the same dates as when some of the shares were first registered."

Phil looked puzzled. "Who were these murder victims?"

Birkett waved a hand. "Oh, just local thugs. The kind of person who would rob you in some dark alley."

"But if murder was pretty common place, what was so special about these murders that caused your father any concern?"

Birkett stood and walked around the office. "It was the nature of these murders that made them stand out. In each case, sometimes years apart, each murder was exactly the same. And, as I said, happened when one of these men was here."

"So what happened to these potential robbers?"

Birkett sat down and looked Phil in the eye. "They were torn to pieces. There were just bits of rags and flesh left in a splash of blood over the walls and sidewalk."

Shivers ran up and down Phil's spine. "Now hold on, you got to be kidding me. This is more like a session of the *Twilight Zone*." Phil stood up, smiling, and collected his papers. "Just tell me one thing before I leave. Were the men who purchased the stock Arabs?"

Birkett smiled and also stood. "I see you are still chasing terrorists, Agent Jones. Do you think they planned to hijack Charles Lindenburg and crash into the Empire State building?"

Phil flushed with embarrassment. "No, but it's more likely than your hobgoblins and monsters. I repeat; were these men Arabs?"

"No." Birkett smiled, looking Phil in the eye. "They were Africans."

"You mean Negros like me?"

"No, I mean they were Africans, like from Africa."

Chapter 6

Bill awoke to find the ball in one hand and a good hard erection in the other. Most men called this occurrence a morning glory or a piss hard. He cancelled the alarm just as it was about to ring, and rolled out of bed.

The first thing to do was to have a pee. These things normally subsided after the bladder was relieved. He tried to push it down, but it only made him stand on tiptoe. Peeing was going to be difficult, unless he could stand on his head and pee downwards. After trying a few contortions at the toilet that resembled a Giraffe's drinking position, he gave up and walked into the shower.

The difference between a gentleman and an ordinary man was that the gentleman got out of the shower to pee. Bill was now doing the opposite. In desperation, he turned off the hot water and had a cold shower. Things started to look a bit more relaxed. *The last resort would have been to lay it on the table and use a tenderising mallet.*

After dressing, he jogged round to the canteen for breakfast, breathing in the fresh morning air.

He lit his first cigarette of the day while talking to Ammed at the crushing plant. It didn't taste so good. *Maybe I'm going through the male menopause; some sort of change.*

One primary jaw liner needed turning. It was worn at the lower end. He called for the crane on the radio and arranged for it to arrive at the crusher in one hour's time.

Bill lit his second cigarette when he saw two large Land Cruisers driving slowly round the stock piles of crushed stone. It was his lordship, the project manager, and his cronies, doing their weekly tour of the site. Why the company spent thirty thousand dollars on cars like that was beyond him. *More of a status symbol than anything else. They always manage to time their visits when the plant is not working.*

The vehicles stopped side by side for a while, and then drove off. Bill flicked his cigarette in the direction of the departing cars.

Maybe they expect me to run over to them with my cap under my arm, smiling and bowing. Sorry, I don't do that sort of thing. If they want to speak to me they will have to step out of their fancy cars and get their shoes dirty.

That evening, Bill drove directly home for a quick shit, shave and shower; ready for the gas station. The change would be nice, but having to go to work every morning put a damper on any night out.

Slipping into a clean shirt and his best jeans, Bill stood in front of the wardrobe mirror. *Not bad at my age. Five foot ten and eighty-five kilograms is a pretty good combination.*

He had seen a lot worse in some of the younger men. Someone had told him grey hair was the fashion now in England. They were calling it steel hair. Bill didn't actually believe this.

He brushed his short, thick, grey hair back from his forehead and checked himself out in the mirror. *Hmm, Harrison Ford? No, Harrison Ford without the money, maybe.*

He put on a more macho expression. *Yes, definitely Harrison Ford.*

It would be cool sitting outside at the gas station. The prevailing wind normally blew from the lake across the town. It could be quite chilly at night. Bill decided to wear his light weight, leather jacket, and then checked his pockets. He had the distinct feeling he had forgotten something. *Money, car key, cigarettes and lighter.*

He walked over to the bedside cabinet and removed the ball from the drawer. It seemed like the natural thing to do, and made him feel more complete. Bill decided to use it like a good luck charm. Why not? He may need some luck while driving in the dark. The local mini bus taxes scared the shit out of him. They usually came at you head on when overtaking or avoiding a pothole in the road. The best course of action was to pull over until they had passed by in a cloud of dust and exhaust smoke. Local trucks were notorious for their malfunctioning or nonexistent auto electrical systems. Sometimes they drove at night with only one head lamp working. It was quite disconcerting to be approached by one light, and then suddenly out of the darkness a huge truck roaring past. Bill called these overloaded trucks 'hundred ton motorcycles'.

The small charcoal trucks were the worst. All of them were a collection of rusty, beat-up lumps of scrap with bags piled up on the back to three times the height of the windowless cabs. They trundled along at walking pace on aeroplane tyres hidden inside their own smokescreen. Four breakdowns to the kilometre was the usual rate of progress. If they pulled into a garage, Bill imagined the driver would say '*Check the fuel, fill up the oil and trim the tyres*'.

Eyes straining ahead, he carefully drove to town with a Don Williams tape playing *Back in my Younger Days*. He had just missed one of the charcoal truck obstructions. Luckily, the driver had cut some branches and placed them on the road behind as a warning, before crawling underneath to sleep. The night sky was overcast and it was another six kilometres to Malenga. Roberto must have been there a good hour already. He finished work at five, not like Bill's seven o'clock finishing time.

The trees and bushes ahead seemed to twist and change into grotesque shapes in the glare of the headlights. *Need my eyes tested.*

He removed the ball from his pocket and placed it inside his shirt next to his skin. For some reason, he liked the feel of it. The road ahead became lighter. *There must be a full moon and the clouds have parted.*

Bill increased his speed. It was nearly light enough to drive with no lights.

*　　　*　　　*

The gas station was situated in the middle of town next to the main road. A better description for the main road would be a collection of potholes. At the end of every rainy season they were filled in, but after the first rain they reappeared bigger and better than before. There had been a heavy shower two weeks ago, so most of the filling had been washed out.

Parking his Hilux, Bill noticed Roberto's Nissan among the dozen or so pick-ups in the car park. The bar owner's old Land Rover was newly-painted in black and white zebra stripes. It stood alongside the bar, which used to be the gas station kiosk-come-shop. Most people sat in what used to be the pump area, at tables under thatched umbrellas. The only things missing were the pumps and their attendants.

Bill walked past the white-tiled Lube Bay, which housed a coin-operated pool table. Music from the sixties blazed out from two large speakers. Otto catered for the expats in every way possible. He had to make hay while the sun shone, before the end of the contract. Without the expats, he would have to drop his prices and revert back to African music to try to attract the local clientele.

On his way towards the bar, Bill caught sight of Roberto waving, seated at one of the tables in the shadows. He had two girls with him and signalled that they were not ready yet for fresh drinks. Bill smiled, remembering a saying from smart asses who had probably never even met an Italian: 'only good for jig a jig and ice cream'. When he had been a young boy on the beach, the summers used to be long and hot. He and his friends had been tanned a golden brown. The local Italian immigrant had a donkey and a two-wheeled cart with a huge tub of ice cream mounted in the centre. That was the most delicious memory of his childhood. *A two penny cornet or a three penny sandwich.*

He had been on that same beach five years ago, and had seen an ice cream van displaying the same logo as the cart used to have.

The ice cream squirted out of a machine and tasted like ice mixed with milk and sugar. *How could today's children know how real ice cream should taste?*

Otto, the fat German bar owner, saw him approaching through the cigarette smoke. "Good evening, Villiam, Velcome. You vaunt the usual?"

"Ja, ja," said Bill sitting on an empty bar stool. "Why the stripes on the Land Rover?"

Otto's bushy blond eyebrows shot up. "For the wisitors," he exclaimed. "They expect that sort of ting when day go game wooing."

Bill was unimpressed. "The only wild game around here is the bunch of hookers you have sitting over there." He nodded towards the back of the room.

"Vell, day are good for business," Otto said, pouring Bill's beer. "The men who come here want a drink and a Voman; it is only normal, ja."

"I suppose so," Bill admitted, sipping his beer.

Otto pointed. "You see that tall von; she will lick your asshole if you tell her to." He grinned with sparkling eyes.

Bill turned to see which one he was talking about. The girl in question smiled back at him.

"Ja, well, it's only normal," Bill replied, giving Otto a strange glance.

He paid for the beer and was propositioned three times by three different girls before he was able to leave the bar. Smiling, he politely refused each one. He had visions of being kissed by one of Otto's asshole lickers.

Eventually, he arrived at Roberto's table, thinking he should have left the beer in the bottle. Some of the hookers were drinking out of glasses. Roberto stood up, grinning foolishly, and swept back a lock of long black hair from his eyes. "Hi, Bill, glad you could make it. This is Monica. Sara's best friend."

Bill smiled and shook hands. "Please to meet you. You are not a friend of Otto's, are you?"

Monica looked puzzled. "Who is Otto?" she asked.

Roberto interrupted, "He is the owner of this bar."

Monica shook her head. "No, this is the first time I have been here."

Bill sat down and exhaled. "Thank God for that."

"What are you speaking about?" demanded Roberto.

"I will explain tomorrow, but rather drink out of the bottles in the meantime."

There was an awkward silence for a moment as Bill realised he had got off on the wrong foot. Roberto came to his rescue and took over the conversation. Bill was uncomfortable in the presence of women, especially meeting them for the first time. He noticed Monica was quite beautiful and must be from the same tribe as Sara. They both had the same facial features and hairstyles. This was obviously pre-arranged match making by Sara and Roberto. Bill was very conscious of the thirty-year difference between his own age and Monica's. He knew African women did not place much importance on age differences, because here they sometimes used the system of prearranged marriages. It was fairly common for an old man to marry a girl of fifteen years.

Bill waved at a waitress and ordered a round of beers, telling her not to bring any glasses.

As the evening progressed, Bill managed to make some small talk with Monica. The beer was making him feel more relaxed. Bill had known Sara ever since he had struck up a friendship with Roberto. She was a sensible, good natured person and it was easy to enjoy her company. He was sure Roberto's initial attraction to her had been purely physical, but the relationship had progressed into permanent companionship. They were at the point of being unofficially engaged, and lived together in Roberto's house. Bill didn't see much future for himself and Monica. He was trying to retire, and a new wife was definitely not on his programme. He wouldn't be able to support another person when retired.

Some people started dancing, and Monica pulled him up from out of his chair over to the open area in front of the speakers. The beer and the music took over. Bill was starting to enjoy himself, and the music was perfect for his age group. Monica looked as if she was having a good time, unless she was putting on an act.

Halfway through the third dance, Bill had the feeling of being watched. Glancing round, he noticed a large African man standing in the shadows near the edge of the pump area. He was not sure if the man was looking in his direction, because of his sunglasses, but from the angle of his head, Bill was quite certain this man was the cause of his discomfort. Only an African would wear sunglasses in a dark place. *It's a wonder he doesn't fall over a chair or something.* They returned to their table and sat down again. Bill leant over to speak to Roberto.

"Don't look now. There is a man standing over near the toilets in that dark area. I think he is checking me out."

Roberto grinned. "Maybe he fancies you."

Bill kicked Roberto's foot. "He is not my type and men stopped fancying me years ago. I'm serious; I can feel something is wrong."

Roberto dropped his cigarette lighter and stooped to pick it up, while glancing in the direction of the toilets.

"I cannot see anything over there. It is in a complete darkness."

Bill raised his eyebrows in frustration. "He is an African dressed in black with dark glasses."

Roberto stared at him. "Katso, how the hell do you want me to see a black man dressed in a black with dark glasses in the blackness over there? Maybe I should wait for him to a smile."

Bill shook his head. "I don't think this man is the smiling type. He looks very antisocial. I can see him quite plainly in the moonlight."

Roberto stared round at the sky. "What moonlight? The sky is full of clouds. Over there is just blackness."

Bill lit a cigarette with a distasteful look on his face. "I think I bought a reject pack of smokes. This tastes like shit." He took a swig of beer from his bottle. "Have you got your keys with you?"

Roberto nodded.

"Your key ring has a small flashlight. Go to the toilet and see if you recognise that man. Take Sara; maybe she knows him."

Roberto stood up and spoke to Sara. "Okay, we will go and look at your invisible man."

He winked and nodded in Monica's direction before walking towards the toilets with Sara. Halfway, Roberto's key ring came to life and flickered to and fro on the ground in front of them. The man in the shadows drew back, but was trapped in the corner with no avenue of escape. His face was illuminated for a second in the beam of light, causing Roberto to stop in surprise. He directed the light back to the ground and continued on his way.

The strong smell of urine was almost overpowering as Roberto entered the toilet. His eyes watering, he held his breath for as long as possible while peeing.

When outside again, Roberto waited for Sara, and only switched the light on when they were making their way back to the table.

"You were right," exclaimed Roberto.

"I have seen him around, but don't know him."

Sara sat down with a grim expression clouding her normally smiling face. "We should leave now. That man is dangerous."

"Who is he?" Bill demanded.

Sara took a gulp of beer and lit one of Roberto's chesterfields with shaking hands. "I do not know him, but I know of him. He works for Nabusano."

"O shit," said Roberto. "She is right; we'd better leave."

"Who is Nabusano?" enquired Bill.

Roberto took the cigarette from Sara and blew out a plume of smoke before answering. "He is the head of the local Mafia. He controls everything here in Malenga, like a Godfather. The locals are a scared stiff of him. That is his crushing plant half a kilometre upstream from yours. He has been working that quarry for years. Finish the drinks and go. We will meet at the pavement restaurant and have some barbeque chicken."

Bill agreed. "That's a good idea. I didn't eat at the canteen, so I'm starving. I will rather risk the screaming shits than sit here being watched. I wonder what he wants."

Roberto shrugged. "You do not know he is watching you. Could be he likes Monica." He raised his eyebrows. "Anyway, Otto has a baseball bat behind the bar."

"Otto's is a tub of lard," Bill retorted. "If he missed with the first swing, that would be the end of it."

They finished their beers and walked into the car park. Bill was waylaid by two African expats from Kenya who wanted to buy him a drink. They were electricians who repaired all the electrical equipment on site. He shook their hands and excused himself.

Roberto and Sara were waiting in the Nissan with the engine running. Bill found Monica squatting between two cars, having a pee, so he climbed into his Toyota and started the engine. She jumped in beside him and they followed Roberto onto the main road.

Driving in the poorer African countries was a completely different concept from driving in a first world country. The object of the exercise was to get from A to B without getting stuck or destroying the vehicle. To do this on a very bad road, one must constantly weave from side to side to avoid the major holes.

Bill's Hilux had an air freshener tied to the rear-view mirror in the shape of a Scott's girl doing the highland jig. When the car was in motion, she was supposed to dance. Bill watched her jerking up and down, turning summersaults. *A trapeze artist would have been more suitable.*

The suspension on his Toyota was very hard. He had toyed with the idea of placing half a ton of sand bags in the back, but had never got round to it. Tomorrow he would remember.

"Ow!" Monica banged her head on the door pillar. He was quite stable due to his grip on the steering wheel, and only bounced up and down as if riding a horse. *Roberto must choose a different route next time. This is no good for the cars or the people in them.*

They left the potholes behind and parked outside a place that looked like a tiny shop. There was no other building in the whole street with lights on. Plastic tables and chairs were grouped on the pavement. The mouth-watering aroma of roasting chicken came from a barbeque positioned in the alley. *A very pleasant change from the gas station's toilet.*

They sat down and ordered a round of chicken and beers.

Roberto breathed deeply. "I am sure Otto is a Nazi."

"Why?" Bill asked.

"He is still running a gas chamber. I nearly died tonight in that a toilet."

"We nearly died following you through those potholes."

"Sorry, I only realised my mistake half way. It was no good to turn a back. Were you serious the other day about that ball?"

Bill fished inside his shirt and produced the silver ball. "Here is the proof, my friend."

Roberto's grin disappeared as Bill dropped it into his hand. Bill immediately felt sense of loss as the ball left his fingers. Roberto studied the ball in the glow from the restaurant window. "Porko Madonna," he exclaimed. "There is no way this has gone through the crusher. It is perfect; not even a scratch. What is it made of?"

He moved it up and down in his hand, feeling the weight. "The lightness is exceptional."

"I don't know." Bill shrugged. "I was hoping you could tell me; you're the one with the university degree."

"I would need to run tests on it before I could give an opinion. Do you believe Joseph?"

Four beers arrived and were plunked in the middle of the table.

"I have no reason not to, and what about the stone?"

Roberto's professional curiosity was aroused. "Bring them both to the lab tomorrow. This is interesting."

Bill slipped the ball back into his shirt and felt the bottles to check if they were cold.

"Shit, she has left the tops on and I'm dying for a drink."

The girls stopped chatting and expertly opened the bottles with their teeth.

Bill smiled. "Remind me not to give you a bottle opener for a wedding present. Although you may need a tin opener."

Roberto laughed. "I do not know. Sara is full of surprises."

She playfully punched Roberto on the arm and he pretended it was broken, to everyone's amusement.

"You look like Jim Carey," Bill laughed.

"Who do you think I look like?" He tried the same expression he used in the mirror.

Roberto's jaw dropped and he pointed his finger at Bill and then said, "I have a no idea."

Bill frowned. "The leather jacket; that's a clue."

Roberto shook his head. "I do not know who you are supposed to be."

"Don't you think I look a bit like Harrison Ford?"

Roberto gaped and then burst out laughing. "You do not think you can pass yourself off as a Harrison Ford." The tears ran down his face as he doubled up laughing. "I can see a Ford, but not the Harrison."

Sara interrupted, "Who is Harrison Ford?"

Bill joined in the laughter.

Monica looked puzzled. "Does he work on the same contract?"

The laughter increased in volume.

"I don't think so," Bill managed to croak, "Not unless his last two movies were flops."

The waitress returned and systematically went from person to person with a bowl of water, in which they all dutifully washed their hands.

"I'm glad to see some sort of hygiene here," Bill remarked. "Maybe I won't get the screaming shits after all."

The food arrived next, on plastic plates. There were two nice pieces of chicken and some sliced tomato. The chicken was grilled to perfection and tasted wonderful. They had obviously got the grilling down to a fine art. Roberto paid for the food, because Bill had paid for the beers. They sat smoking and drinking to the sound of the girl's constant chatter.

The town was almost deserted at this time of night. Bill noticed the odd rat moving around in the shadows. He had never notice them before. The garbage skip on waste ground across the road had rusted through in places. It was a rat Heaven on Earth. In the day, garbage heaps were normally festooned with huge storks from the lake. They stood waist high and were the ugliest things Bill had ever seen. When in flight, they tucked in their long necks and wheeled about the sky quite gracefully. Every now and then, one would crash into the high-tension power lines and black out the whole area. Bill was feeling content, but was worried about the time.

"I have to go. At twelve o'clock I turn into a pumpkin." He asked Monica if she wanted to meet him here at eight tomorrow night. She seemed very pleased and kissed him on the cheek.

Roberto and Sara waved as he drove off down the street, weaving from side to side around the pot holes.

He changed the tape and found himself listening to Phil Collins singing *Another Day in Paradise*. *Well, we will have to see about that.*

Tonight had been very pleasant. Monica had told him she had left her village two weeks ago to find a job in Malenga. She was staying with Sara's parents while Sara lived in the camp with Roberto. At sixty percent unemployment, there was not much chance of her finding work. Maybe she would end up as one of Otto's girls. Most of them would be out of work anyway once the contract ended. Judging from the sparkle in Otto's eyes, he would probably keep the tall one around.

The last girl who had picked him up at the gas station had not been much of a companion. After sex, she had knelt on the bed with a finger up her nose and said 'You no have big cock. You no have small cock. You have medium cock'.

At that point, Bill had realised any intelligent conversation was out of the question, so he smuggled her out of the camp.

He often wondered who she had been comparing him with. The local men he had driven passed peeing at the side of the road swung the thing round and round to remove the last drops. He was not the propeller type; more of the casual 'shake shake' model.

Chapter 7

Phil arrived back at the office in a state of shock. Not only did he have a touch of jet lag, but he was also suffering from stress created by his fear of flying. All through the flight he expected the wings to break off. They gave him a window seat just behind the wing. He watched it flexing up and down, especially when flying through cloud after take off and on decent.

To take his mind off the wings, he read the in flight magazine, but always ended up reading the safety information card instead.

In the event of the aircraft landing on water. *They gotter be kidding. The only aircraft that can land on water is a floatplane.* Airliners had a tendency of disintegrating into a shower of spray and debris as soon as they contacted the surface.

There was another one. In the event of fire, follow the coloured lights on the floor to the nearest emergency exit. *That's no good at thirty thousand feet.* He had a mental image of two hundred passengers sky diving with no parachutes, all leaving a black smoke trail behind them. It would look quite spectacular from the ground.

Now, with both feet on terra firma, he was gradually starting to feel better—then he was shown into John Collins' office.

"Sit down and tell us what you got," the section chief called from behind his desk.

Lozano sat to one side, smiling. Phil's short stay in Chicago must mean the share holdings were legitimate and he had wasted his time and the tax payers' money.

"Birkett and Sanderson are clean," explained Phil. "They have done nothing wrong. All their books are in order; even the IRS are happy."

Lozano interrupted, exclaiming, "I knew it, I knew it!"

"Shut up, Joe," Collins said softly, with a tired expression. "Continue, Phil."

"It is, however, as we suspected; they are not the legal owners of the stock. Most of the shares were purchased in their name one hundred years ago by clients who hold the certificates. They receive thirty percent of the dividends, and Birkett gets ten percent. The rest is reinvested in the same stock that made the dividend."

"So who are the clients?" asked Collins.

Phil scratched his head. "This is where it gets a bit unglued. Birkett doesn't know. He sends the money to Swiss bank accounts. The certificates also ended up in the same bank, in safety deposit boxes. There is a different box for each holding, and also a different account number for each holding."

Collins leant forwards with his arms on top of the desk. "So are you telling me this Birkett has no godamn idea who these mothers are?"

Phil nodded. "Yep, that's about the size of it."

"No fucking idea at all?"

Phil thought for a moment, resisting the temptation to polish his glasses. "Well, he did say he thought they were Africans."

Lozano interrupted. "You mean Negros, like you?"

Phil sighed. "No, I mean Africans like from Africa."

"Bull shit," shouted Collins.

"Africans didn't have two cents to scratch their asses with one hundred years ago. Even now they spend all their godamn time killing each other and begging for money."

Phil swallowed. "Well, that's what he thinks."

Lozano piped up again. "But we are not interested in stock purchase a hundred years ago. Even the Arabs had no money then."

Collins thought for a while. "You're right, Joe. This sounds like some sort of syndicate. Why the different account numbers? Could be Mafia. They have been around for a long time. Who else has been around for a hundred years?"

He looked at the other two for suggestions.

"Ku Klux Klan," ventured Lozano.

Collins closed his eyes and rested his forehead on one hand. "Give me something sensible, Joe."

Phil hid the smile on his face by covering his mouth with a sheet of paper. He cleared his throat. "What about the Germans? I heard they were into a lot of things round about the First World War."

Collins rubbed his nose. "That's a bit late. We need something eighteen-ninety for this to gel. It's a lulu of a puzzle for sure."

He smacked his hand on the desk, making the other two jump. "I beckon it's the Free Masons. They are full of all this secret kind of crap."

Lozano shuffled around in his chair. "The Free Masons are not listed as a terrorist organisation, sir. I'm sure we are wasting our time. We are not interested in this hundred-year-old stock."

"Too right we are," shouted Collins.

"We have a bunch of people holding seven and-a-half-billion dollars worth of American corporations, and we haven't a clue who they are. This law firm is a definite front. I don't know what their game is, but this stinks like a Bronx garbage can in midsummer."

He turned towards Phil. "Get your ass over to Switzerland and get some names and addresses. I will contact our embassy to put some pressure on their minister of finance for full cooperation. After September eleventh, there's no such thing as client confidentiality."

He stood up. "We are at war with these motherfuckers." His fist slammed down on the desk. "Kapish?"

Both Lozano and Phil flinched and answered together, "Yes, sir."

This was one side of John Collins Phil had never seen before. *He sure as hell has got the bit between his teeth.*

"Joe, get Phil organised out of here on tonight's flight. Understood?"

Lozano glanced at Phil, "Yes, sir."

"Contact the embassy and tell them he's coming."

Joe nodded and Collins stared at them for a moment. "What are you waiting for? Go to it. I want some answers."

Outside Collins' office, Phil and Joe were still in a daze. *I've become a travel agent for niggers,* flashed through Joe's mind.

Phil was busy thinking about the overnight flight to Zurich. Washington to Chicago was nothing compared to the next one. Most of it was over the Atlantic. *In the event of the aircraft landing on water.*

At least he had some time to prepare for this journey.

A few sleeping pills just before takeoff would not be a bad idea.

Chapter 8

Bill woke before the clock could ring, and cancelled the alarm. He lay there thinking, with the ball in his hand.

When he was a boy, he used to lie on the grass in summer time with his eyes closed. With the sun shining on his face, everything had looked bright orange. If he shaded his closed eyes, then everything had grown darker. Sometimes he could see strange shapes moving around, over which he had no control. Other times he could see some sort of weird landscape. Just as he began to identify mountains and trees, the picture would change into some other meaningless pattern. It was frustrating not to be able to make any sense of these images. Perhaps a brain specialist or a psychiatrist could explain these occurrences.

If you look out through a window and then close your eyes, the silhouette of the window can still be seen for a fraction of a second. Like an imprint on the brain.

Bill discovered that if you concentrated, the brain could reverse the system of sight and give your closed eyes something to see. He had never mentioned any of this to anyone for fear of being ridiculed, or worse still, thought of as being crazy. Probably everyone else could do the same thing, as far as he knew.

There had been a new development over the last two years. When he closed his eyes in the shower, he could see faces. They were constantly changing. As one face came into view, it would form into some other face. The heads turned like three-dimensional computer images.

At first they had been made from a blurry smoke shape, which became crystal clear for a second. Each individual eyelash could be distinguished on their frozen faces before fading away and reshaping into a different face. The expressions never changed, and most of them were old people. Bill wondered if they were deceased, or just figments of his imagination. Whoever they were, he could not recognise any of them. They were all complete strangers. Needless to say, he hadn't mentioned the faces to anyone, and it never really worried him. He could switch them on and off any time he wanted to.

Except in the shower. There they came to him automatically when he closed his eyes. Probably because he was expecting them.

Lying now on the bed with his eyes closed, something very strange was happening. He could see a clear picture of people actually moving around. More frightening still, he could hear what they were saying. There was a teenage boy in blue jeans and a red pullover. He was cleaning a blue racing bike and explaining to another boy how to tighten the spokes to make the rim run true. The other boy had a red sit-up-and-beg bicycle with a three-speed rear hub. This bike had been modified with a double clangour and chain tensioner. He knew all this because it was his bicycle. The boy in the red pullover was his older brother. Bill quickly opened his eyes in a panic and was back in his park home.

What the hell had happened? He checked the time on the alarm clock. Five minutes had passed. He must have fallen asleep again. It had been a dream. That was the only explanation.

He placed the ball in the ashtray and rolled out of bed. If he had woken up with a hard on this morning, there was no sign of it now. The dream had given him a fright. The term 'scared stiff' did not apply to men's dicks. No cold shower was needed this morning, but as sure as shit he was going to keep his eyes open when he washed his hair and face.

Driving to work, the dream episode played on his mind. Dreams were normally disjointed and confused. What he had seen was clear and precise. A thirty-five-year-old action replay. Everything Bill saw and heard was exactly how he remembered it. The only difference was that he had been a spectator and not part of the action like in a dream.

The Hilux slewed to one side as he braked hard to avoid a local dog. It had trotted across the road, sniffing the ground on its own personal mission, unnoticed until the last minute. *I'm sure African dogs and chickens wait all day at the side of the road and then cross when they see a car coming.*

The same could be said about some of the adult Africans, who would set off to cross a road without even looking. A kilometre further on, he passed a group of huts. Two chickens sped across the road in front of him, frantically flapping their wings. Bill called the local chickens Kamikaze.

The crusher gates came into view round the next bend. A black-uniformed security guard waved him through. How they managed to survive the day in a black uniform was unbelievable. An ordinary person would melt. The guard made eye contact with him as he passed. *That's unusual. They normally just wave the car through without looking to see who is driving. There must have been some sort of 'shakeup' at Medusacor in town.* Bill checked his rear-view mirror and noticed the guard talking into his radio.

Ammed was waiting for him outside the office. They walked round the plant together, discussing a few minor problems. Some lower plates in the primary feed hopper needed changing.

"I will do that on Sunday," remarked Bill, while telling Joseph to top up the oil on the secondary.

He noticed Joseph didn't look well. His eyes had a vacant look about them.

Ammed drove away in a cloud of dust, with a cigarette hanging out of his mouth. Bill wondered what he did all day between sleeping. Judging by the Egyptian picture magazines Bill had found in the office, Ammed wasn't too bright. *Maybe he smokes his 'hubbly bubbly' pipe and masturbates.*

Bill climbed up the makeshift wooden stairway to the office container and got down to some paperwork. He glanced out of the window every now and then to keep an eye on what was happening. There was the usual line of trucks being loaded over at the stock pile area. *More trucks than usual.*

They were actually forming a queue. He stamped on the office floor with his foot to summon the site clerk. The clerk had a small office below in the store container. He entered with a mug of coffee. Bill nodded his thanks. "What's going on over there; why so many trucks this morning?"

The clerk rubbed his chin. "Some of those trucks run from the old crusher. They come here for load. The drivers say to me the gate is locked."

Bill passed a hand through his hair. "Those bastards at the office don't tell me anything. I'm like a fucking mushroom here. They keep me in the dark and feed me shit."

The clerk turned to go.

"Wait. I will find out what's going on."

He picked up the radio. "Pasarani, Pasarani, come in."

He was the earth-moving foreman who controlled all the truck movements.

"Pasarani, Pasarani, come in."

The radio crackled. "Si."

"This Bill. Why all truck come here? Truck too many here. Truck waiting for loading."

There was a long pause.

"Porca Madonna, driver all stupid, who is the truck."

Bill cleared his throat. "The truck old crusher here. They say gate locked."

"Dio Porco. I come you."

Bill addressed the clerk. "Pasarani come me." He slapped his forehead. "I mean, Pasarani is coming here. He can sort this shit out. Tell Joseph I need some men Sunday morning to fix the primary hopper."

"Yes, sir." The clerk turned and left the office.

Bill smoked a cigarette while drinking his coffee. It didn't taste so bad with the coffee.

A double cab charged onto the site in a cloud of dust and raced across to the line of trucks. Bill was sure half the Italians who worked there were ex-Formula One drivers.

A short, fat man leapt out of the pickup and jumped up and down, waving his arms as if trying to fly. The drivers all gaped at him from their open windows, totally confused. The last six trucks in the line eventually understood and all turned round at the same time, causing a huge gridlock. Pasarani threw his cap on the ground and jumped on it.

Bill wondered if the traffic cops in Rome performed like this, and stood up so he could see better. All maintenance work on the plant had stopped while the men moved to vantage points. One truck had managed to reverse into the side of another one. Pasarani lay across the bonnet of his car with his head in his hands. Bill picked up his radio, ready to call the company ambulance in case he'd had a heart attack. He noticed the chubby hands were still moving.

The trucks sorted themselves out and drove off. Pasarani picked up his cap and dusted it off while shaking his head. He climbed into the double cab and drove off in a cloud of dust. Bill sat down again. *Well, that concludes this morning's entertainment.*

Surprisingly, Bill completed his weekly paperwork in half an hour. It normally took him a good two hours. The plant started up. There was a *tap, tap* on the door. "Come in," he called.

Joseph entered, and Bill could see immediately something was wrong.

"What's the problem, Joseph?" he asked, genuinely concerned.

Joseph looked round the office as if to make sure no one was hiding anywhere. "Ball problem; ball make big problem."

Joseph stretched out his arms to emphasise the vast magnitude of the problem.

Bill felt the ball inside his shirt. "How ball make problem?"

"Chief M'ba men asking questions about ball. They come to my house and break many things. Somebody has seen the ball. I do not tell them you have ball, but they will come back."

Bill immediately remembered the man at the gas station. "Who is Chief M'ba?"

Joseph rolled his eyes. "He is a very powerful wizard. His people are everywhere. Even here at the crusher. He knows everything, and can make people disappear anytime he wants."

Bill thought it was a good time to try another cigarette, and lit one up. "I've never heard of Chief M`ba; is that a local name?"

"No, local name Nabusano. M`ba old name from my tribe."

Bill flicked the ash from the cigarette. "Go to the police. Surely they can do something?"

Joseph shook his head. "You do not understand. All things here belong to M`ba. Malenga and everything in it belong to M`ba. He control all the police. The military. The security. All the people here. That is why I must leave now. Need you to give me money. I sign paper for you to pick my pay at month end."

Bill did not like the idea of Joseph leaving. He was a very good worker and had three year's experience at the plant. Joseph looked terrified. In that condition, he would be no use on the job anyway, so Bill reluctantly agreed and gave him what cash he had. Joseph gratefully accepted the money by placing his hands together and crouching down.

"Mr. Bill, you also must go. Big danger for you here. Give ball to M`ba or they will kill you. Tell people me sick or maybe no time for me to go."

Jesus Christ. I expected a malaria problem here, not a fucking mafia problem.

Joseph looked out of the window, then left the office.

"Stone the crows," Bill remarked. He needed to talk to Roberto. *He's been here from the start of the contract, and seems to know the local situation better than most.*

Bill could not believe the police were in this Nabusano's pocket, but in Africa, anything was possible. *What the hell does he want this ball for? Finders' keepers, as far as I'm concerned. I must find out more about it, and quickly.*

Bill stamped his foot on the office floor and another mug of coffee arrived.

"Tell John, the charge hand, to load this morning's sample in the back of my car. I'm going to the lab. Also, Joseph is sick; could be malaria."

The clerk set down the mug of coffee. "Why did he not wait for you before going? It is a long walk to the clinic. I saw him going under the fence near the stock piles."

Bill wondered about this line of questioning. "I don't know. I just decided now to go to the lab. Maybe he's going home for something first."

The clerk left and he drank the coffee. Two men carried a sack of crushed material and lifted it onto the back of his Hilux. He forced the last drop of coffee down and wondered if he would ever sleep again.

Driving out of the gate, he checked his rear-view mirror. The guard was on the radio. *They were definitely keeping tabs on him. Joseph was right. Ball big problem.*

Instead of turning right, Bill turned left towards the quarry. The road passed the old crusher near the river. He wanted to see what was happening there. No dust could be seen coming from the plant, and he could see from his car that the gate was locked. *If they had a major break down, why lock the gate?*

He did a three-point turn at the gate, observed by the guard, and headed back up the hill. The guard at his gate watched him drive past. He decided to collect the stone with the dent in it from his mobile home, on the way to the lab. Hopefully Roberto would come up with some answers.

The Madusacor men at the camp lifted the boom for him to enter. When he left, there were three of them at the gate, all looking in his direction. These men were hired to protect company property and employees. Bill felt like a fugitive. It was either his imagination, or their job description had changed.

The doors on the Hilux danced and rattled on their latches as he drove along the corrugated dirt road from the camp to the lab. He glanced up at the Scots girl hanging from the rear-view mirror. *She's having a major epileptic fit.*

At the lab, he reversed in at the place where they offloaded the samples, and went in search of Roberto.

Bill found him watching the pressure gauge on the hydraulic press used for destructive testing of concrete samples. The needle slowly crept up to just past the halfway mark when the concrete cube in the press crumbled, then broke with a crunch. Roberto wrote something on his clipboard, then removed his safety glasses with a theatrical flourish.

"Yes, how is our rock biter today?" He grinned.

"Not so good. I've got a ball problem."

Roberto frowned. "You must always wear a condom. It is different for Sara and I; we never change partners."

Bill closed his eyes. "No, no, no. The silver ball from the crusher, you numb head."

Roberto opened his mouth wide "Oh, excuse. Have you brought it with you?"

"Yes, I've brought the ball, and that piece of stone, but I want you to have a look at it at lunch time; it appears that Nabusano wants it."

Roberto glanced around quickly. "Come to my office; we can a talk there."

Safely in the confines of the office, Bill explained everything Joseph had told him.

Roberto rubbed his chin. "Hmm, so that's why that man was watching you last night. I can believe what you say for the guards. Nabusano owns the security company. They are a good source of information."

"Is there anything he doesn't own in this Godforsaken town?"

Roberto thought for a moment. "Yes, there are a few Indian shops and Otto's place. Otto built that place as a gas station, but Nabusano stopped the petrol. That's why it is a bar. Then Nabusano stopped the beer, but Otto must have come to some arrangement. That's the only reason he is a still here."

A lab technician entered with two small cups of Italian coffee.

Bill groaned. "Don't you guys drink any tea?"

Roberto turned his palms up. "Why drink a tea if we have Italian coffee?"

He offered Bill a cigarette and lit them both with his petrol Zippo. Bill noticed Zippos were back in fashion. All the Italians were using them.

"Who's this Chief M'ba Joseph was talking about?"

"Yes, I have heard that before. There is a one tribe here that use that name for Nabusano. It belonged to one of his ancestors and has been handed down over the years."

"What's it mean?"

Roberto shrugged. "I do not know, but I can ask Sara. She is from that tribe. Where is the ball? I borrowed some measuring equipment from the machine shop."

Bill placed the stone and the ball on Roberto's desk. "Don't let anyone see the ball. According to Joseph, Nabusano's got spies all over the place."

Roberto picked up the ball. "I wonder why he is interested in this. We do not know even what it is."

Bill stubbed out his cigarette. "Well, we better find out before he knows for sure I've got it."

Roberto placed the ball into the indent in the piece of stone. "This is very strange and quite impossible. Come back in two hours. I will have some information for you. There is an explanation for everything."

Bill reluctantly left the ball with Roberto and drove back to the crusher. If it was true that Nabusano wanted the thing, then he must know what it was. By leaving the ball with Roberto, Bill felt like a smoker who had run out of cigarettes. A thing like that couldn't be addictive. After all, it was just a ball.

Roberto checked his watch. It was nearly lunch time. The laboratory staff were climbing on their bicycles and riding off past the batching plant. He took the ball and stone into the lab and placed them on a work table. Clamping a new sheet of paper on his clipboard, he wrote **'Bill's ball'** and underlined the heading.

Right, let us see if there is a connection between the ball and the stone. The fit seemed to be perfect. He held them together with thumb and forefinger and dipped the pair into a water tank. Removing them from the water, he turned them until the ball was at the bottom, and then separated the ball from the stone. The indent was still dry.

Test one. **Ball and stone perfect fit**; could this be one of Bill's jokes? Roberto had never understood the English sense of humour. Bill must have lapped the two together with grinding paste. The alternative was crazy. A two-million-year-old, metallic-like ball. Roberto shook his head.

Test two. Micrometre measurements taken over a number of different directions, all identical. **Perfect sphere.**

After weighing it, he worked out its density, which did not tell him very much because it could be hollow. Next was a Brinell hardness test, which did not even register. He examined the surface through a magnifying glass. **No visible indentation.** No wonder Nabusano was after the thing. Whatever it was made of was worth a fortune.

Roberto rubbed his chin and decided to submerge half the ball in strong acid while he smoked a cigarette. The halfway mark should show a difference in surface texture. He set up his microscope while waiting. No bubbles were rising from the submerged part. He fished it out with rubber gloves and rinsed it under the tap, then dried it off with a cloth. He could not see which half had been in the acid. Revolving the ball in different directions under the microscope, he was unable to detect any surface corrosion. **Impervious to acid.** *No big deal. Stainless steel would give the same result in acid, but not the hardness test. Right, now we do the coefficient of expansion.*

He placed the ball in the electric oven and deducted the ambient temperature from the thermostat reading on the oven.

Roberto was starting to sweat, so he walked over to the fridge and opened a coke. He drank while standing in the cool air from the air conditioner.

The laboratory people would return in another thirty-five minutes, so he could not waste any time. Picking up a pair of tongs, Roberto opened the oven door and removed the ball. He placed it under the height gauge for re-measurement; same measurement as before. There had to be a discrepancy between the gauge and the micrometre for the measurement to remain the same. Everything expanded when heated. Using the micrometre, Roberto was puzzled. The readings were all exactly the same as before. A bead of sweat fell from his forehead onto the ball. It ran down the side without evaporating. Very slowly, Roberto moved his hand closer and closer to the shinny surface and then tapped it quickly with his fingertip, expecting to be burnt. Nothing. He rested a finger on it. It was more or less room temperature.

"Porca Madonna, this is impossible."

Roberto walked back to the oven. He must have forgotten to switch it on. When he opened the door, hot air spilled out. Slamming the door shut, he walked back to the workbench in a daze and sat down heavily on the stool. **Impervious to heat?** Roberto shook his head. *I am not writing that down; I do not believe it.* He lit a cigarette and noticed his hand was shaking. *Let me try something else.*

After tapping the ball again with his finger, he carried it over to the refrigerator and placed it into the icebox.

"Now let me see how you a like that. Roberto Dimodica is not easily beaten."

While he was waiting, Roberto was deep in thought. *Whoever manufactured this thing did so for a reason. The ball is an ideal form of protection for something inside.* What it was made of, he had no idea. It was possible that the ball was a test sample of a new material that NASA had come up with.

He prepared the portable x-ray equipment that was used for examining the special welding on the powerhouse structure. It would be very interesting to see if there was anything inside. After checking his watch, he removed the ball from the icebox. It was still at room temperature. No change. The NASA theory was becoming the only explanation. He eventually wrote on the report 'impervious to temperature change, material unknown'.

Roberto was in for another shock. The x-ray showed nothing. It did not even show the ball. He placed his cigarette lighter alongside it to see if the machine was working. The lighter was clearly visible, but nothing else. *If there's a lead content in the material it would have shown as a solid blank. Nothing at all is crazy. How did it get into the quarry? Someone would have to be very careless to lose a valuable thing like this. Unless, it just fell out of the sky and the homing device stopped working. A re-entry test from a space shuttle that had been lost over Africa instead of the Nevada desert.* This was just speculation.

Roberto still did not know what it was. He had run out of tests, and looked round the lab for inspiration. His gaze fell on the press, and he shook his head. Bill would not be very pleased if the ball was broken. The crusher had not broken it, so they knew it was very strong. A round object in the press could fly out and shoot right through the wall like a cannon ball.

He picked up a small hammer and held the ball between finger and thumb. Tapping on the side, Roberto held it to his ear. Sounded solid. **Sounded**. *That was it. There still was an ultrasonic test he could do.*

Roberto pulled the equipment from a cupboard and plugged it in.

"This will give me a picture of your insides, my stubborn friend."

He contacted the ball with the handset and moved it in a slight circular motion while observing the screen. Blurred images ebbed and flowed. Nothing he could positively identify.

Roberto suddenly felt dizzy and his stomach churned with nausea. Dropping the handset, he collapsed on the floor, coughing and retching. It passed as quickly as it had started, and he staggered to his feet. Switching off the machine, another feeling started to overtake him. Roberto held his lower abdomen and rushed to the toilet, bouncing off the walls as he ran. Just making it to the pan with a bout of diarrhoea, he sat in shocked disbelief at the sudden turn of events.

*   *   *

Bill arrived at the lab an hour later to find Roberto sitting at his desk looking extremely ill.

"What happened?" he enquired, very concerned. "Are you alright? You look terrible."

Roberto looked up with heavy eyes. "I think I got a reaction from your ball. A very negative one. I am going home to bed now. Please take your ball away. I will see you tomorrow."

Bill drove home that evening very confused. The report Roberto had given him was unbelievable. *Another thing, how could the ball make Roberto feel ill when it makes me feel so good?* Only then, he suddenly realised the ball was changing the way he felt and thought. *We may not know what it is, but I certainly know what it's doing to me.*

Bill hoped Roberto would be recovered by tomorrow. He still had many questions to find an answer to.

*   *   *

Monica was patiently waiting for him, seated at one of the tables, when Bill arrived at the Pavement Restaurant. She gave him a brilliant white smile and waved happily when he stopped the Hilux at the curb. She must have been wondering if he was going to turn-up.

They ordered beer with fish and chips. The first beer of the day always tasted the best. Bill had a rule never to drink before six, unless it was Sunday, and then never before twelve noon.

This system kept him on an even keel, away from the dangers of alcohol.

He had read somewhere that if a man looks forward to even one beer a day, technically he's an alcoholic. *Well, then technically I'm an alcoholic,* he admitted to himself. *Alongside most of the male population of the planet Earth.*

The beers arrived and Bill felt them to see if they were cold. He nodded to the restaurant lady, who then opened them. This was standard practice in Africa and could be compared to the wine tasting ritual in Europe. This time she remembered to bring the opener with the beers, so Monica didn't have to use her teeth.

After a while, the lady returned with a bowl of water and a tea towel for the hand-washing procedure. Shortly after, the fish and chips arrived. The fresh fish from the lake tasted excellent and the chips went down very well with a squirt of tomato sauce on them. Monica finished her fish and then pushed her plate towards Bill for him to eat the chips. He managed to make most of them disappear before lighting up a cigarette and ordering another beer each.

Small talk was difficult. Bill was out of practice. They were two people alone for the first time, with a thirty-year age gap. Their interest and cultures were completely different, not to mention the colour of their skins. Long gaps in the conversation made Bill feel uncomfortable, but Monica seemed quite happy just to be with him. "Let's go to the gas station." Bill suggested. "The music is always good there."

"Will Sara and Roberto be there?" Monica asked.

Bill shook his head. "I don't think so. Roberto didn't look very well last time I saw him."

Fifteen minutes later, they arrived at the gas station bar. Otto narrowed his eyes and gave Monica the once over as she approached the counter. He gave Bill a wink and a knowing look as they both sat on bar stools.

"I never see this one before. She looks like she is very good in da bed, ja."

He said this as if Monica was not there. Bill flushed with anger but Otto didn't notice.

"Two beers without glasses," he ordered.

Otto's wife appeared from the storeroom and greeted Monica. She was very tall, with braided hair that stuck out in spikes like a medieval knight's mace. Patricia was a very nice person and reminded Bill of a black Pansy Potter because of her hair.

"Do you two know each other?" Bill enquired.

Monica smiled. "Yes, we met yesterday in the Indian Bazaar."

She turned back to the more important task of gossiping, completely ignoring him. Bill pushed one of the beers in front of her and took a heavy swing from his bottle. He had plenty of experience at being a gossip bystander. Patricia frowned at the bottle of beer in front of Monica, and reached for a glass. Bill coughed as some of the beer went down the wrong way. *How do you explain to somebody's wife not to use the glasses because some of the other people in the bar have been licking her husband's asshole?*

Bill shook his head and noticed Otto holding a glass up to the light, examining it. He did this five or six times, with different glasses, and then scowled in Bill's direction. Bill lit a cigarette and then swung the stool round to face the other way.

Jimmy, the only other Englishman on site, was approaching the bar. He wore a pink, open-necked shirt, unbuttoned to his chest to show off his collection of gold chains. Bill swung back round to face the bar again. He didn't have much patience with office workers, especially this one. *The fact that he has never been mugged up to now is unbelievable. Probably because he is always one of a pair.*

"I see you have a new friend. How disappointing."

Bill shivered and glanced over to the table Jimmy had just left. A young local man, also wearing a pink shirt with a gold chain, smiled in his direction. "I see you also have a new friend, but I can't say I'm disappointed."

Jimmy pouted. "That's my new garden boy. He's living with me cos he's got nowhere to stay."

"Oh, shame."

"Yes, his father threw him out. Can you believe it?"

"Yeah, I can at that."

"Two larger and limes, Otto darling."

Bill and Otto watched as Jimmy walked back to his table carrying his drinks. He placed one foot directly in front of the other, wiggling his behind from side to side.

"Who is da guy with Jimmy?" asked Otto.

"I think the official job description would be night shift garden boy."

Otto shook his head. "*Got in Himmel.* How did you English *vin da var?*"

Bill thought for a moment. "Well, you Germans called the English Tommy, right?"

"*Ja.*"

"And most Germans are called Hans, right?"

"*Ja.*"

"At the time of the First World War in the trenches, Tommy called out, 'Hans, Hans, Hans.' Hans stood up and shouted, '*Ja.*' So Tommy shot him. This happened six times before they realised what was going on. Then Hans called out, 'Tommy, Tommy.' Tommy shouted, 'Is that you, Hans?' Hans stood up and shouted, '*Ja.*' So Tommy shot him."

Otto did some counting on his fingers, and then walked away scratching his head. Bill had a very high regard for German efficiency and engineering, but had told this joke for Otto's benefit, who was more of an exception rather than the rule.

Monica and Patricia were still in heavy conversation and were now laughing about somebody. Bill hoped it wasn't him. It was a good time to visit Otto's gas chamber. There was no toilet at the pavement restaurant. Most people peed behind the rubbish skip on the other side of the road, which Bill didn't like to do. Good job it was downwind. On his way back from the toilet,

Bill noticed Nikolay and Ivan at one of the tables outside. They were two Russian mechanics who repaired and maintained all the dump trucks on the project. He turned to make a diversion, but it was too late. They had already seen him and were waving madly, both grinning like Cheshire cats.

"Come sit here, English," Nikolay shouted.

"I am with somebody at the bar," Bill tried as an excuse.

"Tell Itie come sit here."

"It's not Roberto; it's a girl."

Ivan laughed. "Girl no good for drink, drink. Only good for fuck, fuck. Tell girl come. I never see you with girl. I start think you same as other English."

Bill gave up. "Okay, okay. I come now."

He knew from past experience it was useless to try to resist these two. He also knew a crushing plant was the worst place to be with a Vodka hangover.

Back at the bar, Monica and Patricia were still going at it. "You like sit outside?" Bill said, and then corrected himself. "I mean, do you want to sit outside? I have to have a drink with two friends."

"No, you go. I will wait here for you." She smiled and then dived back into a conversation about some disco in town.

Just then Otto reappeared behind the bar next to his wife. "Fuck you, Englishman. You think us Germans stupid?" he shouted.

Patricia turned round in surprise. "Calm down, Otto. No shouting at the customers," she ordered. "I am sure Bill was only joking."

"*Ja*, well, yoke no good. I no stupid, ja. I once sold a freezer to a man with no electricity," he said proudly.

"Really," enquired Bill. "How did you manage that?"

Otto grinned. "I told him if he buys a lot of electrical tings, they will put power to his house for free."

He slapped the counter and laughed until tears ran down his face.

"Where was that?" asked Bill.

"On top of a mountain back in Deutschland."

His laughing faulted and then stopped abruptly. A heavy scowl spread across his face. *Time I visited the Russians.*

Bill was thinking about Otto's baseball bat behind the bar.

He arrived back at the table in the pump area and both Russians looked around for his girlfriend.

"Where girl?" they both asked.

Bill set his bottle of beer on the table and sat down.

"Girl no come. Busy talking to wife, Otto," he explained.

"*Da*, women like too much yak yak. Only good for fuck, fuck." They both laughed again.

Bill was glad Monica hadn't come with him to the table. He would have died of embarrassment. Nikolay picked up Bill's bottle of beer.

"What you drink, English? This shit?" He sloshed a triple vodka into one of the glasses on the table.

"Russian tradition, drink," he ordered, pushing the glass towards Bill.

The two Russians shouted '*Nastrovia*' and all three *clinked* their glasses. Bill took a sip, while Nikolay and Ivan downed their drinks in one gulp. Nikolay sloshed more vodka into all three glasses.

"What problem, English? You drink like women."

"Da," shouted Evan, who was drunker than Nikolay. "Only good for fuck, fuck."

"I no like drink too much vodka," Bill explained. "Make big problem tomorrow. I have other problem now, now."

Nikolay looked interested. "What problem now, now?" he asked. "We friend for you. You problem, we problem." He thumped Ivan on the shoulder.

"*Da, da*," Ivan answered, "Only good for fuck, fuck."

He leant forward, placing his head on his arms, and immediately fell asleep. Nikolay sloshed more vodka into Bill's glass, completely ignoring his protests.

"So, what problem for you?" he asked.

"Seems I could have a problem with the local Mafia."

Nikolay narrowed his eyes. "We in Russia know Mafia. Too much bad. Where your Itie friend? He too know Mafia."

Bill took a sip of vodka. "He sick today. Go home to the bed."

"Is malaria or the shits?" Nikolay enquired.

Bill shrugged. "The shits, I think."

Nikolay rotated his glass between thumb and forefinger. "Mafia system same in all place. Control all and everybody. If no possible control then eliminate. Always Mafia want. If no give, big problem. What Mafia want for you?"

Bill lit a cigarette and took a sip of vodka. "I find something they want."

Nikolay gulped down his drink and recharged his glass. "Solution simple. You give, problem say bye, bye."

Bill shuffled in his chair. "Me understand, but me wait a while. These people no understand for sure that I have what they want."

Nikolay shook his head. "No wait too long. Bad people here are strong. I see African peoples here no talk too much. Look like Russian peoples for old government. All afraid. If you look the eyes, you see."

He finished his drink and screwed the cap on the bottle. "Now me take Ivan house. Now he no power."

He shook Ivan awake and pulled him to his feet. Ivan grinned like an idiot and ruffled Bill's hair.

"Only good for fuck, fuck." He laughed.

They staggered away, towards the car park, knocking over some chairs and singing a Russian song. The only time the police bothered you here is if you crashed into something. Even then, it ended up in a financial settlement. Bill was pleased Ivan had passed out. There was no way he could keep up with the Russians. He didn't even like vodka. When he walked inside, Otto was behind the bar frowning in his direction. *I think I've overstayed my welcome for tonight.*

"Come, let's go," he told Monica. "Otto's not very pleased with me. No sense of humour."

Patricia smiled. "Do not worry. I can handle him. He is like a small boy."

Back in the Hilux, Bill noticed it was still quite early, and asked Monica where she wanted to go next.

"Me, I like disco," she said, making big, round, pleading eyes.

Oh my God, thought Bill. *That's the worst place I can think of.* He remembered some years before, the last time he had been to a disco. While dancing, he had caught sight of himself in a large mirror. He had been moving around like the tin man from the wizard of OZ. Now it was going to be grandfather tin man with young girl. The pleading eyes changed to Bambi eyes and a soft smile. "Okay, okay, we go to disco, but not for too long," he conceded irritably.

She gave him a hug as they drove off, weaving down the road while the Scots girl somersaulted.

The Tropica disco was still fifty metres further down the street when Bill heard and felt a heavy beat vibrating through the vehicle. He also started to feel ill. *Must have been the bloody Vodka.* Monica was also looking a bit drawn, and rubbed her forehead. He stopped the car, wondering if he was going to throw up.

"Are you alright?" he asked Monica.

"I do not feel well."

Her eyes were showing her discomfort. Bill suddenly remembered Roberto's report and quickly reversed the pick-up back down the street to stop in front of a café. Monica was puzzled.

"Need cigarettes," he explained. "Do you need some aspirin or anything?"

"No, I am feeling fine now," she answered. "You can buy some condoms for later."

He had pulled the keys out of the ignition, but now dropped them on the floor. If that wasn't a promise he didn't know what was. He was also feeling fine now, but decided to buy some aspirin anyway. The Tropica was going to be one hell of an ordeal. Bill swallowed two aspirin in the shop, then the Indian behind the counter asked him if he wanted ribbed or plain.

"Err, ribbed, I think." He felt himself blushing.

The shopkeeper was looking past him towards Monica sitting in the Hilux.

"How many packets? There are four in a packet."

"Err, one's okay, I think."

"You can take more. Save you having to keep coming back."

Bill was feeling uncomfortable. "Alright, give me six," he said in a commanding voice, slapping some money on the counter.

The Indian was doing this on purpose. He handed Bill a plastic bag and his change. Bill turned at the door. "Keep an eye on my car. I'm leaving it here."

Outside, he threw the bag on the seat and pulled the bonnet catch. There was no way he could take the ball inside the Tropica, so he was looking for a safe place to hide it. *Inside the air cleaner is ideal.* There was a bar across the inlet opening, so it wouldn't fall inside the manifold or block the air flow.

While he was under the bonnet, he pulled off one electrical wire from the injector pump to immobilise the engine. This was just a precaution. *If someone steals the vehicle the ball will be lost.* He slammed the bonnet closed and waved at Monica to get out of the pickup. "Come, let's walk. The car is better here."

Bill locked all the doors and they set off down the street. *Into the valley of death,* he thought. *Or should I say deaf?*

Monica held onto his arm and gave him a strange look. "Why buy so many condoms?" she asked. "You have other girl friends."

"No, no. They are all for you. I mean, err… The man in the shop make mistake."

She smiled up at him. "No problem. I did not know you were so powerful." She clung to his arm and squeezed his hand.

The *thud, thud,* of the music increased in volume as they approached. Bill imagined rolling the ball inside. *Everyone will come staggering out puking and shitting.* The difference between the gas station and the Tropica would be the number of decibels. If you rode a motorcycle fifty metres behind a 747 on takeoff, the volume of noise should be equivalent to an African disco. He paid the entrance fee and they proceeded into the animated din.

It was a scene from Hell. Illuminated by flashing strobe lights, groups of men danced around in staccato motion. Some of them wore baseball caps, sunglasses and gum boots. Any white clothing burnt with its own blue light in the dark areas. Some of the dancers were like the invisible man, wearing a white shirt and trainers. These items seemed to be jigging around by themselves.

Bill was rooted to the spot in shock, and gave Monica a look of despair. The heavy beat was vibrating the air inside his lungs. She pulled him forward, deeper inside the turmoil, and pointed to a bar situated away from the dance floor. He hoped there was less noise over there, and made his way in that direction. The hookers smiled and waved until they realised Monica was with him. After that they gave him a flat stare.

Bill was desperately looking for somewhere to sit as far away as possible from the gigantic speakers. The girl behind the bar came to his rescue with two plastic chairs. He shouted into her ear, "Two beers, please."

This whole town must be sitting on plastic garden furniture. At least he didn't have to worry about the small talk; every communication was sign language. Monica fiddled with a plastic ring on her finger. To Bill's amazement, it started flashing.

Being here, he was a definite fish out of water, whereas Monica was in her element. He noticed a white-haired Mazungu dancing with a young local girl. He looked ridiculous, moving one foot at a time forwards and backwards while lifting one hand and then the other. Bill realised that's the way he normally danced, unless he was drunk.

The beers arrived and he downed half the bottle without stopping. Monica stood up and started swaying around to the music. Bill lit a cigarette and pointed at it when she beckoned to him dance. He was stalling for time and needed to get drunk very quickly. There was no way he wanted to look like that other idiot. The beer and cigarette was finished, so he downed half of Monica's before standing up. She moved slowly backwards, still swaying to the music, and beckoned to him again. He followed her into the crowded dance area and glanced around. Thankfully, nobody was taking any notice of him. They were all doing their own thing.

Bill wondered if the flashing lights would brainwash him like Michael Cain in the *Ipcress File* movie.

Monica started dancing. He stood for some seconds, completely at a loss. How anyone could move around so much while standing in one place was beyond him. Her natural beauty and sensual movements held him spellbound. All thoughts of incompatibility disappeared as he tried to imitate some of her movements. She smiled in approval, helping him to relax. This enabled him to flow easily to the beat of the music.

Must have been the two triple vodkas I was forced to drink with Nikolay, he thought as he began to warm up. Well, I'm sure I'm not dancing like the tin man or that other Mzungu. Probably more like the scarecrow. Monica was now smiling in surprise, and moved very close to him. Bill could feel the sensual heat from her undulating body, and actually started to enjoy himself. Something else also started take an interest in Monica's body.

The music changed to a slower number and the men with no partners left the floor. He suspected this change was probably to give the dancers a breather and the extractor fans time to clear the air. There was a strong smell of sweat and body odour present in the atmosphere.

The strobe lights were turned off and a spot turned on to shine on a revolving, mirrored ball. Tiny flecks of light passed over the dark floor. It was an ideal opportunity for some heavy smooching. Monica's body brushed against his as they swayed together in the darkness.

It wasn't long before John Tomas muscled in between them. To Bill's amazement, the little head had taken over the thinking from the big head and there was nothing he could do about it. The throbbing was painful. He expected Monica to slap him any minute. To his surprise, she smiled mischievously and pushed closer to him, breathing quite heavily. Her left hand pressed into his lower back while her right slid in between them and squeezed him through his jeans.

Bill cleared his throat and gripped her shoulders. The situation was now completely out of control and his temperature was rising.

"Let's go," he managed to croak into her ear.

She squeezed him a few more times as if deciding, and then nodded her head while looking up at him with sleepy eyes.

Bill followed her towards the crowed entrance and was pleased it was dark everywhere except for the bar. His problem would have stood out in a well lighted room. Monica struggled to progress through the groups of people because of an influx of new revellers. Every time she stopped, Bill collided with her backside as if to prod her to keep moving. The little head was enjoying this immensely, until a heavy hand rested on his shoulder and something hard passed into his back.

The large man from the gas station suddenly appeared in front of him and frisked him ,bumping into John Thomas in the process. At that point the little head lost all interest in the proceedings and handed control back to the big head. The large man leered into Bill's face and handed him an envelope.

"Have a god time, Mr. Parker."

His breath wasn't very pleasant. He then nodded to the man standing behind Bill. The hard object stopped pressing into his back, and the hand released his shoulder. Bill turned to see the second man, who could have been the others twin, except that there was no sign of a smile on this one's face. Monica sensed he was not standing behind her and looked round.

"Good night, Mr. Parker." The first one smiled again.

"Good night," Bill replied, holding the envelope and walking past him.

"Good night," called out Monica, oblivious to any sort of problem.

Walking back to the pick-up, he realised with apprehension just how easy a target he was. He would have to make himself less vulnerable in future. Just how he was going to do this, he didn't know. It all depended on what was in the envelope. Was it possible they knew for sure he had the ball?

Bill unlocked the Hilux door and placed the letter in the glove box. He leant across and opened the other door for Monica. She crouched down between the sill and the open door, and started peeing. Bill sighed and rested his head on the steering wheel. Just when he needed a quick gateway. No, wait. If he were being watched he should act naturally. Obviously Monica was.

The rear-view mirror was twisted round, so he reset it. Strange, it wasn't like that when he had left the car, unless Monica had been using it for lipstick or something.

"Did you move my mirror?" he asked as she got in, slamming the door.

She shook her head and snuggled up to him. He turned the key and panicked. The engine wouldn't start. Shit, he had forgotten about the solenoid wire that he had pulled off the injector pump.

Bill jumped out and felt around under the bonnet. Eventually, he found the detached wire and pushed it back onto the fitting. Climbing back into the cab, he had the feeling of being watched. Bill started the engine and drove off. He had no intention on checking to see if the ball was still there while he was still in that dark secluded place. The Indian shop owner must have locked up and gone home. Bill was going to turn round, but decided to drive passed the Tropica. The *thud, thud,* of the music had resumed. Feeling ill again, he stopped and did a quick three-point turn. *The ball was still in the car; of that he was now sure.*

As he drove back down the street, the nausea left without a trace. The twinkle of broken glass reflected back at him from the headlights as he drove past the café. He hadn't noticed that when he had visited the shop before.

During the ten-minute drive from town to the camp road, Monica became more and more amorous. She started by playing with the hair at the back of his head and neck. Then she was stroking his ears, which sent shivers up and down his spine. It was not long before her hand was inside his shirt, pinching his nipples and rubbing his stomach with a circular motion. He stopped worrying about the incident at the Tropica. A more urgent need was overtaking him. His body reacted surprising rapidly to Monica's stimulation, causing him to be painfully confined inside his jeans. She soon understood the situation by doing some prospecting with her elbow, and quickly liberated the trapped member only to engulf it in the liquid warmth of her mouth. Bill slowed down dramatically, remembering how easily she could open bottles with her teeth. The last thing he needed right now was to hit a large pothole.

He turned into the camp road on the corrugated surface. At this slow speed, the Hilux was jumping like crazy. It was the first time he had enjoyed driving on a corrugated dirt road, but was finding it very difficult not to press the accelerator.

As he approached the camp turn off, he was undecided whether to enter the camp or to continue to the crusher on the dirt road. The corrugations were causing him to grit his teeth in pleasure. Bill turned in anyway, and the security guard waved him through. It looked as if he was alone in the pick-up. He passed his park home and drove round the camp twice before jerking to a climatic stall near Roberto's house. Monica wouldn't stop. She was like a septic tank suction hose. Things were starting to happen again, so Bill decided it was a good time to try to drive to his park home while he was able.

Inside, they urgently undressed and ended up in the shower. She rolled a condom on him and then, laughing, turned her back to him and placed her hands against the wall with her legs spread. Her laughing soon turned to moans of pleasure. Bill was so hard it felt like it was made of stone. Their frantic passion seemed to last forever under the tingling spray of water.

Chapter 9

Phil slowly moved forwards in the queue of passengers entering the Boeing 747. Some of them carried rucksacks on their backs and pulled luggage with wheels. How they could pass this off as cabin hand baggage was unbelievable.

The progress of this queue was held up by persons attempting to fit these large items into the overhead storage lockers. One man, trying to extract himself from two overcoats, accidentally punched him on the side of his face. He rechecked his boarding card for the seat number. C 25. Phil was now standing at row twenty, and as far as he could see, every overhead locker was full. The guy behind him pushed him up the ass with a small suitcase. Phil pursed his lips and closed his eyes while he counted to ten.

Eventually, he arrived at an emergency exit and noticed row twenty-five was the next one down. Squashing his shoulder bag flat around his laptop, he managed to ram it into a small slot in the nearest locker. He felt something give way inside his bag. *Holy shit, that must have been my new sunglasses.*

The small suitcase thumped him on the knee with one of its metal corners before he could sit down. Phil did not actually sit down; he sort of sank down slowly, because he was wedged into a confined space. His kneecaps were jammed up against the back of the seat in front. Removing the small pillow and blanket from behind his ass, he pushed back in his seat as far as possible. The pressure on his knees was less, but still there. *How can anyone have such a small space on such a gigantic aircraft? Not only are they persecuting the smokers, they are also subjecting the tall or bigger man to mediaeval torture.*

He glanced around and noticed everyone else had a space between their knees and the seat in front. The guy in his row, sitting in 'A', didn't have a seat in front of him. An elderly woman next to him in 'B' had short legs. A small guy sat down in front of him in '24 B' and placed his cabin bag on the floor. There was about two metres of space in front of this row, due to the emergency exit.

That is the one you jump out of when the plane's a ball of fire in a vertical dive, he reminded himself.

A stewardess blustered up the isle, slamming the doors closed on the overhead storage. Some of them bounced back open, but after wrestling with the contents she managed to get them shut again.

Phil raised his hand to complain. There was no way he could spend ten hours sitting like this. She then noticed the guy's bag in front on the floor and wagged her finger at him, smiling. After some polite conversation in French, she picked up the guy's bag and rushed off to the rear of the cabin.

Phil lowered his hand and stared at the sign in front of him. Half of it was in French. Fasten your seatbelt while seated. *If the Godamn pilot flew upside down, there is no way I could fall out of this seat. I would probably need a tyre iron just to stand up.*

A male cabin attendant rushed passed from behind, bumping his arm.

"Wait up," he called out, but he was gone.

Phil was fuming. He had to get a hold of this situation and turn it around. A screen came to life on the next bulkhead forwards. It showed a happy, smiling row of passengers demonstrating leg and foot exercises. They were actually crossing and uncrossing their legs. He stared at this in disbelief. Cramps had already started to take over his imprisoned legs. A woman cabin attendant was walking down the aisle with a clipboard, doing a head count. As she got to Phil, he blocked her way with his arm.

"This seat is quite something," he complained. "I can't move. It's for children or circus midgets. I am not staying in this seat."

She raised her eyebrows. "Give me your boarding card."

He handed it to her and she ran her finger down the clipboard.

"Ah, Monsieur Jones. You cannot change. You requested this seat when you booked."

Phil was confused, and then he recalled Joe Lozano's sadistic smile when he had handed him his ticket. At that critical point in time, the guy in front decided to test his seat to see how far back he could recline. During the next five minutes of shouting and struggling, while he was being arrested as an 'air rage' passenger, he managed to ID himself as FBI. Some nervous cabin attendants and what look like a flight security guard led him away to the rear of the aircraft, where there were three empty seats together.

Phil swallowed four sleeping pills while the plane took off, and then pulled up the armrests and lay down. The next thing he remembered was being shaken awake as the Boeing started it's decent.

*   *   *

Charles De Gaul Airport was divided up into different terminals, which are called A, B, C, etcetera.

Buses continuously drove round and round, stopping at each terminal. A transit passenger like Phil had to disembark and follow the signs for transit, then to board one of the buses to the terminal stated on the ticket. In theory, this was quite simple, but for a novice like Phil it was a confused nightmare. He tried asking a plainclothes security officer for directions and was promptly told, 'Icy France. In francsais vous parly francsais'.

So much for an international airport. The women in airport uniform were more helpful, and must have been employed because of their wonderful smiles. The smiles, however, soon disappeared if Phil asked a second question or asked them to repeat the directions.

Arriving at the right terminal, he was subjected to a very tight security check before being able to continue to the correct check-in counter. When it was his turn at the desk, the attractive girl produced her wonderful smile as he handed her his ticket.

He smiled back at her, showing off his own set of white teeth. She quickly ran her fingers over the consol keys while examining his ticket.

"The gate for this flight is closed. There will be another one in eight hours."

Phil's white teeth disappeared as he stared at her. She made some adjustments to his ticket and handed it back to him. The wonderful smile reappeared. "Here are two free meal tickets for the restaurant. Have a nice day."

"But I came straight here. I gotter be able to hook up with the next flight."

Her expression changed. The wonderful smile was nowhere to be seen. "The gate closed fifteen minutes ago. The flight is not possible. You are making a blockage. Restaurant that way." She pointed to a downward escalator behind the queue of passengers.

Two policemen standing to one side had started to take an interest in him. Phil picked up his bag and walked away in a daze.

In the restaurant, he checked out his ticket. There was only forty minutes between landing and takeoff. In an airport of this size, one hour would have been possible. Forty minutes was crazy. Phil removed his glasses and slowly polished them. *I don't know how or when, but I'm gonna get you for this, Joe Lozano.*

Outside, the sky was a uniform dark grey. The airport vehicles moved around with white vapour puffing from their exhausts. Temperature here was similar to the states. All he needed now was a snowstorm or an airport strike. The French were always going on strike. He removed his laptop from the shoulder bag. The new pair of sunglasses was broken in the middle. They weren't prescription glasses, but had looked very stylish in the shop. *Somehow a band aid in the middle could possibly ruin the effect.* He slid them back into their plastic pouch and threw them into the nearest rubbish bin. *Probably some hobo in Paris will end up wearing them.*

He sat down again with the laptop in front of him and spent most of his waiting time condensing the facts. *Birkett's clients were defiantly some sort of consortium, or group, but what type?*

Who the heck was around over a hundred years ago? The other side of the coin was Birkett himself. He had come across as being very helpful and sincere; or was he a nutcase? Lunacy ran in the family. That last bit Birkett said about the murders had sent shivers up and down his spine. If it was true, the timing and the method was very disturbing. Today's homicide investigators placed a very high importance on the so called 'trade mark' of every murder. Any connection or similarity was a clue. Let's see, murders all happened in same city. Victims all murdered in the same unusual way. All the victims were thugs and roughnecks. All the murders happened when the clients' man was around. All the murders happen in dark allies where one would expect to be robbed.

Yep, I reckon we have a few similarities here. You don't have to be Perry Mason to figure this one out.

If the information is true, the cops of that time really fucked up. They were probably happy as a hog in shit to be rid of the victims.

Phil compiled an email to one of his academy friends who was working in FBI homicide and kidnapping. *This sure needs some checking out. If this African guy was a murderer it might shed some light on who the heck he had been working for. It sure as hell wasn't the Ku Klux Klan.* Thoughts of Joe clouded his mind for a while. He forced himself to concentrate.

Right, two African guys with the same little finger missing. Definitely not cut off by accident. Must be a sect or cult, like the Japanese mafia with their tattoos. They had diamonds. High value and light to carry. No foreign exchange to worry about; same value internationally. Diamonds originate from Africa. Okay, we have one connection. Africans and diamonds. Who was in Africa? Brits, French, Germans, Portuguese, Belgium and Spanish. Every man and his dog were trying to grab a piece.

Let's try a different approach. How did they know which shares to buy and where to buy them? What was the main factor that increased the values?

Phil chewed on his nails. *Nostradamus had been dead for a while, so we can rule him out.*

"Bingo," he called out. The other people in the restaurant glanced in his direction. *The war. The godamn First World War.* America had been neutral. Even after the Lusitanian had been torpedoed. The Zimmermann telegraph urging Mexico to declare war on America had clinched it. *Before and after we joined in, we made a whole heap of bucks. Same with the Second World War. It's wars that made America powerful and increased all our stock market values.* War turned companies into corporations. Even the cold war and every international war afterwards; America was usually involved and industrially expanded. *Who could possibly know the First World War was going to start? Out of those colonial powers in Africa, we have the Brits and the Germans, who were the main participants. They were in a major arms race, which started round about the time the first shares were purchased, but nobody could have known what would happen twenty years later.*

The other thing that didn't fit was the Africans. *Why give a bag of diamonds to an African and send him off to America? The only Africans going to America before that were slaves. Why not send one of your own people?*

Phil pulled on the lobe of his ear. *This African was no mere messenger. Birkett said he was well educated and drew up the agreement. The African who had first met with Birkett's great-grandfather must have been a key figure in their organisation.* To Phil's reasoning, this African was a real 'Nigger in the wood pile.' He fitted perfectly with the African-diamond theory but not the Brit – German Scenario.

The high school Phil had attended was ninety percent black. The history teacher had really pushed them on learning about their roots and the African slave trade. This had resulted in him knowing all about the Slave Coast and Zanzibar, but not a lot about the rest of Africa. The British Empire had been built by the slave trade just as America benefited from war. Namibia was owned by the Germans and is very rich in diamonds. Kimberly was a diamond mine and was owned by the Brits. As far as Phil knew, there was no diamonds in North Africa; only in the middle and the south could one find them in large numbers. His photographic memory was no use if he had never been instructed on or read about the subject in the first place. Phil's brain storming was interrupted by his mobile beeping. Lozano's name appeared on the screen. Not wanting to give Joe any satisfaction, he took a deep breath to calm his anger before answering, "Hi Joe, how are you?"

"I'm okay. How is it with you?"

"Oh, same shit, different day."

"Where are you at? Did you make Zurich okay?"

"Not yet. I'm still in France. Missed my connection."

"No kidding. That is a bummer. You have to step lively at these big airports, my boy."

"Yeah, I guess so. I will remember that next time around. Anyway, gives me a change to do some homework on the case."

Lozano grunted. "A guy from our embassy is meeting you at Zurich. I will tell him you will be coming in on the next one. Give me a call on progress if any. I think this whole thing is a load of crap. Hope you realise I'm doing your work at the office while you're globetrotting."

"Sorry about that, Joe. Could be you will appreciate me a whole lot more in future. Having a nice time, wish you were here. Love Phil."

He pressed the end button with a smile on his lips. *Joe will eventually see from the paperwork for this trip that the next flight was changed to business class.*

"Fuck you, too, old buddy."

That afternoon, he arrived in Switzerland on a Swissair flight. Smaller plane, but very comfortable. The extra seating space made a heck of a difference. Sitting at the front was also an advantage. You couldn't see the wings flexing up and down. Emerging from the arrival gate, he noticed his name displayed on a card. It was held up by a young blond guy in suit and overcoat, who introduced himself as Garry.

"Sorry I'm late," Phil apologised.

Garry looked puzzled. "How do you mean late?" The flight came in on time."

"You weren't told I was arriving eight hours ago?"

"No, why?"

"I was booked on the morning flight from Charles De Gaul."

"It's not possible to make the transfer from Air France to this morning's Swissair. Why didn't you fly direct from DC to Zurich on last night's United Redeye?"

"Good question," fumed Phil. "My travel agent's an asshole."

"Sure looks that way." Garry smiled. "Follow me; the car's out front. No problem with dip plates."

He turned, grabbed Phil's trolley and pushed it towards the main entrance.

"By the way," continued Garry. "I made an appointment for you with the manager of Zurich National for ten tomorrow morning. You will be staying at the embassy tonight, in Bern. It's a good place to chill out and only one hour's drive from Zurich. That overnight flight is quite something."

"You got that right," answered Phil. "I don't recall much about it, but I am feeling bushed. Glad to meet someone who is on the ball?"

Garry shrugged his shoulders. "It's my job. That's what Uncle Sam pays me for. I do this all the time, in between routine admin work. Gets me outta the office for a change."

Phil nodded. "Yep, I know how you feel."

They arrived at the car and Garry opened the trunk.

"By the way, you will be dining with the ambassador tonight at seven. It's not often we have got the FBI visiting. Saturday night is our usual get together anyways."

The embassy building in Bern was old and elegant, with enormous rooms decked out with chandeliers and thick carpets. Wood panelling was everywhere. It was a cross between a five star hotel and a scene from *Gone With the Wind*. A more modern office building stood next to the old one.

After a relaxing bath in a king-sized tub, Phil spent the rest of the afternoon sleeping in one of the guest rooms. The phone beeped at six. It was Garry, giving him a wake-up call. His case had been unpacked and his shirts were all neatly pressed, hanging in the wardrobe.

"This is the life," he said as he began to feel human again.

He should have got a job with the Diplomatic Cor. Phil dressed for dinner and opened the heavy purple drapes. A mixture of snow and rain was falling outside. The centrally-heated room he was standing in was a much more inviting place to be. This time of year, it was cold everywhere. He remembered the icy wind he had left behind in DC. Pity this trip hadn't taken him somewhere a little warmer. Monday he would be flying back home again, and this change of scene would be over. *Oh well, back to Joe and the office, I suppose.* A tapping on the door interrupted his daydreams.

"Yeah, come on in," he called out.

Garry walked in. "Let's grab a couple of beers in the bar before dinner."

Phil smiled. "Yep, sounds good to me."

He followed Garry down to a huge dining room. The long table glittered with polished silver, and in the adjoining room was a small bar complete with pool table.

Garry waved to the young barman as he approached. "Two beers, please."

Phil parked himself on top of one of the stools and helped himself to some cashew nuts from a silver bowl. The first mouthful of beer went down very well. Just when he thought it couldn't get any better, it already had.

"After dinner the guys will come in here to talk shop," Garry explained. "I'm pretty sure the ambassador will have a word with you about tomorrow."

Three or four other staff members entered the bar with their wives. Garry introduced Phil to everyone, and then the ambassador himself arrived. At that moment, a bell was rung and the gathering filtered from the bar to the dining room to be seated.

The dinner was a long, drawn out affair with some small talk between courses. Phil was confused by the number of knives and forks, so waited to see what Garry picked up and then followed suit. No one picked up a fork in their right-hand, which was normal, as far as Phil was concerned.

The Swiss house staff was very prim and proper, serving from the left every time.

"This is good practice for official dinners," whispered Garry. "We don't want to look like slobs in front of foreign big shots."

Eventually, the eating and small talk was finished and the ambassador announced that the bar was open. He stood and made his way back to the bar, followed by the other six staff members and Phil. Eight brandies were waiting on the counter. The ambassador steered Phil towards two armchairs and a coffee table, and motioned him to sit down.

"I just wanted to fill you in about tomorrow."

He took a sip of brandy and pulled a cigar from his top pocket, which he lit with a match.

"I picked up this habit when my father did his stint in Cuba." He turned his head and blew a plume of smoke away from Phil. "A mite before your time, I would think. Collins reckons it's important you get your information from the bank, so I persuaded the minister of finance to have a word with the bank manager. He is pretty pissed off at having to meet you on a Sunday morning. Don't expect any pleasant chitchat when you and Garry get there. The Swiss are very serious people, especially when it comes to banking. Their whole economy is built on confidential numbered accounts. Every tin-pot dictator or money-grabbing president stashes their bucks here for that reason. Most of the time they get rubbed out or snuff it, and the money just sits here forever. Usually, the people they are supposed to represent are starving. It's a crazy world, Agent Jones."

Phil sipped his brandy. "Have you found much opposition in the giving of information?"

"Oh yeah, they sure as hell don't like it, but since Nine Eleven things have changed. They know we will be really pissed if they don't co-operate. We have enough financial clout to manipulate world markets and currencies. They are dead scared of that. When John Foster of South Africa co-operated with Kissinger over the Rhodesian war, the gold price doubled. We got rid of the minority white government in Rhodesia, but we didn't know what would replace it. The people there are actually worse off now than before."

Phil stared at the ambassador. "Did we do that?"

"Officially no, but you don't have to be a smartass to put two and two together. Ian smith would have lost the war eventually, so could be we saved a few lives. Anyway, this won't be the first time we have put pressure on the Swiss banks and I'm as sure as hell it won't be the last time."

Phil sipped his brandy, deep in thought. If the American government was doing things like that before Nine Eleven, just what was it doing now? With the Russians virtually out of the picture, the US had a free hand. They could manipulate the world though military might and financial power. He sure hoped the politicians knew what they were doing.

Yawning, he stretched out his long legs. The ambassador had left, and was talking to three guys at the bar. Tomorrow would be a piece of cake. He would have all the information he needed on the account holders. *This calls for another one of these excellent brandies.*

He drained his glass and headed back towards the bar, smiling at everyone in general.

Chapter 10

Bill awoke with the usual problem, but Monica was on hand and eagerly took control of the situation. On Sunday mornings, he usually arrived at the crusher at eight. Ammed stayed on after the night shift for a while, because the next night shift would only be on Monday night. It was just as well this particular morning. Monica was busy trying to break a world record in the sex Olympics and it seemed like her energy was inexhaustible. Eventually, she collapsed on top of him and they both managed to shower. She promptly crawled back into bed and fell asleep.

Bill could not remember much about last night, but two packets of condoms were missing. Normally, his sex life resulted in his condoms expiring before he used them. This was quite a pleasant change. Some of the condoms floated round and round in the bowl after flushing. He coked them into the s-bend with the brush and flushed again. Maybe the people who say life begins at fifty were right.

He made himself a cup of tea and toasted some bread before leaving the park home. His unusual sexual appetite was satisfied, but now he was desperate to hold the ball. Outside, the camp was deserted. Bill was the only expat to work on Sunday morning. He removed the ball from the Toyota's air cleaner and drove to the crusher.

After checking on the progress of the repairs, Ammed drove home and Bill retired to the office to read the letter that had been given to him at the disco. It was a single sheet of A4 paper, which was typewritten by a computer printer.

*   *   *

Mr. Parker,

I know that you are in possession of an item that belongs to me. It is legally mine because I own the land and the mineral rights in the whole of the Malenga region. You will deliver the item to the police station not later than Monday evening to the office of the officer commanding. You will be paid a substantial amount of America dollars as a reward for finding the object. Failure to comply will result in drastic action taken against you.

The ball is in your court, Mr. Parker.

Do not disappoint me.

Nabusano.

*   *   *

Bill read the letter three times. There was no mistaking the fact that they knew for sure the ball was in his possession. Joseph had left the area, so someone else must have seen him with it. He removed the ball from his shirt and rotated it between his thumb and fingers while thinking about the options left open to him.

Number one: give them the ball and receive some cash.

Number two: keep the ball and make a run for it.

Number three; keep the ball and stay here.

The first option seemed like the best way to go. That second man in the disco had stuck a gun in his back. Even if he gave them the ball, they could still kill him to keep him quiet. A sudden thought occurred to him. Maybe he had put Roberto's life in danger by involving him. Nikolay had said 'give them what they want and problem say bye bye'.

The nature of the ball had complicated things. Could be it wasn't as simple as that. Joseph had said 'give ball and leave'.

With a pocket full of money—that didn't sound such a bad idea. Nabusano had mentioned a substantial amount of dollars. For a rich man to say that, it would surely compensate him for the loss of his job.

His thoughts were interrupted by someone running up the office stairs. He quickly dropped the ball into his shirt pocket, thinking it was one of Nabusano's men, who had come to kill him.

John, the charge hand, burst into the office. "Come quick, Mr. Bill," he shouted. "The welding man has trapped his leg."

Bill rushed out with the charge hand. There was a commotion near the primary hopper. He ran over to the hopper and climbed the steel ladder to the top. Looking down inside, he could see the welder with his leg stuck between the two large rocks.

"Shit," he exclaimed.

Why hadn't Ammed emptied the hopper this morning while the crusher had been running? Bill cursed himself for not checking. He had been too preoccupied about the ball. The welder looked as if he was in quite a lot of pain.

He shouted back down the ladder, "Bring some bars and long pipes. We need to force the rocks apart."

The men below stopped milling around and ran for the items requested. While he waited for a bar, Bill could see what had happened. The welder must have pulled on his cables, causing the one rock to slide down the side of the hopper while he was busy welding. Someone below him on the ladder handed him a long crowbar. Bill climbed over the edge of the hopper and carefully slid down the inside, towards the trapped man at the bottom. The welder's face was contorted in pain.

"Don't worry. We will have you out just now," Bill told him.

He placed the end of the bar in a small opening and pulled with all his might. The bar bent, but there was no movement.

"Get down here with a long pipe," he shouted at two faces peering from above.

A long pipe came over the top and slid towards Bill, followed by two men.

"Be careful. Don't loosen anymore stones," he called. The men arrived safely and Bill directed them on where to insert the pipe.

"Here." He pointed to a gap just large enough for the end of the pipe to enter. "Put it in there and all pull together."

This they did without much success. Both the pipe and the bar were bending. To move a one-and-a-half-ton rock up a forty-five degree slope was not going to be easy.

"Try again," he shouted.

If this failed they would have to rig up a chain block, which would take time. They all pulled again, as hard as possible, and this time there was a slight movement. The gap had widened. Bill frantically looked round for something to place in the gap so it wouldn't close again. Sweat ran into his eyes, blinding him. He shook his head, flinging the drops from his forehead. A wedge-shaped stone was just out of reach. His one arm was pushing against his shirt front pocket. He could feel a hard lump inside. The ball. If he could remove the ball from his shirt without releasing the force on the bar, he could place it in the gap.

He exerted more force on the bar, and carefully removed the ball, telling the men to pull harder. At that moment, when the ball was in his hand, all three of them fell backwards in a heap.

"Christ!" *The bar and the pipe must have broken.*

Looking back towards the rock, all three of them were amazed to see it hovering a good half metre above the welder's leg. The welder stared at the floating rock for a moment and then quickly pulled his leg from underneath, and backed away on all fours. The urgency of the situation was over. Bill wiped the sweat from his eyes. He couldn't believe what he was seeing. The rock fell back on top of the other one with a crash that shook the hopper. All three of the men were galvanised into action by the sound of the collision, and scrambled out of the hopper in a shower of dust and stones. *Can't be much wrong with him.*

Bill watched the three disappear over the top. He sat where he had fallen in a daze, and lit a cigarette. His tongue felt like a dead animal resting at the bottom of his mouth. *What the hell happened? The only unknown factor in the equation was the ball.* By having skin contact with the ball and a high level of concentration, he could actually move things. *Fucking heavy things.*

Bill concentrated as hard as he could, and focussed his attention on a small rock. It slowly lifted. He was so surprised that the stone fell back immediately. Knowing what to expect, he tried again. The stone lifted and stopped in midair. He then swung it over to the left and slowly set it down. John's head appeared above the edge of the hopper. Bill dropped the ball into his open shirt and continued to smoke, trying to stop his legs from shaking.

"What has happened?" John called down to him. "Those three men have run off into the bushes."

Bill blew out a cloud of smoke, thinking of something to say. "I lost my temper and shouted at the men. I don't want any accidents happening on my job."

John didn't look too convinced. "I have never seen men run so fast. They were very frightened."

Bill stood up, rubbing his back. "Yes, well sometimes I get very angry. Tell somebody to pull these welding cables out of here. We will do this job next Sunday."

Bill climbed up the sloping side, with the help of the welding cables. The other men were standing in a group, muttering to each other. He shouted from the top, "It's not safe to work in here today. Finish the other jobs, then go home."

He climbed down the ladder on rubbery legs. The men seemed pleased at the prospect of an early finish, and went off to finish the other two small jobs.

"John," Bill called. "I don't feel well. I'm going home. Check the men finish, then lock up. I'll see you tomorrow morning."

"Yes sir," answered John, also pleased to finish early.

Bill collected Nabusano's letter from the office and locked the door. By tonight the whole of Malenga would be buzzing with stories of moving rocks and silver balls. With any luck, the three men who had been in the hopper would not be believed. Nobody in Europe would believe them. It was different here. The local population was very superstitious and would probably swallow the story hook, line and sinker. Nabusano would certainly hear about it, and any doubts about Bill having the ball would be dispelled once and for all.

As he walked to the Hilux the uncomfortable feeling returned. He noticed two black-suited security guards with old 303 Lee Enfield's slung over their shoulders. They were watching him intently from the shade of a tree on the other side of the fence.

There's nothing unusual in that, he told himself. That's what they are supposed to do. He climbed into his pick-up and started the engine, waiting for the air con to cool the interior.

Who am I trying to fool? This feeling has never been wrong before. It has something to do with the ball. Like a warning system of some sort.

He closed the door and drove back to camp. The feeling left him about half a kilometre down the road. He would make his own report on how the ball was affecting him, and discuss it with Roberto. It was too late to keep him out of it now, anyway.

Arriving back at the park home, he was warmly welcomed by a smiling Monica. She had made some sandwiches, and now switched on the kettle to make some tea while he showered. It was a nice change to come home to somebody. *She really has some body,* he thought as she washed his back. She then slid her hand round to his belly. John Thomas, who had been innocently studying the plastic floor of the shower, took a sudden interest in the ceiling.

"Here we go again," sighed Bill.

There was no stopping the series of events about to happen once set into motion. Luckily, the kettle was able to switch itself off.

Bill normally ate at the canteen, but Monica would not be allowed to enter. The expats with regular girlfriends usually changed from eating in the canteen to receiving a food allowance, and then cooking and eating at home. Also, an expat could acquire a camp gate pass for a girlfriend from the admin office, on the understanding that he would be held responsible for any problems. This system was to discourage the men from bringing hookers into the camp, which would result in a major breach of security. The majority of them would steal anything that was not screwed down, if given the chance.

Monica made a nice sandwich, but Bill gulped a bit when he tasted the tea. She had made it African style. Lots of sugar and milk. It was more like a very sweet and milky bedtime drink than tea, but it certainly made the cigarette taste better. He could only smoke if he was drinking something, otherwise they tasted like shit. That was another thing that had changed; probably due to the ball. He then remembered the insect bites that had disappeared overnight, and also being able to see in the dark.

To test his theory, he stuck his head under the bedclothes while holding the ball. At first it was dark, and then gradually became lighter, until he was able to clearly see the ball in his hand.

"What are you doing?" asked Monica, standing behind him.

He ducked his head out from under the bedding and stood up.

"I lost my good luck charm," he replied, with the ball in his hand.

She gasped and backed away. "What is wrong with your eyes?" she cried. "There is no white; only blackness."

He walked over to the mirror in the bathroom and could see his pupils were enormous. They nearly filled the whole of his eye sockets, but were gradually reducing in size.

"It's no problem," he replied. "I got a flash from the welding today. You see now they are alright again."

He tilted his head back and used some eye drops. They were the ones for washing the dust from his eyes. Looking back into the mirror, he saw his eyes were now normal again.

"You see, nothing to worry about." He smiled.

She wasn't so sure. "You frightened me. I have never seen eyes like that. Not even on a cat."

He walked over and hugged her, feeling guilty about scaring her. "Get ready; we are going over to Roberto's house. Sara will be there."

She smiled at the mention of Sara's name. "Sit down while I wash the dishes."

She pushed him back into the armchair and brought him a coke from the fridge. "I cannot leave a mess in my husband's house."

Bill shook his head, smiling. "We have just met and already you are hearing wedding bells. I have no plans to marry again."

She hummed a tune while washing the pots. "We will see. You will not want to leave me here when it is time for you to go."

Bill relaxed to the clinking sound of the dishes being washed. He took a swig of coke from the bottle. *A guy could quite easily get used to this, especially after being alone for so long.*

When Monica was ready, he took a quick look around outside. Every now and then, some of the guards went on foot patrol round the perimeter fence. He called for her to get in the Hilux and to keep down, because she had no pass yet. The last thing he needed was problems with Medusacor, especially on Sunday afternoon. The admin office would be deserted. He climbed in and started the engine. She immediately started fondling the front of his jeans.

"No, no, no," he ordered desperately.

He had visions of having to drive round and round the camp again.

Roberto's house was one of the permanent buildings that had been built for the staff of the hydro electric plant. They would move into the camp once the contractor's left. The house was a two-bedroom bungalow situated in one corner of the camp. Over the past two years, Roberto and Sara had established quite a nice garden. There was a vegetable patch round the back between the fence and the house. At the front were a number of banana trees, which had started producing small bananas. These trees grew very quickly in this climate, and also look very attractive, with large, hanging leaves spouting out of the central stem. The grass at the front and sides was cut every now and then by a garden boy with a local grass-cutting tool. This was like a steel, flat bar, one-metre long, with a handle at one end. The other end was bent at ninety degrees and sharpened on both sides. This tool was then swung backwards and forwards in one hand, slashing the grass to the required length. These tools were aptly called slashers, and at least provided some employment for the local young men.

Bill was relieved to see Roberto's Nissan parked under the carport and, with tyres crunching on the crushed stone driveway, he pulled in behind. A curtain moved and then Sara came out onto the veranda, smiling. She laughed when Monica surfaced from the passenger side, probably thinking the worst. Bill followed the chatting pair into the coolness of the house, not understanding a word they said. He wondered what on earth they were talking and laughing about. They had switched to the local language for a reason. He suspected that they discussed all the intimate details of their love lives. After a few surprised glances from Sara in his direction, he was sure of it.

Roberto emerged from the bedroom looking like Rip Van Winkle. With ruffled hair and bleary eyes, he managed a crooked smile. "On Sundays I catch up on sex and sleep," he explained.

"I think you have had too much of both. Over the last twenty-four hours I have managed to screw my brains out. I won't need sex for another year now."

They both sat in lounge chairs on opposite sides of the coffee table, on which Sara plunked two ice cold cokes. She quickly walked out to the veranda to resume the interrupted conversation with Monica.

"I think they are talking about us," Bill remarked.

"I am sure they are," Roberto surmised, taking a sip of coke. "What do you think about my garden? It is looking good, no?"

"Yes, very nice. Not much thanks to you, I'm sure. If you knock a stick in the ground the right way up it will grow here."

Roberto snorted. "You are only jealous of my talent. This evening I am cooking outside. Then you can see my other talent at barbeque."

Bill was unimpressed. He had attended some of Roberto's barbeques. If left to Roberto, they would have all turned into disasters.

He leant forward. "I need to talk to you urgently about the ball. The situation has escalated since yesterday."

Roberto's expression changed. He remembered the last encounter he'd experienced with the ball.

"So, what has happened?" he asked as he lit a cigarette.

Bill handed him Nabusano's letter. "They gave me this in the Tropica last night. I'm sure one of them stuck a gun in my back."

Roberto read the letter with a grim expression. "This sounds as if he knows for sure you have the ball." He read the letter again. "He also says that he has a legal right to the ball, which is true. The company pays him a royalty on every ton of rock from the quarry. There is even a rumour that he is financing the construction of the dam, but this I do not believe. It is a 150 million US dollar project. Nabusano is rich, but cannot be that rich. As far as I know, the customer is the electricity board, which is government owned."

Bill nodded. "Okay. So the ball is legally his and he knows for sure that I have it. The only course of action is for me to give it to him tomorrow night. There are two things I want to know before I give it away.

"One; I want to know what the hell it is, and two; I want to know how Nabusano knows about it. I found it a few days ago and this Nabusano knows exactly what it is and was probably expecting it to be found more or less where it was found. This I don't understand."

Roberto rubbed the end of his nose "Yes, you are right. He must know what it is, because he wants it. The other theory is quite interesting. There is good stone closer to the dam, but Nabusano insisted on the quarry being next to his old quarry. His lawyer attends all the meetings, and this point was not negotiable. I remember it because of the extra transport cost involved. His lawyer said 'no problem'. They would pay the extra cost. For me, that was stupid. All the royalty from the rock is paid back to us for a longer haul, which is not necessary. Cazzo, a business man not looking for a profit. This is crazy, no?"

Bill lit one of his own cigarettes. "Since I found the ball, his quarry has closed. Their crusher is not working and the gates are locked."

Roberto laughed. "What are you suggesting? That he was crushing for the ball?" Roberto laughed again and pointed. "And that he couldn't find it so he hired us to open a new quarry." Roberto waved his hands around in the air and laughed again. "And so this whole construction project is to find a silver ball."

His laughing gradually died away, enabling him to drink some coke.

Bill had sat motionless, thinking, while Roberto had made fun of him. "Yes, that's exactly what I am suggesting."

Roberto coughed and choked on the coke, which had gone down the wrong way, and the stared back at Bill.

"Vafanculo, you expect me to believe we have all been working here to find a fucking ball."

Bill exhaled a plume of smoke. "Yeah, that's exactly what I believe."

Roberto stared at him as if he had gone mad. Bill removed the ball from inside his shirt front. Roberto stiffened and pushed back in his chair, not wanting to get too close to it. Bill made sure the girls were still outside before switching his attention back to Roberto.

"This morning I found out something else the ball can do."

"What you mean do? The material is very valuable, but it cannot do anything." Roberto smiled and shook his head. "Give Nabusano the ball. All it is doing is making your brain into spaghetti."

Bill held the ball up in front of him. "This thing heals insect bites on my skin. This thing allows me to see in the dark. This thing gives me a warning of any danger within half a kilometre. This thing is trying to get me to stop smoking, and it also allows me to lift things up and down."

Roberto shook his head. "Cazzo, I can lift things up and down. I do not need a ball for that."

He picked up the ashtray and set it down again. "See, no problemo."

Bill concentrated on the ashtray. It lifted in the air and then floated down again. There was no reaction from Roberto, except his face was paler than before, so Bill lifted it up and down again. Still no reaction from Roberto, so Bill continued by lifting up and down all the items on the table. Roberto's eyes followed the movement of each item. The cigarette lighter spun round like a top, then did a figure of eight before landing back down on the tabletop. Roberto rubbed his eyes.

"I am dreaming. I did not get up from my bed yet. This is all a restless dream."

Bill stood and walked over to Roberto's drink cabinet. He poured two double whiskies and carried them back to the table. "You are not dreaming. Have a drink. I know how you feel. I was just as shocked as you when it happened to me the first time."

Bill lifted the glass to Roberto's mouth and tipped a little of the whisky inside. Roberto sat motionless for a moment, and then started slapping his own face.

"You are not dreaming," Bill repeated.

Roberto pushed his chair back and knelt down to look under the table. "How did you a do that? There is nothing under here and I did not see any strings."

Bill shook his head. "It is not a trick; the ball is doing it. Watch."

The book shelf in the corner lifted up and down and then a cushion floated round the room.

"Stop, stop," Roberto cried. "This is like the movie *Poltergeist*. It is making me a dizzy."

He picked up the whisky glass and emptied it in one gulp.

"So you believe me now?" Bill asked.

"Si, si, I believe you, but I do not understand how it works. Let me try."

Bill reluctantly handed the ball to Roberto. "You have to have a special concentration," he explained. "Or you can't do it." He placed a pencil on the table. "Try to move that, but concentrate really hard."

Roberto held the ball in both hands as if he was praying, and stared at the pencil. It started wobbling around, but didn't lift. Roberto looked like a constipated man trying to take a shit. He reminded Bill of an old joke. *What's the definition of strain? Teeth marks on the shithouse door.*

Eventually, the pencil spun round and flew off the table. Bill held out his hand. "Give it back to me. I think it's addictive. If it's not touching my skin, I feel empty." Bill dropped it back inside his shirt front. "Roberto, I need your help in trying to determine what this is, and the connection with Nabusano."

He refilled the two glasses and sat back down at the table. Roberto stood and brought a pen and notepad. He returned to his seat and lit a cigarette.

"The best way of solving problems is brain storming. We did this at university with a group of people and a blackboard."

He started writing on the pad. "Okay, what is the ball? Material unknown. Power source unknown. That remains a blank. What does it do? All those crazy things you mentioned. Anything else?"

Bill thought for a moment. "I can work things out much faster. It's improved my mental capacity."

"Okay, let us test that with a calculator. Right what is 6482 multiplied by 581?"

Bill narrowed his eyes and said, "Three million seven hundred and sixty-six thousand and forty-two."

Roberto raised his eyebrows. "Correct. What else can it do?"

Bill shuffled around in his chair. "Well, my sex life is much better and I think my dick is bigger."

Roberto looked very interested. "You are a joking, right?"

"No, its true, but I'm not showing you my dick. You will have to speak to Monica about that. I'm sure by now Sara knows all there is to know about my sex life. Let's just say if Jimmy was the proud owner of the ball, his night shift garden boy would have a poop hole like the channel tunnel by now."

Roberto cleared his throat and raised his eyebrows again. "Do you think I can borrow that thing before you give it to Nabusano?"

Bill shook head. "Sorry, no can do. Let's get back on track, shall we?"

Roberto rubbed his chin. "Well, whoever has a one of these; they have a distinct advantage over the have not. If you did not make that hollow in the stone, then I am starting to think this thing is one and-a-half to two million years old. Why not believe that? Everything else is unbelievable, anyway."

"There was no one around here two million years ago," Bill remarked.

"Yes there was," countered Roberto. "They were not men. They were ape-like creatures walking around on two legs."

"Good enough to manufacture the ball," Bill said, shaking his head.

"No, no, no, we even now could not manufacture it. We may have some materials like that, of which I have not heard of, but it's impossible to make it even do one of the things its doing. It does not even follow the laws of physics."

Bill lay back in the chair. "So it is not man-made."

The following silence was only broken by the flicking of Roberto's Zippo.

"Yes, I think we can safely say that," Roberto conceded.

Bill took a sip of whisky. "This has been fairly obvious to me since this morning, but I wanted to hear it from you. Tell me everything you know about this part of the world one-and-a-half to two million years ago."

Roberto screwed up his eyes. "Well, we have the Darwin Theory. This is basically one group of apes coming down out of the trees and walking around on two legs. They started standing up because the grass was too high for them to see over the top. The other apes carried on as apes and evolved into today's' monkeys, gorillas and chimps. Darwin thought that this one family of ape that stood up evolved into man. We now know this is not a strictly true. Three million years ago, there were three different types of apes walking around in this area. One they called 'Lucy, and another one they are calling Flat Face. The third one, which had a better physique for running and walking long distances, they have called *Erectus*. This is the one they think evolved into man. Lucy and Flat Face seemed to die out. There were two other lots that came along later. One they called Nutcracker because of his huge jaws, and another was called Goliath because of his a size. He was six-foot tall, which was one and-a-half times as tall as *Erectus*, but he also died out; or did he come after *Erectus*? I cannot remember. Anyway, *Erectus* was still going strong. There was another one called Robustus. He lived mostly by eating termites. Very good protein, but not in a big volume. It took time to dig into the termite's hills. They all lived together on about the same level, until two million years ago, then something happened. They found piles of round stones in places where *Erectus* was living. These stones had been removed from riverbeds and stock piled. They were just the right size for throwing. Then they discovered traces of cooking fires and some charred bones from Robustus in *Erectus* old camps. The cooking of the meat meant that *Erectus* could chew and swallow far more protein than any of the others, enabling his brain to grow larger. One-and-a-half million years ago, *Erectus* spread north into what is now known as Georgia. This is the Out of Africa theory."

Bill sipped his drink and puffed on his cigarette. "Did you learn all this in university?"

"No, I watch channel sixty-six on DSTV."

"There could be a connection here between *Erectus* and the ball." Bill continued. "Two million years ago *Erectus* suddenly became top dog. He was throwing stones and controlling fire. The others never even got around to doing any of that. Do you remember that old movie called *Two Thousand and One*?"

Roberto leant forwards. "You mean the function for the ball is the same as the obelisk?"

Bill shrugged. "Why not? It all fits. The ball is just the right size for *Erectus* to carry around. It's a shiny silver to attract some creature like that."

Roberto shook his head. "Yes, but to make it move things you have to concentrate. *Erectus* had a very small brain and a very little concentration."

Bill held up his hand. "No. Wait a minute. When I said concentration, it wasn't strictly true. It's more like a reflex action, as if you're trying to push something away. It first worked for me in a panic situation, quite by accident. If *Erectus* had a ball, he could push a predator away in a panic. All the other things, it does by itself automatically, to whoever has contact with it. Everything fits exactly. Even the higher sex drive is to promote the species. Seeing in the dark. Quick healing of the skin. Higher intelligence. Premonition of approaching danger. The only disadvantage would be if *Erectus* was a regular at the disco."

Roberto smiled and shook his head again. "Bill, you are forgetting one crucial thing. If this is a two thousand and one device and E.T. dropped it off two million years ago, what's it doing here now? Out of Africa happened and you have only discovered this ball a few days ago."

Bill rubbed his forehead. "I don't know, but I'm sure there is a reason. There must be. Everything else fits perfectly. It could have done its job and then been lost."

Roberto lit another Chesterfield. "Okay, that is a possibility. Now the other thing is Nabusano. How is he involved? What's his interest in the ball and how can he know about something that's just been found?"

Roberto poured a drop more whisky into their glasses while waiting for Bill to answer.

Bill lay back in the chair and stared at the ceiling. "I am sure my theory about him searching for the ball for a long time is right. How he is involved, I have no idea. It's not logical for him to be looking for something that has been hidden here for two million years."

Roberto nodded. "Yes, that does not make any sense. The old quarry of his is about fifty years old. If your Nabusano theory is a correct, then he has been looking for your ball for at least fifty years."

Bill brushed back his hair with the palm of his hand. "The only way we can hope to find out is to know as much as possible about Nabusano and this area. The answer must lie in the past."

Roberto glanced at his watch. "I must start preparing for the barbeque. Two of my guests have lived here for twenty possible years. I will introduce them for you to interrogate."

Billed smiled at Roberto's use of the English language, but decided not to correct him. Technically, he was right. The definition of interrogate would be to ask questions.

"How much do you know about Nabusano? I only know what you and Joseph have told me."

Roberto stroked his eyebrows with the tips of his fingers. "Everybody knows he is bad news. There is rumour of people disappearing if they make any sort of problem, but there is no proof. According to that letter, it looks as if he has a strong connection with the police in town. If you were drunk and ran over a little old lady, they would probably let you go for a case of beers."

"So basically what Joseph told me is good advice. He said to give them the ball and leave here. He also mentioned the police and the military working for Nabusano."

Roberto stubbed out his cigarette. "He has more brains than you. He is out of here. We could also be working for him if that rumour about the project funding is correct."

Bill leant forward in his chair. "So what does he look like? You must have seen him at the monthly meetings."

Roberto shook his head. "No, his lawyer attends all the meetings that concern them. His name is Gwasa, John Gwasa. Funding is never discussed at the head of department level. All we talk about is day-to-day problems and progress. The admin manager has his usual complaints about expenditure. If I think about it, Gwasa only asks questions about the quarry. I presumed his interest was because of their quarry and crushing plant supplying some of the stone."

"What other meetings does Gwasa attend?"

Roberto rubbed his chin. "I have seen him in the project manager's office. I do not know what they talk about."

Bill nodded. "The project manager sends me letters about where to drill and blast. I bet that's what they talk about. Sometimes we stop drilling and blasting where there is a good face, and move to a fucked up part of the quarry. I was thinking the project manager was an asshole, but now it's starting to make sense. Nabusano is telling him where to drill and blast."

Roberto checked his watch again and stood up. "You could be right, but do not forget it is their stone. They have the say so about the source. I only check the quality. Now I must prepare the fire for the cooking outside."

Bill also stood, reluctant to end the conversation. "So nobody sees Nabusano? Not even in the town?"

"No, he is a recluse. He lives on an island in the middle of the lake. Speak to Ken and James. They will be here in one hour."

Roberto walked outside, anxious to commence lighting the fire. Bill grabbed a cold beer from the kitchen fridge and headed for the veranda. He passed the girls on their way in and they both started giggling as they arrived in the kitchen to make salads. Bill had the feeling he wasn't actually famous; more like infamous.

He sat down in a veranda chair so he could observe Roberto's fire lighting performance. It was usually quite entertaining, unless it reached a stage where the meat would never be cooked. If that happened, some of the hungrier men would formulate an excuse to get Roberto to leave the fire while they quickly got it going properly. On his return, he would say, "See, I told you the fire is okay."

The standard construction site barbeque was usually made from an oil drum that had been cut in half vertically, and some legs added to raise the open part of the drum to waist height. These half-drums could cook meat for about fifteen people at one time, and were always topped off with a piece of steel mesh from the crushing plant. Roberto was now trying to balance small pieces of wood on top of a large bundle of compacted newspaper. As a teenager, Bill had been a boy scout. He could have produced a blazing pile of wood in about five minutes. Once the wood was burning really well, it was then possible to start adding the charcoal. It usually took Roberto an hour to reach this stage. After three or four failed attempts, he would smother the burning wood with half a bag of charcoal dumped on top. If the charcoal managed to start burning, he would prematurely start poking it, fascinated by the flames. This invariably caused the fire to die and Roberto then to reappear, armed with an electric fan. For some unknown reason, he wouldn't accept any help or resort to using fire lighters. It could only be some sort of macho thing. Roberto was now busy coughing and choking, hidden in a cloud of black smoke. Sara arrived with another cold beer for Bill. She kicked his foot lightly and nodded towards a large flower pot on the veranda.

Roberto's black face emerged from the smoke. "Where is my beer?" he asked while fanning the source of the smoke with a piece of cardboard.

"I am looking after our guest. You can get one yourself."

She rolled her eyes toward the plant pot and went back inside. Roberto followed her, licking his dry lips.

"Can you not see I am a very busy?" he asked, grumbling.

Bill quickly reached inside the plant pot and removed a plastic bottle, which had a strong smell of diesel fuel. He sloshed it on the smoking pile of charcoal and replaced the empty bottle inside the pot. The black smoke of the fire turned to a grey colour, but did not ignite. *Shit, if Roberto comes back now he's going to lose his eyebrows.*

Bill lit a piece of paper with his lighter and tossed it into the fumes while sitting down with the beer in his hand. Roberto arrived back on the veranda with an electric fan, trailing an extension lead behind him.

Vump. The barbeque was transformed into an orange ball of fire. Roberto took a step back inside the house and peered round the door frame with round eyes. "What a happened"?

Bill wiped some beer from his lips. "Must have been wet charcoal. It's probably just dried out."

Roberto went back into the house and returned with a beer. He sat down next to Bill and took a long pull from the bottle. "That explains everything. Other people do not a fight like I do to start a barbeque. Sara must be buying damp charcoal all the time."

There was a red glow on the western horizon as the sun started to set. The two of them sat together, drinking beer, content with each other's company. Roberto turned his smoke-blackened, tear-streaked face towards Bill. "Your ball is the greatest discovery mankind has ever made, but promise me one thing."

"What's that?"

"That you will definitely give it to them tomorrow night. Do not get any crazy ideas about keeping it."

Bill took a swig of beer. "Yes, I promise. It's the only way I can get out of this mess."

The flames began to die down as the diesel fuel was consumed. Red embers of charcoal glowed from the centre of the fire. Roberto felt an irresistible urge to poke the embers with a steel rod, but was a bit apprehensive after witnessing the ball of fire a few minutes ago.

"Do something for me," Bill added. "Check on your computer about the history of this area. Look for anything out of the ordinary."

Roberto nodded. "I will do that tomorrow. Google or Yahoo search should have some information on record." He thought a while. "Also, the British Ministry of Defence. They had soldiers here in the colonial days. It should be educational, if nothing else."

Lights swung across the garden as two cars arrived in the driveway.

"I think you had better wash your face," Bill remarked.

"You look like a refugee from the Black and White mistral show."

"The what?"

Bill waved his hand. "Never mind. That was before your time, on English television."

Roberto ducked inside while Sara came out to welcome the visitors. She looked at the glowing fire and smiled at Bill. "I see Roberto's fire lighting is getting better."

Bill nodded. "Yes, but I'm glad you didn't put petrol in that bottle. My name would have been Guy Fawkes by now."

Sara shook her head. "You expats forget that we African women have spent our whole lives cooking outside on wood fires."

"Yes, you're right," Bill agreed." You women are experts at fire lighting."

Monica came out and smiled at Bill. She had that look in her eyes. *This is going to be a long night*, he told himself, and stepped forward to meet Roberto's guests.

The first vehicle had parked next to Bill's Hilux. It was an old Toyota Stout; a very strong single cab pickup truck. Bill recognised the man walking towards them. It was Ken Marshal, who he had met twice before at the golf club bar. He was an ex-Rhodesian Airlines pilot who made his living by flying the odd tourist round the lake in his old float plane. It was difficult to guess Ken's age.

He looked about sixty-five, but his monthly consumption of whisky was probably more than his plane's avgas.

His red-nosed face lit up into a smile when he saw them coming to meet him.

"Those blighters at the gate are full of shit," he complained. "Made us all sign a bloody visitors' book, of all things. Never had to do that before."

Ken stroked his white moustache in anticipation of being handed a whisky, then made his way to the house to help himself. He was followed by a short, middle-aged African man and his wife. Ken, who lived on the shore of the lake at the other side of town, had given the couple a lift to the camp. They were introduced to Bill by Sara. The short, stocky African's name was James Boama. His wife's name was Brenda. He was a school teacher in Malenga and had probably left his car at home to save petrol. Roberto emerged from the front door, fresh and clean. All trace of the recent struggle with the fire was washed away. He stood proudly next to the barbeque, grinning foolishly with a bottle of beer in his hand.

Ken came outside with a double whisky on the rocks and stood next to Bill. "Roberto's managed a jolly good fire for a change," he remarked.

Bill winked and tapped the side of his nose with his index finger.

"Oh," Ken lifted his head knowingly. "Some stout chap has assisted him, no doubt." He called over to Roberto, "Jolly good fire you have there. We should be able to start braaing in half an hour. It's too hot for the meat just now."

Roberto stuck his nose up in the air and strutted importantly round the barbeque.

Ken smiled. "I think I have just made his day."

"Yes," Bill agreed. "Don't go and burst his bubble. He has a macho thing about lighting fires. I think if he wasn't a geologist he would have been an arsonist. A very unsuccessful one. He would be arrested with a can of petrol in one hand and an electric fan in the other."

The second car that had arrived belonged to the workshop manager. He quietly stood next to the fire, smiling, with a beer in his hand. Bill introduced him to Ken and they talked about the weather. They all agreed the rains were due any day now. The two contractors listened intently to Ken's predictions as to when the rains would start and how heavy it would turn out to be. Bill was worried about crushing and screening wet material, whereas the other was worried about his truck transmissions. The girls were busy circulating with the snacks and drinks, but ended up chatting with Brenda, the school teacher's wife. After that it was a 'help yourself' situation.

By the time the fire was ready for braaing, the last two cars had arrived, with four more Italians. They all went inside and sat round the dining room table, with Roberto as master of ceremonies.

"Nice, quiet sort of chap, that workshop manager," Ken remarked as he sipped his whisky

"Yes," Bill answered. "He's very good at his job, but don't judge a book by its cover. I've heard he sleeps with two girls at the same time. He's the only man in Malenga who can get pussy on credit."

Ken coughed into his glass. "Good lord, I wonder where he gets the energy."

"By all accounts, it's the pasta."

"Hmm, would be a waste on me. I'm a bit past that sort of thing. The only one that shares my bed is Patch, my dog. By the way, remind me to take some bones away with me when I leave. I'd forgotten already."

Roberto returned, wearing a cook's hat, carrying a tray of meat. "Tadar," he shouted, plunking the tray on top of the patio table. Ken and Bill gave each other a sideways glance. Roberto's braaing usually ended up with burnt or dried out meat.

"I'll do that for you," Bill offered. "A good friend of mine taught me how to braai in South Africa. The Afrikaaners are experts at this. They do it all the time."

Roberto looked a bit crestfallen and unsure.

"Yes," chimed in Ken. "You must look after your guests. Your impression of the project manager talking on the radio is quite famous. Very amusing, in fact."

Roberto's face broke into a foolish grin. He plucked off the cook's hat and plunked it on top of Bill's head, then rushed back inside. Bill smiled back at Ken. "Well done. That was a stroke of genius."

Ken looked into his empty glass. "I have my moments, you know. Right now I need a refill."

Ken walked inside, aiming towards the refrigerator in the kitchen. All the Italians were laughing while Roberto spoke into a handheld radio, imitating the project manager. "Pasarani. Pasarani," he shouted. "Si, si," he squeaked in Pasarani's voice.

The Italians roared with laughter.

"I hope that thing's not switched on," Ken remarked as he walked passed.

Roberto's expression instantly turned to one of horror as he examined the radio in a panic. There was a deadly silence around the table until Roberto clasped a hand to his heart and blew out a sigh of relief. Immediately, the laughing erupted even louder.

The project manager had the habit of listening to the radio broadcast at night and would surprise the night shift every now and again by issuing an instruction.

Roberto was smiling on Ken's return from the kitchen, but Ken could see he was badly shaken. To get on the wrong side of any project manager was occupational suicide on any contract.

Two lab technicians arrived on foot from the other side of the camp. They didn't have use of company vehicles after working hours. There was quite a lot of inequality in the company system, but it was motivated by practicality rather than prejudice. Firstly, there were never enough vehicles for everyone, and secondly, some Africans viewed company transport as a means of making money. Car equals taxi, equals money, equals drink, equals upside down car in the bush. As it was, now and again, the odd drunken expat recruited a friend to pull his car out of a ditch early the next morning. Hopefully before anyone found out. Usually by lunch time everyone else knew about it.

The Africans examined what was cooking on the fire and then made a beeline for the fridge. While Bill turned the meat on the grill, Ken walked up with whisky in hand to see how he was doing.

"You lived here long?" Bill enquired.

"Oh, about fifteen years or so," Ken smiled, stroking his white moustache.

"What do you know about this Nabusano character?" ventured Bill, while turning a coil of sausages.

Ken's smile disappeared. "Why do you ask?" he demanded.

"I have something he wants."

"Best to give it to him as soon as possible, old chap. He has a group of thugs in his town that makes sure he gets what he wants. Owns everything here. He tolerates Otto and I like a man who would let a fly walk on the back of his hand and do nothing about it. There are also one or two Indian cafes and shops, but that's it. Only last night one of them had his throat cut. I can bet the police are doing nothing about it."

"Which shop was that?" Bill asked as he took a swig of beer.

"Oh, that small café near that godawful disco place. He owns that, as well. Won't catch me in a place like that. Blast out your eardrums from half a mile away."

Bill felt his stomach tighten. "You mean the Tropica?" he asked.

"I don't know what its name is. Thank God I live out of town near the lake. Nice and quite there."

"How did you find out about the cafe?"

"I passed there this morning and stopped when I saw them load the body into the back of a police van. They say it was a robbery, but any fool can see the broken glass is all on the outside. If you ask me, I think it was Nabusano's men. They were probably inside, demanding protection money, and broke the bloody door window from the inside after killing the poor sod."

Bill cleared his throat. "Is there much crime here in Malenga?"

Ken snorted. "Nothing that hasn't anything to do with Nabusano's thugs. The local criminals are too scared to try anything. Even the odd fishing boat mysteriously burns to the waterline every now and then."

Ken tapped the side of his nose. "That's because they've been too close to Nabusano Island."

Bill wondered if Ken was a little paranoid about Nabusano. At least he was acquiring quite a lot of information. Bill waved and caught Sara's attention. The first lot of meat was ready. He started removing it from the grid, placing it into a large aluminium dish. The lab technicians immediately followed her, with a beer in each hand, as she carried the food into the house. Bill started to lay the other half of the meat on the grid. "Have you ever been to the island?" he enquired.

Ken laughed. "You must be bloody joking. No one sets foot on that place unless he invites them. Actually, a better way of putting it would be 'sent for or ordered to see him'. Five years ago I used to fly over there. That place of his is built like a Moorish fort. I didn't like flying over it, but the tourists were quite impressed. I've seen the flash of sunlight from more than one pair of binoculars while passing overhead. The last time I was buzzed by that bloody great white helicopter he parks on his roof. Scared the shit out of everyone, and then later the police hand delivered a letter from his lawyer. Violation of air space. Invasion of privacy. Possible loss of my license, etc., etc.. I was going to go back just for the hell of it. His lawyer, John Gwasa is his name, must have read my mind." Ken dropped his voice to a whisper. "He came to see me the next day, quite unofficial sort of, because he told me not to mention his visit to anyone. He pleaded with me, with tears in his eyes, not to fly over the island again. Rumour has it that he is as queer as a nine bob note, but I honestly think that man saved my life."

The noise from inside the house rose in volume as all the Italians were talking at the same time. Every few seconds, one of them shouted 'allora', which means 'and then'. At least they didn't seem to have a care in the world, and were having a good time.

Ken smiled and shook his head. "Italian conversational volume is directly proportional to how much bloody vino they drink."

Bill nodded and started turning over the meat with a large fork. "Yeah, I know exactly what you mean. What else do you know about Nabusano?"

Ken pursed his lips and squinted. "As I said, he owns nearly everything here in Malenga. Everything and anybody he wants to own, that is. The businesses in town are run by his sons, of whom he seems to have plenty. They are the only regular visitors to the island. It's strictly off limits to anyone else. If the locals ask too many questions or step out of line, they simply disappear."

Ken lowered his voice. "There was one reporter from Mabarta doing an article on Nabusano. He only lasted a week. No one knows what happened to him. The hotel said he'd checked out, but the paper he worked for said he'd vanished. It's a bit different for people like us with foreign passports. The British government is not too amused when their citizens just vanish off the face of the Earth. They would send someone to investigate. I think for a foreign passport holder, Nabusano would go to a bit more trouble and have something fabricated, like an allegation of rape or child abuse. He could have anyone deported in a couple of days. Once you understand the situation, the only way to survive here is to keep a very low profile. Lord knows how I've managed that. I'm not usually the kind of chap that keeps his trap shut."

The second batch of meat was ready, so Bill started to remove it to the outer edges of the grid. Monica came up behind him and slipped an arm round his waist. Bill introduced her to Ken, then asked her to find the meat dish. Ken watched her walk away.

"I see you've been doing a bit of integration. Hope you realise a single expat is quite a prize for a local girl."

"Yes, I've only known her two days and she's talking about marriage already. Can't really blame her. It's the situation here."

They each picked up a piece of meat that had cooled down, and started chewing.

"A huge improvement on Roberto's ruddy efforts, I must say."

"What do you know about Nabusano's crushing plant and the quarry?" Bill persisted.

Ken emptied his glass and rattled the half-melted cubes about in the bottom. "Been there a good fifty years, as far as I know. Never been on the same scale as you have now. Even so, over the years he's over produced for the local market. There's a bloody great stockpile of concrete stone on the far side of town near the Mabarta road. You can only see it from the air. God knows what he's going to do with that. That island of his must have thousands of tons of concrete structures all over the place. Stone used to go over there by barge until the dam project started. Why don't you people start a new quarry nearer the batching plant? Seems not too clever to run it seven kilometres for no reason."

Bill shrugged. "Search me. Roberto says there's good stone much closer than the quarry."

Monica returned with the aluminium dish and waited until Bill filled it, keeping some aside for Ken and himself.

"That's the perks of braaing," Bill remarked. "You get to choose the best bits."

Ken nodded and examined the bottom of his glass.

Bill could see he was about to head for the kitchen again. "How long has the Nabusano family been here?" he quickly asked.

"The Nabusano family has been on that island for as long as anyone can remember. I think his great-grandfather was called Chief M'ba by the locals. That means 'great father' or something or other. Supposed to have been a great warrior and sorcerer. Vanquished all their enemies and all that rot. The name has been passed down from generation to generation, but the head of the Nabusano family is now more like a mafia godfather than anything else. Do yourself a ruddy favour and give him what he wants."

With that, Ken dashed off for a refill. Bill continued eating meat from the grid until Roberto appeared with a fresh beer for him.

"I must buy meat from that same place in Mabarta again. It tasted excellently good this time. Verbeni. Have you talked to Ken about you known who?"

"Yeah, he's given me a lot of information, but he doesn't know much about Nabusano history. If he hasn't exaggerated, I'm in a lot of trouble," he added.

Roberto made a crooked face while he thought, and then pointed to the other end of the garden.

"Go over there and get James to the one side. Get the African point of view. People of a different culture normally have a totally different sighting of the same problem. I tried to talk to Sara, but when I say 'Nabusano' she looked to me like I am a snake."

Bill could see the party had become a group round the garden table, while the Italians had taken over the house. Judging by all the used paper plates, most of the eating was finished in the garden. They must have climbed into the first lot of meat. Bill nodded and Roberto went back inside to the 'allora' shouters.

The women had formed a small group of their own, so at the moment James was virtually standing alone. Bill picked up his bottle of beer and casually walked over to him. They shook each other's hand and reintroduced themselves again. James showed a pleasant smile, but Bill noticed a tired look to his eyes. Even in the dim light, Bill could see the other's jacket was rather threadbare and out of shape. He estimated the teacher's age as close to his own, because his tight, black, curly hair was starting to grey at the sides. It's not normal for Africans to prematurely go grey, so it's a fairly good indication of age.

"We have never met, but I have heard some good things about you." James smiled.

Bill was surprised. "Really, how's that?"

"Some of my pupils' fathers work at your crusher and say you are not like the one before. He was one for making big noise with no thinking. They named him after a certain bird from the lake. It flies round in circles making a horrible noise."

James stretched out his arms and turned round and round, making a loud bird noise. "Caw, caw, caw," he shrieked.

The other African men laughed from across the garden. "Yes, Mr. Bill. That is your predecessor," one of them shouted. He immediately started doing an impression of a chicken, walking around, periodically scratching the ground with his feet.

"Who is that?" Bill asked.

James smiled. "That is your workshop manager looking for spare parts in the scrap yard."

Bill shook his head. "I'm not going to ask you what my name is."

James laughed. "Do not worry. They just call you the silent one. The exact translation is quite a compliment. Your Italian friends are not as fortunate. Roberto is something of an exception. His name means 'the clown with the wise head'."

Bill held up his hands. "Don't tell me any more. I'm liable to start laughing when I meet these people."

The workshop manager did actually look like a chicken with a large, Roman nose and staring eyes.

"What subjects do you teach?" Bill enquired as he took a swig of beer.

"I teach all subjects, because my school is very small and I am the only one. I cannot afford other teachers. My school is private, so I am able to teach what the government schools dare not."

Bill looked shocked. "What on earth are you teaching that is banned in the other schools?"

"You must understand, Mr. Parker; the people in this part of the country are like lost souls who are floundering in quicksand.

The more they struggle, the more they sink. I am trying to raise them from the depths of superstition and ignorance, but there is a powerful force here pushing them down."

The conversation seemed to have developed serious undertones. Bill decided to light up a cigarette. "I am very interested in learning about local history." Some of the smoke stung his eyes and made them water.

"For what reason would an expatriate contractor be interested in local history?" James inclined has head to one side, waiting for Bill to answer. Bill took a heavy drag on the cigarette and exhaled.

"I need to know all I can about this Chief M'ba."

James pulled Bill to one side and led him into the corner of the garden.

"That is Nabusano you're talking about," he hissed.

Bill nodded. "Yes, I suppose so."

James composed himself and addressed Bill in a stern voice. "You should leave well enough alone. Do not involve yourself with that man."

"He is the one who has approached me," Bill explained defensively.

"What does he want?" James snapped.

"I have something he wants."

"Then give it to him and think yourself lucky if that's the end of it."

"Yes. I'm going to do that, but I would like to know more about him. It's important," Bill added.

James paced up and down in the corner of the garden as if trying to make up his mind. He passed a hand over his sweating face and eventually stopped.

"I will answer your questions to enlighten you as to the gravity of your situation purely because I am concerned for your well being."

Brenda, his wife, looked anxiously across from the talking women. James raised his hand to signal her to stay where she was, and then continued. "I came here twenty years ago to be married to my future wife, Brenda." He inclined his head towards the women. "We met each other at a roadside shop in Malenga Main Street. It was on my way from Mabarta to the border. It was love at first sight, but she refused to move to the capital, so I had to start a new life here. Her father demanded a heavy dowry, thinking I would be unable to pay. Strangers are never welcome here in Malenga.

"It was not easy at first, because I am from a different tribe. The tribe here is suspicious of outsiders. After five years, I was gradually accepted because the school was very successful. Some of my pupils went on to university in Mabarta. It was not difficult to shine against the government schools. Nabusano discouraged education and, as you probably know, he controls this town. Uneducated people can be controlled easier by fear and superstition. One night there was a terrible noise from the school room next to my house. I found four men breaking everything, and tried to stop them. They produced a pair of pliers."

At this point, James stopped and removed a set of dentures from his mouth. "Have you ever seen an African with false teeth?" He slipped them back in and continued, "My screams eventually woke the whole neighbourhood, and they came in ones and twos to see what was happening. Normally they would have huddled behind locked doors, but they came because of the school. The school had given them some hope for their children's future. Eventually, one of the bystanders picked something up and threw it at one of the men. They were so surprised that they stopped pulling out my teeth and stared at the crowed. A miracle happened. The people went into frenzy and threw anything that came to hand at the men. They fled in confusion and never returned. They could have killed me at a later stage, but they did not. This was the one and only time people reacted to Nabusano's henchmen, and it must have made him think twice. The last thing he wanted was a martyr. Many others have not been so lucky."

James paused to wipe his face with a handkerchief.

"If the police are corrupted here in Malenga, surely the police commissioner in Mabarta can do something," Bill insisted.

James shook his head. "You still do not understand. The president of this country is Nabusano's puppet. Two of his sons are permanently serving as advisors in the president's office. Presidents come and go, but Nabusano just continues. They are not chosen by the people. Nabusano chooses them."

James walked over to the table for his glass of wine to give Bill time to absorb the statement he had just made. When he returned, Bill was puffing on a second cigarette.

"Are you telling me this local recluse is controlling the whole country?" Bill asked.

"Yes. This is exactly what I told you, and I am sure his influence does not stop at our borders."

"Have you any proof of this?"

"No, but I have lived here long enough to understand what is happening. I am only telling you these things in case you run foul of Nabusano and go to some government official for help. You would be snuffed out like a candle. The rebels in the north are fighting for a change of government, but even they do not know who the real villain is. All they have achieved is the death of a few innocent people. They are too afraid of the M'ba legend to even come into this area."

"What does the legend say? M'ba means 'father', doesn't it?"

"Yes, but it is the language of the west coast. Our local word for father is 'baba'."

"What does the legend say about the Nabusano family?"

James shook his head. "This is precisely the kind of thing I am trying to stamp out. To uplift our people into the modern age."

"Tell me anyway. I am from the modern age and will not be influenced by what you tell me."

James looked a bit doubtful, but decided to tell Bill what he had heard. "Let's go and sit down at the table. I am tired of standing in the corner like a dunce."

The lab technicians had gone home. Only the women were left at the table, talking. James addressed them. "You women go inside. I want to speak to Mr. Parker." He pointed to Monica. "And you; fetch your man a beer." All the women rushed off together and went inside the house.

Bill sat down, amazed. "I must try that on a group of white women sometime," he remarked to no one in particular.

James refilled his wine glass from the bottle on the table. "If you do, call an ambulance ten minutes beforehand."

Bill looked back at James, but he seemed deadly serious until he suddenly burst out laughing. Monica arrived with Bill's beer. She knelt down on the glass, bowed her head, and placed the beer on the table, then left. Bill stared at the beer. "How on earth did you manage that?"

"You must start off on the right foot, but eventually they take over without you noticing."

"So, tell me about the Chief M'ba legend," Bill persisted.

James rested his hands on the table, palms facing up.

"I only know what my wife has told me. As I said, I am not of this tribe. I forced her to tell me because in a fight against superstition, one has to know one's enemy." James started laughing. "There is even a story in the town about you being a magician." He shook his head and then continued. "She said that a long time ago, long before the first Mzungu came to this land, her tribesmen were fishermen and lived here on the shore of the lake. There was another, larger tribe, close by, of hunters and warriors. The fishermen were no match for the hunters and were constantly raided by them.

"That was the normal African way of doing things. I think we are still trying to grow out of that system, but have not quite managed it yet. Anyway, one day a young boy arrived at the village near to starving. The chief decided to keep the boy because in some years he would be an extra man to defend the village. He gave the boy to a family that had lost its son. Their son had been killed by the hunters. The name of that family was Nabusano. The boy had terrible dreams at night and constantly cried out 'M'ba, M'ba'. So the Nabusano family gave him the name of M'ba for that reason. He grew up to be a very strong young man, physically far superior to the tribe of fishermen. The chief had great plans for breeding from this stranger, and ordered that he have many wives. One girl in particular, M'ba fell in love with. As soon as all the wives were pregnant, he spent all his time with the one he loved. The chief did not object, because all the others were with child.

"One day, M'ba had taken a group of young men into the forest to teach them the ways of a hunter when the other tribe attacked the village. His favourite wife was raped and then murdered because she resisted and fought back. When M'ba returned, he found that his wife and the chief had been killed. His mind was destroyed with grief. He spent many days alone on the riverbank, just staring into the fast-flowing water. He attacked anyone who ventured close to him. This all sounds quite normal up to now, but then the story changes into fantasy.

"After many days, M'ba returned to the village quite sane. He told them the God of the river had honoured him with a gift and he was now the new chief. No one argued with him because he was bigger and stronger than any of them, so they gave him the staff of the chief. Then he showed them the gift of the river God. They bowed down and worshiped him as a prophet. After some time, they say he changed into a powerful wizard and performed all kinds of magic.

"A year later, the tribe of warriors returned for their usual raping and stealing. M'ba went out to meet them alone and was gone for two days. He returned with the head of the warrior chief and threw it into the river. M'ba told everyone that the other tribe was totally destroyed and would never return, and that their village had been made as if it had never existed."

James poured some more wine into his glass and shrugged. "You see what sort of thing I am up against."

"Did the fishermen believe him?"

"Not all of them. Some of the braver ones followed the river in the direction M'ba had come from and they say they saw the most terrible sight. The hunters had been destroyed in a most terrible manner. According to the story, they were all torn to pieces. The bits in the river, the crocodiles ate. The bits on the ground, the jackals ate. The bits in the trees, the birds ate."

Bill lit up a fresh cigarette while James paused. "So you see, that's how the Nabusano family came to rule this tribe and that's why there is a Nabusano controlling everything today."

Bill rubbed his forehead with his left hand. "Do you believe any of this?"

James shook his head. "No sane person would believe this legend, but the people here do. That is why they are so afraid of Nabusano. They say the power of M'ba still continues."

"What was the gift from the river God to M'ba? Why did they bow down to him?"

James spread his hands. "I have no idea. Either my wife does not know or she would not tell me. Anyway, what does it matter? The whole story is a figment of some old women's imagination."

Bill blew out a plume of smoke. "Sometimes there is some truth in these tales, but most of it is changed from one generation to the other."

James shook his head. "You see, I should never have told you anything. Even you believe some of the crazy legend."

"Why did Nabusano choose to live on an island?"

James waggled a little finger inside his ear.

"They have been there a long time. It was purchased from the British after they had pronounced this part of Africa was theirs. I suppose the British had no use for an island in the middle of a lake in the middle of Africa. The only use for such a place is if you do not want contact with anyone. That must have been in Nabusano's grandfather's day. M'ba was supposed to have a great hatred of all people except is own offspring. That is probably why Nabusano's grandfather split the tribe in two and one half stayed here while the others moved to the island. M'ba called his offspring the true followers. I have heard they still worship the god of the river, even today. That is the reason why they have to control the president. If not, the government could declare the island as the property of the country to chase the Nabusano family from it."

Bill nodded. "Yes, I never thought of that. I'm starting to believe your conspiracy theory."

"If you believe anything, believe that. I know what's going on. I am an educated man who can read between the lines. Most of the population only believes what they hear on the radio or read in the newspapers. All are controlled by the government."

Bill finished his beer. "Have you ever met Nabusano?"

"No, I have seen him from a distance. About ten years ago, I saw him where your quarry is now. He was standing alone, looking across the river, not moving for a long time. He was holding something, but I could not see what it was. Eventually, one of his men saw me, so I quickly moved off."

James emptied the wine bottle into his glass. "Now I have a question. What is it that you have that Nabusano wants?"

Bill stubbed out his cigarette. "If I told you, you wouldn't believe me. It is far crazier than your legend. All I can say is, its very important to him."

"Then you are in far more danger than I realised. I will help you in any way I can."

He gripped Bill's forearm in a gesture of support and looked him in the eye. Bill smiled and covered the man's hand with his own.

"Thank you. You can only help me by finding out what you can of Nabusano's history. I need to know how and why he wants the thing that I have."

Music started playing inside the house. Monica appeared on the veranda. "Come inside," she shouted. "I have found some rock and roll for you."

Bill raised his eyebrows. "At least she understands how old I am."

James released his grip. "Good luck, my friend, and God be with you."

Inside, clouds of toxic smoke rose from the Italian table. They were all playing cards. Roberto was sprawled out on the couch, snoring with his mouth open. All the women stood up and started dancing to the rock and roll music. The workshop manager's attention was redirected towards the gyrating woman. His beak-like nose swung from side to side as he checked out the wiggling backsides, first with one eye, then the other.

Oh lord, Bill thought. *Someone better not play the Funky Chicken or I'm going to collapse in hysterics.*

He and James danced with one partner, then the other. The Italians put down their cards and joined in the dancing. *Time to go*, Bill thought. *I think the pasta has started working.* There were more men than women and they were all spoken for. It could end up in a punch up.

He winked at Monica and flicked his head towards the door. She seemed puzzled for a moment, then that look spread over her face. *Here we go again. But at least I'm getting her out of here.*

They danced through the door onto the veranda. Bill didn't like saying goodbye to drunken people. Sometimes it proved quite difficult to actually depart. When they reached the Hilux, he found he was parked in, so they set off walking down the road. He only hoped the security guards weren't prowling around inside the camp. There was a shout from behind.

"Shit," Bill cursed under his breath and stopped.

James was trotting down the road from the direction of the house. Unexplainably, Monica looked frightened until Bill realised she couldn't see who it was.

"It's only James," he told her.

She still looked confused until James appeared out of the darkness. He was breathing hard, not used to the exercise. "I spoke to Brenda," he panted. "She says she has an old woven mat that depicts the legend of M'ba. I have never seen it, but she is willing to show it to you if it will help."

"Thanks very much," Bill replied. "I need all the help I can get."

"Alright, I will bring it here tomorrow and leave it at Roberto's house with Sara. Brenda says it is not a good idea for you to come to our house." James lowered his voice. "She is afraid for the children."

"I understand," Bill replied. "Thanks again."

They shook hands and James held on.

"We are all tired of living in fear here in Malenga. I have a strange feeling you can change that."

Chapter 11

Phil opened his eyes and stretched lazily in the sumptuous double bed. Sleeping naked between silk sheets gave him a luxurious feeling of pleasure. He languished for another half an hour before forcing himself to throw back the covers and half bury his feet in the thick carpet. Flames danced among the logs in the fireplace across the room. *It must be gas. It was exactly like that last night and there's no sign of any firewood anywhere.* He walked across the room towards the bathroom, feeling the thick carpet push up between his toes. Tomorrow he would be back home. Sleeping in the spare room of his parent's modest house in a quiet Washington suburb was going to be a letdown after this.

Phil paused at the window and moved back the heavy curtains to peak outside. Down in the street, the Sunday traffic was just getting underway. The sky was a dark grey and wet snow was continuously falling. Phil shivered in the warm room and let the drapes fall back into place. He wondered if Swiss people spoke Swiss or German. The only thing he knew about Switzerland was William Tell and the Red Cross.

Surprisingly, the floor ties in the bathroom were warm. He looked longingly at the huge bath, but decided to shower. *The last thing I need this morning is to fall asleep again and miss my ten o'clock appointment at the bank. The manager would really be pissed if I pitched up late.*

Phil towelled himself off briskly in front of the fire after the refreshing shower. The phone at the side of the bed beeped.

Garry wished him good morning and said he would come to the room in ten minutes to show him where the breakfast room was. Phil whistled as he dressed. *After ten o'clock it will be mission accomplished.*

132

He removed his overcoat and scarf from the wardrobe and surveyed the room. *Sure wish I'd fetched a camera. Ma would of been tickled pink to see this place.*

He would have enjoyed showing Joe where he had stayed. Garry arrived at the door. "You sleep well?" he asked.

"You gotter be kidding. Best night's sleep ever."

"I thought I'd hook up with you here or you wouldn't know where you're at in this building."

"You got that right. Some place you guys live in."

Garry led the way along three corridors and down two stairwells before entering a cafeteria.

"This is where we normally chow," he explained. "I hope you didn't think we eat in the dining room all the time."

"Oh no, that would be crazy."

Phil was disappointed, but didn't show it. The scrambled egg and flap jacks with maple syrup tasted great. Garry checked his watch.

"Okay, let's move. The car should be out front."

Wet snow melted instantly on the limo's windshield and was flicked off by the wipers as they sped along the freeway towards Zurich.

"Sure as hell not much traffic on Sunday morning," Garry remarked. "Everyone's in bed catching a screw. Different ball game tomorrow."

Phil nodded as he checked out the speedometer. "This driver sure doesn't waste any time," he said apprehensively.

"No sweat." Garry inclined his head towards the chauffeur.

"These guys are used to driving in worse crap than this."

*   *   *

The Zurich National was housed in a building just as grand as the embassy in Bern. The security guards had been expecting them, but seemed disconcerted and edgy receiving visitors on Sunday. Two of them with side arms accompanied the pair up to the manager's office in the lift. Phil noticed cameras everywhere. More than one pair of eyes was following their every move from control rooms throughout the bank. Eventually, they arrived outside the manager's office. One security officer slid his pass card through the lock and the door swung open. He waved them inside while he and the other guard took up positions on either side of the door.

Phil and Garry entered the office and interrupted the managers pacing behind a huge rosewood desk. He dropped a pocket watch back inside his waistcoat and gave the two of them an icy stare.

"Four minutes late," he snorted. "Place your identifications on the desk."

This they did without saying a word, and stood waiting while the manager examined each document. The office reminded Phil of an antique furniture show room. He had never seen anything like it before. Garry was less impressed and yawned behind his hand while waiting for the manager to say something.

"So, you are agent Jones." The stony grey eyes were fixed in Phil's direction.

"Yes, sir," Phil answered, feeling as if he was back in school.

The manager looked old and fragile, but his voice sounded like the prosecutor in a supreme court case. "I do not suppose you realise the amount of trouble you have caused us. Banking in this country is based on client confidentiality. If you people persist in forcing us to reveal our clients, the whole structure of banking in Switzerland could collapse. In the old days, this type of thing would never have been allowed."

He removed a large brown envelope from his desk draw and slapped it down on the polished surface. "The request for certain information, which came to me via our minister of finance." He paused for effect at this point. "Is all contained inside this envelope. Nothing more and nothing less. I entrust this information to you unwillingly and I sincerely hope you will treat such information in strict confidence. I am not obliged to give you computer access to our files, and this I will not do. The request to examine some of our safety deposit boxes has been refused. Even we do not know the contents of those boxes. All the other information you require is in that envelope."

Phil moved closer to the desk, eager to have the envelope in his possession. "If I have any queries about the contents, can I get back to you?" Phil ventured.

The manager sighed and sat down behind the desk. "I am not sure whether you are afflicted by deafness or are just too uneducated to comprehend what I have just told you. There is the envelope. Take it or leave it."

Garry cleared his throat. "Being a might more civil 'aint gonna cost you any bucks yaknow."

A patch of red appeared on the banker's check bones. "I have just been forced to break our banking traditions and rules of protocol, which I have done under very strong protest . In my opinion, your country would by vastly improved if you imported more tradition and culture from Europe."

Garry took a step forwards. "I'm proud of being an American and we are just trying to do our job here. We have plenty of tradition and culture back in the US of A."

The manager's lips formed a superior smile. "I know something of the American people. I had the unfortunate experience of seeing some of the Jerry Springer show. I was so shocked it was a good five minutes before I could change the channel."

Garry face darkened. "Now see here. You can't judge the American population by the people on the Jerry Springer show."

Phil picked up the envelope before things got out of hand. "Come on; you're not going to win with a guy like that," he whispered. He pulled Garry towards the door. "You're supposed to be looking after me," he added.

The banker stood and pressed a button on top of the desk. "Good day gentlemen. I can recommend a good teacher of English if you have a mind to learn the language."

The door slid open and the two guards entered. Garry was fuming as Phil bundled him through the door. "You fat cats piss me off," he shouted. "You're all sitting on a whole heap of Nazi gold."

The door slid closed and they made their way to the lift between the two stone-faced security men.

"At least I got the last word in."

Phil shook his head. "Like water off a duck's back. That guy will never change his mind. Jerry Springer has a lot to answer for."

*   *   *

Back at the embassy in Bern, Phil made straight for his room and placed the envelope on the writing desk. He switched on the reading lamp and sat down, polishing his glasses in nervous anticipation. "Right, let's see who you guys are," he said, slitting open the flap and tipping out the contents. "Okay, first, the account holders."

He checked the top of the page. *This account is owned by a business.* He frowned and quickly shuffled through the other twenty-six pages. *They are all held by businesses.* He stared in amazement. All twenty-seven account numbers belonged to a different company name, but all of them sounded similar.

Plato Enterprises.
Cyclops Transportation.
Zeus Construction.
Phoenix Engineering.
Hercules Holdings.
Academes Water Treatment.

What the hell is this? He still didn't know who the godamn account holders were. *Collins' going to crap himself. The next step is to find out who the hell owns all these cock sucking companies. Where the heck are they?*

He shuffled through the papers again, writing down the postal addresses. After writing down the first three, he just glanced at the others and whistled. *Different box numbers, but same town.*

That makes it a bit easier. Now let's see what sort of money we are looking at.

He added up all the bottom lines and reached a total of over one hundred million.

On each account statement, the last withdrawal had been transferred two years ago. All on the same day, and all to the same account in Italy. A total of fifty million dollars to some construction company in Milan. It was obvious all these accounts were owned by one group of persons working together. The word 'mafia' came to the forefront of his mind. Other than that, no major amounts had been withdrawn over the years. *These companies are using the accounts like savings rather than current accounts. They must have their own source of income for their day-to-day expenditure.*

He placed his laptop on the desk and opened it. *Now let's see if Birkett's info ties up with some of this.*

After a moment of using the mouse, he found what he was looking for. *Yep, these accounts were opened just after the African's last visit to Birkett's grandfather. They were just a means of receiving the dividends.*

For some reason the African didn't want to visit the states anymore. The accounts are more convenient, anyway, than carrying cash around. Hell of a risk of being robbed, especially in Chicago.

That jogged Phil's mind about the Chicago murders, and he checked for incoming email from his academy friend. There was a reply, which Phil punched up on his screen.

'Hi old buddy. I was so interested in your request I spent Saturday afternoon on my computer. Hope you realised I missed an important ball game. There have been heaps of unsolved murders in Chicago where bodies have been cut up. Only four where the victim was reduced to small pieces. I don't know where you're going with this but here are the dates.'

Phil wrote down the four dates in his notebook and read on. In each case, the police had had nothing to go on. The only thing in common with the victims was that three of them had known criminal records, and the fourth consorted with criminals. The medical examiner had stated that some sort of machine was needed to rip up the bodies. Something like a concrete mixer with rotating arms. There had been no motive, and no machine anywhere near the scene of the crimes. One witness of disrepute had stated he heard a scream and found what was left of the body one minute later. He had been questioned for two days as a suspect ,but he never changed his story.

'The perps must now be long dead but let me know what is cooking. I'm curious. You owe me one. Regards Benny.'

Phil compared the dates with the stock purchases and found that all of them coincided within a day or two of the murders.

Maybe the African was a cannibal and had chopped them up for food. No body parts were reported missing and besides, they weren't chopped, they were torn. Nobody is that strong. No wonder Birkett's father couldn't sleep.

Phil sat a while, polishing is glasses, deep in thought, and then picked up the phone. Garry's number was on a list mounted on the wall. He drummed his fingers on the tabletop while the phone rang.

"Hi Garry, Phil here. Oh fine. I need some info. Yeah the banker gave us everything, but it's not what I expected. Can you come and collect me at my room? I need some info from the embassy computer, and to send a report back to my chief. Okay. Thanks."

Garry tapped on Phil's door five minutes later, looking a bit dishevelled. He was still blinking some of the sleep from his eyes as he passed a hand through his ruffled blond hair.

"Sorry to wake you," Phil apologised.

"No problem. This is Sunday siesta time, so we will have the communications room to ourselves. We should be hooked up pretty quick, then I can crash out again."

Phil followed Garry up to the top floor and came to a door that required Garry's pass card to open. He was amazed at the amount of equipment installed in the room. "Holy shit, now I know why you embassy guys have all that crap on the roof."

"Yep." Garry smiled. "This is pretty standard. You wonna see what they got in some of the more sensitive countries? Twice what we have here. Okay, what are you looking for?"

"First, I need what you can dig up on this Italian construction company, and why they received fifty million dollars two years ago. There is the exact date of transfer." Phil handed Garry a sheet of paper.

"Hum, this could take a while. If they have nothing to hide, it could even be on their website. What else do you need?"

Phil handed him another sheet of paper. "The location of this town. That is the address of all the account holders. I'm gonna make out a report and fax it to my chief's house. He is an old fashioned kinda guy. Only likes computers if someone else is using them. Hope he don't bite my head off for calling him on Sunday."

Garry nodded. "Okay, will do. You draft your report while I get to it."

Two lots of keys rattled away in the communications room for the next half an hour while Phil typed his report. He paused every now and then to clean his glasses and chew on a fingernail.

Collins had told him to report to him directly as soon as he had something, so that was just what he was doing. He scanned through his two-page report. Collins didn't like anything long winded, so he had made it clear and precise just with the main facts. The only thing missing was what Garry was working on.

"Where are you at Garry? You come up with anything?"

"Yep, all finished. It's coming out the printed just now."

He pushed himself away from the console and swivelled round to face Phil.

"You know on the ride here from the airport, when you were bitching about coming from a Washington winter to a Swiss winter?"

Phil nodded. "Yeah, I remember. So what?"

"Well, you could be climbing out the fridge just now and stepping into the frying pan."

Phil was confused. "What the hell you talking about?"

"It's midsummer just now in Africa. Your town is slap bang in the middle of it."

Phil stared at him. "You're kidding."

Garry shook his head. "Nope, and guess where that Italian company is building a hydro electric project? The job they got paid fifty mil up front for."

Phil's jaw dropped open. "You're shitting me."

"Nope, same little town. Malenga."

Garry wheeled himself back to the printer and tore off the protruding piece of paper. He flicked it in Phil's direction. Phil leapt out of his chair and grabbed it before it reached the floor. *Here it was at last. The African connection. The shareholders were African.*

Phil finished his report, then faxed it to Collins' home number.

Garry spun round and round on his swivel chair, quite proud of himself. "Well, you can't complain about the service round here." He checked his watch. "Time we grabbed some chow. I'm hungry. Not used to Sunday work."

Phil checked out the fax report. It had gone though okay.

"Thanks, Garry old buddy. You're a star. Could have done it myself if I wasn't typing my report."

Garry continued to swing round on the chair like a school boy. "Oh, now you have hurt my feelings. Come, let's get some lunch."

"No. I need to phone Collins now. I need instructions from him."

Garry stopped swinging. "You sure you want to do that, old buddy?"

Phil shrugged. "I don't see why not."

He dialled Collins' direct line and waited. There was a muffled reply on the line. "Yeah. Collins."

"It's Phil Jones here, sir. I have just faxed you my report."

"Who?"

"Phil Jones. I'm in Switzerland."

"Oh yeah. Now I remember. Have you got the shareholders names?"

"Not exactly, sir; it's all in the report."

"Okay. I will read it and get back to you. I will just check to see if it's come through. Hold on." There was a muffled thump on the line. "Shit." Then a pause. "No. You go back to sleep."

Phil heard Collins shout. "No godamn it. Get back to sleep."

They must be having a siesta in Washington, too.

"Jones."

Phil flinched. "Yes, sir."

"There are three pages, and it looks legible. I will get back to you in few hours. Stay close to your mobile."

"Yes sir. Thank you, sir."

He heard a click on the other end. Phil replaced the handset and turned to face Garry. "He sounded like a bear with a sore head. I wonder what has got into him."

Garry pointed to a row of clocks mounted on the wall. They were calibrated in twenty-four hours.

"You see the one marked Washington DC?"

Phil stood up and stared at the one Garry had mentioned. "Holy shit. It's still night time there."

Garry nodded. "Well, you sure have bigger balls than me. The only way I would phone my boss at that time is if World War Three was about to start."

Phil removed his glasses and polished them furiously. "I needed instructions. I may have to jump on a plane to Africa."

"Yeah, I guess so. Come on, let's find some food."

The chief of the FBI research department was on his third cup of coffee before he noticed it was beginning to get light outside. He would have to cancel his usual round of golf that morning.

Even if he made it to the clubhouse on time, he would be too bushed to be able to play properly. Collins could be a real pain in the ass sometimes.

He now stared at the two sheets of paper his number two had given him. "Is this all we have for Collins?" he asked in disbelief.

"Fraid so, boss. This must be the most boring, run-of-the-mill, third world town in existence. Nobody's even heard of the place."

The research chief grunted. "Collins is going to invite me for breakfast."

"How come?"

"He is going to chew my balls while I eat his shit."

"Maybe I can get some spy in the sky shots from my buddies in Langley. They work twenty-four hours, seven days a week. All depends who's on duty."

"Yeah, good idea. At least Collins will have something to look at."

* * *

Phil lay on his bed dozing when his cell phone made him jump.

"Phil, Collins here." He sounded tired. "I will fax you everything we have on Malenga. Afraid it is not much. Our people here suggest you go to the capital, Mabarta, and then the registrar of companies. They will have nothing on computer. Probably never seen one. Find out which people own those shares. After that, go to Malenga and eyeball them. A good percent of the population is Muslim, so we could be back to the Arab thing again. You get black Arabs jaknow. You could bump into Bin Laden himself out there, for all we know. If you do, ask no questions; just shoot him."

Phil swallowed and nodded. "Yes, sir."

"I know you're not a field operative. Never even been there myself, so the CIA reckoned you go to South Africa first and meet up with a guy called Watson. He is the CIA expert in that area and will give you good advice. Don't mention CIA to anybody, otherwise we will all be in crap with the South Africans. Now then, this Malenga is in the asshole of the world. There is no airport, but there is a strip; you will have to go with a private plane from Mabarta, or by road. You need a cover there, so we think you should go as a bird watcher. That's Watson's idea. He says there is one Limey out there who takes in the odd tourist, so he is going to fax him to book a holiday for you. I have told Joe to organise you a ticket to Johannesburg."

"Oh, don't bother. They can do that from this end."

"Okay. I will tell Joe to cancel. Watson will organise you from Johannesburg to Mabarta. The embassy in Mabarta will organise you from Mabarta to Malenga. If you don't want this one, say so now. We can send an experienced guy from the states. After South Africa, you can't travel as FBI. No badge and no shooter. You got that?"

"Yes sir, I understand. I don't want to give up on this one, sir. I'm slowly getting there."

"Okay, it's your call. I will keep in touch with Watson. If you get into crap he is the only one who can bail you out. Good luck."

The phone went dead. Phil stared at it sometime before setting it down. He picked up the embassy phone and called Garry.

"There is a fax coming through from my boss. He says I gotter haul ass to Africa."

"Yeah, I guessed as much. I have already done some enquires with the airlines. Air France has a flight to Mabarta on Wednesday from Paris. They cover most of Central Africa. There are also two flights a week from Johannesburg to Mabarta, with a private airline called Interair. They stop at quite a few places; a sort of flying taxi service. They seem pretty reliable."

"When is the next one from Zurich to Johannesburg?"

"There is one tonight, but it's a bit short notice. Probably only business class available."

"That's fine; book me on that."

"Okay. It departs at nine forty-five, so start packing. We have to leave here at five-thirty. I will go upstairs and collect your fax. Be ready to go. We will pick up the ticket at the airport."

Phil packed in quite a panic, and then checked his watch. There was still one hour before Garry would collect him. He lay back down on the bed and wondered if he had made the right decision. This situation reminded him of a show he had seen on TV, called the *Amazing Race*. Phil used to get stressed out just watching. It had been one of his mother's favourite programmes, so he had had to endure it or go to his room and read a book.

His cell phone made him jump again. It must be Collins phoning to cancel everything.

"Yes, sir." answered Phil expectantly.

"Glad to see you're showing a little respect for a change."

It was Joe's voice.

"Don't kid yourself. I thought it was Collins. What do you want?"

"I hear you changed your travel agent. Just as well. I didn't like the job anyways. Give my regards to your African brothers. Good opportunity to search for your roots, if nothing else. Could be there is a chimpanzee somewhere that is family. Learn to pick your nose every five minutes and you should blend in okay. Don't forget your mosquito net."

Joe rang off before Phil could tell him to shove it where the sun didn't shine. He lay there thinking about home. His mother would be preparing the Sunday dinner just now, with his father helping to peel the potatoes. Phil had longed for this type of assignment. Now he didn't want it anymore.

The feeling of home sickness caused his eyes to water. He removed his glasses and dabbed his eyes with his handkerchief. A sudden thought made him walk about the room. *If my father could see me now, he would be very disappointed.* He had even let Joe get to him.

Angry with himself, Phil rinsed his face and blew his nose. *What is there to be afraid of?* He had got used to flying and this

Watson sounded like a good guy who knew all the 'ins and outs'.

Flashing his FBI badge, he examined his reflection in the bathroom mirror.

"Special Agent Jones, reporting for duty," he said loudly.

He pulled his jacket straight and walked briskly back into the guest bedroom to do a final check on all the cupboards and drawers.

*　　　*　　　*

That evening, Phil boarded a South African Airways 747 for Johannesburg International. Business class was in the nose, and it didn't take him long to settle in. Garry's last words at the check in, before he had said goodbye, were a little disturbing. He had warned Phil not to expect too much from the Mabarta Embassy. *Guys normally get posted to an asshole place like that because they fucked-up somewhere else.*

With that thought in mind, he fastened his safety belt and sipped on his welcoming cup of orange juice. It was no good worrying about the future. He must learn to take things one step at a time.

He remembered the trapped fly buzzing fanatically against his office window. If it had escaped the confines of the centrally-heated building, it's life expectancy outside would have been very limited. Could be he was now in the same situation.

Chapter 12

The crushing plant workers had all arrived on site, except for the three who had witnessed the episode inside the hopper. Bill had been worried about the possibility of a general stay away. Maybe the three men had left the area for a while without telling many people what they had seen. Even James had heard the rumour that he was a magician. It would have been rather difficult to explain a stay away to the management. The site clerk gave Bill a strange look when he brought him his morning mug of coffee.

"Give those three men eight hours a day until they return. It's not their fault that they are not here."

The clerk raised his eyebrows and nodded.

"Don't tell the others, or there will be nobody here tomorrow."

"Yes, sir," he answered and turned to go.

Bill checked his watch. "Tell the charge hand to start at normal time, unless he has seen something else that needs fixing before tomorrow morning."

"Yes sir."

The clerk was halfway through the door.

"Oh, and give me last week's production figures," he shouted after him.

The coffee tasted good and he lit his first cigarette of the day. His consumption was down to about half of what he used to smoke. He wondered if it would go up again without the ball.

Outside, the plant started in sequence from the product end.

Finally, the generator growled with a plume of black smoke as the jaw started. The flywheels turned faster and faster until the jaw was up to running speed. *Crump, crump, crump.* The first stones from the half empty hopper were fed into the machine. That stone he had lifted with the ball must now be in small pieces.

Bill knew the Africans could run the crusher without him, but eventually the plant would be crippled with a series of breakdowns. There weren't many of them who could visualise the big picture when it came to machinery. One just had to look at the privately owned trucks in the area to see what would happen. There was also tendency to take money out of a system without feeding some back in to keep things going. Even new plants, which had been donated by some European countries, ground to a halt after the expats had handed over and left. The money from product sales would disappear, so no fuel could be purchased. Scheduled maintenance would be zero, and then all the batteries would be stolen to put the final nail into the coffin.

Bill shook his head to clear these depressing thoughts from his mind. *If only there were presidents who thought more about their people instead of lining their pockets. The change could only start at the top and work its way down to the population. Easier said than done.* Bill had heard of one president in West Africa who had tried to change a corrupt system. When the gravy train had stopped for the officials in the civil service, he had soon been voted out of office.

Why hadn't Nabusano made himself president when he was younger? For some reason, he didn't want the job. According to James, he didn't even leave his island anymore. From all accounts, Nabusano was quite old, and from Bill's calculation, he must be the original Chief M'ba's great-great-grandson. Maybe the next Nabusano in line would be more sympathetic to the people's needs.

Bill mashed out his cigarette and quickly finished last week's production figures.

He then drove down to the quarry to check on the drilling. Everything was progressing according to plan and on schedule. Another twenty thousand tons of rock could be blasted before the weekend. Bill climbed up to the highest point on the edge of the quarry so he could survey the whole operation. His weekly meetings with the plant operators were starting to pay dividends. He nodded in satisfaction. All the men and machines were working well.

Before climbing down again from his vantage point, Bill examined the sky to the south. A huge bank of dark clouds was building over the lake. Ken's forecast of the coming rains seemed to be on the nose. He had predicted they would start tonight or tomorrow. There was stillness in the air and the atmosphere was heavy with humidity. The calm before the storm. *Could be a few days of no production once the elements are unleashed.*

Bill scrambled down the rocky slope. Making his way to his pick-up, he waved at each operator as he passed the machines. Driving up the hill, he noticed the gates were still locked at the old crusher.

"I need some answers," he said to himself. *If this plant is not going to work anymore, I'm going to have to of recalculate the number wearing parts for my plant.*

He turned into the site and stopped outside his office container. Bill blew his horn to summon the clerk. "I'm going to the administration office and then the lab. I will be back this afternoon. Fetch the production figures. They are on my desk."

The clerk ran up the stairs and returned with the papers. Bill waved and drove off, closing his window. He knew from experience that the first rains were always heavy. *There will probably be some flash floods because the ground is dry and hard, especially the road. It is as hard as concrete.* Gallera, the contracts manager, would order all the roads to be graded after a couple of days' of rain. At least he wouldn't have to drive on a washboard for a few weeks.

In the reception of the main office, Bill placed the production figures into the quantity surveyor's post box and then walked through to the admin manager's office. They greeted each other warmly. Bill had found this manager to be a perfect gentleman. They were few and far between in the contracting business.

"What is the story with the old crushing plant? Is it not going to produce anymore?" Bill asked.

"Take it that it will not. I spoke to the owner's lawyer this morning on the phone. He said they have closed down indefinitely. Whatever that means."

Bill nodded. "Okay. As long as I know. Bit stupid of them to lose out on the production money."

"Yes, I cannot understand it, but it is more money in our pocket at the end of the day. Thanks to you, we have a good stockpile of material, so we are not too worried about the closure."

Bill had the impression the admin manager was descended from Italian aristocracy. He was certainly a cut above your normal contractor.

"There is one other thing I wanted to ask you," Bill continued. "I know its not encouraged, but I seem to have found a steady girlfriend who I would like to stay with me in the camp."

The manager smiled knowingly. "It must be difficult for you single men. I make these decisions on merit. In your case, it is not a problem. Give me the girl's details."

Bill handed him a piece of paper with Monica's full name, which the manager copied onto a form.

"This is a temporary pass for one month. Maybe you make a change before it expires, like our workshop manager. In the beginning, he was in here every other day for passes for different women. Eventually I had to refuse. I have heard that he is so well known by all the prostitutes that he is the only man in Malenga who can acquire pussy on credit."

They both laughed. Bill had heard that before. The workshop manager was quite a hero among the Italians. He decided not to tell the admin manager what the workshop manager had told him the previous night. He had said he had found a use for the hotel room Bible. You wedge it between the wall and the headboard to stop the bed from squeaking.

Bill picked up the pass and made for the camp. It was nearly lunch time and Bill was eager to give Monica her gate pass. He knew she would be very pleased. One step closer to marriage, in her way of thinking.

Monica put the kettle on as soon as Bill walked through the door. There was also a plate of sandwiches.

"Where did you get the bread?" he enquired.

"Sara brought some food here this morning. Roberto did not eat breakfast."

"I wonder why? I'm surprised he made it to work judging by the state of him last night."

After the snack, Monica pulled him towards the bed. Bill pretended to resist, and then checked his watch. "Promise me, only half an hour, then I must go."

She nodded while urgently stripping off his clothes. Half an hour turned into an hour before he managed to step into the shower. He must have sounded like the white rabbit from *Alice in Wonderland*. "I'm late, I'm late," he repeated while quickly dressing.

Outside, on the road that passed his park home, the contract manager's wife was walking her small, white dog. Bill smiled and waved as he climbed into the Hilux. That was all he needed. *She will probably give a full report to Gallera and anyone else who would listen about Bill Parker being in the camp at two pm.*

She inclined her head in acknowledgement and continued down the road. Monica opened his park home door, wrapped in a towel, and shouted, "Buy some more condoms. We are using them very quickly."

The contract manager's wife stared and nearly fell over her dog. Bill drove away rapidly with his head down, before Monica could shout anything else.

Outside the camp gate, he stopped and called the crushing plant on his car radio. The plant was running alright, without any problems. Bill turned in the direction of the laboratory, eager to know what Roberto had found out about the history of this area.

Roberto had rescheduled his daily routine work so he could spend most of the day on his computer. It was after nine before he felt well enough to start. The lab technicians had not disturbed him in his office after seeing him arrive. He could have quite easily been in the cast of an old zombie movie titled *The Walking Dead*.

The internet was able to supply the recent facts and figures about this area, but the information began to dry up as he progressed back in time.

Everything seemed normal. The usual struggle for power and border disputes. Presidents coming and going. No mention of the Nabusano's, obviously because they were not in the political arena. There was some information about the colonial days, but not much. Three different governors over a fifty year period. The building of the railway running north to the south in the eastern part of the country. A main road from Mabarta to the western boarder, passing through Malenga. It gave access to the lake's fishing industry. Some of the towns had had different names in those days. Christianity had converted most of the population in 1880. Before that, there were the Arab slave traders operating from the east coast of Africa. Livingston had passed through the area a few times until he died in 1872. Stanley had been searching for him in 1871. Before that, nothing. Unexplored darkest Africa.

Roberto rubbed his forehead and swallowed another aspirin. *Christianity equals missionaries. Livingston equals explorers. Explorers equal Royal Geological Society. Let me see what records they have.*

There was a detailed account concerning Burton and Speak, but not quite in the area under investigation. Speak had been killed by natives, so some of the tribes had been hostile at that time. A couple of other explorers had disappeared. Must have got lost or come down with Malaria.

"Cazzso," Roberto exclaimed. *Missionaries also disappearing.* These were separate incidents, complete with guides and porters. The same for the explorers. *No survivors.*

151

Roberto's calculating mind swung into action as he accessed more details about these expeditions. Bill walked into his office.

"Have you found anything out?" he asked.

Roberto held his head in his hands. "Stop shouting," he whispered.

"I'm not shouting," exclaimed Bill in a raised voice. "Next time you have a party, stick to beer like I do. You were drinking Cintsano and Vermouth and all sorts of shit. If you were in the army, your condition would be classed as 'self inflicted wounds'."

"Okay, okay. It was my own fault. Now lower your voice."

"Have you found anything interesting? Anything out of the ordinary?"

Roberto nodded slowly. "Yes. I think I have found the Bermuda triangle, but it is nowhere near Bermuda. It is a right here."

Bill pulled over a chair and sat next to him. "What the hell are you talking about?"

"Look." Roberto pointed to the notepaper in front of him. There was a group of names and details listed under explorers in the top half of the page. Lower down was another group under the heading of missionaries. Bill scanned the sheet of paper. "So what does this tell us?"

"All these expeditions and missions, or whatever you want to call them, happened right here, within a ten year period."

"So?"

"Add up all the people involved, including the porters."

Bill quickly did this in his head. "I get one hundred and sixty-two. So what?"

Roberto turned to face him. "They all disappeared in this area. Every last a man. Never to be heard of again." He whistled the tune from the *Twilight Zone*.

Bill stared at him. "You're kidding. All of them?"

"Yes. I am not kidding. It is from the computer."

"But then, somebody would have gone to look for them."

"Yes. It is so. Most of these are people searching for the first people. Then the disappearing just stopped."

Bill thought a moment. "What did the government do?"

Roberto shrugged. "What government? This was when you British were just starting to take over here. Taking over from what, I do not know. There must have only been small tribes here. Can you imagine? No government. No laws. No roads. No telephone."

"Huh. Not much different now, if you ask me. When the rains start, there won't be any roads or phones. There must have been soldiers here. The military keep good records. See what you can access from the British army archives."

"Hmm, this will take some time. There must be a mountain of information to sift through. I only hope the connection keeps working."

Bill walked to the fridge and opened two cokes. "Things go better with Coca cola."

Roberto swallowed another aspirin with his coke and got down to work. Bill lit a cigarette to smoke while he drank his coke. By the time it was finished, he was getting impatient. It was nearly three o'clock. He would have to return to the crusher. A strange feeling came over him.

"Let me have a go," he said to Roberto. "For some reason, I think I can operate that thing."

Roberto turned in surprise. "You are not computer literate. It is not possible you can do better than I am. You cannot even type."

Bill pushed Roberto away in his swivel chair and sat down in front of the computer. The screen showed Roberto had already accessed the military records. Bill removed the ball from inside his shirt, holding it in both hands, staring at the screen.

"What are you doing?" taunted Roberto. "Are you praying for a miracle?"

All of a sudden, the keys started dancing and the mouse jerked around as if it was possessed. Roberto backed away into the corner of the office, spellbound. Some five minutes passed with the keys chattering while the mouse swung backwards and forwards. Roberto's mouth was dry. He then realised it was wide open and snapped it closed. Three printouts emerged in quick succession from the machine, which then fell silent.

Roberto grabbed another coke from the fridge and lit a Chesterfield. Bill started to move his glazed eyes, as if coming out of a trance.

"Did I do okay?" he asked as he slipped the ball back into his shirt.

"Reasonable," Roberto croaked.

"Right, let's see what we have. I'm running out of time."

Bill spread the papers on top of the desk.

They discovered that two British patrols in the Malenga area had also disappeared shortly after the missionaries. It had been presumed they had killed their officers and deserted. The whole thing had been hushed up.

"That now makes it two hundred and four missing persons," stated Bill.

The first governor, who had sold a small island in the centre of the lake to a local chief, had been dismissed. He had retired a very rich man. Nothing unusual had happened after that, until the First World War. The Germans had had some steamers and a gunboat, which was patrolling up and down the centre of the lake. All the land south-east of Malenga and from the shore of the lake to the east coast of Africa, belonged to the Germans. The lake was their western border with the Belgium Congo. The out-numbered Germans had been commanded by Colonel Von Letton-Vorbeck. With their well-trained African Askari soldiers, they proved to be a much superior fighting force than the South African led allies. They had given a good account of themselves until they had been vastly outnumbered by Indian and Belgium troops. Even so, with no supplies or reinforcements, they played a cat and mouse game until the end of the war. The gunboat had inflicted a lot of damage on the west coast of the lake and captured a number of machine guns.

Bill pointed to the paper in front of him. "This gunboat. It patrolled up and down the lake. They must have come across Nabusano Island eventually. If the Nabusano clan started building there, the Germans would have noticed."

Roberto shrugged. "Possible they only started a building after the war."

Bill shook his head. "You can't tell me that they lived there for thirty years without building anything. What happened to the German boat?"

Roberto checked through the third printout. "They say here, scuttled at the end of nineteen fifteen."

"And the crew. What happened to them?"

"They say here, one crew member washed up on the British side to the north, was found by tribesmen, and died of malaria while being transported by a British patrol back to Kisumu."

Bill stood, then paced up and down Roberto's office. "That's a load of horse shit. Why scuttle it before the end of the war without a fight? They weren't threatened in any way. That boat was king of the lake. Humphrey Bogart wasn't around to sink it with the African Queen. That was fiction."

Roberto was still busy reading. "It says here, the British were transporting two fast motorboats overland to the lake, each armed with a small three pounder. Because of their speed, they were capable of sinking all the German steamers. The Derflinger, that was the gunboats' name, was fitted with the latest quick-firing 105 mm gun. Possibly, they did not want it to fall into enemy hands."

"Bullshit, they could have tossed it over the side, and besides, the British had already captured some of those guns. The same type of gun was fitted to the U-boats."

Roberto looked up in surprise. "How do you know that?"

"You may watch channel sixty-six, but I like watching sixty-eight. I've seen it on the history channel."

Roberto lifted his hands. "Okay, but in the Second World War, the captain of the Graff Spay scuttled his battleship in the battle of the river Plate."

"That's different," Bill counted. "He thought he was trapped by a superior force. He did it to save the lives of his crew. How many crew aboard the Derflinger?"

Roberto ran his finger over the print out. "Twenty-two."

"You can't tell me this captain scuttled his boat with a ninety-five-point-five percent loss of his crew."

Roberto shrugged. "It must have been an accident then."

Bill shook his head. "It's one hell of an accident when you lose virtually all your crew. I think we can add the crew of the Derflinger to those other missing persons."

Bill checked his watch. "I must get back to the crusher. See what else you can find out. I will tell you after work what James told me. He's bringing a mat or wall hanging round to your house as soon as he can. It's all about this chief M'ba. The first of the Nabusano line."

With that, he rushed out of Roberto's office. "See you later," he called over his shoulder.

Roberto seated himself in front of the computer again and massaged his forehead. What Bill had done with the computer had been quite a shock. Just what else was he capable of? His reasoning about the gunboat made some sense.

Roberto decided to see what he could find out about the one survivor. *There must be some mention of what he said before he died.* What all these missing persons had to do with the Nabusano's, he did not know.

After a while, he gave up on the survivor. It was a dead end.

There was no connection, except that they were all in the same place during the same period of a time. Anyway, Bill would give them the ball tonight and that will be the end of it. He hoped.

Chapter 13

The old man sat high above the waters of the lake, gazing out towards the setting sun. Over the years he had learnt how to defend the followers. At a moment's notice, he could strike and destroy the cities of the buyers of slaves. Make them pay for their ancestors' crimes. Death and destruction would rain down on them at the time of his end, or the time of renewal. Either way, they would pay for their forefathers' sins.

The renewal must come soon. His power had faded and he was dying. For the first time in his life, doubt had entered his mind. The sleeping dragon in the west had been awakened twice. Once by the Japanese, and now by Arabs. He had not foreseen the destruction of the Trade Centre.

His organisation, built up and put into place over the years, could not be changed overnight. He had received a call from Switzerland. A danger was approaching from the north, which had been sent by the dragon of the west. This danger could be stalled or eliminated, but eventually it would arrive. The dragon was awake. Wheels were turning that could not be stopped. Of all these things, he was sure.

The doubt that had crept over him concerned the white man named Parker. How could he have underestimated this man?

Recent reports indicated Parker was using the power. This he had not thought possible. Parker was an unbeliever.

Long ago, the people of Malenga had chosen to worship the false gods and had been cast out. The only true followers were of his blood. They had moved to the island to be safe from contamination. The followers were of a greater stature than the men of the mainland. Bariba blood of M'ba flowed through their veins.

Parker was unpredictable, a wild card and lose cannon. All white men bowed to intimidation and bribery. The addiction of the ball should not have overcome Parker's fear and greed. Even so, the doubt could not be dispelled from Nabusano's mind.

The beginning of the end was in motion. Could the same be said about the start of the new beginning?

The cold wind from across the water was growing stronger, and penetrated the chief's cloak, which wrapped his frail body. A storm was approaching and the sun had sunk below the horizon.

A glass door slid open at the other end of the stone balcony. It was time. He pushed the switch on his armrest over to the left, causing his wheelchair to turn. The tyres squeaked on the polished marble tiles every time the chair changed direction on its journey into the huge apartment. Warm air surrounded his body as the automatic door slid shut behind him.

His latest wife had come with the female children to bid their farewells. This was the custom every ten years for all the followers on the island. The females would depart and start a new life in Mabarta, leaving the male children behind. They would change their identity and keep a low profile, receiving a substantial living allowance every month. The senior sons chose new wives of different blood for the younger men. They only found out that they would be prisoners on the island for ten years after they had arrived. Most accepted the situation willingly. The standard of living on the island was far superior to that of the mainland. The others were sacrificed to the god of the river in the temple below the fortress. They had insulted the Supreme Being by refusing one of his followers.

Nabusano's physical condition had deteriorated rapidly over the last ten years. He would not be taking a new wife.

After the sinners in the west had been punished, the island would cease to exist. It would be vaporised by their swift retribution.

Chapter 14

Magyenzi, the officer commanding Malenga's police force, like James, was also from Mabarta. But unlike James, he had found no problem settling into his new location. A few days after his arrival two years ago, he had been visited by John Gwasa, Nabusano's lawyer. He had heard of Gwasa. Some years previously Gwasa had been one of those 'do gooders', a champion of the poor in Mabarta. What an idiot the man had been, working for people with no money.

An understanding was soon reached, resulting in him receiving a salary supplement of twice what he was being paid by the government. This supplement was paid promptly every month by Gwasa in cash, in the privacy of the lawyer's office.

OC Magyenzi was very pleased with this arrangement because his government salary was usually far from prompt. His huge bulk increased as a good part of this extra money was spent on food and beer. The only concession he had been asked to make was that Gwasa would advise him on certain cases that affected Mr. Nabusano.

After the first year, in which a nosy reporter had disappeared, Magyenzi had been presented with a brand new Mitsubishi Colt four by four by the local oil company. Technically, the vehicle was now owned by the government, but the OC didn't see things from a technical point of view. His old, broken down police van, which permanently listed over to the driver's side, was passed on to his second in command. The first week, he drove round the town every day until the novelty wore off. Since the day of the 'handing over' ceremony, the smile on his chubby face had not worn off. It seemed to be a permanent fixture. His small eyes remained hard and calculating, assessing every situation that could be turned into personal gain. The odd interruptions in his investigations by Gwasa had become irritating. A few chances of extortion had been missed by dropping the case in question. Magyenzi knew from experience that every case contained some sort of financial reward for the investigating officer.

The main annoyance at the moment was the four thugs who received instructions from Gwasa. They were starting to be too familiar. He had walked past them the other day on his way to the garage, where his car was being serviced. All four were standing outside a bar with nothing else to do. All four smiled and formed their lips into a kiss as he trundled passed in the heat of the day. His smile had remained fixed, but his hands had formed into fists, clenching and unclenching until he reached the garage. The boy who ran towards him with his car keys was knocked unconscious. Owner and mechanic said nothing. They could see OC Magyenzi was not in a good mood.

He now sat wedged behind his desk, trying to think of a way to rid himself of his tormenters. If it wasn't for his arrangement with Gwasa, the four guerrillas would now be rotting inside jail cells with their features rearranged. Ten of his officers with batons would soon make short work of them. If they pulled a pistol, an AK 47 could solve the problem permanently.

These pleasant thoughts ran through his mind while the ceiling fan made some of the peeling, green paint hanging from the walls flutter in its breeze. He wasn't afraid of Gwasa. The young lawyer looked frightened every time they met. Like a rat facing a snake that wasn't there.

Normally, in any town, the local OC was the most feared and respected man around. Malenga was different. Something was out of step here. The population was terrified of some old businessman nobody saw.

That morning Gwasa had phoned him. A white expatriate who worked for the Italians was due to call in at his office this evening. This white man was going to exchange something that Nabusano wanted for an envelope full of American dollars. The exchange was going to be handled by Gwasa's four gorillas. He was just an observer. The police station venue was to give an official atmosphere to the proceedings, for the benefit of the white man. If there were any problem with the exchange, he was to intervene on the side of Gwasa's men. Magyenzi shook his head. *Not only am I prevented from locking up these animals, but Gwasa wants me to work with them.* He wondered what the white man possessed that was so important to Nabusano. It certainly must be very valuable to go to all this trouble. Maybe he should eliminate these four assholes and take this thing for himself. The only problem was the white man. When they disappeared, someone always came looking for them, asking awkward questions.

Magyenzi was not a stupid man. He would wait and see what happened. There was more to this than Gwasa was telling him. It did not smell right. His nose for trouble had earned him this promotion. In Mabarta, he had been appointed by the chief of police himself. Not this Nabusano. The secret of success in the police was to solve the case by finding the culprit. If you couldn't find the culprit, you found somebody else. It was easy.

Magyenzi leant to one side in the tight-fitting chair and farted loudly. There was an hour before the exchange was due. He pressed the buzzer on his desk and waited for his number two to arrive. There was the sound of boots running up the stairs from the charge office and then a knock on his door. The sergeant entered and saluted smartly. Magyenzi surveyed him with a critical eye. The man was so small and thin he looked like a Boy Scout in his kaki uniform.

"In one hour's time I am expecting a white man to come here. His name is Parker."

"Yes sir," the sergeant replied.

"Direct him to my office. Also, those four animals who work for Gwasa will be coming. If there is any trouble, I will press my buzzer. You and six other officers will burst in here with automatic rifles." Magyenzi paused. "Six officers bigger than you."

"Yes sir," the sergeant blinked.

"Do not shoot the white man. I don't mind if you shoot the others, but do not shoot the white man. Understood?"

"Yes sir, I understand."

"Now go and prepare yourselves."

The sergeant saluted and left the office. Magyenzi prised himself out of the chair and walked over to an old refrigerator in the corner. He removed a bottle of beer and bumped it open on the edge of the door. At the first gulp half the bottle was empty. He looked down at the bicycles passing by on the main street. Most of them were taxis with women behind, sitting side-saddle.

"Yes, downtown Malenga. All I have to do is to wait. Everything is under control. I am now prepared for anything."

Chapter 15

After work, Bill picked Monica up and dropped her off at Roberto's house. He didn't go in because he was running late. It had been dark for a good hour already and he wanted to get the exchange over with. They had failed to find out how Nabusano knew about the ball. It was obvious why he wanted it. A thing like that was worth millions of pounds, but how did he know its value and where to look for it? That was the burning question in his mind.

The Scot's girl jiggled around like a porno star on fast forward. *Too late now to worry about unanswered questions.* Bill felt as if he was on his way to the dentist with a broken tooth. Hated going, but something he had to do.

The uncomfortable feeling of danger mounted quickly as he approached the police station. He pulled over and parked, deciding to walk the rest of the way. The danger feeling was making him feel sick. It had mounted too fast while he had been driving. Walking would give him time to become used to the sensation gradually.

Opposite the police station entrance, Bill noticed a parked, badly-dented, black saloon with two men inside. They wore dark glasses. It was Tweedle Dumb and Tweedle Dee from the disco.

The sergeant in the charge office said, "Mr. Parker, I presume?"

"Well I'm not Doctor Livingston," Bill answered.

The sergeant's blank expression didn't change as he directed him to the stairway. "OC Magyenzi is expecting you."

No sense of humour. Unless the man has no idea who Dr. Livingston was.

The stairway was dark. They were either saving electricity or the light didn't work.

The switch on the wall clicked up and down uselessly. At the top of the landing, one dim light was working, illuminating three green-painted doors. The end one, nearest the main street, had the letters **'O.C. OFFICE'** painted on it. Bill took a deep breath. *Let's see what's behind the green door.*

He knocked and entered. The fat policeman sitting at the desk smiled broadly. "Welcome, welcome, Mr. Parker. I am OC Magyenzi. Please take a seat."

Bill could see the officer commanding would have some difficulty extracting himself from behind the desk, and walked over to the chair indicated.

"Do I give you the thing Nabusano wants?" Bill asked.

Magyenzi contemplated this for a moment. He looked undecided until he shook his head.

"No, no. Four other men are arriving with some money for you. I am just an observer to make sure everything goes smoothly. I am sure you feel a lot safer here in the police station rather than some dark alley."

The OC's belly jiggled up and down as he laughed. Bill stood, holding the back of the chair. He didn't feel like sitting down.

"Why four men? This is a simple exchange. I am willing to cooperate."

"Yes, yes. Do not be alarmed." Magyenzi placed his hands on the desk and leant forwards. "It is not safe to carry money around after dark. I am sure that is the only reason that four men are coming."

He leant back again smiling, twiddling his thumps round and round. "I can always escort you back to your camp. Just to make sure you arrive safely."

Bill was reminded of the nursery rhyme, in which the spider was talking to the fly. "No thank you. I will be okay."

There was a knock on the door and the sergeant appeared. "Some more visitors to see you, sir."

Four large men pushed their way passed the sergeant into the room. Magyenzi scowled at the intruders.

"Yes. You may go," he commanded the sergeant.

The first two, Bill had never seen before. One carried a small wooden box. Tweedle Dumb carried a cardboard carton, which he placed on the floor. Tweedle Dee closed the office door and stood in front of it, blocking off the exit. Magyenzi raised his voice in a show of authority.

"Mr. Parker has agreed to cooperate fully. There will be no trouble here."

The first man placed the wooden box on the desk and reached inside his jacket pocket. A chubby hand concealed the buzzer, ready to press at a moment's notice. He then produced a large brown envelope and the contents were tipped out on top of the desk. Magyenzi stared in amazement. He had never seen so much money. *It's US dollars. Real money that could be spent anywhere in the world.*

The hundred dollar bills were restacked and pushed back into the envelope.

"You are to place Nabusano's property into this box."

The man slid the small wooden box over to where Bill was standing. Bill reached inside his shirt and reluctantly placed the ball into the padded interior of the box.

Magyenzi could not comprehend what he was seeing. He rubbed his eyes in disbelief, forgetting about the buzzer. *How in God's name could anyone pay this amount of money for a trinket, a bauble that's usually hung on a white man's Christmas tree?*

Bill picked up the envelope and thrust it into the front of his shirt. "My business here is finished," he said while fastening his shirt buttons. "I am leaving now."

Tweedle Dee remained stationary in front of the office door. Tweedle Dumb picked up the cardboard carton and placed it on the OC's desk.

"To be sure of your full cooperation, Mr. Nabusano has decided to give you a present."

Bill shook his head. "I don't want anything else."

Magyenzi's nose started twitching. He could smell trouble, and placed his hand over the buzzer again.

"This belongs to you anyway. We just want you to identify the contents."

Bill was puzzled, and angry at being detained. Maybe it was something that been stolen from the crusher. He rapidly tore open the top of the box, but stepped back when he breathed in the stench from inside. The four men laughed at his discomfort. One of them stepped forward and tipped out the contents, which rolled around on top of Magyenzi's desk. The OC pushed away in disgust and fell over backwards with a crash. He looked like an upturned beetle trying to right itself. The laughter turned into an uproar at the sight of Magyenzi's legs waving in the air.

Bill stared at the human head, which rolled around on the top of the desk. Before it rolled off and fell onto the floor, he caught sight of the features in the dim light. An anger he'd never experienced before now consumed him. He grabbed the ball from the box and turned to face the laughing men, who instantly reached for their firearms. Two of them flew backwards through the air, crashing through the windows in a shower of glass and timber. The other two slammed into the wall with such force it shook the whole building.

Magyenzi had managed to free himself from the chair and was now peeping over the top of the desk with wide eyes. The silence in the room was only broken by the rocking of Joseph's head in the corner.

Tears of rage and sorrow ran down Bill's cheeks as he stared at the head in the darkness. Holding the ball, he could now clearly see the look of surprise on Joseph's face. He was distracted by whimpering from the direction of the desk, and swung round to face the sound. OC Magyenzi's round eyes stared into the face of Bill Parker. The eyes he stared into were completely black, and shone with tears. He moaned and curled himself into a ball under his desk.

Screams from the street below awoke Bill from his trance. He would have to get out of here very quickly. Police officers were in the street, pushing through the crowd. Two broken bodies were hanging from the building across the road. Bill opened the door and descended the stairs, four at a time.

All the policemen were in the street, trying to make some sense of the situation. It was only when the sergeant looked over his shoulder that he noticed the windows missing from the OC's office. He started to push his way back through the crowd towards the police station. Bill slipped out of the entrance and turned the first corner into an alley. He would have to get away before the alarm was raised. The sergeant knew his name and probably where he lived.

Magyenzi made himself as small as possible. He hoped he was invisible. The sergeant ran up the stairway and entered the OC's office. At first glance, it was empty, but then he saw two men standing against the wall at the other end of the room. They stood perfectly still, with their feet apart, a few inches from the floor. The sergeant drew his sidearm. These men were armed, but were pointing their pistols upwards, without moving. He advanced cautiously. What could be wrong with them? A loud moaning from under the desk stopped him in his tracks. He went to investigate. "Sir, sir. Are you alright? What happened here?"

Magyenzi slowly lifted his head and peered round the side of the desk. "Is he gone?" he asked.

"Is who gone?"

"Parker, the white man who was here."

"Yes. There is no one here except us and those two over there." The sergeant pointed with his pistol towards the end wall.

The OC stared at the two men, then stared moaning again. "I should have listened to her. I should have listened to her," he whimpered.

"Who?"

"My mother. She told me to go to the church."

"What happened here? Do you want me to arrest Parker?"

167

"No, no, no," wailed Magyenzi. "I do not want him here. I order you not to arrest him. He will kill us all. We must escape before he comes back. He is the Devil."

The sergeant shook his head and walked over to examine the two men. They looked frozen. It was only when he got closer that he discovered they were half-embedded in the wall.

Chapter 16

The phone in the charge office rang a long time before it was picked up by a breathless constable. "No. OC Magyenzi is not available. We have a problem here."

The line went dead. Gwasa held the silent phone for a while. Something had gone wrong. Magyenzi was not even answering his cell phone. *How could those idiots mess up a simple transaction with one man?*

He should have conducted the exchange here in his own office at home. Nabusano had insisted on handling this matter himself. For some reason, he hadn't wanted John involved in the actual exchange. His only function after setting up the meeting was to receive a small box, which was to be locked in the safe. The enforcer and his men hadn't returned. They were thirty minutes late. He would have to go there himself to find out what had happened. There was probably some mess that needed cleaning up.

Six years ago, John Gwasa had been blackmailed into Nabusano's service. He had set out to help people like Magyenzi's falsely accused, and the down trodden of Mabarta. His one year of victories over an unjust society must have attracted Nabusano's attention.

Because of his lifestyle's dark secrets, he was an easy target for manipulation. The truth would have destroyed his parents' pride in their son's success. This, he could never allow to happen.

In Mabarta, he had become an embarrassment to the corrupt politicians and the system of injustice. If he had not agreed to the move to Malenga, and to work for Nabusano, he felt sure he would have been eliminated. Financially, now he earned more money than the president's official salary. The wall safe in his bedroom was overcrowded with foreign currency.

Even after paying back his parents for his overseas education, he had accumulated more money then he knew what to do with. *Inside*, John was an empty shell. The years of doing the opposite of what he yearned to do had eaten him away. He was trapped like a hamster running on a treadmill.

Malenga lay in a state of neglect and decay, whereas all the father's business flourished. There was no opposition. Compared to Nabusano, Al Capone was a saint. The evil old man's tentacles reached far into the rest of the world.

Two things, apart from the blackmail, stopped John from bringing down this criminal empire. First of all, the proof was unobtainable. It consisted of thousands of files and tapes, which lined the shelves of an underground vault on the island. John had accessed some of these, to bring pressure to bear on certain people worldwide. He was only allowed in and out naked. Even his rectum had been searched before he could leave. Sometimes this would cause him to experience an erection. The guards would look on in contempt before handing back his clothes.

Secondly, there was the fear. On the occasions he had met Nabusano face to face, his heart had stopped beating. The foul smell of evil had seeped out from the man's body, but the worst was his eyes. They had radiated hate like a light from within.

He shivered while sitting behind the wheel of his 280 SE. John found that the older Mercedes Benz was stronger than the new ones and rode better on the broken roads of Malenga.

He slowly made his way down the hill to the poorer part of town. There was a problem ahead. Crowds of people were blocking the high street.

Chapter 17

Bill reached his Hilux safely. People were running in the direction of the police station. He could hear them talking excitedly about the thugs who had been killed. To them, this was a major event, like a football match. Even a small road accident usually drew a crowd of people. He drove to the camp, because he couldn't think of anywhere else to go. His passport was in his park home. He would collect that before telling Roberto what had happened. The camp would not be a safe haven for very long. Security guards at the gate would know exactly where he was.

Lightning danced among black clouds that were approaching from the lake. He drove so fast over the corrugated road he felt as if the pick-up was floating. It drifted sideways twice before he managed to reach the turn off for the gate. Slowing down, he entered the camp while the guard held up the boom. *Everything is still normal here.*

At the park home, he collected his passport and slipped on his leather jacket, then drove quickly round to Roberto's. The tyres crunched on the gravel driveway before he came to rest behind Roberto's Nissan. He switched off the engine and sat behind wheel sweating. What the hell was he going to do? His mind was in turmoil.

A tapping on the window made him jump. Roberto was standing there. Bill wound down the window and faced him, not knowing what to say.

"Tella me you gave them the ball?"

Bill nodded. "Yes. I gave them the ball."

Roberto blew out a sigh of relief. "So what is the problem? You are looking ill." He lifted his hands, waiting for an answer.

"The problem is, they gave me a box with Joseph's head inside."

"What?" Roberto didn't understand.

"They had killed Joseph. They gave me a box with his head inside."

Roberto's jaw dropped open. "Dio Porko. I cannot a believe it."

"It is true. Joseph was murdered."

Roberto lit a Chesterfield and walked round in circles beside the car. "That is to frighten you. To keep you quiet."

"Yes, but they laughed. They all laughed. I took the ball back and killed them. I killed all four of them with the ball."

Roberto stopped walking. "Porka Madonna. You must go. You must run."

Bill nodded. "Yes, but where? They will be waiting at the border. Even the airport, if I make it that far, they will be watching for me."

Roberto started walking again and pushed back the long hair from his forehead. He stopped and returned to the window, raising his finger like Bin Laden. "I have a plan. It is your only chance."

A crash of thunder shook the ground.

"Go to Ken's place. Hide there until he can fly you out." He stepped back from the Hilux. "This car is no good. It has the company sign on the doors. Take my motorbike. Hide it in the back and drive to the bus station. Leave this car there and ride to Ken's house on the bike. Hide the bike in the trees. They will think you have taken a taxi, but won't know in which direction."

Bill jumped out of the pick-up. At least now he had a plan of action. They pulled the dust sheet from Roberto's Honda scrambler and laid it down in the back of the Hilux. Bill recovered it with the sheet. It wouldn't matter if it blew off once he had left the camp. Roberto ran inside the house. He returned with the helmet and the keys.

"With this on, nobody will see it is you. Here is Sara's cell phone. We can keep in touch. Do you need any money?"

Bill patted his stomach. "No. I'm loaded with cash. I have US dollars."

Roberto embraced him. "Go now, or they will stop you at the gate."

Bill seized his hand in gratitude and leapt back behind the wheel. Roberto waved from the carport as the Hilux reversed onto the road. He caught a glimpse of Bill's determined face in a flash of lightning as he changed gears and pulled away.

Chapter 18

Gwasa, like Bill, also parked one block away from the police station. This was not by choice. He was unable to progress any further. The street was packed with shouting people and unmoving cars. *This does not look at all good.*

Nearing the police station, he pushed his way through the crowd. His feet crunched on broken glass. The constables baring the entrance recognised him and let him through. On the charge office floor, four broken bodies lay in a huge pool of blood. He could see they were the same four who had collected the money from his house earlier that evening. Two of them were cut to ribbons. The back of the others' heads were flat. John swallowed. *What could have happened? A truck must have run over them.*

"Where is Magyenzi?" he asked.

The sergeant pointed to the ceiling. "OC Magyenzi is indisposed. He is not himself and does not want to be disturbed."

Gwasa pushed his way back out of the charge office and climbed the stairs. He had to determine where the box and the money were.

There was an officer guarding Magyenzi's door with a Kalashnikov. "No one is to enter," he informed John.

"I am Magyenzi's lawyer. What happened here?" he asked.

The officer looked frightened and confused. "I do not know. First the OC said 'do not shoot the white man'. Now he says 'shoot the white man if he comes back'."

"What about the bodies downstairs?"

"Two are from across the road, and two are from this office. I saw all four go up the stairs. None returned. There has been some magic here."

John could smell beer on the man's breath. "You have been drinking on duty. Let me pass."

The policeman hesitated and then moved to one side.

Magyenzi was seated at his desk, surrounded by empty beer bottles. He grabbed his pistol and pointed it in John's direction as he entered. "How dare you come here? Did you want to gloat over my body?"

John walked forward, unafraid. He had seen Magyenzi intoxicated many times before. "Where is the box for Nabusano and what happened to the money I sent here?"

The OC laughed. "There is your precious box." He pointed towards a cluster of empty bottles half-hiding the box.

"The devil you sent here took your money."

John picked up the small wooden box. It was empty.

"Didn't Parker bring something to go inside this box?"

Magyenzi rolled his eyes. "Yes. He brought the ball from a Christmas tree, and then he took it back when he saw inside the other box."

John frowned. "Which other box? There was only one box."

The OC waved his pistol at a cardboard carton on the floor. "What was in this box?"

The pistol swung to a round object in the corner. John walked over to it and pushed it with his foot. The next thing he saw was a face staring up at him. He jumped back in surprise.

Magyenzi struggled to his feet, waving the gun from side to side. "Yes. I know you do not like me. You tried to kill me. You sent the ghost of this man in the box to turn the white man into a devil. I saw it all before my eyes. I have heard stories that Nabusano is a wizard. He made this possible and you are his servant. Now you are going to die."

John suddenly became worried. He could see Magyenzi believed what he was saying. *The drunken buffoon has transformed into a snarling madman.*

Two shots rang out, kicking plaster from the wall above John's head. He ran through the door, pushing the policeman out of the way. Two more shots whistled past as he leapt down the stairway out into the street. Hysterical laughter echoed from above, followed by a hail of bullets from the assault rifle.

John looked round to see if anyone was injured. The street was deserted.

Chapter 19

Nabusano listened to Gwasa's voice on the phone.

"None of this was my fault," he repeated continuously.

He advised Nabusano to forget about whatever he wanted from Parker and just cut his losses. The situation was getting out of hand. Magyenzi had gone mad and tried to kill him. None of this was his fault.

Nabusano ended Gwasa's call in mid-sentence, cutting off the whining voice. He pressed a button on the side of the wheelchair, then dialled a number on the phone. Marco, the chief of the security company, answered.

Nabusano kept his voice steady "Are your men tracking the white man, Parker, as instructed?"

"Yes, father."

"Where is he now?"

"He left the construction camp five minutes ago."

Nabusano cursed. "Search the town. Use as many men and vehicles as possible to locate him. When you do, report back to me."

He ended the call and pressed the button again on the side of the wheelchair. Two of his son's entered the bedroom and waited for him to speak. Each had a bird tattooed on the palm of their left hand. Nabusano turned the wheelchair to face them. "Our existence is being threatened by an Englishman by the name of Parker. He has stolen something that is rightfully mine. He is now probably in Malenga, trying to hide or flee the country. The two of you are to take the helicopter and one cruiser, with as many followers as possible. They are to be dressed in the uniform of Medusacor. Use their office as your headquarters. When you locate Parker, shoot him and retrieve the object. It is silver in colour and in the shape of a ball."

The two men nodded and left the room.

Nabusano made another call to the commandant in charge of the local militia.

"Place the Malenga area under marshal law. Tell your men a group of rebels have moved down from the north. I will instruct the minister of defence to make an announcement on Mabarta radio. The police cannot be trusted. Magyenzi has failed. He is of no more use to us." Nabusano said this last sentence very slowly. "Set up roadblocks immediately on all the roads leaving Malenga. We are searching for a white man called Parker. He is to be killed by your special soldiers. You will report it as an accident or blame the rebels. In his possession you will find a silver ball. This, you will bring directly to me. Do you understand?"

"Yes, father," replied the commandant.

"Place a curfew on Malenga. Your brother, Marco, will carry out a house to house search. Do not fail me."

Nabusano ended the call. His throat was dry. He sipped a little water through a straw. All his resources must now be directed against the Englishman. He should have found out more about his adversary. The events at the police station had been totally unexpected. It was probably a sign of his failing powers. What could have changed Parker's attitude of cooperation to one of hostility? Surely not the head of his foreman. The idea was incomprehensible to Nabusano's way of thinking. There could be no other answer. If this were so, then it was a weakness that could be used against him.

*   *   *

Ten minutes later, the commandant gazed down through the window in the nose of the military helicopter.

Below, vehicles were pouring out of the compound's gate. Some were driving in the direction of Mabarta. The others would drive towards the western border. He had ordered the pilot to land at the airstrip next to the Italian's plane. Three of the special soldiers with maroon berets would be left there. The rest were destined to be dropped halfway up the Mabarta road and halfway on the border road.

To the south lay the vast expanse of the lake. The radar station on the island would detect anything moving upon its surface. There was no way out. *This man, Parker, is trapped.*

Chapter 20

Bill stopped the Hilux under some trees in an unlit area near the bus station. This was not difficult, because half the street lighting had stopped working long ago.

Three or four minibus taxis were unloading and loading people. The rest were parked for the night next to one large bus in the corner.

He dropped the tailgate and pulled the Honda out behind the pickup. The dust sheet had blown away on the road into town. Bill propped the bike on its side stand and closed the tailgate. He found the bike's keys in his pocket and pushed them into the lock. The helmet; he had nearly forgotten the helmet.

He removed the helmet from the cab and decided not to lock the door. If the car was stolen, it may lead them away from him. Before donning the helmet, he heard the distant throb of rotor blades from the direction of the army camp. *Why take off at this time of night with a storm approaching? They must have started searching for me.*

He pulled on the helmet and flipped the tinted visor down over his face. He could easily pass for an African, dressed like this. There weren't many Europeans resident in Malenga. A Mzungu would stand out like a sore thumb.

He looked down at the handlebars and cursed. His hands. The backs of his hands were white.

Bill took a deep breath. If he was to survive, he would have to start thinking. Gloves, forget gloves. He didn't have any.

With a flash of inspiration, he pushed two fingers into the Hilux exhaust pipe and massaged the backs of his hands. *Yes. This would prove he was black. This grunge wouldn't even wash off in the rain. Anyone stopping him would take one look at his hands and wave him through.*

Bill climbed back onto the bike, opened the petrol tap, switched on and gave it a kick. The engine roared into life on the second try. Now he must get away from the company car as soon as possible. The gear lever wouldn't lift. He tried to flip it up with his right foot and then discovered it was the brake pedal. Bill hadn't ridden a motorcycle for years. *This Japanese shit has everything back to front.*

He flipped up the lever on the left and pulled away in second gear. Changing gear would be a problem until he became familiar with this bike. The throttle was also very delicate. He could feel the front wheel rising if he gave it too much power. *This was never a problem with the old British bikes, unless you owned a Vincent or a Bonnie. At least it was a four stroke. It isn't making that horrible two stroke noise.*

Bill chose to ride through the northern part of town. The only other route to reach the west road to Ken's place would be down the main street.

The north side had been the more opulent part of Malenga, but it was now a mere shadow of its former self. He rode up the hill and along a tree-lined avenue. Bill had noticed before that most of these large houses bore the date of nineteen forty to fifty on their stone facades. Their previous colonial owners would turn over in their graves if they could see them now. Scrap cars littered the driveways in different stages of being dismantled. The iron gates had long since fallen down, or had been stolen. Six or more families now lived in each of these elegant monstrosities. More a case of economics than anything else.

A deafening clap of thunder shook the bike, causing a huge cloud of bats to rise up from a wooded area ahead. Large drops of rain began to splash onto his visor.

Chapter 21

Patch, Ken's Jack Russell, barked twice at the vivid flash of lightning. He then scuttled back up the wooded slope to the cabin after a crash of thunder.

"Yes Patch, my boy," gasped Ken. "This is going to be a 'lulu'. Even a little chap like you could get zapped out here."

Ken wasn't used to physical exertion, but he had managed to secure the float plane with four extra lines before the rain started. He glanced around at the night sky. *No stars.* To the south, it looked like a giant's workshop with ten of them welding at the same time.

He rested his hand on the plane's pontoon. "You should be all right now, old girl."

A heavy drop of rain splashed onto his bald patch, prompting him to walk quickly back to shore along the old jetty, then up the hill.

Ken contemplated driving up to the golf club for a couple of whiskies, then dismissed the idea. The place was like a morgue through the week. He might as well stay at home and talk to the dog.

The *chug, chug* of the Lister engine could be heard from the outhouse, behind the cabin. *If the ice cubes in the fridge are solid, I will stop the engine and light a couple of candles.*

Expensive way of making ice, but the visitors he had now and again expected electricity. One of the old paraffin fridges would be more cost effective. He needed power, anyway, for the electric water pump down here at the jetty. It filled a plastic storage tank further up the hill, which usually lasted him a week.

Of course, all the drinking water had to be boiled. Especially for the ice. The whisky didn't kill all the nasty things in the water.

Even the water in the town had to be boiled, unless you spent a fortune on the bottled stuff.

The locals drank water from the tap. Ken was convinced an African stomach was different to that of a Mzungu's.

The cabin was halfway up the slope, and had a splendid view of the inlet. It was also an ideal place for mooring the old girl. She was quite sheltered down there, bobbing up and down against the rubber tyres of the jetty.

The ice cubes were solid, so Ken lit some candles and then went out of the back door and stopped the generator. He ran back into the house because of a sudden shower.

A half bottle of cheap whisky, a glass, and the ice bucket he set up on the veranda table before settling himself into the old armchair. He poured himself a stiff one, and then waited in anticipation for the storm to really begin. A sudden gust of wind swirled leaves and dust into the air around the cabin, and hailstones rattled on the veranda's tin roof.

Ken passed most of his time out here sedated by whisky, in tune with nature. The main event was just starting. He enjoyed a good electrical storm at night. To witness God's awesome power sent shivers up and down his spine. *The armchair is the best thing to fly in weather like this.*

Chapter 22

Bill was making good progress through the town. Security vehicles were out in force, slowly patrolling up and down the quiet streets. They didn't pay him much attention. Dust and paper rose high into the air, and he was buffeted from side to side. Locals ran for shelter, with fixed expressions on their faces. Some of them ran across the street without looking as he descended the hill towards the west road. His stomach tightened when he approached the intersection. A security van was blocking the way. They flashed their lights for him to stop. A convoy of army trucks trundled over the intersection, heading out of town. Bill pulled up and stopped alongside the white van, waiting for them to pass. He noticed a small boy standing on the pavement in the rain. The boy seemed fascinated by the olive-green vehicles, and even the hailstones didn't drive him away. The occupants of the van looked across at Bill. *Probably because they have nothing else to do.*

After the last truck, one of them waved at him in a manner that said 'fuck off'. Bill was quite happy to do this, and pulled away, turning right, with the bike nearly stalling. The small boy waved at him and jumped on the back. Bill didn't mind. *They were searching for a white man in a pick-up, not two locals on a motorcycle.*

One kilometre out of town, he encountered a roadblock. Two soldiers dressed in waterproof capes stopped him. They both had their fingers on the triggers of their assault rifles and started asking questions in the local language. Unexpectedly, the boy behind him chatted away in a singsong voice, waving arms around. Bill was under the impression that the boy was asking them questions. Every now and then they nodded or shook their heads with bored expression. Eventually, one of them pointed down the road with his weapon and walked back to the shelter of his truck. Bill set off this time without a problem. He had learnt first gear was down on this contraption. *Where are the police?* He hadn't seen one policeman so far. Maybe the weather was keeping them indoors, or they didn't have any vehicles in running condition.

Five minutes further on, the boy patted his arm in a signal to stop. Bill pulled off the road next to a group of mud huts, and lifted his visor.

"Ah. Mzungu." The boy smiled up at him.

"What did you say to the soldiers?" Bill enquired.

"I asked many questions." The boy stuck out his small chest. "I want to be a soldier."

Bill ruffled the boy's wet, curly hair. "I think you will be a good soldier. What's your name?"

"Sunday; my mother calls me Sunday. I was born on Sunday."

Bill smiled and closed his visor. *This boy may well have saved my life.*

The golf club turn off was not far from the village. Large, deep pools of water now covered most of the road, and the turn off looked like a lake. He slowed and inched his way forward, turning off his lights. They were just for show anyway. If he rode off the road here he could disappear into a ditch.

Now he was riding south towards the lake. The bike was handling the gravel surface very well. *I must keep a close watch on the right-hand side bush.* According to Roberto, the track to Ken's place was unmarked and overgrown.

$$* \qquad * \qquad *$$

Roberto explained the situation to Monica and Sara. They gave each other frightened glances at the mention of Nabusano's name. He only described the ball as something Nabusano wanted.

Monica burst into tears. "I will never see my husband again."

Roberto was going to remind her that she wasn't married, but decided not to.

Chapter 23

Magyenzi had calmed down enough to start thinking rationally. He knew he could not tell the truth about the nightmare events that had occurred in his office. The sergeant would probably lock him up in one of his own cells.

He had finished writing the official report and signed it with a flourish. Basically, it read that four armed men of ill repute had entered his office to try to intimidate a white man who was assisting him with some enquiries. These men had a box with a human head inside in their possession. The identity of the deceased was at this point unknown. They had threatened to kill the white man with firearms. He himself had thrown two of the culprits out of the window and beat the other two to death in self defence. *Case closed.*

Magyenzi smiled and nodded in satisfaction. The chief of police may even award him with a medal for his heroic actions.

He pressed the buzzer and waited for the sergeant to appear. The sergeant tapped on the door and entered slowly, not knowing what to expect.

"File this report and send a copy to Mabarta." He handed him the paper. "They will want to know about four fatalities and a human head. It is late. I am going home. Get something to cover these windows. The rain is coming in."

The sergeant was pleased that the OC was back to his normal, pompous self. Magyenzi twiddle his thumbs and smiled. "If you want to, when you type this, you can say you assisted me."

The sergeant read the report and stared back at the OC in disbelief.

"There could be an increase in salary for you. I will personally recommend it."

186

The sergeant nodded and started to leave the office. "Sir, there is something you should know. On radio Mabarta, they are saying this area is under marshal law."

Magyenzi scowled and signalled the sergeant to leave.

This is Nabusano's doing. One of his sons is the commandant at the army camp. For marshal law to be declared, there has to be an emergency.

The population was not rioting and the rebels were far north in hiding. Could this be a way of supplanting his authority? It was a sham. He had not requested assistance.

They had bypassed him. He had become dispensable. To become dispensable instantly gave him a high rating on the endangered species list.

Chapter 24

Patch jerked up his head and started barking. *Who could be visiting on a night like this?*

The Jack Russell was an excellent watchdog. He only barked like that when someone was coming. Never gave a false alarm and always shut up at a word from Ken. The dog's hearing was exceptional. Due to the state of the winding track down the hill, Ken usually had two minutes advance warning before any visitor actually arrived. This was handy, because the place was normally in such a mess. Ken galvanised into action. He dashed round the house, picking up and putting away anything out of place. After two minutes of animated motion, Ken stopped like a rundown clockwork toy.

"Must keep up appearances. Can't afford to let the side down, you know," he panted.

Patch cocked his head to one side, then followed his master out onto the veranda. A motorbike arrived and the helmeted rider leant the steaming machine against the front of the veranda.

"Oh. Roberto," called Ken. "What brings you here at this time of night?"

"It's me, Bill," said the figure in a muffled voice as he removed the helmet.

Ken was surprised. Bill had never been there before. "Come in out of the rain, old chap. You're flipping-well wet through."

Ken walked back inside the living room to fetch another glass and a towel. Something was wrong for anybody to be out on a motorcycle at that late hour in the foul weather.

"Where's your car?" Ken enquired on his return.

"I had to leave it at the bus station."

Ken poured Bill a whisky, which he downed in one gulp and held out the glass for another one. *Something is very wrong here,* thought Ken as they seated themselves. *Bill usually nurses a drink like that for half an hour.*

"So what seems to be the problem, old man?" Ken smiled, sipping his drink.

Bill decided to tell Ken everything. It would be the only way he would be able to convince him to help him.

"Remember I told you I had something Nabusano wanted?"

Ken wasn't smiling anymore. "Yes," he said apprehensively.

"Well, tonight, I went into town to give the thing to that gang of thugs of his. They had killed my foreman. All hell broke loose and the four of them are dead. I need your plane to get out of here."

Ken choked on his whisky. "I beg your pardon," he gasped.

"Four men are dead. The security company and the army are searching for me."

"Hold on, hold on." Ken stood and raised his hand. "Let's take this one step at a time." He held up one finger. "First, you say four men are dead."

Bill nodded, looking very miserable. "Yes."

"How did they die?"

"I killed them."

"Good lord," Ken exclaimed, becoming very agitated. "Now let's stay cool and calm. There is normally a logical way out of this type of mess. Point two. Were there any witnesses?"

"Yes, one."

"Okay. It's not good to have a witness, but one can be discredited. Who is the witness?"

"OC Magyenzi."

"What, the commanding officer of the bloody police force," Ken gasped.

"Yes." Bill lit a cigarette.

Ken held up his hands again. "Let's stay calm. Let's stay calm." He cleared his throat. "Point three. Where did all this happen?"

Bill blew out a plume of smoke. "In Magyenzi's office."

"In the OC's office at the fucking police station," Ken yelled.

Bill took a sip of whisky. "Yes."

Patch started to take an interest in the conversation. He knew from experience his master only used the 'F' word in times of high stress. Like the time his toolbox had dropped into the lake while he'd been working on the plane's engine. Also, the time he had thrown the aluminium anchor over the side, only to discover it wasn't tied to the plane.

"Now, let's stay calm. The thing is not to panic," Ken continued. "You say you killed those four thugs. How on earth could you manage that? I've seen those men hanging around town. It's not physically possible. They would make mincemeat out of you."

Bill flicked his cigarette over the veranda railing. "I used the power of the ball," he said flatly.

"Ball! What fucking ball?" Ken yelled.

"This fucking ball," Bill shouted, placing it on the table.

Ken stared at the ball and realised with horror he was in the presence of a raving lunatic.

Just then Sara's cell phone buzzed in Bill's pocket.

"Yes, Roberto, I've arrived safely at Ken's place."

Bill listened while Roberto explained the area was now under Martial Law. "Some shit of the bull story about rebels. The security guards searched the camp. I don't think they noticed the Honda was missing. All company people were confined to the camp for their own safety. The girls were very frightened."

Ken kept signalling that he wanted to speak to Roberto, so Bill said, "Here's Ken. He wants a word with you."

Ken took the phone and retreated inside the cabin. "Hello, Roberto," he said pleasantly. Then he whispered urgently. "I don't think Bill is quite right in the head. He came here two sheets to the wind. I think the poor chap's got a loose tile."

"What do you mean?" asked Roberto.

"You know. I think he's got a slate missing."

"A what?"

"Maybe he fell off your bike and banged his head. He's gone a bit crazy."

"Why do you say that?"

Ken chuckled. "He's talking about killing four men with the power of a ball." He laughed nervously, waiting for Roberto to answer.

"Oh yes. We think the ball was left on this planet by extraterrestrials two million years ago. They could have a thrown it out of a flying saucer."

Ken was frozen. "A flying what?" he asked eventually.

"Flying saucer. Everyone knows what that is. The thing with the little green a men on the inside."

There was dead silence.

"Hello, hello, are you a still there?" Roberto enquired.

"What the fuck are you talking about?" Ken yelled.

"Ask Bill to give you a demonstration."

"Demonstration. Demonstration. What fucking demonstration? Are you fuckers selling vacuum cleaners?" he shouted.

Bill came into the house and removed the phone from Ken's hand, who took a couple of steps backwards in the process. "Roberto, it's me again. Ken is not taking this very well."

"Yes. I got that impression. You will have to convince him. Hide the motorcycle in the trees. It is only a time before they think about Ken and his plane. You will have to hide until you can get away. I do not think he can fly in this a storm."

Bill nodded. "Yes. I think you are right. We must call each other if something comes up."

"Be careful," Roberto replied and ended the call.

Ken was standing in a corner of the room. "All you fuckers are mad," he shouted. With any luck, he would wake up in bed, sweating.

Bill went outside and brought in the whisky and the glasses. He was cold in his wet clothes. "Come and sit down. Have another drink," he suggested.

"That's the only reasonable thing you said since you fucking arrived," said Ken slowly, taking a seat.

"I'm sorry. All this must sound crazy, but it's true. Roberto and I felt the same as you in the beginning. I found this at the crusher." He held up the ball between thumb and forefinger. "After a while, I found out you can move things with it. There are a lot of other powers it gives the owner. That's why Nabusano wants it. I think he's been looking for this for a long time. Now he's moving Heaven and Earth to get his hands on it."

Ken poured himself another drink. "You don't expect me to believe that. I may be senile, but I'm not stupid."

"Watch. I'll show you."

The whisky bottle lifted from the coffee table, then started spinning like a top. It stopped spinning, then returned to the table. Ken continued to stare at the bottle for a moment, then rubbed his eyes. His red nose contrasted with the whiteness of his face.

"I didn't see that. I didn't see that," he repeated. "Where are the pink elephants? That's all I need now." The last case of whisky he had bought was not his usual brand. It was a local blend that was half price. *I'm not buying any more of that muck*, he thought.

Ken was still not convinced. He waved his hand from side to side over the top of the bottle, and eventually picked it up, pouring himself another drink. "How the bloody hell did you do that? There's no string anywhere. If this is your idea of a joke, it's not bloody funny."

Patch barked at the cigarette packet on the table. The top was opening. A cigarette slid out and floated up to Bill's mouth. The lighter then lifted and lit the end. Ken turned to face Patch. "Did you see that? I'm not going crazy. Patch saw that."

The dog growled and snapped at the lighter, which circled his head.

"I'm not hallucinating. Patch doesn't drink whisky."

The lighter returned to the table, then Patch yelped as he lifted into the air. With staring eyes, the dog paddled round the room as if he was swimming. He must have enjoyed the experience, because his stubby tail wagged and he now sported an erection.

"What's he supposed to be," Ken remarked. "A flying fuck."

Lightning flickered at the windows, followed by thunder, which rolled and boomed around the surrounding hills. Bill shivered and pointed to the fireplace. "Do you mind if I make a fire?"

Ken shook his head as if in a trance.

"I'll take that as a yes," Bill said as he prepared the paper and wood. The rain was even coming down the chimney in the form of granules of soot.

A blazing fire was soon warming up the small living room. Bill placed the envelope full of dollars on the floor. He then removed his wet jeans, which he hung over the back of a chair, and rubbed his hands together.

"Let's have a cup of coffee, then I'll tell you the whole story."

Ken's head nodded up and down vigorously. Bill smiled. *He just needs a hat with a bell on it.*

*   *   *

The thunder exploded over the water with a blinding flash of lightning. There was no repetition of sounds by reflection out here in the middle of the lake.

Nabusano was weary. Two assistants bathed him and lifted him into bed.

A report had been received that Parker's Toyota had been discovered near the bus station. The roadblocks had long since been in place. Even at the border and airport, his agents were waiting and watching. It was only a matter of time.

Time was the one thing he did not have.

Chapter 25

James was worried. He watched the military truck with the loudspeaker blaring drive by from behind the curtain. The message was repeated. "Stay indoors. Malenga is under marshal law. A curfew is enforced during the hours of darkness. Curfew breakers may be shot on sight. Stay indoors."

The obtrusive noise faded away down the street. Security vans slowly passed by. Obviously, the curfew didn't affect them. None of this made any sense. Where were the police? According to the radio, a group of rebels had infiltrated the area. *This is Nabusano's doing. He may be able to fool the uneducated majority of the people.* James knew the rebels stayed close to the northern border. Their method of operation was to raid a village to capture young recruits, then march them back over the border before the army could react. *Down here the rebels would be completely out of their depth. There would be nowhere for them to run. It would be a suicide mission.*

A rumour had spread from house to house. The four gangsters who had terrorised the town had been killed at the police station. Could it be that Magyenzi had at last decided to do something about them? It seemed unlikely. Since he had been stationed at Malenga, he spent half his time covering up their crimes. Why change now?

James had a feeling change was taking place. *Nabusano is losing control. Why else this show of force, unless he is fighting for his survival.*

Brenda came from out of the bedroom and interrupted his thoughts.

"I have found the mat that Bill Parker is interested in."

"I will look at it tomorrow," he told her.

"It cannot be of any great importance."

Chapter 26

The commandant and three of his personal guard stood under the trees by the side of the Mabarta road. No vehicles had been observed driving towards Malenga.

Most people avoided travelling at night. The last taxi to leave Malenga was due to pass by in a few minutes. It had already been searched at the roadblock and was headed this way. The capital lay another twenty-five kilometres further on. Passengers reaching this point would be feeling quite safe.

Rain dripped from the commandant's nose and ears. "Only two of you will fire." He addressed the men standing nearest to him. "You, take position at the side of the road. Aim low. We need these people alive to tell their story. You…" He pointed to a second soldier. "Shoot from here as the taxi comes towards you. Aim high. Do not disable the vehicle. Understood?"

"Yes sir," they responded, and took up their positions in the wet foliage. Once they stopped moving, they became invisible.

Headlights swept over the embankment as the minibus rounded the bend. The commandant stepped back behind a tree and shielded his cigarette inside a cupped hand.

Most passengers were sleeping. Their heads rocked from side to side with the motion of the hard-driven taxi. The driver breathed a sigh of relief as he passed the twenty-five kilometre marker.

Phut, phut, phut. Holes appeared along the inside of the bus. Two or three people pitched forward without a sound before the others realised what was happening. Shouting and screaming broke out inside the packed interior. Confused, the driver started to slow down.

Chink, chink, chink. Three holes magically appeared in the windscreen. The driver jammed his foot on the accelerator and started screaming with his passengers.

Chapter 27

Bill finished giving Ken a brief summary of the whole story regarding the ball. Ken sat unmoving, staring into the fire, with a mug of coffee clutched in his hand. Patch copied his master by also staring into the fire. Bill looked from Ken to Patch and then back again. He had the feeling he was examining figures in a wax museum.

Giving up on receiving any sort of reaction, he found a plastic raincoat and went outside to hide the motorcycle. It started on the first kick, probably due to the warm engine. He rode it directly up the hillside and lifted it, using the ball, into the middle of a dense clump of thorn bush. No one could reach it on foot, not even some self-conscious person searching for an ideal place to take a shit.

Back at the cabin, Bill found Ken in exactly the same position he had left him in. Patch hadn't moved around much, either. After Bill had placed some larger pieces of wood on the fire, which cracked and popped, sending sparks up the chimney, did Ken finally start moving. He lifted the coffee mug to his lips and drank.

"So," Bill enquired. "Do you think you can help me?"

Ken's blue eyes rested on Bill's face. "This is one hell of a bloody mess. If they find you here, they will shoot the both of us. Maybe you should have stayed in the camp. The Italians would have protected you."

Bill shook his head. "You don't understand. They would have told them they need me for questioning. If the Italians refused, then all the people in the camp could be killed. The rebels would be blamed. With this marshal law Nabusano can do anything he wants to. He has a free hand."

Ken stared into the fire again. "Yes, I suppose you're right. I don't want to get involved, but I'm involved already. On the other hand, we Mzungu's have to stick together when the shit hits the fan. It's different for me. This country is my home. I ruddy well live here."

Bill ran a hand through his hair. "Yes, I know. I'm very sorry for all this, but Roberto and I couldn't think of anything else."

Ken faced him again. "I will do what I can to help, because none of this is really your fault, but I can't promise anything. I can't fly in this weather, but it should clear up by morning. The other thing is, the old girls' tanks are empty and I'm financially embarrassed at the moment. I picked up a fax today from town. Some Yank bird watcher is due to arrive tomorrow evening. I can only fuel up after he pays me something in advance."

Bill picked up the large envelope from the floor. "Money is not a problem. This thing is full of hundred dollar bills. I'll give you enough to fill your plane ten times over."

Ken stared. "Good lord. Well that's a step in the right direction. I will fill her up in the morning. Also, I will just happen to show them the fax at the fuel depot. It gives me a good reason for buying the two drums of avgas."

Bill nodded. "The only other question is where I hide. I suppose I could conceal myself in the bush until you are ready."

Ken raised his hand. "I have an idea. This cabin is built on a slope. Under the veranda is a storage space. As far as I know, nobody else knows about it, except for the previous owner. It's a bit damp, but it's a ruddy sight better than the bloody bush."

Ken pulled back the rug on the veranda to reveal a trapdoor.

Bill smiled. "This is ideal. They should never find me down there."

Ken scratched his head. "If I remember rightly, there should be an old mattress down there. I would give you a candle, but maybe the light will shine up through the floor boards."

"Light down there is one thing I don't need."

Chapter 28

The next morning after breakfast the 747 started it's decent. Phil's excitement mounted. He would soon be looking down on Africa itself. The mysterious, dark continent full of elephants and lions. He had formed his own preconceptions of what he was about to find below. They were a blend of scenes from the Serengeti and the Camel Trophy, where Land Rovers crossed rivers on rafts.

The airliner passed through the thick layer of cloud, shuddering as the decent continued. Once through the cloud layer, the shuddering stopped and he had a clear view of the ground. They were flying over a range of hills. *Too high to make out any wild animals.*

The pilot's voice interrupted his thoughts. "We shall be landing in fifteen minutes' time and are twenty minutes ahead of schedule. The temperature on the ground is twenty-seven degrees. To our left is Pretoria. We shall soon be approaching Johannesburg from the north. Our flight path will take us round to the west and then to approach from the south for landing at Johannesburg International. The crew and I hope you have had a pleasant flight and thank you for flying SAA."

Phil pressed his head against the window and peered out over the landscape. In the distance, he could make out office buildings. That must be Pretoria, where he would meet Watson. Switzerland had been a similar scenario. Land at Zurich, then travel to Bern. Here, land at Johannesburg, then travel to Pretoria.

Below, he could make out a network of roadways. Sunlight glinted from car windscreens. *Surely the wild animals would be run down with all that traffic.*

The light came on for 'fasten your seatbelt'. Phil stopped peering down for a while. The view from this height was starting to make him feel dizzy.

After another five minutes, the plane tilted to the left and he turned back to the window. As far as the eye could see were roads and buildings. Further over to the left was a section of high rise offices and hotels, with two tall telecommunications towers. The freeways were packed with traffic. Phil removed and polished his glasses. "But this is not Africa," he said.

A large man sitting close to him smiled. "No, my mart. This is not Africa. This is South Africa."

Phil wasn't quite sure what the man was implying, so decided not to say anything.

The aircraft tilted again to the left, turning around the southern part of the city. This was certainly not what he had expected. After another five minutes, they turned again to the left and started the final decent. Industrial areas with large factory roofs sped by as the altitude became lower. Individual houses were now clearly visible in the suburbs. Most of them had gardens with blue swimming pools. The aircraft flew into a large, clear area and touched down with a bump and the deafening noise of reverse thrust. Gradually, the charging plane slowed and taxied passed a system of different runways.

A woman's voice instructed the passengers to remain seated. Eventually, they came to rest and the seatbelt light blinked off. Phil breathed a sigh of relief. *Well, that wasn't so bad.* Flying was quite something, but becoming more routine every day. It sure looked like he'd got a handle on his fear of flying.

The airport terminal was still some way off from this aircraft parking area, so the passengers boarded a line of buses. His overcoat had become obsolete, so he doubled it up and laid it over the top of his overnight bag. *This is kinda like a summer's day in the states, except there is no humidity.*

The terminal was on par with a first world international airport, and was pretty well jacked up. There were about ten lines of passengers at immigration, so it didn't take long to pass through. He told them he had some business at the embassy, but should be leaving again this afternoon. His passport was stamped for seven days in case he was delayed.

After collecting his suitcase from one of the 'merry go rounds' he pushed his trolley, following the exit signs. On the other side of the automatic doors, a crowd of people stood waiting behind a chromium hand rail. A few held names up before them, clearly waiting for the passenger in question to identify themselves. Phil saw his name held up towards the back of the crowd and pushed his trolley in that direction. The African man with the sign introduced himself as Geoffrey, then dialled a number on his cell phone.

"Mr. Watson told me to phone him on your arrival."

He spoke for a moment, then handed the phone to Phil.

"Hi, Mr. Watson, This is Phil Jones."

"Okay, now listen up." A stern voice instructed him. "First off, my job here is officially an environmentalist. As far as Geoffrey is concerned, that's what I do. Have you got that?"

Phil swallowed. "Yeah, loud and clear."

"Secondly, you are an expert on birds and fish. Geoffrey is going to buy some gear for you. He knows where things are at locally. I'm pretty much tied up as of now, but I'll brief you later at the embassy."

"Okay, I understand."

"Now hand me back to Geoffrey."

The African nodded and said 'yes' a few times on the phone before placing it back in his pocket.

"Let's go," he said setting off with the trolley. "The car is in the basement parking."

Phil's feeling of being a tourist had ended abruptly after listening to Watson. "Is Watson always like that?" Phil enquired.

Geoffrey laughed. "Only when he's worried about something. Come on. We have some shopping to do. I hope you're not afraid of needles."

They walked past a number of restaurants and shops before coming to the elevators.

"Where are we going?" Phil asked.

"B2."

"No, I mean in the car. Where are we going in the car?"

Geoffrey checked his watch. "The traffic is not bad now. We will go back to Pretoria. It's easier to drive around there. We will be there in one hour. It's only fifty kilometres from here."

On the second level, Geoffrey inserted his parking card and some money into a machine, then they walked off in search of the car.

"How long have you worked for Watson?"

Geoffrey pressed the button on his remote and the hazards blinked on a Jeep Cherokee ahead. "Oh, about five years. The other embassy people come and go, but Mr. Watson is more permanent. He has his own department. The pay is good. He's a good boss. He knows what he wants. Sometimes I travel north with him if there are things to carry."

"What's it like up there?"

Geoffrey laughed again. "You will see. It's very different from here. I can say, after been up there, I am very happy I live down here in the south."

Phil wasn't feeling very reassured. He climbed into the car and found the steering wheel in front of him. Geoffrey laughed, holding onto the door for support.

"I don't think you want to drive in Jo'burg. If you make a mistake, the other cars will kill you."

Phil climbed out again, feeling very foolish. Geoffrey wiped the tears from his eyes.

"Don't worry. I wait for all you Americans to get in the wrong side. I'm not joking about the traffic. They are very aggressive drivers here. In the old days, they used to shoot at each other."

Phil climbed into the left hand side and fastened his seatbelt. The Cherokee's tyres squeaked on the painted floor of the underground parking at every ninety degree turn until they emerged into the early morning sunlight.

Geoffrey followed the A19 Pretoria signs until he was cruising on the three-lane, northbound freeway at a steady one-thirty kilometres per hour. A BMW closed in from behind and flashed his headlights. Geoffrey jerked his head. "See what I mean?"

He pulled into the next lane as the BMW accelerated past. Further on, Phil noticed a speed cop on the centre island, peering through an eyeglass on a tripod. Further on, the BMW was pulled over next to a police car.

Geoffrey shook his head. "Expensive way to show me his car is faster than mine. They sometimes flash their lights when the freeway is full. I don't know what they expect me to do. Maybe they think I'm a helicopter."

Phil pushed his seat back to make more space for his long legs. "Everyone's driving pretty well as far as I can see."

Geoffrey braked suddenly as a minibus taxi changed lanes and pushed over in front of them.

"Wait until it rains. Then you'll see some real fun."

The freeway now blended into the N1 and was still surrounded by blocks of company offices.

"Where are all the animals? All I can see are buildings and roads."

"Which animals?"

"The wild animals. This is Africa."

Geoffrey laughed again. "You think everyone has a lion in the back garden. Even the farmers wouldn't like wild animals on their land. They are all fenced in reserves or national parks for the tourists. The only animals in the city are in the zoo. Even a dog has to be on a lead."

Phil was disappointed. "And further north. There gotter be animals walking around up there."

Geoffrey nodded. "Yes, northern Botswana is full of wild animals. If you are stupid enough to drive at night, you have a good chance of crashing into an elephant. It's all a national park protected by the Botswana defence force. Even in the south of Botswana, you don't drive at night."

"Are there elephants there?"

"No, donkeys. They stand in the middle of the road, waiting for you to hit them. In the day, they stand there looking down at the surface. Mr. Watson calls them road inspectors."

"Are there animals where I'm going?"

"You will be very lucky to see anything in the poorer countries. They all end up in the cooking pot. Even rats, bats and snakes are eaten."

Geoffrey smiled. "There's one zoo in Brazzaville. It's completely empty."

Phil turned towards the driver. "You gotter be kidding."

Geoffrey shook his head. "No. In times of war it's open season on everything. If you're a soldier with a gun and you're hungry, what are you going to do?"

Phil remained quite while digesting this latest information.

"Don't worry. I've never been to Malenga, but I've heard there are thousands of birds and fish to study at the lake. The only thing that's likely to be eaten is you."

Phil stiffened in his seat. "Cannibals?"

"No." Geoffrey smiled. "Mosquitoes. That's where we're going first. To a travel clinic to get you fixed up."

The Cherokee was now cruising through open farmland. Both of them flipped down the visors to shield their eyes from the glare of the morning sun. Phil wished he hadn't thrown away the broken sun glasses.

"Pretoria is north of Johannesburg, right?"

Geoffrey nodded. "Yes. We are nearly there."

"Then the sun is in the wrong place."

"No. here the sun shines from the north."

Phil shook his head. "My sense of direction is all scrambled."

"Where you're going, it passes more or less overhead. There, you must just think about it rising in the east and setting in the west. That never changes."

"Yep, that's a good pointer."

"That reminds me," said Geoffrey distastefully. "At Mabarta airport, you will be met by an embassy staffer by the name of Simon Pointer. We don't like each other. He thinks he is God's gift to the world."

Phil couldn't imagine anyone not liking Geoffrey, and decided the fault must lay with this Pointer guy.

"I'm surprise at the number of white people here. Where did they all come from?"

Geoffrey laughed. "Most of them were born here. This is their home, same as us black people. The whites have two main tribes. One is the Afrikaners and the other is the English. We have all fought each other at one time or other, but now we're all working together. Is not easy, but most of us are trying."

Phil nodded. "I know what you mean; even in the states we still have our own problems between black and white."

Geoffrey smiled. "Yes, well, you Negro's are in the minority. Here, we Africans are in the majority. You need to get plenty of girlfriends and start fucking."

They both laughed as the Cherokee slipped onto an off-ramp and drove under the freeway.

The city of Pretoria was situated in a slight hollow, so the approach was down the side of the surrounding hills. From this vantage point, Phil had a good view of the city spread out below. He could see the streets were lined with tall trees covered with purple flowers. This was a sharp contrast to Johannesburg's concrete steel and glass.

"What are those purple trees?" Phil asked.

"They are from South America. They are not African, but they grow really well here."

Phil smiled. "They are beautiful."

"Not if you have any allergies. You're here at the wrong time of the year and that's for sure."

Phil now viewed the trees with some apprehension, instead of bemused wonder. He was allergic to dust and cats. They parked outside the travel clinic and Geoffrey checked his watch.

"We have to push to make the flight this afternoon."

Inside, Phil was jabbed with three injections and received a plethora of pills, lotions and leaflets. He was dismayed to find out he could die from about ten different fatal diseases, which were resident in the location he was visiting. Back in the car, Phil was feeling dizzy.

"That's the yellow fever injection," Geoffrey explained. "Should wear off in half an hour." He rubbed his hands together. "Now for some shopping."

They drove to one of the large shopping complexes that housed every type of store imaginable. Geoffrey signalled to one of the many car park attendants to keep an eye on the Cherokee.

"You have to be on your guard at all times. In the evil apartheid days, crime wasn't so bad. Now we have the 'have nots' rubbing shoulders with the 'haves' and African people don't need passes anymore. Anybody can walk anywhere they want to. Crime is a small price for freedom, but a problem we hope to solve."

After one hour Phil was kitted out with boots, jeans, waterproof jacket, checked shirts, shorts, trainers and a baseball cap. He wanted to buy some of the military-looking bush shirts, but Geoffrey advised against it.

"You don't want to change your appearance from a missionary to a mercenary," he told him.

Phil had got the last word in by buying a pair of sunglasses on his way of out the store.

"The things you don't need up there, like your overcoat and black suits, you can leave at the embassy."

"Now, let's have an early lunch. From the embassy I'm taking you straight back to the airport."

I must be back in the Amazing Race *again,* thought Phil as they hurried over to one of the restaurants.

Twenty minutes later he was enjoying a large fillet steak with fries. He declined to order any lager and settled for a cold glass of fresh milk instead. The last thing he wanted was to meet Watson smelling of beer.

Geoffrey tipped the car park attendant, then drove to the east side of the city before the lunch time traffic started.

The embassy was situated in a quiet avenue that was filled with parked cars. In front of the high perimeter wall, it was a no parking area. Phil noticed an electric fence on the top, backed up by razor wire. The security guard examined both their identity cards and carried out a routine search of the Cherokee. After checking under the car with a mirror, he nodded towards a camera mounted on the wall, and the gate slid open. There was a separate pedestrian gate for visitors and South African employees. Geoffrey parked under the shaded internal parking area and carried Phil's baggage over to a side entrance. The stars and stripes hung limply in the still air above the main doorway.

Inside, the African placed everything on top of a table, then pressed a button on an intercom. "Mr. Jones to see Mr. Watson. We are expected."

The baleful eye of another camera fixed above the next set of doors stared down at them. A voice came from the intercom. "Leave all those things on the table and come through. Mr. Watson is out back."

Geoffrey pulled down the handle on the door and waited.

"Mr. Watson usually has lunch out at the pool. He says he suffers from claustrophobia."

A heavy *clunk* vibrated through the door, allowing Geoffrey to push it open. Phil followed him along a corridor that led out into a large garden at the rear of the embassy. A fair-sized pool was situated to one side, surrounded by umbrellas and tables. Sunlight glinted from its quivering surface as the pool cleaner vibrated its way up from the deep end. Phil removed his glasses and changed them for his new shades.

A small, middle aged man with sandy hair was the only person seated at the poolside. He glanced up from the newspaper he was reading and raised his eyebrows.

"If I didn't know any better, I would say you were Will Smith from the men in black movie."

Phil smiled in embarrassment and held out his hand. "Phil Jones, sir."

The hand was ignored as Watson turned his attention to Geoffrey. "For Christ sake, go and fetch something sensible for Mr. Jones to wear. He can dress in the changing rooms out here."

Watson pointed to the chair next to him. "Sit down or I'm goner end up with a pain in my neck. I'm already suffering from indigestion over you."

He stuck out his hand after Phil was seated.

"Keith Watson. I know this is none of your fault, but I think John Collins is a darn fool to send a paper shuffler out here. I've just come off the horn trying to get him to pull the plug on this one. That guy is one stubborn sonofabitch. Where you're going is a different world. You are going to be completely out of your depth and virtually on your own. The only thing going for you is that you're black. You may be able to pass for a local if the crap hits the fan. Only so long as you keep your trap shut. Your accent will be a dead giveaway."

Watson opened a tin of coke and pushed it over to Phil. "As far as I know, everything is cool up there, but don't make any waves. You will be travelling as a private individual. Give me your badge and ID now, before Geoffrey comes back. You can't just pitch up in a foreign country to start waving that around."

Phil placed his FBI ID on the table, which Watson pocketed. He immediately felt naked.

"Okay, now this is the plan. You will arrive in Mabarta this evening. A guy called Simon Pointer will meet you. Just tell him you're doing some fact finding. I don't trust him. He's been feeding me info over the last six years that pretty well pans out, but his boss has told me that he is living way over his means. He's on the take from somebody. But we don't know who."

Phil removed his sun glasses and polished them.

"Tomorrow go to the registrar of companies and do your thing. It's supposed to be open to the public. Might cost you a couple of bucks to speed things up, but that's normal. Then Pointer is to organise you to Malenga. There, you will just be a tourist staying with a Limey called Ken Marshal. He has a float plane that may come in useful. We sent him a fax. He knows you're coming. Get what info you can about these shareholders, then get out. Do not confront anybody. You got that?"

Phil nodded. "Sounds pretty well straightforward."

Watson shook his head. "You don't know where this is going to lead. If you find anything interesting, one of my guys can follow up."

Geoffrey appeared at the back of the building. Watson raised his hand for him to wait there. He reached under the table and placed a small bag on the top.

"In this bag is a special cell phone. It can communicate in areas of poor reception. If you dial one-eight-one-two-six-nine it gets you straight through to me, via our dish on the roof here."

Phil removed a pen from his pocket.

"Don't write it down. Remember the eighteen twelve overture and the relative sex act."

Phil was feeling a little dazed.

"Also, this phone has a homing device fitted. If we have to come and bail you out, we will know exactly where you're at. Give or take a yard or two. There are a couple of books about birds. Read them on the plane. There's a pair of binoculars and a camera with a zoom lens. Last, but not the least, is a tape recorder. The underside is specially made to house a nine mill automatic. If you press both sides at the same time, the bottom opens. Pointer will give you the shooter tomorrow at your hotel. You can't fly with a gun from here. Don't tell anyone about the recorder. If you're caught with a gun up there, you will end up in the slammer and they'll throw away the key. The gun's only as a last resort. You got that?"

Phil nodded a couple of times. It didn't sound so straightforward now. His throat was dry. He finished off the tin of coke and removed his necktie. Watson waved Geoffrey to come over.

"I have taken out everything Mr. Jones won't need up there and managed to get everything in one case. Here's a casual change of clothes for him now."

Geoffrey handed Phil a shirt with a pair of jeans and some trainers.

Watson checked his watch. "You gotter be outer here in fifteen minutes so go get changed."

Phil walked over to a small building next to the pool to rid himself of his Will Smith suit.

Keith Watson walked round the pool stroking his chin. Like it or not, this green horn was now his responsibility. Could be this was a straightforward paper chase, but he didn't think so. Somebody was hiding something. It was unbelievable that anybody in Malenga owned stock in American corporations. That town was a third world backwater. Nothing ever happened there. For that reason, Watson didn't know anything about the place.

Phil emerged from the changing room feeling much more comfortable. He could now easily blend into the silent majority of any country. Phil handed Geoffrey his clothes and shoes, then picked up the bag from the table.

"You look a whole heap better now," Watson commented. "Give me your old cell phone. I'll have someone take messages for you. From here on in, you're on your own. That phone I gave you is an important lifeline. Don't lose it."

He turned towards Geoffrey. "Educate Phil here about the 'dos and don'ts' on your way to the airport. We sure as hell don't want him catching something nasty."

Watson shook Phil's hand. "Good luck. I hope you have an uneventful time up there."

He smiled, but Phil noticed genuine concern in his eyes.

"Thank you sir. I promise not to start a war."

*   *   *

Phil had just learnt from Geoffrey that the N1 freeway runs all the way from the Zimbabwe border to Cape Town. If they drove another one thousand three hundred kilometres south, he could be sitting on the beach. Geoffrey changed the subject. "The two main dangers up in the north are mosquitoes and women."

"How come?"

"They both eat you and you have to swat them on the head to stop them sucking."

Phil managed a half-hatred smile to Geoffrey's joke. He wasn't in the mood for idle chit chat.

"So what are the real dangers up there?"

"Like I said, mosquitoes and women. Any mosquitoes from north of South Africa up to the Sahara carry malaria. It's like a band that runs round the world. You're going right in the middle of it."

"I've got pills for malaria."

Geoffrey shook his head. "That's a preventive that doesn't stop you catching it. You might as well throw them away. If you're taking that and catch it, it doesn't show up well on the blood test and time is critical. You need to take the cure as soon as possible."

"What's the cure?"

"Pills you get from any clinic up there. You take them for three or four days, then you're over it, if you start soon enough."

"How do I know if I've got it?"

"If you get a headache with sore joints in your body, go straight to the clinic for a blood test. The best preventive is to spray your room before you go to sleep. Especially cupboards. Anywhere the mosquitoes can hide. If you're outside at night, use the white cream they gave you."

"What about yellow fever?"

"You can't get that now. Put that card in your passport. They will ask for it at Mabarta. Without that, they will turn you back or make you pay. If you get muscle cramps, take a salt tablet. Don't drink the water up there or you won't be able to blow your nose without shitting yourself. If you get the shits, drink plenty of coke."

Phil rummaged around in the plastic bag from the travel clinic and found the yellow fever card.

"Mosquitoes are clever," Geoffrey continued. "They are attracted to you by your breath. Sleep with a fan running. That confuses them. Don't count on the fan. The power goes off regular up there. They also go for your ankles. The blood pressure is higher there. Put cream on your ankles and wear socks and long pants in the evening."

Phil felt as if he was preparing for a battle. "What about women? You mentioned women."

"As soon as they find out you're a tourist, they will come after your money. Split your money up into different pockets. They use sex to rob you. If you have one in your room, get rid of her before you fall asleep. Always use a condom. You can rub some of that white cream in your pubic hair and round your balls to stop the crabs from transferring."

Phil stared at Geoffrey. "Surely all the women are not crab-infected thieves."

"No, but I'm just preparing you for the worst. The condom could save your life. Africa is the AIDS capital of the world. Mainly because a lot of African men won't wear them."

"I don't think I will get it on up there after what you have told me."

Geoffrey smiled. "What you plan and what happens are two different things. Some of the women up there are fantastic and perform very well."

"Ah. The voice of experience," exclaimed Phil.

Geoffrey covered his mouth with his hand. "I'm not saying any more. My wife would kill me."

*   *   *

Keith Watson entered his office and found Chuck Henderson the ambassador waiting for him.

"What's the story with this FBI guy from Washington?"

Watson shrugged. "Some wet behind the ears paper shuffler. He's working for John Collins in the financial intelligence department. They're following a paper trail that's led them to Africa. Could be something, or could be zilch. We will have to wait and see."

"You don't look happy about it, Keith."

Watson shrugged again. "Could have been worse. They could have sent him direct from Switzerland. He doesn't know his ass from his elbow about Africa. At least now he's better prepared. Collins won't hear of one of my guys being involved. He's as stubborn as an old mule. He reckons it's an FBI matter."

"Could be he's right. You worry too much."

Henderson helped himself to a cup of coffee from the percolator. "Are you still keeping track of that bunch of Muslims in Cape Town?"

"Yep. They've done nothing wrong so far, but a couple of them are in and out the UK regular. I think you should have a word with our Brit friends down the road. They're living in a fool's paradise. British passport holders are in and out of England via France. They just wave 'em straight through on the Brit side. The only stamp they get is when they leave and enter RSA and France"

Henderson raised his eyebrows. "You're kidding."

"Nope. I kid you not. I've got a hunch some crap is about to happen over there."

Henderson nodded. "Okay, I'll get right on it."

He finished his coffee and stood. "Lighten up. I'm sure the FBI guy will be okay. See you later. We're going to try that Greek restaurant tonight in Klerk Street."

Watson sat for a while, rubbing his chin. It was crazy, but he had the same feeling about London and Malenga. Something was about to happen.

Phil fastened his seatbelt on the Interair 737 and started reading 'Birds of Central Africa'. Watson was right. He didn't know a stork from a blue tit.

The aircraft flew north as the light was fading. He felt as if he was now really en route to the Dark Continent.

Four hours later, he woke with a start. He had been dreaming of a flock of Marabou storks pecking him to death. The stewardess continued to tap his arm until he was fully awake. She indicated that he must fold back his table and adjust his seat to the upright position. This he did mechanically, like a robot. The stewardess nudged her colleague as they strapped themselves in, ready for landing.

"That man in A 16 looks like he's going to his own funeral."

The other one smiled. "They all look like that. You check out the ones tomorrow going back to Jo'burg. They will be smiling."

The plane shuddered and bucked from side to side as it came into contact with the warm air rising from the darkness below. Phil started to feel queasy. In front of him, the heads of the other passengers rocked from the side to side like prize fighters doing a synchronised neck exercise. Everyone groaned as the aircraft suddenly dropped. The contents of Phil's stomach pushed at his throat, trying to escape. He was sure he had changed colour from black to a sickly green.

A small African girl in the next seat smiled up at him, enjoying the bumpy ride. He fished for the paper vomit bag in the pouch in front of him, but decided he didn't want to make a fool of himself. The rocking heads in front were making him dizzy. *Left, right.*

Right, left, left. They all moved together. He was pushed down in the seat as the plane suddenly lifted.

The white pilot had smiled at him when he had boarded. He was doing this on purpose just for Phil's benefit. *I'll teach that nigger to fly on my plane.*

Left, left. Right, left. Phil's head banged against the window. The little girl squealed in delight as the aircraft dropped again. Her mother didn't look so good. She held a crucifix in her hands and was murmuring something.

A man's voice came over the speakers. "Please remain seated. We have run into some slight turbulence."

Slight turbulence. Slight fucking turbulence. He was like a bean in a Mexicans rattle. *Left, right. Right, left, right.* The aircraft's tail suddenly lifted, caught in an updraft. *It's the size of the plane. That's the problem. All the other planes were bigger. If I get out of this alive, I must remember never to fly on small planes again.*

He closed his eyes and pulled the seatbelt tighter. A nursery rhyme started running through his head. *Star above, burning bright. Help me make it through the night.* Or was it a pop song? He couldn't remember.

Phil knew that if he continued to look at the rocking heads he was sure to throw up, so switched his attention to the window.

Let's analyse the situation, he told himself. *The pilot is trying to kill me. To do that, he would have to be suicidal.*

Okay, so we have a suicidal pilot flying though turbulence in the dark. That's not crazy. The girl's mother knows we're going to die.

White streaks of light appeared and disappeared in a regular sequence near the end of the wing. *What the heck is that?* He suddenly realised it was rain lit up by the flashing light.

Okay, so we have a suicidal pilot flying though turbulence in the dark in the rain. There was nothing else out there. Only darkness. He checked his watch and did a quick calculation. *They said we were landing in another five minutes. Where's Mabarta? There should be a capital city down there.*

The bouncing plane tilted to the right and then levelled up again. *At least the pilot knows where we're going. Or does he?*

*Okay, so we have a lost suicidal pilot...*Just then the aircraft touched down with a gentle bump. The runway lights flashed by in quick succession. A cowling flipped over the back of the engine and the air brakes sprang up along the length of the wing. *Holy shit! The wing is disintegrating.*

Phil looked round wildly at the other passengers to gauge their level of panic. Surprisingly, they were clapping their hands with smiling faces. He turned his attention back to the window.

The plane had slowed down and the wing put itself back together. Phil's anxiety attack slowly subsided with the plane's speed.

"Welcome to Mabarta," a bored female voice told him.

"Please remain seated until the aircraft comes to rest. The temperature is 31 degrees and local time is eight-twenty."

Phil checked his watch. It was an hour wrong.

"Do not leave any personal possessions on the aircraft. Thank you for flying Interair, and enjoy the rest of your evening."

A two-storey building came into view with a tower next to it. The plane turned right, towards the building, under the direction of a man waving two table tennis bats.

An old, yellow fire engine started up and drove away. *No business for them tonight.* Phil wondered if they were disappointed.

A small truck with a stairway on the back reversed up to the side near the front. Everyone stood up and started removing their baggage from the overhead lockers. He decided to stay where he was until he had stopped shaking. He held *Birds of Central Africa* while keeping an eye on the locker that held Watson's bag. *To lose that would be something at this stage.*

He collected the bag and followed the last ones down the aisle. The cockpit door open ahead of him and out stepped the smiling pilot. People were shaking his hand before disembarking. Phil was the last one. He smiled and shook the pilot's hand.

"Neat flying."

The pilot nodded and winked at him. "Catch you later."

Phil remembered he had a return ticket and quickly made for the exit. At the top of the stairs, he felt as if he had walked into an oven. The fact that the rain had stopped was one blessing, the other was to get his feet on the ground. He trudged after the heavily-laden passengers making their way to a door marked 'arrivals'.

The heat and humidity were oppressive. He was thinking he should have worn his shorts, then he remembered about the mosquitoes.

After filling out the arrival form, everyone waited in two lines. One for residents, and one for non-residents. Some of the building's windows were broken, which was another blessing. The overhead fans stood motionless, mocking the people below. Phil noticed a rat scuttle past, down one corner of the grimy tiled floor. No one batted an eye, but stood patiently waiting for the officials to arrive.

Two fat guys in uniform squeezed themselves into the small glass-fronted boxes marked immigration. When Phil reached the window, Fats Domino eyed him suspiciously.

"American, what are you doing here?"

"Visitor..

"I know that; I can read. Who are you visiting and why?"

The fat official squinted, waiting for an answer.

"I'm studying birds. Tomorrow I'm going to Malenga, to the lake. I'm staying with Lake Tours."

The immigration officer tapped a podgy finger on Phil's form. "Where are you staying tonight"?

"Mabarta."

"I know that. Which hotel? You must fill in the address."

Phil shrugged. "I don't know. I've never been here before."

Fatso pushed the form and Phil's passport back through the small opening in the glass window and clasped his hands together. He looked up towards the stationary ceiling fan. "If you don't fill in the forms correctly, you cannot enter."

An impatient voice behind him called out, "The Central on Main Street."

The official glared past Phil, trying to see who had spoken. "I know where the Central is." He shouted at no one in particular. "Next, go to the back and fill out the form."

By the time he joined the queue again, there were only four people standing in line. 'Welcome to Mabarta', said a sign on the wall. When he reached the window again, Phil pointed at the form. "Tonight I'm staying at the Central on Main Street."

Fatso searched his face for any sign of a smile, but couldn't find one. "When are you leaving?" he asked.

"Maybe after one week."

His passport was stamped with a bang in the middle of an empty page. The next obstacle could have passed for Fatso's sister wearing a barrette with no badge. "Yellow fever," she demanded. An expression of disappointment spread across her face after checking Phil's card.

Next he progressed into a large room full of passengers waiting for their luggage, and was amazed at what started coming along the conveyor belt. Everything was arriving, except for the kitchen sink. The most popular items were new refrigerators and televisions. Some of the cartons had their arrows pointing down, next to an inverted wine glass. Phil blinked. *So much for the international coding system for the handling of freight.*

A number of new bicycles and bales of material of some sort followed. *A cargo plane must have landed, but why are they offloading here where the passengers are standing?*

His question was soon answered. Passengers started lifting the cartons on their trolleys. Phil repositioned his glasses on his nose. *All this stuff is baggage.*

Phil moved to one side for fear of being run down by one of the jostling trolleys, and joined a group of six Europeans.

They all waited patiently with bored expressions until a variety of luggage emerged through the hole in the wall. Phil was pleasantly surprised to recognise his suitcase, and stepped forward to retrieve it from the revolving belt.

A small African man touched his elbow. "I will carry your bags for you."

Phil shook his head. "I only have one suitcase. It's no hassle."

The man, dressed in what could only be described as pyjamas, made from a bright, patterned, curtain material, smiled up at him. "If I carry bag, no stopping at customs."

Below the exit sign were long tables littered with open cartons and suitcases. Half a dozen customs men rummaged among the debris as if frantically searching for buried treasure.

"I don't have any local money," explained Phil.

"No problem." The little man grinned, revealing his missing front teeth. "Dollar good. I saw your passport." He hoisted Phil's case on top of his skull-capped head.

"Follow close. The man at the door must see we are together."

They passed the long tables where heated arguments had erupted between the customs men and some passengers. The man at the exit, wearing an ill-fitting dark suit with a plastic airport card clipped to his top pocket, nodded as they continued through the door into the main building.

A small crowd of people waited at arrival gates. Most of them seemed to be cab drivers shouting 'taxi, taxi'. Pyjamas exposed his gums again after being handed a five-dollar bill, and then trotted back inside for his next customer. Phil pushed his way through the encircling cab drivers, heading for the glass doors. There was no white face among the waiting people. *Where the heck is Simon Pointer?*

Outside, a line of green and yellow cabs were pulled up along the curb. They looked like survivors from the junkyard wars. Some of the drivers were busy tying large cartons onto the roof, and then competing for a new Guinness world record. *How many fat women can you cram into a Toyota corolla?*

It started raining again, so Phil remained under cover near the entrance. A cool wind sprang up, fluttering the national flag on the other side of the road. An army truck was parked below. A few soldiers stood in pairs, sheltering against the outside of the terminal building.

The Kalashnikov was evident everywhere, even on the flapping flag above the truck. Phil noticed the rifle butts were made of cracked wood. *A very old model.*

He had no intention of finding out if they were still in working order. The soldiers ignored him. Nevertheless he was starting to feel very conspicuous. *Maybe he should take a cab to the Central and phone the embassy in the morning.*

The sweet, strong smell of hashish carried on the wind. A man, dressed in a white shirt and slacks, stood in the shadows upwind of him.

"Yo," the man called out. "Are you Jones?"

Phil rolled his eyes in exasperation. "Yeah; why the heck are you standing there? We were supposed to hook up inside."

The man walked forward with a stupid grin on his face, and raised a joint between his finger and thumb. He waved it towards the glass doors. "There's no smoking in there, my man. I'm Simon Pointer. Glad to meet you, bro."

Pointer stuck out his left hand. His right was otherwise engaged. Phil was annoyed. "How long have you been standing there? You're taking a hell of a chance smoking that shit in public," he added.

Simon put on the hurt expression. "Chill out. Most everybody smokes up here. Do you smoke?"

"No I don't."

Simon reached into his pocket. "Okay, so have a Marlboro."

Phil shook his head. "I don't smoke at all."

Pointer raised his eyebrows in surprise. "Okay, so nobody's perfect. Anyways, how was I supposed to know you? You look like all the other dudes, except taller."

Phil had taken an instant disliking to Pointer. They were opposites in every way. Pointer looked like a middle-aged John Travolta with a ponytail, selling washing powder.

"Where's your car at? I by passed customs and these soldiers make me nervous."

"No sweat. There are always soldiers here."

Simon surveyed the front of the building. "Tonight there's more than usual. Must be something to do with the marshal law."

"What marshal law? Watson never mentioned marshal law."

Simon smiled as he picked up Phil's suitcase. "That's because God Almighty Watson doesn't know about it. It's just been announced on the radio. Malenga area is under marshal law."

He threw the joint down on the paving. "Come on, let's blow this joint."

He giggled at the pun and strode off in the direction of the line of taxies. Phil trotted behind, carrying his shoulder bag. "Wait up," he called after Pointer. "Marshal law is quite something. How will it affect my mission tomorrow?"

Simon stopped abruptly, causing Phil to bump into him. He was enjoying the tall Negro's insecurity, and smiled broadly. "Okay, now listen up, my man. This is your first time in Africa. You can't count South Africa. That's different. Any dude who goes to a marshal law area in Africa has shit for brains. I will organise your flight to Malenga for two o'clock. I will give you a shooter at lunch time as per the great Mr. Watson's instructions." Simon raised his hands as if praying to Allah. "If the situation's the same tomorrow, I would butt out and head for home." He pointed at Phil "You do what you want. I can see you're the eager beaver type, but don't cry when your ass's in a sling."

Simon strode off again and banged on the roof of an empty taxi. The driver ran over from the airport entrance and grabbed the suitcase.

"In the front, in the front," Simon shouted. "Not in the trunk with all the goat shit."

He was in his element, showing off in front of Phil.

"Where's your car at? This junk won't get us very far." Phil kicked the bald back tyre.

Simon folded his arms. "My white, highly-polished Land cruiser is in its garage, ready to take me where it's at down town. I'm sure as shit not riding it the five miles from Mabarta to here on this crappy road in the rain. Also, cabs don't stand out. They're a dime a dozen."

Phil nodded, starring at the Toyota Corolla. "I can see that."

He tried to open the rear door, which was stuck fast. The driver signalled for them to get in from his side, which they did.

"Talking about standing out, why are you dressed all in white?"

"This kit is a real pussy magnet. I'm going to the disco after I drop you. Everything is a happening there."

Phil shook his head in disbelief. "I pretty much get the feeling you don't take this job very seriously."

"Whoa." Simon held up his hands. "Smoking grass gets me a whole heap of info I wouldn't normally latch onto. Me and the weed work hand to mouth, so to speak."

He giggled while lighting up another joint. Phil didn't object. The interior of the car smelt like a wet dog. Anything else could be an improvement. The driver removed a stone from under the front wheel and started pushing, with the front door open. Phil polished his glasses, wondering if the driver was going to make it back in the car before it picked up speed down the slope.

Simon sat giggling next to him, blowing smoke out of the open window. "See, my man. African handbrake and African starter motor."

Phil would be interested to see what an African footbrake was. *Maybe the driver throws out an anchor or just jumps out before impact.* He suddenly remembered the door on his side was jammed shut.

The driver expertly leapt inside and slammed the door. There was a grating of gears, then the car jerked twice before the engine coughed into life, accompanied by backfiring. A huge cloud of blue smoked obscured the road behind. Phil noticed the two red lights on the dash dimmed and flicked, but didn't go out. *So much for oil pressure and charging. They don't seem to be essential to running a car here.*

"What happens if we break down?" he enquired.

"No sweat. We give the driver a couple of bucks and flag down another cab."

Phil began to notice an uncomfortable feeling in the seat of his pants. As well as the spring sticking up into one cheek of his ass, the seat was wet. The driver must have left the window open in the rain. Pointer didn't seem to notice. Judging by his eyes, he was on another planet in a different galaxy.

Two miles from the airport, the road disintegrated into a series of potholes and small lakes. The taxi with the cartoons tied to the roof was marooned in the middle of one of the larger ones. As they skirted round the edge, Phil had the impression he was watching a mud-wrestling tag match. Four fat ladies were illuminated in the dim headlight as they systematically beat up the hapless driver. Simon and the cabby started laughing. He handed the driver his half-smoked joint and lit another one.

This is really great, thought Phil. *We are driving through a swamp in a piece of junk with barely any headlights, so let's get the driver stoned. What a great idea. Why didn't I think of that?*

Every time the driver lifted his foot from the accelerator, the gearbox sounded like it wanted to climb inside and sit next to them. Phil was feeling more and more convinced the cab wouldn't make it to Mabarta.

The driver opened his window and leant out with a gas station-type windscreen cleaner to brush off the raindrops in front of him.

"What's he going to do if it comes down heavy?" asked Phil sarcastically. "I suppose he could take out the screen and start wearing goggles."

Simon blew some smoke in Phil's direction. "Lighten up. We're over halfway there. Here you just roll with the punches, my man."

Phil grabbed Simon's arm. "Let's get something straight. First off, I'm not your man. Secondly, I think you are using a cab just to piss me off because you don't like Watson."

Simon pulled his arm away. "I don't give a shit what you think. You assholes don't have to live here. I'm just getting you sort of acclimatised, that's all. Watson's not my boss. I'm doing him a big favour here, so chill out."

They rode in silence for the next mile. Phil's head occasionally thumped on the underside of the roof when the driver was unable to avoid a submerged pothole.

Simon clapped at a couple of mosquitoes, which were circulating the interior. "I should have brought my spray," he conceded. "This car needs fumigating."

Phil thought incinerating would be more suitable, but didn't voice his opinion.

Bright headlights flashed ahead of them, lighting up the inside of the taxi. Something big was approaching from the other direction. The lights were closing rapidly. Whatever it was, it doesn't seem to be handicapped by the flooded road. The driver quickly rolled up his window and slowed down. Simon followed suite and wound the handle on his door. Nothing happened. He tried the opposite direction to no avail, then started cursing. A huge, six-wheel army truck was bearing down on them.

The nearer the truck came, the faster Simon wound the window handle. Phil watched the proceedings with interest and tried the handle on his side, which was working, but came off in his hand. "Here, try this one."

He offered the handle to Simon as the truck roared past like a speed boat from hell.

For the next few seconds, Phil thought he was in a submarine. Simon sat next to him, frozen.

Phil cleared his throat. "I know you don't care what I think, but you should cancel the disco tonight. A change of venue would be in order. Try a find a fancy dress ball. You could go as Dalmatian."

Phil replaced the handle back on his door and started laughing. The cabby stepped out and cleaned the mud off the windscreen, looking a bit apprehensively in Simon's direction. "It's not fucking funny," he muttered, smacking the back of the driver's head as he got back in.

"Oh, chill out," remark Phil with tears in his eyes.

"Lighten up. It could have been worse. I could have been sitting there."

Phil tried very hard, but was unable to stop laughing until they reached Mabarta. The streets gave the impression a flash flood has passed through the city. Some roads were still underwater. The drainage system was incapable of handling the volume of water and rubbish that was evident everywhere. Many houses were only half built. Phil presumed this was due to lack of funds on the part of the owners.

He could see most of the structures were built by erecting thin concrete pillars containing steel rods. The walls were filled in by cement blocks and steel window frames on each level. None of them looked very safe, especially the three- and four-storey ones. He hoped the hotel was more substantial.

The odd cab roamed the deserted streets. This was probably due to the rain and the late hour. Simon tapped the driver on the shoulder. "Go to the park," he commanded.

"I told immigration I was staying at the Central." Phil interrupted.

"Don't matter. You can stay anywhere you want. I've booked you in the Park," came the sullen reply.

They turned left and stopped outside a hotel two blocks down. Simon got out and pulled the suitcase from the front seat. Phil could see steam rising from the piebald shirt.

"The first night is already paid for. I'll see you tomorrow at lunch. You must decide what you're gonna do."

Simon climbed in next to the driver and told him to go, without as much as a goodnight. Phil was left standing next to his case, coughing in a cloud of blue exhaust smoke. Could be he had laughed a bit too much. He smiled, thinking about Simon's shirt. *It was so godamn funny when the window wouldn't close, I couldn't help but crack up.*

Still smiling, he carried his case into reception.

The Park had seen better days. *This was going to be another one of Simon's tricks.*

The girl at the reception sat on a high stool reading a magazine. Occasionally, she pushed a finger inside her nose and waggled it around. *Maybe Joe Lozano was right about the nose picking.* Phil didn't like to think so. *Could be this girl has nothing more than an itching nose.*

He stood in front of her for a couple of minutes, feeling really bushed. "Hello, hello."

On the second attempt, she looked up from the magazine and stared at him.

"I'm Phil Jones; I have a reservation for tonight."

The girl opened a ledger and ran her moist finger down a list of names. She turned on the stool and removed a key from a hook behind her, which she placed in front of him. Mission accomplished, she switched her attention back to the magazine.

"Where is the porter?" He was feeling a bit neglected.

She started banging her hand repeatedly on top of the bell next to her, without taking her eyes from the magazine. The continuous ringing sound was like someone striking Phil on the head with a hammer. Eventually, a sleepy porter emerged from a door marked 'linen'. Phil presumed that must be the bedding testing room.

"Where can I get some chow?"

She raised her eyebrows with a puzzled expression.

"Food; where can I eat?"

She pointed to a door marked 'dining room'. Phil noticed another door opposite, through which loud music penetrated, marked 'ladies bar'. That was one door he would give a miss tonight. The porter picked up the keys.

"Two-o-six," he said. "You must be Mr. Jones?"

"That's right." Phil was happy somebody was talking to him.

"Follow me." The porter picked up the suitcase and made for the stairway. An 'out of order' sign was taped to the elevator door. Phil didn't mind. He needed the exercise. He thought it strange the porter had known he was arriving, whereas the receptionist hadn't.

"How did you know my name?" he enquired.

There was a pause before the porter answered. "Mr. Pointer said you would be arriving."

They were now on the first floor landing.

"So you know Mr. Pointer?"

"No, I don't know him," came the quick response. After another pause he added, "He phoned; he phoned the desk when Joy was not there. That is how I know your name."

Phil didn't know why, but he was getting the impression the porter was making this up. *How come he knew who I was from the room number, unless Pointer prearranged everything with the him?*

They were now on the second floor and the stairs didn't go any higher. "How many rooms on each floor?" he asked.

The porter fumbled with the key at two-o-six. "This hotel has forty rooms. We never get full unless there is an important football match at the stadium."

He pushed inside and switched on all the lights. The room was a fair size with a double bed and bathroom en-suite. When the porter started the air conditioner, it sounded like a tractor with a loose engine cover.

"If you need anything, I will be near the reception."

Phil nodded. "Thanks."

He gave the porter a five-dollar bill. Halfway out, the man stopped and smiled. "I know a very nice young lady."

"No thanks; I'm bushed. What's your name?"

"Samuel." He removed the key from the door and handed it to Phil. "The door locks itself when you close it."

"Thanks; good night."

Alone at last, Phil slipped off his shoes and lay on the bed. *The porter seemed quite helpful.* Could be he was imagining some sort of conspiracy. Samuel may have easily checked out the hotel book at the desk. That would explain the connection between the room number and his name. Phil realised he needed some chow urgently. He would freshen up and head downstairs. Simon's story about marshal law in Malenga was disconcerting. Could be a load of bull. He would check it out in the morning.

Simon Pointer walked into his shower fully dressed. *Whatever Mr. Philip Jones decides to do tomorrow, he's dead in the water.* He would make sure of that.

He had to. The payment to stop him was already in the bank.

*   *   *

Phil was busy following Geoffrey's advice. He pulled back the bed covers to check for any fleas. The sheets were clean and nothing visible was jumping around. Next, he pulled the bottom sheet from the mattress and sprayed it with doom. According to Geoffrey, this would stop any bed bugs in their tracks if they emerged from the mattress. By all accounts, they were attracted by body heat. *Now for the mosquitoes.*

He remade the bed and sprayed underneath, also between the headboard and the wall. Two mosquitoes flew out of the cupboard when he opened the doors. He sprayed inside and closed the doors. Next, he sprayed in all the corners and the bathroom, then started coughing. They would find him in the morning buzzing around the floor on his back. He remembered he should have sprayed the room just before going out. It was too late now.

Phil didn't like to sit on any plastic toilet seat. It didn't feel secure. He lifted the seat and wiped the top of the bowl with toilet paper. *Now for a good crap.* Airplane toilets, he wouldn't sit on. He had a fear of being stuck on the top with the vacuum, and the slurping noise in the bowl scared him to death.

Phil removed his cloths and settled himself on the toilet. The cool of the porcelain felt good. To his dismay, he found that when he lifted up on the one side to wipe his ass, the whole toilet tilted over. *So much for feeling secure.* The toilet wasn't fastened properly to the floor.

He turned on the shower and soon realised that there was a plumbing problem. The water changed from medium to hot, to cold, to nothing, back to medium, in a regular cycle. Because the cycle was regular, he managed to shower by jumping in and out at the correct times, yelping when he miscalculated the sequence.

This is probably how the circus trains animals to do tricks. The shower must have been imported from a KGB interrogation room. It would have the strongest man confessing to anything in no time. He was lucky to not break his neck on the wet floor. At least he was clean and his reaction times were down to milliseconds. He would be able to beat anyone on an arcade star wars machine.

After towelling himself off, he rubbed some white repellent cream on his face, arms and legs. Discovering two itchy bumps on his arms and one on his ankle, he hoped the cab mosquitoes weren't carrying malaria. According to Geoffrey, there was a two week incubation period before the disease manifested itself. He would be out of there long before then.

Dressing himself in some of his new clothes, Phil almost felt human again. Darkest Africa wasn't so bad after all. As Pointer had said, you just had to chill out and roll with the punches.

When he walked down the stairs, the repetitive jangling music from the ladies bar grew in volume. The girl at the desk was still busy with her magazine and the exploration of her nose.

The busiest guy in the whole place must be the barkeep next door. He sat down in the dimly lighted dining room and waited, and waited, and waited. Eventually, he poked his head through the swing door into the kitchen and switched on the light. It was deserted. The kitchen was closed.

Back at reception, Joy pointed to a time table. The kitchen had closed just before he had arrived at the hotel. Why anyone had named this girl Joy was unbelievable. She had as much joy as a freeway pile up.

Phil knocked on the door marked 'linen' and wasn't surprised when Samuel appeared. "Can you find me something to eat, and a beer? It's worth ten dollars extra to me."

Samuel pointed to the ladies' bar. "You can buy a beer and a snack in there."

Phil told him to wait where he was, and poked his head into the bar. The noise immediately attacked his eardrums and what he saw didn't do much for his sanity. *This was either a New Year's Eve party that had got out of control, or a celebration in a nuthouse.*

Phil quickly closed the door, shutting off most of the noise, and returned to Samuel. "I am not going in there," he stated.

Samuel shrugged. "The bar has a door onto the street. That is our best money making. Wait in the dining room. I will bring you something."

Phil nodded. "Okay, deal."

His tiredness was flowing over him waves. "I'm not happy with the service here." He pointed to the receptionist. "That woman is fucking useless; what's wrong with her?"

"She is deaf and dumb. She can see what you say if you talk slowly."

"Oh." Phil felt like an absolute asshole. "I'm sorry."

He went back into the dining room and found an easy chair. The noise was muted to an expectable level in here, but still jangled his nerves. At least he wouldn't hear it from two-o-six. He stretched out his long legs and tried to relax. After some chow and a beer he would feel better. The music momentarily rose in volume as the door opened and closed. Phil sat up, expecting Samuel, and was surprised to see a young girl had entered the room. She was obviously wearing a wig that was totally out of place, but the whole concept oozed sex appeal. An eighteen-year-old Tina Turner.

She came over to where Phil was sitting, walking on tip toe in her high heels.

"The kitchen is closed. There's no food here," he announced.

"I know. I want to sit here with you." She smiled seductively.

His brief visit next door seemed to have attracted some attention. This must be one of the girls Geoffrey had mentioned. He was about to tell her to 'fuck off', but then noticed she was twirling a hotel key on her finger. She was a guest and had as much right as him to be there.

"Will you buy me a drink?"

She cocked her head to one side, waiting for him to answer.

Phil shrugged. "Yeah. No problem."

Samuel entered the room carrying a tray with something that looked like a hamburger and two bottles of beer. One of them had a straw sticking out the top. Phil realised that this must be the girl he had tried to proposition him with before. The porter pulled a chair over for the girl.

"This Freda. Very good girl, and very clean."

Phil took a heavy pull from the bottle of beer. "I told you before. I'm very tired. I don't want a girl tonight."

Samuel smiled and left the room. Freda walked over to the chair. She was wearing tight-fitting white jeans with the black letters 'TNT' printed all over them.

"No problem if you tired. I like to go on top and do all the work."

Phil choked on the bread he was trying to swallow. He was feeling tempted. The tight TNT jeans were showing off her slender figure. *A major sex bomb. Somebody will get a real bang out of this girl.*

She sat down and started sipping her beer through the straw. Occasionally she would remove the straw and run her tongue around the lip of the bottle. Phil was experiencing a tingling sensation in his balls.

He had always been self-conscious and awkward when it came to girls. His girlfriend in Washington had been a real challenge. She was just as awkward and self-conscious as himself. Eventually, after one year, they slept together. Phil found the whole thing disappointing, because she just laid there without moving. He gave up the relationship as a lost cause and reverted back to stroking himself in the shower. Attempting that in the shower of two-o-six was out of the question. He would end up with second degree burns on his dick.

The chunks of dark meat inside the roll had hair on them, but tasted alright. He wondered what it was. Fatigue pushed him down into the chair. He finished his beer and stood with an effort. Freda nuzzled into the front of his jeans "You like blow job or fucka fucka?"

He pushed her away. "Maybe tomorrow night. I don't feel good."

It wasn't an excuse. The truth was, he did feel dizzy. He needed to lie down as soon as possible. On the second flight of stairs, he stumbled, but managed to make it to the top. It took a while to open the door, and he felt relieved once he pushed it closed behind him.

Something is wrong. Some motherfucker has drugged me.

Phil wedged a chair under the door handle. The bulk of his money, he hid inside the air conditioner grill. Watson's cell phone, he shoved under the mattress where his head would lay. That was the best he could do under the circumstances. Phil managed to hit the light switch before collapsing onto the bed.

*   *   *

Later that night, he became aware of being in a dreamlike state. Someone had removed his trainers and was now pulling off his jeans. His skin was alive to the slightest touch, but he was unable to move. Phil could feel something like a small pair of scissors snipping his underpants on each side. He was now in a state of panic, not knowing who this person was. Cool air surrounded his privates as his under jocks were unfolded. A lightning flash illuminated a naked female form crouched over him. *Thank God.* For a horrible moment he had thought it could even be the porter.

Thunder rattled the windows as he felt long hair caressing his belly and chest. Lightning flashed again and lit up a blonde wig as Freda kissed his lips. Phil sneezed involuntary as the hair brushed his nose. It smelt like a dusty old tom cat sleeping on his face. Freda tossed off the wig and got down to some serious business below his waist. Phil could hear lapping and slurping in between the rolls of thunder. The sensations he was experiencing were exquisite. If this was a wet dream, it was the best he'd ever had.

A hand grasped his engorged member and waved it around in triumph. Phil wondered if she was trying to smash the light fitting on the ceiling. He could now feel something being slowly rolled down its entire length. The figure crouched over him and lowered itself onto him, then started bouncing up and down as if attached to the ceiling on a spring. If Phil had the power to stop this bobbing giant spider, he wouldn't.

He had read a ghost story the year before, about a female spirit that raped men in their beds. *Incubus.* Yes, that was the name. *Could be this is one of them.*

The bobbing continued until Phil went into spasm, and coughed. Then the spider changed position slightly and moved further down until it was just above his thighs. This bent Phil's penis backwards, causing it to swell even more. Now the motion started again in a fierce forward and backwards movement, which increased in speed until the incubus cried out.

This is how it continued in silence, except for Phil's coughs and the incubus' cries. Eventually, the spider faded away and left him in peace.

Chapter 29

Another day was starting to force itself into the world, and Parker had not been found. The previous night's rain had stopped, but the sun was unable to lever its way through the leaden sky.

Nabusano was finding it difficult to concentrate after a restless night of storms and dreams.

He was falling into an abyss of decay, and could even smell the decomposition of his own body.

The dreams had been of past glories and triumphs, but always ended in the same way. *Parker must be found or the renewal will slip through my fingers. The phoenix will not rise again.*

According to the latest reports, Parker had been seen leaving the construction camp. His vehicle had been found near the bus station. The roadblocks had found nothing. Between the bus station and the roadblocks, Parker had disappeared. Either he was in hiding near the road, or still in the town. The only person willing to conceal him would be a friend. One of his own kind.

Nabusano opened his eyes. *But of course; the white man with the airplane.*

He pressed a button on the side of the bed.

Chapter 30

James awoke to the sound of his wife making breakfast. He was sure she rattled the pots and pans on purpose.

The smell of the slowly-boiling green bananas filled the three-roomed house.

He had slept badly, probably due to the uncertainty of the situation, and was still tired. The invasion of his house by the security company late last night hadn't helped. James had allowed them to search his house without any protest .Why not? He had nothing to hide. They must be looking for the man who had killed those thugs. *Where were the police?* That was puzzling.

A few bicycles passed by the window. *At least they are allowed to move around in daylight.*

The children were still sleeping soundly in the other bedroom when his cell phone buzzed. One of the parents called to inform him a sign was hanging on the school gate— 'Closed until further notice'.

James swore and called out to Brenda. "Even the children are suffering now. They have closed the school."

Brenda shook her head while stirring the breakfast porridge. "It is just as well. We must stay together. It's safer for the children."

James snorted. "You are always full of wisdom." He thought for a while. "I will drive us to the market. We must stock up on food. You never know what these idiots will do next."

He walked back into the semi-darkness of the bedroom to dress for going out, and stubbed his toe on something under the bed. "Ow," he exclaimed, sitting down on the bed.

Rubbing his toe, he looked down and saw the corner of a wooden box. "Brenda," he called angrily. "What is this box doing here?"

"That is the box with the mat inside that Mr. Parker wanted to see," she answered defensively.

"Oh yes. I had forgotten about that. Where did it come from?"

"I took it out from my trunk yesterday," she called back.

Curious, James pulled out the box and opened it. The old, long, narrow box had been made exactly to the right size. He spread the mat on the bed and drew back the curtains. It was divided into square pictures, like a comic book. After switching on the light, he saw it was in very bad condition. The colours had faded and insects had eaten holes in it over the years.

"How old is this?" he called to Brenda, and waited impatiently for her to answer.

"It was made by my grandmother's grandmother. It was the way of the women of my tribe in the old days to make such things."

James did a rough calculation in his head and whistled. Even taking into account the short life expectancy in those days, this thing must be two hundred years old.

"They are always given to the eldest daughter at the time of marriage," she added.

James wondered why he had never seen any of these hanging on people's walls.

"Come here and explain the pictures to me."

Brenda entered the bedroom, more interested in going shopping than anything else. Her face dropped, and she dashed over to the window and quickly closed the curtains.

"What are you doing, woman?"

She lifted the corner of the curtain and peered outside. "Mb'a ordered all these mats to be destroyed at the time he took his followers to the island."

"You stupid woman," James taunted. "He is not around now to see what we are doing."

"Yes, but even now, the Nabusano's will burn one of these if they hear of one."

James shook his head, perplexed. "I will never understand how the mind works with your tribe. Now explain the pictures for me."

Brenda closed the bedroom door and locked it.

"You must understand. My mother told me to keep this hidden."

James raised his eyes to the ceiling and shook his head. "Now, will you explain the pictures to me? I need to explain to Mr. Parker what it is about."

She came over to the bed and pointed to a picture of a boy holding a bow and arrow. "This is Mb'a before he was Mb'a. He showed our tribe the skill of hunting."

"That does not make sense, but I know what you mean. So in the beginning they called him Nabusano before Mb'a."

Brenda nodded. "Yes. He came from the setting sun and could not speak our language. The family of Nabusano adopted him. Later, they called him Mb'a because of his dreams."

James nodded. "I know the legend. You told it to me before." He pointed to the next picture. "What is happening here?"

"That is when Mb'a was given the power of the river God."

James opened his mouth and rubbed one eye. "You believe all this?"

"Yes, it is all true. Why would the grandmother of my grandmother lie?"

James stroked his chin. *Brenda has a point. If this mat is two hundred years old, then it was made shortly after the events were supposed to have taken place. There was no time for the story to be twisted by being handed down.*

He looked at the picture with renewed interest. A man was kneeling at the edge of a river with both his hands immersed in the water. James scratched the top of his head. The next picture showed some sort of ceremony.

"That is Mb'a being married," Brenda pointed out. "You can see the chief is there by the staff and the cloak."

James nodded, and was surprised by the next picture. It showed a man and woman joined together by a very large penis. "Do not show the children this," James stressed.

"They will learn soon enough about such things."

He pointed at the next one. "Who is this woman on the ground, full of arrows?"

"That is M'ba's first wife. The hunters killed her because she resisted their chief and spat upon him."

"No wonder, after having sex with a thing of that size."

Brenda kicked James on the shin. "Do not make fun. This is serious." She started to roll up the mat.

"I am sorry. Please let us finish. I really am interested."

She stopped and scrutinised his face. Satisfied, she unrolled the mat again.

"You insult my family by making fun," she scolded.

"I said I am sorry. That kick you gave me is making a lump." He rubbed his leg with a pained expression on his face.

"This next one is where Mb'a killed all the hunters."

James raised his eyebrows. The picture was full of body parts, with Mb'a standing in the centre, holding something. One of the insect holes had obliterated whatever he was holding.

"What is he holding in both hands?"

"It is the power of the river God."

"Yes, but what is it? You cannot see anything because of that hole."

Brenda shrugged. "I do not know. It was like that before. It had many holes in it before it was given to me."

James shook his head impatiently. "Did not your mother tell you what was there?"

"No, she did not know."

James rubbed a hand across his forehead. "Well, we cannot ask your grandmother. She is dead. You have left me with a puzzle which cannot be solved."

"It is not my fault. You told me you were not interested in such things."

James scratched the top of his head again. "Alright, it is not your fault. What is happening in this last picture?"

Mb'a was standing in the middle of a group of kneeling people.

"Here, the tribe is worshipping Chief Mb'a as the prophet of the river God. They still practice that religion on the island."

"Yes, I have heard that said. The people on the island are very strange."

James examined this last picture closely. The only thing he was holding here was the chief's staff in his right-hand. The left hand was spread against his chest.

"Why is the little finger of the left hand missing?"

"That was the custom in those days. If a man lost the woman he loved, he would cut off his little finger and bury it with the woman."

James looked at his wife. "I hope you do not expect me to do that if you die."

"Oh, so you do not love me?"

She rolled up the mat and replaced it back in the box.

"Of course I love you. Whatever happens, you must never doubt that. You and the children, and, of course, the school, are everything in my life."

She stood and encircled him in her arms. "Do not worry, my darling. That custom, even then, was very uncommon. I think Mb'a was the last one to do that, as far as I know."

She kissed him on his cheek. He raised her chin with one hand and kissed her on the lips.

"Oh, so maybe you do love me a little?"

She pushed his other hand away. "There is no time for that. The children are awake, and besides, we have some shopping to do."

"The legend is very sad, and also very puzzling," he told her.

"Why puzzling?"

"Because the mat tells the same story as the legend, and I do not think your grandmother's grandmother was a liar."

"If you are so interested, my cousin has another mat made by her grandmother's mother. That one is not so old, and is in much better condition. I saw it once when I was a little girl. It shows the chief of that time also destroying the tribe's enemies."

She placed a finger over her lips. "If I remember correctly, there is a boat on it."

Chapter 31

Bill awoke suddenly with a growing sense of unease. The storm had blown itself out and daylight filtered through the gaps in the floorboards above. All was quiet except for the intermittent croaking of a few frogs.

He pushed open the trapdoor and entered the house. Patch lifted his head, interested by the early morning intrusion. His master never moved around at this time of day. Bill shook Ken, trying to achieve some response. "Wake up. They're coming."

Ken groaned and squinted up at him. "Who's coming?"

"Nabusano's people. They are coming."

Ken peered with one eye at his watch on the night table. "It's only half past bloody six."

He looked like a leftover from an all night party.

"Patch isn't barking. How do you know someone is ruddy well coming?"

"The ball tells me when danger is approaching. I just want to get rid of that glass and empty the ashtray. You don't smoke."

"Oh yes. The bloody ball. I'd forgotten about that ruddy thing."

Ken sat up on the edge of the bed and held his head in his hands. "So the ball tells you when some blighter is coming?"

"Yes."

Bill emptied the ashtray and rinsed it, then dried it with an old towel. "Hurry up. I need you to cover the trapdoor with the carpet again."

Ken staggered to his feet, making smacking sounds with his lips. "Where's the cat?"

"What cat?"

"The one that shat in my mouth."

Bill rinsed the second glass and glanced around the room. He opened all the curtains so that anyone sneaking up to the cabin would be able to see inside.

"Right, that's it. Cover the trapdoor and go back to bed. Pretend you're still asleep."

Ken shuffled after Bill and slid the small carpet into position. He placed a chair on top for good measure. *At least that's got rid of him,* he thought. *Pretend to be asleep. I still am a-fucking-sleep.*

He shielded his eyes from the daylight and looked around outside. Not a sausage. He cocked his head to one side and listened. Nothing. *That Bill is a bloody nutter. It's like a graveyard out here.*

He shuffled back into the house and closed the door. Patch had laid his head on top of his forelegs and gone back to sleep.

"You've got the right idea, my boy," Ken mumbled on his way back to the bedroom. "Next time I have a late night visitor, I'm going to tell them to bugger off."

He climbed into bed and pulled the blanket over his head. Ken grunted once or twice and then turned over.

*   *   *

Two vehicles slowly freewheeled down the track from the golf club road. They stopped some distance from the cabin and the doors quietly opened. About fifteen black, uniformed figures armed with Lee Enfield riffles abandoned the two vehicles, leaving the doors open. They crept forward, with the security chief in the lead, and surrounded the cabin. Patch lifted his head and woofed once quietly. He wasn't sure if he had heard something. Faces appeared at all the windows. Patch saw one and started barking like crazy, jumping up and down below the window like a yoyo. Ken threw back the covers and sat up. "Good grief. What the hell is going on?"

Nabusano's son strode purposely up to the back door and started hammering on it.

"Open up. Security check," he shouted.

Ken appeared at the door with wide eyes and tuffs of white hair sticking up. "What's going on? What do you want?"

"We have to check the house. The military have reported some rebels in the area."

"What are you doing here? That's a job for the police or the army."

The security chief narrowed his eyes in determination.

Ken had met this man before, in the company office in town. That was the time he had been enquiring about prices to guard the plane. Marco; yes, that was his name. Marco Nabusano.

"The military have requested our assistance to guard the town. They are busy on the roads and at the airport."

"Oh, and who is paying for all this? You people are a private company."

"My father has agreed to assist the community in this time of need."

Ken smiled. "That's very kind of him, but as you can see, I am alright."

"Until we check the house, we do not know. You could be held at gunpoint."

Ken thought a moment. "Yes. I see what you mean. Come inside."

He waved Marco to enter and stepped to one side.

"Shut up, Patch. Stop that barking. This man is our friend."

Patch wasn't so sure, and skulked off, growling from the back of his throat.

"The only problem is your timing," Ken remarked.

Two other guards entered the cabin and started searching anything big enough to hide a man.

"I'm afraid the rest of the world has a different timetable than you, Mr. Marshal."

Marco scanned the interior of the room, then turned his back towards Ken. "Do you have a motorcycle, Mr. Marshal?"

"No. Why do you ask?"

He turned round, holding a motorcycle helmet. Ken swallowed, his confidence now totally destroyed. "That's Roberto's, from the construction camp. He forgot it here one night."

Marco gave Ken a searching look, then set the helmet down. "We are very worried about Mr. Parker. It seems he has disappeared from the construction camp. All expatriates are confined to the camp for their own safety. If you should hear from him, please call me. Here is my card."

Ken swallowed again and took the card. "The last time I saw Bill Parker was at Roberto's barbeque on Sunday night."

Ken felt his face flushing. He was useless at telling lies.

"If you say so, Mr. Marshal. I will leave one man at the top of the hill with a radio. It's for your protection, you understand."

Ken nodded. "Yes. I understand. Thank you very much."

Marco signalled for his men to vacate the cabin. Bill lay under the veranda, listening to the heavy boots pass overhead. From the doorway, Ken could see two guards looking into his water tank on the hillside. Another one was walking back from the old girl, checking under the jetty at every step. *These blighters know what they are doing. It's not rag tag and bobtail.*

Marco called out to his men. "Spread out and make your way up the hill."

He turned back towards Ken and bit his bottom lip thoughtfully. "Can I talk to you in confidence?"

Ken stared at him in surprise, then nodded. "You can if you want to."

Marco was quiet for a while, probably choosing his words. "The son's of Nabusano obey our father's command. We have no choice. We are never told why we must do a certain thing, and we dare not ask. For some reason, Mr. Parker is very important to our father. Like a life and death struggle. The younger sons, like me, were trained in our duties overseas. We still follow our father, but some of us question his methods. Mr. Parker has something our father desperately needs. He will stop at nothing to attain it. Our father has deteriorated in mind and body. He is very old.

The wind of change is blowing. I am interested to know what our father needs from Mr. Parker. How this will affect my life. I am not like the followers who live on the island. It is important that I know what is happening. I need to shape my own destiny." He paused for a moment. "Would you be surprised to know we have orders to kill Mr. Parker?"

Ken coughed and took a step back. "Why are you telling me all this?"

"Because I think talking to you is nearly the same as talking to Mr. Parker. Tell him not to underestimate the father. Good day, Mr. Marshal."

Ken watched Marco climb into his black BMW X5, then the two vehicles drove off up the track. The men on the wooded slope were halfway up the hillside, poking their rifles into the bushes. With the thicker ones, they donned gas masks and threw in tear gas canisters.

"Hmm. Very professional," Ken mumbled.

He turned to Patch. "If they find the ruddy motorbike, we are in the bloody shit."

He made a cup of tea, then went and sat on the veranda. "Bill, can you hear me?" he asked softly.

"Yeah, I can hear you perfectly," a voice answered from below.

"We made a right cock-up. They found the helmet. I hope you hid the bike really well. Those buggers are searching the hillside."

"Don't worry. It's in the middle of a thorn thicket. They can't get in there without being torn to bits."

Ken thought a moment. "How did you get the bike in there?"

"I lifted it up and then lowered it into the middle. I used the ball."

Ken nodded. "That's a relief. You'll never guess what their boss Macro said to me."

"Yeah, it was interesting. I heard every word."

Ken raised his eyebrows. "How could you possibly hear from down there? We were standing next to the back door. Oh, don't tell me you used that bloody ball, right."

"Right, I can hear really well, and also see in the dark."

"Good lord. I feel like *Alice in Wonderland* with you around."

Ken sipped his tea. "Later on I will go and get two drums of avgas. I will take that fax from the Yank. Push two thousand dollars through up through the floor. I'm also out of whisky."

Ken looked around, then leant forward as hundred-dollar notes appeared one by one at his feet.

"This is handy. Could you stay down there forever?"

Ken felt like James Bond in a spy movie. He pushed the money into the top of his long socks. His hands were shaking. *Double-o-seven's hands never shook.* He needed a drink.

Chapter 32

Phil shuffled to the toilet with a full bladder and a pounding headache. He sat down and started to pee. The sitting position was far more efficient, especially when naked. Something gently tugged his dick downwards. Perplexed, he looked down between his legs just in time to see a urine-filled condom disengage itself from his penis. It slid into the pan like the launching of a torpedo. *Holy shit, last night's dream was real.*

He glanced at his watch to see what time it was, and found it missing. *Shit.* A moment of panic overcame him. He rushed back to the bed and lifted the mattress. Thankfully, the cell phone was still there and showed a time of eight-thirty. The loss of the phone would have been one hell of a hassle. The money inside the aircon hadn't been touched, but the camera from his shoulder bag wasn't there. Also, the few bills from the night table had gone. It could have been a whole heap worse, but how in the heck had she got in? The chair was still wedged under the door handle. This was like a Sherlock Holms mystery. *The case of the locked room.*

He checked the window. All the latches were secured and besides, it was a straight drop down to the busy sidewalk below. Phil sat on the bed trying to think, and stared at the wall in front of him. There was a door in it. He opened the door and found an identical room to his, except opposite. The key was on the other side. *Elementary, my dear Watson; adjoining rooms.*

Removing the key, he locked the door from his side. *Like closing the stable door after the horse had gone.* Samuel had set him up. Freda had been staying in two-o-four next door. There wasn't a whole lot he could prove, and besides, the police would ask plenty of questions.

Did you have someone in your room last night? Err, yes and no. I wasn't sure whether it was a person or a spider. Had you been drinking last night? Err, yes. Phil picked up his glasses and polished them. *Could be that this is another of Pointer's fuck-arounds.* There was no time to dwell on the situation. If he was successful at the registrar of companies, he could be flying to Malenga in another five-and-a-half hours.

He braved the KGB shower again. If it had been a normal shower, he would probably have whacked off thinking about last night.

There was a different woman at reception. This one smiled a lot and could talk. She told him Samuel wasn't due on duty till the afternoon. He had phoned in saying he was sick, so probably wouldn't be there till tomorrow. What a surprise. *That camera was worth a sack full of greenbacks.*

Phil explained he could be checking out after lunch and needed a quick breakfast. She recommended the continental breakfast from the buffet and, if he was pushed for time, to leave his case with her behind the counter. After lunch with Pointer, he would be able to leave directly for the airport.

She frowned and shook her head when he mentioned Malenga. It wasn't advisable. A taxi had been shot at only twenty-five kilometres south of Mabarta. Two people were dead. Nobody knew what was happening in Malenga. The military was in charge.

He was going to ask her where the company registration building was, but decided not to. Could be Pointer would phone, asking questions.

After breakfast he went back to his room to collect his suitcase, and phoned Watson. He told Phil not to worry about the camera and not to go ahead with the Malenga trip until he had checked back with him. The information he was receiving was conflicting. Some of his contacts in the field had told him there had not been any movement of rebels from the north. Rebels always left a trail of looted stores behind them.

"Who have you got in the field?" Phil asked.

He couldn't imagine Americans sitting around in the bush out there.

"There's a couple of flag wavers in the Peace Corps. They tell us what it's like on the ground, locally. Do what you need to do in Mabarta for now. Make sure nobody finds the shooter Pointer gives you, or you'll end up in the slammer. There's no baggage check on local flights, but loose it before you fly international."

Watson ended the call. He sounded pretty busy. Phil placed his cell phone back in his pocket. As an afterthought, he viewed the street from behind the curtains. The scene below was in stark contrast to the streets of last night. Hundreds of bicycles and small motorbikes milled around between the green and yellow cabs. Some of the bicycles carried forty-four gallon drums and single beds tied on behind the riders. Others were taxies with the women sitting side-saddle on the back. He could see the bicycles were making better progress through the packed streets, and decided it would save time if he made use of one of them.

Peering directly below the hotel, he could see group of beggars rattling their bowls and mugs. Some of them shuffled around on small boards fitted with wheels. Others had bandaged hands with no fingers.

He recoiled from the window with a jerk. *Leprosy. Those are lepers down there. Holy shit. I thought that was just a bunch of stuff from the bible.*

Phil approached the window again. "Welcome to the real world," he mumbled.

Half a block down, to the left, on the other side of the road, a white Toyota Land Cruiser with tinted windows caught his attention. It was conspicuous, because it was the only thing not trying to move around. Phil pulled the binoculars from the shoulder bag and focussed them on the vehicle. Pointer had said he drove a white Toyota Land Cruiser. Could this be him, waiting for Phil to leave the hotel? Half the car was hidden by a roadside stall. Even so, it was impossible to see through the tinted windscreen. A second white Toyota Land Cruiser made its way slowly past, then turned down a side street. There was definitely more than one of these cars in Mabarta. The one behind the stall had green plates. He observed the traffic for a while. *Cabs had yellow plates. Trucks had red plates; most other cars had white plates starting with letters MAB.*

He made a final check on the room, then proceeded down the stairs to the desk.

"If a car had green plates, what does that mean?" he asked the receptionist,

"Green what?"

"Green number plates," he repeated.

She thought a moment, with her finger on her lips. "That is when there is no customs duty on the car."

"So who uses cars with green number plates?"

She shrugged. "Some businesses that are doing work for the government, but mostly NGOs and foreign diplomats. They do not have to pay duty to import the car."

"Thanks." He placed the room keys on the counter. "I'm going out, but I have a lunch appointment here with a guy named Simon Pointer. I could be booking in again for a second night. I don't know yet."

She smiled again, showing off her white teeth. "No problem; we have plenty of room. I will look after your suitcase."

Phil hesitated at the entrance. He was reluctant to go outside. "Flag me down a cycle taxi," he asked the doorman.

"You want Buda Buda or motorcycle?"

"Buda what?"

"Bicycle or motorcycle?"

"Err; motorcycle, if you can get one."

The doorman stepped out into the street and waved his arms around, whistling above the noise of the honking horns. Phil slipped the strap of his shoulder bag around his neck and donned his sunglasses. He couldn't see very well without his normal glasses, but the less he saw of this journey the better.

A small red and chrome bike pulled up at the curb, puffing out blue smoke from the tail pipe. Phil dashed out through the beggars on the sidewalk and jumped onto the pillion seat. "Go," he called to the rider.

"Go where?"

"Just go quickly. I will tell you where later."

The bike pulled away with a jerk and started weaving in and out of the honking cabs. Phil glanced over his shoulder. *Shit.* The cruiser with the green plates was pushing its way into the traffic.

"Go quickly, and I will pay two times the money. Someone is following me."

The rider speeded up, *peeping* his horn among a crowed of bicycles. "Go quickly where?"

"I need to go to the office of the registrar of companies," Phil shouted

"I do not know that place."

Phil bit his lip and cursed. "It's an office for the government."

"Okay, all office for government same place. Freedom Square. I get you there in five minutes."

Phil bumped his knee on a Pajero's taillight and pulled his long legs in tighter. The bike was just missing things by inches on both sides. Beeping his horn continuously, the rider cut through the people on the sidewalk and turned into an alley. The bike swung from side to side as it dodged piles of rubbish and pools of water.

"Small road quicker than road for cars," the rider called "People follow you in car or on motorcycle?"

"In car," Phil shouted.

"Good, car no can come here."

They joined a main road and rode alongside a truck loaded with bags that hung over the body. Phil expected to be buried by tons of bags at any moment. There were even people riding on top and clinging to the sides. They turned down another alley and stopped at the end.

"Turn left and go into big office, then look at the names on the board."

"Thanks." Phil gave the man ten dollars and asked him to wait.

He nodded and propped his bike against the wall, holding out his hand. "Need money for waiting."

No problem. Phil gave him another five dollars.

At the centre of Freedom Square was a bronze statue of three figures. The middle one waved a sword in a menacing manner while the other two held up AK47s. Phil wondered whatever had happened to the simple spear and shield. *The soviets have a lot to answer for.*

He turned left and entered a glass-fronted old office block. The office he wanted was on the fourth floor. A few people were walking up and down the stairway. No one stood in front of the elevator doors, probably for obvious reasons.

Phil climbed the stairs two at a time and soon reached a doorway marked 'Registrar of Companies'.

The place was virtually deserted, except for an old man sitting at a desk reading a newspaper. A fat lady pushed a bucket round the floor with her mop. Phil placed the list of companies in front of the old man and tried to explain what he wanted.

"What did you say?" The man turned off his small portable radio and cupped a hand to his ear. "I am not hearing very well."

Phil was still out of breath from the four flights of stairs. He pointed to the list on the desk and spoke very slowly. "This is a list of Malenga companies. I need copies of the registration certificates for all these companies."

The old man nodded and examined the list. "If you want copies of all of these, you will have to come back tomorrow. We also need money for Photostatting."

Phil checked the clock on the wall. "If you can do this for me in one hour, I will give you one hundred American Dollars."

The cleaning lady jerked her head up and walked over to the desk with a hand on her hip. She counted the number of companies on the list. "This is a lot of work. These names are filed here in alphabetical order. My father cannot do all this work in one hour."

Phil counted one hundred dollars out on top of the desk.

"I will give you one hundred now and another hundred when you finish."

Father and daughter looked at each other. The fat lady snatched up the notes, then folded the list in half. She cut down the crease with a pair of scissors, giving one half to the old man. "After we find the certificates, you can go with me to have them copied," she said. "None of the machines in this building are working."

Phil nodded in agreement. "When you give me the copies, I will give you the other hundred dollars."

The old man stood and limped towards a double glass door.

"I can help you, if you want," Phil offered.

He shook his head and pointed to a sign above—'No admittance to the public'.

"Wait in the Solar Café next to the pharmacy. My daughter will meet you there."

He disappeared into the room that looked like a library, except for the fact that it appeared quite dark. Most of the strip lights in the ceiling were not working. The fat woman turned a sign around on the door to the stairs, which said 'Closed'.

She followed her father with the other half of the list into the dimly lighted room, and started signing.

Phil walked back down the stairway. *The fat lady's singing, but it's far from over.*

Chapter 33

Roberto stubbed out his second Chesterfield in the ashtray and lit another. The canteen was buzzing with unanswered questions.

All the company expats had assembled on instructions from the contracts manager, who now stood up. Being only five-foot-two tall, most of the gathering hadn't realised he was standing. He banged a metal salt pot on the table for order. The buzzing conversation continued until automatic firing could be heard in the distance. During the following silence, another burst of firing was clearly audible to everyone gathered in the canteen.

Galleria cleared his throat, "Attention, attention. I have called this meeting because of the situation."

The workshop manager's head flicked from side to side as he first observed the contracts manager with one eye, and then the other.

"As some of you already know, our aircraft left this morning for Dar with the women and children."

It had also contained all the senior staff, with the exception of himself. He thought it best not to mention it at that point in time.

"I have just returned from a meeting with the commandant of the army. He assures me that everyone in the camp is safe and that the situation will be back to normal after a few days."

He stopped to clear his throat again and took a drink of water. "Work is suspended until further notice. As you all know, we are not allowed to leave the camp for our own safety. Mr. Parker, the crushing plant manager, is missing. The military is busy searching for him. If anyone knows his whereabouts, they are to speak to me after the meeting."

Roberto swallowed and tried to look normal.

"We all hope for his safe return. The commandant has agreed to escort company transport to Mabarta for those of you who wish to leave the camp."

He pulled himself up to his full height. "I myself will be staying to monitor the situation for the company." The project manager had told him that this morning. He felt as if he had been deserted. "No one will be permitted to travel on company transport unless they are legally family members."

The contracts manager glanced in Roberto's direction, but dropped his gaze when Roberto made eye contact.

"The company will house its employees in a three star hotel until such time as they can return. Only one small bag per person is allowed. All those wishing to leave will now raise their hands."

The only expats who didn't raise their hands were the ones with local women staying with them. Including Roberto, there was about four. The contracts manager counted the show of hands.

"Transport for thirty-two persons will leave the camp at twelve o'clock."

The workshop manager raised his hand a second time. "I need one person to check the generator every morning." He certainly wasn't going to stay confined to the camp. There were plenty of fresh girls in Mabarta just waiting for him.

One of the men staying was the Portuguese service mechanic. He was the obvious choice, so he raised his hand. The contracts manager forced a smile. "Alright. So everything is settled. The convoy will leave the camp at twelve sharp."

Roberto walked back to his house deep in thought. By allowing the expats to travel to Mabarta, the military had effectively removed ninety percent of foreign nationals from the area.

Gunfire rattled in the distance. Roberto checked his watch. *The gunfire is too regular. It is as if someone is firing into the air every half an hour.*

Chapter 34

Ken's old Toyota Stout rattled and growled its way up the winding track towards the golf club, with Patch riding co-pilot. The two empty forty-four gallon drums rolling around in the back accounted for a small portion of the noise. The majority was attributed to the Stout itself.

One day, driving to town, Ken had been overtaken by a wheel. He had stared at the departing wheel in amazement as it had scatted some oncoming bicycles.

"Some daft bugger has lost a wheel," he exclaimed to an unconcerned Patch. The next moment the rear end of the Stout had pitched over to one side, solving the mystery. Patch was quite helpful in locating the rogue wheel in the dense bush, although a string of F words had not helped his concentration.

They turned right at the top of the track, and ended up in the golf club car park. Ken tooted his horn three times as a signal. The grounds man appeared from one of the ramshackle out buildings and waved. He walked over and climbed into the back of the Stout. Patch didn't like giving up his window seat without a commotion, so it was easier for the man to ride with the drums.

This was a ritual all three performed when Ken's plane needed fuel. The drive into town was uneventful, except for two roadblocks manned by the army. Ken stopped at a small supermarket where he normally purchased his provisions, and winked at the Indian proprietor. The owner's expression of mundane boredom changed to one of keen interest. He beckoned Ken to follow him into the backroom. After a certain amount of customary haggling, they agreed on a rate of exchange for the American dollars. The Indian wouldn't mention the exchange to anyone, because it was illegal to change money on the black market.

After buying a carton of decent whisky and a large cardboard box full of groceries, they proceeded to the oil depot. Ken showed the salesman the fax from Johannesburg. "About time I had a paying customer," he laughed. "I'm going to enjoy a spot of flying once the weather clears up."

The salesman hesitated, then made out an invoice for four hundred and twenty litres of Avgas.

"Will you be flying today, Mr. Marshal?"

"Oh, no; this American is only arriving late afternoon. If he cancels, I won't be flying at all."

Ken drove into the yard and exchanged the empty drums for full ones. He breathed a sigh of relief once back on the road to the lake.

At both roadblocks, he was made to get out while they searched the Stout. On the way back down the hill Ken, noticed the security guard in the trees speaking into his radio. Marco would now know that he'd been to Malenga for fuel. He wondered what sort of adverse effect that would have on their plans.

The grounds man opened the tailgate and guided Ken backwards until he had reversed up to a small wooden ramp. He rolled out the two drums while Ken collected the hand pump from the plane. The sun was shining strongly through the broken cloud, raising the humidity in the air. If it wasn't for the cooling effect of the prevailing wind from the lake, it would have been quite oppressive. Ken guessed another storm was on its way. Both drums were now standing on the wooden jetty in front of the aircraft. Ken broke the seal and unscrewed the cap. The hand pump was screwed into the aperture and an earth wire connected from the pump to the plane. A spark from static electricity could ignite the volatile Avgas fumes.

The first time he had refuelled, assisted by the grounds man, Ken had repeated his lecture about sparks and explosions just to be sure. He had then climbed on top of the wing to place the end of the plastic pipe into the filler cap. After instructing the man to start pumping, Ken had turned round to see him puffing on a lit cigarette while working the pump. Ken had leapt head first from the top of the wing, like a screaming Apache, to knock his new assistant into the water. After the two sodden men had reached the shore, Ken had taken a deep breath and added 'no smoking' to his instructions.

The idea now was to pump the same amount of fuel into each wing tank. When one drum was empty, they would open the other drum for the other side. If the first wing tank became full, they would just continue and fill the other side.

Ken stood on top of the pontoon under the wing and pushed a glass tube up to the spring-loaded drain value. If there was any sign of water, he would repeat the process until the fuel was clear. Condensation was a major problem with an empty tank in this climate.

The wearisome task of pumping the fuel from the drums seemed to be underway without the possibility of a catastrophic explosion.

Ken walked back along the creaking jetty towards the Stout. He smacked his lips in anticipation. The new case of whisky was now foremost in his mind. *One double with ice and soda would go down quite nicely just about now.*

Chapter 35

Phil sat on a high stool at the counter of the café, quite close to the window. From this vantage point, he was able to see the main entrance of the office block, which was about a hundred yards away to the left of the square.

A hand cart on the sidewalk blocked his view momentarily. It was festooned with every nick knack imaginable. Some cheap plastic digital watches caught Phil's eye. *Anything is better than nothing.* He was getting really pissed off checking an empty wrist.

The peddler tried to sell him a Rolex that had a ticking second hand, but Phil settled for an imitation Seiko. It was supposed to be waterproof. There was some condensation on the inside of the glass. *Could be it was supposed to keep the water inside. At least it's working.*

There were a number of baseball caps and cheap nylon jackets hanging from the canopy of the cart. Phil purchased one of each. Most of the locals wore the same type of thing. Sitting down, he could easily pass as a resident of Mabarta. Standing, he was a good head and shoulders taller.

Back at his window seat, he was on his third coke before he saw a familiar figure make her way down the office steps. She turned in his direction. He also saw something else that caused him to pull down the peak of his cap. A white Land Cruiser with green plates doubled parked outside the office. The fat lady was now halfway to the café, making good progress on the crowded sidewalk. A white man wearing a white shirt and trousers stepped out of the cruiser and hurried inside the building. A large local man followed, then remained at the doorway. The cruiser pulled away, releasing the 'bottle neck' of accumulated traffic. The crescendo of blaring horns died away as the vehicle slowly circled the square. Phil replaced his glasses with the shaded ones. He had seen enough to know Pointer was working for the opposition and had been tipped off about Phil's mission.

The fat lady entered the café and glanced round the room in confusion. It was only when Phil raised his hand that she stared in his direction and removed a wad of papers from her handbag.

"Come with me next door." She beckoned. "The pharmacy has a copier."

Phil walked amongst the people outside with his legs slightly bent. All he needed was a cigar and he would be doing an impression of Gaucho Marks.

Inside the pharmacy, the fat lady engaged the women behind the counter in some local chit chat. They were obviously friends. Phil wondered how long before the old man told Pointer where they were, and frantically tapped a finger on his new watch. The fat lady gave him a distasteful look, then placed the papers on the counter with some local money.

"One copy of each," she explained.

Phil kept an eye on the entrance of the office through the store window, expecting Pointer to run outside any minute. The fact that the elevators were out of order would slow him down. At the office block, the man at the entrance lifted his cell phone to his ear, then unexplainably entered the building. Phil could not understand why the man hadn't come over to the café.

It can only mean the old man isn't cooperating with Pointer.

Eventually, the photostatting was finished and Phil completed the deal with the fat lady. He wanted to leave that area of town as soon as possible. Folding the copies four times, he pushed them into his back pocket.

*   *   *

Inside the registrar of companies, Pointer was fuming. When things didn't go according to plan, he always lost his temper. Jones had been there alright, but that was as much as the stupid old man would say. A bit of persuasion had caused an unforeseen negative result. Simon checked his watch as their footsteps echoed down the stairway. In half an hour he would be able to turn the situation around. *Mr. Jones' life is just about to become totally unravelled.*

He emerged into the sunlight and lit up some weed. "Let's blow this joint," he remarked to his companion. "The service is dead here anyways."

$$*\qquad*\qquad*$$

Phil saw Pointer wave at the circling vehicle while doing his Gaucho Marks impression in the crowds on the sidewalk. The people nearest to him were giving him some funny looks. He held his back as if he was in pain, which wasn't far from the truth. *Pointer has drawn a blank and is leaving.*

Phil checked his watch. *The lunch date at the Park is in half an hour.* He would be able to get there ahead of him on the motor cycle and act as if nothing had happened. Phil didn't feel safe in Mabarta with Pointer on the loose. He would get the flight information from Pointer and leave without saying anything. There was plenty of time to reach the airport before two o'clock. Tonight he would be on holiday with lake tours. It would be a welcome change to the stress he was experiencing now.

The motorcycle was still waiting for him in the alley. Phil stood upright once out of sight from the square, and flexed his back muscles. The rider had made good use of his time by polishing the bike with a dirty rag.

On the way back to the Park Hotel, Phil turned his cap back to front to stop it blowing off, then closed his eyes. He pretended he was in a flight simulator with a black screen, or maybe one of those rides at Disneyland. Close your eyes and hang on till it was finished.

The bike stopped and Phil opened his eyes. Miraculously, they were outside the hotel. Phil dismounted and spoke to the rider.

"Okay, now listen up. At half-past-twelve I want you to take me to the airport. You must get me there quick, to domestic flights. I am taking an airliner to Malenga."

The rider looked puzzled. "Airliner?"

"Yes. Airplane." Phil pointed to the sky and held out his arms.

"Yes. I know airplane," the man nodded.

"Okay, keep my cap and jacket and fill up with gas."

The rider looked puzzled again. "Gas?"

"Yes. Gasoline. Petrol." Phil pointed to the tank. "Once I get on the bike. No stopping. We go straight to airport."

"Okay. No problem, but now need more money."

Phil paid him twenty dollars. "This for waiting. At the airport I'll give you another fifty. Go and put petrol in now."

The man smiled and rode off into the traffic. Phil entered the hotel and gave the receptionist five dollars. "This is for you. At half-past-twelve I'm leaving. Don't tell anyone. It's a surprise."

She seemed very pleased with the tip and pushed the bill into her bra. "Thank you, Mr. Jones. I hope you have a pleasant journey."

He went into the washroom next to the dining room and freshened up. Checking himself out in the mirror, he smiled. "Okay Simon, my man. Let's see how smart you really are."

Phil was hungry. The continental breakfast hadn't filled much of a gap. He went into the dining room and ordered a three course lunch from the set menu. There would be no telling what the chow would be like on the plane to Malenga. He checked his new watch. It was five to something. The little hand had fallen off.

Halfway through the soup Pointer walked in smiling, carrying a rolled up newspaper. "Hi Phil; how you doing?"

Phil smiled back. "Oh, okay. Mabarta takes some getting used to. And you. How was your day up to now?"

Simon sat down and also ordered from the set menu.

"Coulder been better. I have got something for you." He let the newspaper unfold by the side of the table. Phil stiffened. He was looking down the barrel of a nine millimetre. Pointer smiled at Phil's discomfort.

"No sweat. I'm just following orders from that prick Watson."

He reversed the weapon and handed it to Phil under the table. Phil placed the gun next to him on the bench seat and covered it with the newspaper. Simon reached into his pocket. "Here's a spare clip in case you want to start something down there."

Phil took the clip in his hand and slid it under the newspaper.

"I don't expect I'm going to need a shooter down there. I'm just checking up on a few things. Mostly paperwork."

Simon shrugged. "Oh well, you never know. Good insurance as a last resort. How did you sleep last night? I hope you haven't been a naughty boy?"

Simon's soup arrived with Phil's main course.

"I slept like a log. I was really bushed after all that flying. Some girl sneaked into my room and stole a few things."

Pointer laughed. "Who are you trying to kid. I knew you've been a bad boy. Some of the girls here screw like crazy. No sweat, a cell phone in this burg is dirt cheap. You can pick one up for a few cents."

Phil glanced up in surprise. "She stole my watch and camera. I've still got my cell phone. How come you think she stole my phone?"

Simon's smile was fixed, but a hardness had entered his eyes. "They always go for phones." He pushed his empty plate away and folded his arms. "So have you spoken to Watson about going to Malenga?"

"Not yet. I think he's going to tell me to stay here. I haven't finished my work here anyways."

The hardness left Pointers eyes. "So you didn't manage anything this morning?"

"Not really. I was just checking out the lay of the land. Where the places are at. What's the info on that flight to Malenga? Just in case Watson says go."

Pointer's main meal arrived.

"Makes no diffs to me whether you stay or go. Just let me know what's happening. That's all." He pushed a piece of paper over to Phil. "That's the pilot's name. He's available most days. If you bug out, it's no sweat. You can always go another day."

Phil checked his watch. It was nearly half-past-something. He held his stomach. "I've got a little gut problem since I've been here."

Simon laughed, showing the food in his mouth. "That's normal, my man. Every new guy spends half his life on the crapper."

Phil slipped the piece of paper in his shirt pocket and packed the gun into his shoulder bag. "I need the washroom and I can't leave that thing lying around. See you just now."

Phil stood up and left the dining room with a pained expression on his face. Pointer was still laughing as Phil closed the door behind him.

In one of the cubicles, Phil checked the handgun. It was fully loaded and fitted perfectly inside the bottom of the tape recorder. There was no space for the clip. He supposed he could always throw it away on the ride to the airport. The washroom windows were all barred with a heavy metal grid. Phil unloaded the bullets from the clip and threw them one at a time though the small squares. The clip itself just managed to fit through the window bars. The time now was dead on half past.

He picked up his case from reception and found the motorcycle waiting for him at the curb. After dressing in a jacket and cap, he slipped the shoulder bag onto his back, holding the suitcase in front of him between himself and the rider. The white Toyota was packed outside, but there was no sign of any of Pointer's companions. Phil breathed a sigh of relief once the bike had joined the flow of traffic and left the Park Hotel one block behind.

Simon finished his main course, then both sweets arrived on the table. He ate the ice cream slowly while watching Phil's ice cream start to melt. Jones must have died in the crapper. He glanced at his watch. *Nearly ten to one. If Jones is going to leave Mabarta today, he would have to be setting off for the airport about now.*

He stood and made his way to the washroom, only to find it empty. *So, Mr. Jones has taken a gap.*

He checked out the whole of the washroom, looking inside all of the water cisterns. The place was clean. Jones hadn't stashed the shooter anywhere.

The receptionist told him Mr. Jones had checked out. Back in the dining room, Simon sat before Phil's ice cream and quickly ate it. He dabbed his mouth with a serviette and pulled out his mobile. *Time to make that prearranged call to airport security.* His friend, Captain Komenda, would be expecting it.

On the road to the airport, Phil was dismayed to see a heavily-armed roadblock. Two personal carriers with machine guns mounted on top were parked on either side of the road. A queue of about ten cars was slowly filtering through. The motorcycle overtook the waiting vehicles and stopped in front of the soldiers. A handful of Europeans were having their passports scrutinised at a small wooden table. Phil was surprised when the motorcycle was waved through. *They only seemed interested in stopping white people.*

At the airport, there were twice as many soldiers than there had been last night. The rider turned off down a side road, following the perimeter fence. He stopped the bike in front of a gate manned by four bored-looking soldiers and a security guard. After paying the rider, he gave him the jacket and cap. Phil had his own jacket and cap inside the case. Only the security guard was interested in Phil's arrival. After being shown the piece of paper, the guard pointed to the aircraft parking area.

"You will find Mr. Van Eck over there near that white aeroplane."

The only decent-sized plane in the whole area was the aircraft the guard had pointed out. Phil couldn't see any other passengers around. He must be early; could be they would come along later. As he neared the white plane, he could see it was a whole lot smaller than the ones he'd flown in up to now. It looked like some type of executive Learjet. Very sleek and very fast. The midday sun reflected off its polished surface.

By the time Phil reached the bottom of the stairway, he was soaked in perspiration. "Hello," he called up the stairway. "Anyone there?"

A very smartly dressed European pilot appeared in the doorway. The sun glittered from the four gold strips on his epaulettes, matching his shining grey hair. His whole appearance radiated confidence. "Can I help you?" he asked.

"Yes. I am Mr. Jones for Malenga."

The pilot shook his head. "This aircraft doesn't fly to Malenga. I only do long haul flights for government officials."

Phil pulled the piece of paper from his pocket. "I have a flight number here. AVDZ."

The pilot smiled. "That's not a flight number. That's an aircraft."

He turned and shouted back into the cabin. "Alpha Victor Delta Zulu. Your passenger has arrived."

Another man appeared at the top of the stairway, dressed in kaki shirt and shorts. He reminded Phil of a huge orang-utan with gingerbread. He scowled at Phil with fierce eyes. "Who the bliksem is jy?"

"I'm Phil Jones. I'm looking for Mr. Van Eck."

"That's me. I was expecting a white oke. American is what I wus told."

Phil waved his passport around in front of him. The kaki-clad figure descended the steps and checked the passport. "Sorry, my maat. I wasn't expecting a black Yank. By the way," he called back to the man with the golden epaulettes. "Can you sommer land this 'ear aerospace contraption on a dirt strip?"

The pilot raised his eyebrows, then disappeared inside without saying a word. The gorilla picked up Phil's suitcase. "Didn't think he could. Too frightened to get his paintwork fucked up. That there thing's full of fucking leather armchairs."

"Where are we going?" Phil shouted after the departing Van Eck.

"My plane's parked behind this un. Come on, we can get an early start before any bad weather. I've already filed the flight plan with the tower."

Phil walked round the aero space jet and stopped. Van Eck pushed his suitcase though a small door, halfway down the smallest plane he had ever seen.

"I can't fly in this," he called. "It's only got one propeller."

"Geen probleem. If one engine stops on a twin, you still sommer falls down. Just takes a bit longer, that's all."

That statement didn't make Phil feel any better. The pilot was now carrying something that looked like foot pump and connected it to the front wheel. "Heer, come and puts your size fourteen on this 'ear pump while I checks the controls."

Phil walked over to the plane in a daze and started pumping. The front tyre was half flat.

"Couldn't you get a bigger plane?"

Van Eck poked his head out of the window. He looked as if the aircraft had been built around him. "This is a bigger plane. It's a Cessna 210. The one I 'as before was a 180. It could only sommer carry four persons. This one is for six and also has a turbo. She is a lekker size, eh."

"What happened to the 180?" Phil asked while still inflating the front tyre.

"We were all sitting inside ready to take off, when the cabin, all of a sudden like, sommer fills up with smoke. So I said to the passengers. Please vacate the aircraft. I've never seen three groot okes move so fast since."

Phil decided not to ask him any more questions.

The pilot struggled out of the plane to check on the front tyre.

"That looks lekker now. It was only flat on the bottom. My first name is Johannes. Folk call me Jan. What is your name?"

"Philip. Folk call me Phil."

They shook hands and then Jan stowed the pump back in the luggage compartment. Phil was starting to like this ginger-haired gorilla, but was panicking about flying in his plane. The other option was to return to Mabarta and risk another day with Pointer. That was out of the question.

"Why are you going to Malenga? There is supposed to be some kak down there with the rebels."

"I'm an ornithologist."

"A what?"

"A bird watcher."

"Well, why didn't you say's so."

"I'm going to stay with Lake Tours."

"Oh, Ken Marshal." Jan beamed. "Die Engelsman and ek is groot pals. Hy is my personeel sout peel. We sommer get lekker drunk if I ever gets that way. I used to fly north for the mining okes, but they don't use me so much now. My company is Central African Mystery Tours, because we never knows where we is going to end up."

Phil didn't know if Jan was serious, but didn't want to ask. A small army truck pulled up in front of the plane and six soldiers spilled out with assault rifles pointed in their direction. An NCO and a man in a dark suit stepped out of the cab.

"Wat maak jy nou!" Jan exclaimed.

"I am Captain Komenda of airport security," the small man in the dark suit announced. "We have reason to believe your passenger is carrying a firearm. Remove everything from this aircraft."

Jan gave Phil a hard look, then unlocked the luggage compartment. Two soldiers emptied the compartment and laid everything on the ground. The man in the suit strutted up and down , then addressed Phil. "Which are your bags, Mr. Jones?"

Phil pointed to his case and shoulder bag. Komenda nodded to the soldiers, who tipped everything out onto the ground while the NCO stood watching from the side of the truck. After a while, the soldiers stopped searching. "There is nothing," one of them said.

"That is impossible," the suit shouted. "Search the other bag."

"Hey, that's my bag," Jan protested.

They opened it and tipped everything out. The soldiers sifted through the jumble of items on the concrete. Nothing, they reported.

"Not possible nothing. Check again."

The NCO started tapping his swagger stick against the side of his leg. He didn't like the way this civilian was shouting at his men.

"Search the aircraft," Komenda commanded.

The two soldiers checked under the seats and in every aperture, and came up empty handed. A note of uncertainty had crept into Komenda's voice. His tone wasn't so commanding anymore. Jan took advantage of this and started a big spiel about complaining to the embassies.

"I is going to complain to the South African embassy and this oke's a Yank. He can complain to the American Embassy so you oke's will have two loads of kak coming in your direction".

"Search both of them," Komenda ordered.

"I is going to write a letter to Mr. Mandela. He will be phoning your president next week."

The soldiers started glancing towards their NCO while they searched the two men. The officer raised his stick.

"Enough. There is nothing here."

Komenda picked up the empty shoulder bag and felt the sides and the bottom. He threw down the bag in frustration. The officer rested his stick on Komenda's shoulder. "I think you had better check the source of your information."

He jerked his head for the soldiers to board the truck. Komenda was the last one to climb back into the truck. He had made a fool of himself in front of the military. The next time he would use his own men.

Phil and Jan started repacking their bags.

"Who the fuck has told them you has a gun? You're not even a hunter. This is a groot gemors and that is for sure."

"Why did you mention Mandela? Mbeki is your president now."

"Ek weet, but these clowns have probably never heard of 'im. Everybody knows Mandela. Why didn't you mention Bush? He sommer starts a war for fuckall."

The bags were all repacked in a fashion and stowed away.

"Let's hast to before them clowns decides to come back. What time is it? My watch needs a new batteray."

"It's ten past something." Phil checked his cell phone. "It's ten past two."

"Hgot, we is now running late. This time of year, you are liable for groot storms late in the day."

Jan opened the right side door for Phil. He pushed back the seat and told him to get in. He then pulled out the chocks from under the wheels and climbed in the other side. After switching on the ignition, he flipped some switches and pressed a button. There was a whining noise, causing the two-blade propeller to move slowly.

"Ghot." Jan slapped himself on the forehead with the palm of his hand. "Die donnerser batteray is pap. Get out; I'll show you how to starts the engine."

Phil sat there, unmoving, just staring ahead.

"If you want to get to Malenga today, you have to starts the engine. I have to sit inside to operate the throttle and keep my foot on the brake or you becomes mince meat."

Phil gave his glasses a quick polish, then climbed outside. Jan met him at the nose of the plane.

"Okay. Kyk wat I does. Turn the prop so it's at ten o'clock. Puts your fingers on top. Pulls down and step back or you lose your face. Don't forgets, pulls down, steps back."

Phil swallowed and nodded. Jan climbed back in and, after a moment, nodded at Phil. Phil took a deep breath and pulled down, taking a huge step backwards. *Phut, Phut, Phut.*

"Again," Jan shouted. "Turn the blade back where it was." *Phut, Phut, Phut.*

"Again." He nodded. *Phut, cough, cough, phut.*

"Nearly there. Again." *Phut, cough, cough, cough.* The propeller kicked backwards.

"Again." *Phut, cough, broom.*

The engine roared to life. Phil back peddled and then ran round under the wing to climb back inside. With the windows open, the wind from the propeller started drying the perspiration on his face. Jan donned a set of headphones.

"Now that weren't so bad, was it?"

Phil didn't answer as he strapped himself in. His eyes had a glazed look about them.

"Make sure that the door is closed. It has a bad habit of popping open."

Phil reopened the door and slammed it shut, then pushed hard against it with his shoulder.

"Okay, okay. Don't break the donners a ding. You black okes sommer breek alles. Keep those groot feet of yours away from the pedals."

Jan pushed the throttle all the way forward, with the brakes on. The whole aircraft strained forward with a deafening noise. He did this a few times while tapping his finger on some of the gauges. Phil's eyes did a quick search of all the instruments. He realised his life depended on what they indicated and didn't like the fact that Jan was tapping some of them.

He now signalled to Phil to put on the other set of headphones. "Alpha Victor Delta Zulu to tower come in."

Jan repeated this again before the tower answered. A metallic voice crackled in the headphones. "Tower to Alpha Victor Delta Zulu, go ahead."

"Request permission to takes off. Pilot plus one to Malenga; over."

"Proceed to holding area. We have one transport arriving in eight minutes. After that you will be clear, over."

"Thank you, tower. Over and out."

Jan released the foot brake and they started rolling across the concrete towards a tarmac road that ran parallel to the runway. He smiled and nodded at Phil. "So far, so good," he shouted as they trundled along the road at a good running pace. Jan continued to tap some of the gauges.

"What's wrong?" shouted Phil.

Jan shook his head. "Nothing. I just makes sure they're not sticking. Die batteray is charging. Oil and fuel pressure okay. Alles is okay up to now."

"What do you mean up to now?" Phil shouted back.

"Well, anything can happen up there. You fly in small planes before? I gets the feeling you are a bit nervous like."

"No, and I don't like flying in big planes either. At least you don't have to pump the tyres and start the engine."

"Oh, you in for a groot experience, my maat. After you've flown in a small plane, you don't worry any more about groot airplanes. If you feel sick, use that plastic bag in the door flap."

Just then a huge, four-engine jet screamed past, rocking the Cessna with an ear splitting noise. The aircraft was painted grey and had a huge tailfin. It touched down, kicking up a cloud of smoke from the numerous groups of wheels underneath.

"What the heck is that?" Phil shouted.

"Russian transport. See, no markings. It's bringing a load of obsolete guns for these okes to kill each other with." Jan shook his head and shouted, "Let em get on with it, I says."

They reached a circular area at the end of the runway.

"Alpha Victor Delta Zulu to tower, come in."

"Tower receiving, go ahead."

"Permission to takes off, over." There no answer. so Jan repeated. "Permission to takes off. over."

There was still no answer.

"Something is wrong. Can you see any sign of those clowns again?"

Phil rummaged around in his shoulder bag and brought out the binoculars. He trained them down the approach road in the direction of the terminal buildings. Phil could just make out a white vehicle travelling at some speed towards them.

"I think it's the same guy who told them I have a gun." Phil shouted.

"Vok daaie oke? We is going to takes off."

Jan taxied the Cessna onto the runway. "Alpha Victor Delta Zulu. I am ready to takes off and not receiving yous over."

"Tower to Alpha Victor Delta Zulu. Stay on hold, over."

Phil could make out the green plate on the white vehicle. "It is the same guy," he shouted.

"Close your window. We is going," Jan shouted back.

"Alpha Victor Delta Zulu to tower. I am not receiving you. You told me it was clear after the transport, so I'm taking off, over and out."

"Negative, negative, stay on hold."

It was now quieter in the cabin with the windows closed, until Jan pushed the throttle fully forward and released the brakes. The Cessna moved forward and started to gather speed. Jan pulled a lever on his side to full flap position. The white cruiser turned left across the runway and stopped.

"Kyk daaie oke. Hy's vokkin mal. Hy's on the bliksermar runway." Jan gritted his teeth and narrowed his eyes. "Fuck him. Who the donner does he think he is?"

Phil removed his glasses and started to polish them furiously. "Can we make it okay?"

The engine noise vibrated through the cabin as the Cessna charged towards the parked 4x4 saloon.

"Nie panic nie. We is not overloaded so I should be able to lift off without blikseming die oke."

Jan started to sweat. The air speed indicator needle crept agonisingly slowly towards the green area.

Two black men jumped out from the cruiser and ran away. A white man stood in front of it, waving his arms to and fro above his head. Eventually, he also ran away. Phil's asshole was clamped shut so tight he thought he would be able to break his finger off inside. A bead of sweat dripped from Jan's nose.

That's a good indication to start worrying, thought Phil. *When you see the pilot sweating, it's time to bail out.*

The Toyota was starting to fill the windscreen. Phil placed his head between his knees. Jan saw the pointer reach the green.

"Daar sy," he exclaimed and pulled back on the controls.

The plane leapt into the air with a buzzer sounding inside the cabin.

"Vot maak jy nou?" Jan called.

"I'm bracing for impact," Phil shouted above the noise of the buzzer.

"Ghot, that's only good for crash landing. Not for collision with full tanks."

Phil slowly lifted his head and saw clear sky in front of them. Jan mopped his face with a handkerchief.

"Alpha Delta Victor Zulu to tower," he said in level voice. "I doesn't knows if you is receiving me, but I wish to report a obstruction on your runway."

Chapter 36

After the shopping James relaxed in the broken down, old armchair in front of the fireplace. Shopping with women always exhausted him. The fire was only lit at night during the short, cooler part of the year, or to help with the cooking when they had visitors. Brenda had tried to get rid of the armchair on numerous occasions, but James would not hear of it.

"I want something comfortable, not something nice to look at," he would reprimand her. Besides, they could not afford a new chair. He had heard the expats were confined to the construction camp and all the local workers had been sent home. Maybe visitors could still enter. He did not see why not.

"Brenda," he called. "Are you busy?"

"Not really. Just doing some mending. Why?"

"How would you like to visit your cousin? You know, the one with the other mat. I was thinking of going to the camp to see Roberto and Bill."

Brenda appeared from the bedroom.

"Yes, what a good idea. I haven't seen my cousin for weeks."

James removed the mat from the box and laid it out in the boot of the car. He covered it with old newspapers and wasn't surprised to see that Brenda and the children were quickly ready.

Traffic in town was very light. Security people and the military were everywhere. The odd policeman stood around. They looked like observers.

"I didn't know Medusacor had so many men," Brenda remarked.

"You're right. I have never seen the taller ones around before. I wonder where they came from."

They drove up the hill and passed the large, old houses and came to an area where small houses clustered together. This was the northern outskirts of the town, where most of the local construction workers lived. They were the only ones with any sort of money in their pockets.

Brenda's cousin was delighted when she saw her and the children, and immediately launched into the gossiping. Her husband, who drove a truck for the Italians, offered James a warm beer. The electricity in this part of town was out due to the previous night's storm.

They sat and played two games of checkers before James started to get a headache. It was a combination of the warm beer and the raised voices in the bedroom.

"Ask her about the mat," James shouted.

He was eager to leave. The truck driver was no match for him at checkers and at least he would have something cold to drink at the camp.

"In a minute," she called back impatiently.

"No; now. You can talk after I have gone. I will pick you up before the curfew."

The truck driver wanted to go with James to escape the gossiping, but James did not want any complications at the camp gate. Eventually, Brenda appeared with a rolled-up mat. She offered her cheek for James to kiss. He pecked at the side of her face, self-conscious in front of the other man. With both mats covered up in the boot, he drove off, leaving the truck driver to his fate. After buying a packet of cigarettes from a roadside vender, he set off towards the camp.

The gate guard recognised James. Two of his children attended the school, but his attitude was quite hostile. "What do you want here?" he demanded.

James forced smile. "I am visiting my friend, Roberto Demodica."

The guard eyed the cigarettes on top of the dashboard. "You can have those if you want. I do not smoke."

The man snatched the packet off the dash. "Most of the Italians have gone, but your friend is still here. Open the boot."

The guard patted the newspaper and was satisfied the boot was empty. He raised the boom for James to pass.

How we can ever succeed as a nation when a man is bribed by a pack of cigarettes, James asked himself as he drove into the camp.

There was no car outside Bill's park home, so James carried on to Roberto's house. He found Roberto and the two girls watching television. They all looked very depressed.

"Where is Bill? I have brought the mats for him to see."

Nobody answered. Roberto stood up and switched off the television. "What would you like to drink?"

"A glass of coke with an ice cube and an aspirin."

Roberto pointed to a chair at the dining table. "I will a join you just now."

James sat down and waited in the silent room. *Something is wrong here. It's like a gathering after a funeral. Maybe Bill Parker is dead.*

Roberto returned with two glasses of coke with ice cubes, and sat opposite to James. He pushed an aspirin over the table and swallowed one himself.

"The night of my barbeque, did Bill talk to you? He told me you were going to bring something here. What did he a tell you?"

James took a sip of coke to remove the taste of warm beer from his mouth. "Basically, he asked about Nabusano. He said he had something that Nabusano wanted. I advised him to give Nabusano what he wanted. There is no telling what that evil old man is capable of. He has a great influence in this country, especially here in Malenga."

Roberto nodded. "I advised him to do the same thing."

James swallowed the aspirin and drank some more coke. "So what seems to be the problem? Where is Bill now?"

"I can't tell you where he is. It is better you do not know. The problem is, Bill went to the police station to give the thing to Nabusano's men. Everything went wrong and now he is a trying to escape."

"Good God! Did Bill kill those four men?" James exclaimed.

"He told me it was an accident. I believed him. It was a not his fault."

"And the thing Nabusano wanted. Where is that?"

"Bill still has it."

James sat quietly for a moment, staring at the ice cube in his glass.

"This explains many things. Nabusano is using the army and Medusacor to search for him. The police do not seem to be interested, so there is probably no formal charge against him. What on earth has Bill got that Nabusano wants? It must be a thing of great importance."

Roberto lit a cigarette and hesitated before he spoke. "I cannot tell you what it is. You would think me mad. It may even place your life in a danger if you know about it. Bill and I understand the thing's value, and probably where it came from. What we do not understand is how Nabusano knows about it. We think he has been searching for it for many years. That is why Bill wanted to find out everything about the Nabusano family. We do not know the picture Nabusano fits into."

James rubbed his forehead with his fingers. His headache was not getting any better. "Bill was very interested in the old legend of Chief M'ba. That is why I brought the mat he wanted to see. We found a second one of a later date, so I have brought both of them. According to Brenda, the Nabusano family wanted all these mats destroyed."

Roberto mashed out his cigarette in the ashtray and lit another one. "There must be a reason for that. Show me the mats. If I discover anything, I can phone Bill and instruct him what we a find."

James went out to his car and returned with the two mats rolled up together. He opened them out on top of the table. Sara and Monica gathered round to see that James had brought.

"These are the mats the old people used to make," said Sara. "The tradition stopped a long time ago. This is the first time I have seen one."

James explained the legend of Chief M'ba for Roberto's benefit. The girls had heard the general outline of story before, but had never seen it portrayed in picture form.

"What is he holding "? Roberto asked.

James shrugged. "Brenda does not know. The answer has been lost with the old people of her tribe. All she knows is that it is the gift from the god of the river."

James smiled and shook his head. "This is the very thing my school is fighting."

"What is on the other mat?" Roberto asked.

"I don't know. I have never seen it. Brenda says there is a boat on it."

The word 'boat' prompted Roberto to experience shivers up and down his spine. James rolled up the first mat to expose the one underneath. The hair on the back of Roberto's neck stood to attention.

"Hmm, very interesting. Quite a work of art." James stroked his chin and tilted his head from side to side. "Look at the detail. It is very well done. I wish we knew what it is about."

The girls crowded round and started touching the mat with their fingers.

"Look at the way the smoke and fire has been made," said Sara. "I wish my needlework was as good."

"Oh, look at this man standing at the front." Monica pointed. "He is holding a ball like the one Bill has." Roberto took a step backwards and then disappeared into the kitchen.

"What is wrong with Roberto? He is looking ill," James said.

Sara followed Roberto to the kitchen, then they all heard a glass breaking. Roberto returned with a glass half full of whisky and sat down on the settee, closely followed by Sara.

"What is wrong with you"? she asked.

James pointed at the mat. "I think this picture has upset him. I do not know why. We do not even know what it is about."

Roberto mumbled something and then gulped down half the whisky in the glass. "It is the Derflinger," he said at last.

"The der what?" James asked.

Roberto lit a cigarette with shaking hands. "It is the Derflinger," he repeated in a louder voice. "It was a German gunboat that was sunk on the lake in nineteen-fifteen."

James smiled and raised his hands. "How could you possibly know that? These mats are only old wives tales."

"Look at the front of the ship and tell me what you see." James examined the picture again. "It is gun of some sort."

"Now look at the back of the ship."

James bent over the table. "There is a flag there. I have seen that flag before, in a history book."

"That is the ensign of the German imperial navy."

James was fascinated. "Well, I would not expect these mats to depict an event that actually happened. This boat has exploded. These are only two pieces sticking out of the water. Nineteen-fifteen was ninety years ago. Brenda said this mat was made by her grandmother's mother."

He did some counting on his fingers. "That's about right for four generations. Brenda said both mats show Chief Mb'a destroying the tribe's enemies. This must be the grandson of Mb'a on this mat."

Roberto shook his head. "No, I do not a think so."

James did some more counting on his fingers. "Alright, it could be his great grandson."

Roberto shook his head again. "Look at the man's hands."

"What is he holding? Monica said Bill has one."

"That is the same thing Nabusano is after. That is what M'ba is holding on both mats. The power of the river god."

James shook his head in disbelief. He had always thought Roberto was a scientific person who arrived at his conclusions from facts. "Who do you think this second man is?"

"It is the same man. Look again at his hands."

James' mouth fell open. *The little finger of the left hand was missing.*

Chapter 37

Nabusano's anger ebbed and flowed through his whole being. His body was in a state of decay, but the fire of a raging volcano shone from his eyes. His personal valet and attendants glanced at each other nervously. They had never seen him this agitated before. He dismissed them with a snarl, then screamed his defiance at the empty room. An uncontrollable fit of coughing cut short his outburst. His sons, the most trusted of the followers, were starting to fail him at this most crucial time of all. Marco had not found Parker at the house of the white man. It was logical; Parker was there, just waiting to escape. It was time to implement stronger measures. Measures that would make use of Parker's weakness. Before this was over, Parker himself would deliver the power to its rightful owner. The great Chief Mb'a would be resurrected even stronger than before.

Nabusano grinned and wiped the spittle and blood from the corner of his mouth with the sleeve of his robe. The other, less important matter was that of the dragon's agent. Pointer, the mercenary had failed. The descendent of slaves was now en route to Malenga. Nabusano despised these black Americans. They had allowed themselves to be corrupted by the white man's ways. Their forefathers had bowed down to slavery instead of ending their lives like true warriors. His own father had died before his eyes in defiance of the oppressors.

These Negros were black men with the way of thinking of a white man. Neither one thing nor the other. Some of them were half breeds. Their blood was contaminated. He smiled again. "I will make the world a better place by ending this one's existence."

Chapter 38

Listening to the monotonous *clunk, clunk* of the pump down on the jetty Bill, began to doze. He felt quite safe under the veranda, but if Medusacor returned with dogs, things would take a sharp turn for the worse. Was it possible that Marco had not brought dogs on purpose? Their use was a normal means of searching for people. As things stood, he and Ken had a good chance of escaping after dark. There was only one security guard to deal with. With the ball in his possession, he could probably take on a whole army under the cover of darkness.

Clunk, clunk, clunk. Bill's chin eventually dropped onto his chest. He drifted off into a state of semi-consciousness. That's when the visions started. It was like watching a sequence of movie previews all jumbled together with no sound track. At first he tried to fight the unwelcome incursions into his mind by constantly waking up.

Clunk, clunk, clunk. The pump drove him back to the borderline of sleep. With great effort, he removed the ball from his shirt and laid it next to him. The space under the veranda faded into darkness and the clunking of the pump retreated into the distance. He felt like a man dying of thirst with a glass of cold water standing next to him. Bill's stubbornness hardened his resolve. *Why must some alien beings of two million years ago be in charge of my will? Fuck them. Bill Parker is his own man.* The battle of control over his body started to make him feel physically sick. He had now become an alcoholic dying of thirst, and the ball a glass of cold beer. With a shaking hand, he fumbled around in the darkness and picked up the ball.

"Okay, you win, whoever you are."

Light filtered back under the veranda and the clunking of the pump grew more distinct. The feeling of nausea gradually left. If he gave away the ball now, he wondered how long it would take for him to rehabilitate. Nabusano would kill him anyway. The situation had gone too far. He may as well get used to it. The ball was now an extension of himself.

The clunking of the pump soon returned him to his dozing. He let the visions wash over him without any resistance. The reception of the vision was opposite to that of an old television. Instead of receiving the sound first and then fiddling around to get a good picture, Bill received the picture first. The sound came later. He couldn't make any sense of the quickly-changing scenes, and decided he wasn't relaxed enough. There was no time to visit the nearest massage parlour for a blow job. He would just have to force himself to relax.

Clunk, clunk, cluck. Bill descended into another level of semi-consciousness. A city street with no traffic. Large tinted Perspex tubes of about ten feet diameter were attached like leeches to the front of the tall white buildings. The tops were curved where they entered the skyscrapers on different levels. At the lower end, they all disappeared into the ground. People dressed in white robes sat in what looked like a roller coaster train. These trains constantly ran up and down the faces of all the buildings with a quiet hissing noise. Where they went to once entering the ground, Bill had no idea. The automobile had disappeared and people were pressing their thumbs on things that reminded him of parking metres. This could only be the future. The people in the street stood on fast-moving conveyor belts, which slowed down at each intersection. These were also covered by tinted Perspex. Everyone wore wide-brimmed hats and some sort of dark eye protection. They had overcome pollution, but were still suffering the effects of a damaged ozone layer. No fat people were evident. Medical science or an improved diet must have overcome that problem. Bill felt as if he was actually standing on the street, but no one could see him. Vapour trails crisscrossed high in the blue sky.

Aircraft of some sort were still in use. The picture faded and another took its place.

A brightly lighted warehouse of immense proportions now appeared before him. Large polystyrene boxes trundled along miles of travelling ways, which focussed upon a loading bay area. The boxes closest to Bill were marked 'Fam 4 Day 10'.

He interpreted this as meaning 'family of four for a ten day period'. If it wasn't a holiday package tour for midgets, it could only be a standard box of provisions for ten days.

Bill was interested to see what type of transport was used to deliver the goods. He seemed to float off in the direction of the loading bays. Large flat cars about the size of a truck formed a queue in each bay. The carrying area of each was interlaced with sets of rollers positioned at different angles. A box trundled onto the back, and was then rolled into whatever placed was available. Bill couldn't see any people inside the building. Everything was fully automated.

His biggest surprise came once the car was loaded. Red beams of light flicked from the front to rear of the car and round the back. The beams looked like a means of securing the boxes. With a loud humming noise, the flat car lifted and sped off through the open doorway. *Anti-gravity.* This was much further forward in time than the roller coasters he had previously observed. They were probably driven by a system of electro magnets. Anti-gravity was a completely different kettle of fish, and far more advanced. Bill examined the boxes to try to find some sort of date stamp, but failed. Everything was only bar-coded for the eye of a computer. Human eyes were no longer required.

He started thinking about the countryside, and wondered what changes had taken place there. The picture blurred, then cleared.

He was standing in what appeared to be a dense forest of saplings. *No,* he thought. *More like a tall plantation of bamboo.* The ground was littered with fallen branches, which looked uncommonly straight. *More bamboo,* he presumed. Then he noticed many round objects, similar to hen's eggs, scattered about on the floor. He tried to pick one up, but his hands just passed through the object. Now he knew how Scrooge felt in the story by Dickens called *The Christmas Carol. Where did these round things come from?* He looked up and saw that the tops of the saplings ended in massive ears of corn. He was standing in a wheat field. For a horrible moment, Bill thought he had shrunk. He expected a huge rat to dash out at any moment carry him off in its jaws. A noise startled him. It was a bird. A bird of regular size. *The only thing out of proportion here is the corn.*

A faint humming was audible, similar to the noise the flat car had made in the warehouse. It was growing louder.

Something big is approaching. The humming was now vibrating the ground. Bill didn't know whether he was actually feeling the vibrations or just sensing them. In reality, he wasn't even there.

Whatever was coming, he couldn't see because of the corn. Stepping back into a small clearing, Bill was able to see a machine like a huge tanker floating towards him. At the rear, a series of sprays jetted out some atomised liquid. At the front, there was a red beam similar to a laser, swinging to and fro among the corn. A klaxon suddenly went off and the machine stopped.

"All humans to vacate the area. Spraying is in progress."

A pleasant female voice repeated the instruction. Bill glanced around, expecting to see someone. Eventually, he moved further back to the edge of the field. The voice stopped and the machine started moving again. How could the machine have seen him? He was under the floor of Ken's house back in 2005. The sensors must have indicated some sort of presence or disturbance.

Whoever was monitoring this machine would have to put the stoppage down to a glitch. The vibrations were definitely real and undulating in waves. They were now focussed on the thigh of his right leg. He awoke with a start. Sara's cell phone was buzzing in his pocket.

In an excited voice, Roberto explained all about the mats that James had brought over for him to see. He voiced his opinion that Chief Mb'a was the same man on both mats and that the Derflinger was definitely destroyed by the ball.

"Okay. I agree the Derflinger was destroyed by them. There obviously must be two balls in existence, but Mb'a being the same man is a bit too farfetched. Maybe all the chiefs after Mb'a cut off their fingers. That makes more sense than a two-hundred-year-old man."

Roberto agreed. "I probably overreacted," he confessed.

Bill continued, "At least it explains how Nabusano knows about the ball. The first ball may have indicated the area in which there was another. The ball I have is making me experience visions."

"What sort of visions?"

"It's a bit like second sight, only happens when I'm semi-conscious. I have seen some flashes of the future, or what the future could be. One small change in the present would alter the future drastically. If Corporal Hitler had been killed in the First World War, the world would be a hell of a different place now.

"Maybe not," Roberto interrupted. "Possibly another hundred different men could have taken his place."

"This sort of second sight," Bill continued. "I'm thinking is the factor that enabled *Erectus* to start throwing stones and controlling fire. I have also had glimpse of the past, which was dead accurate. Maybe that's just a spin off from seeing into the future. There was no use for *Erectus* to see the past."

Roberto went on to explain the situation in the camp. "Most of the expats have gone to Mabarta. We seem to be quite safe inside the camp. Galleria is the only senior staff member left behind. I can see he is not a happy about it. His wife left this morning on the company plane. She took their dog, but left him behind." Roberto forced a laugh. "I think the dog is more important. Half the woman's bags came back in the company's bus from the airstrip. Michel, the pilot, weighs everything with a spring balance. He does not take any bullshits from his passengers."

Bill also forced a chuckle. "Well tonight, I hope to see how professional Ken is. He's busy refuelling. There's only one guard on top of the hill." He thought for a moment. "Somehow, I don't think Nabusano will leave things like that. He's not stupid."

They wished each other good luck and he ended the call.

Chapter 39

Still climbing, Jan swung onto his westward heading. The buzzer stopped sounding off.

"'Holy shit!" Phil exclaimed. His hands were shaking. Jan reached behind Phil's seat, flipped the lid off a cool box and handed him a can of beer. "Here, gets one of these down ja. No extra charge for refreshments."

Phil pulled the tab and gulped down half the tin. Jan raised his bushy eyebrows. "Strange, all my passengers drink quick."

He offered Phil two buns in a cellophane bag. "Would you likes chicken or beef?"

Phil shook his head and finished the beer. Then he gripped both hands on the underside of the seat. The plane was bouncing up and down vigorously in the updraft of hot air. Because the Cessna was a top wing aircraft, Phil had the impression that both he and the seat could fall through the floor at any moment.

"As soon as we is above the cloud, she will starts to settle down."

Jan reached behind for another beer and opened it. *So much for drinking and driving,* thought Phil, watching the pilot tip his head back.

"What was that buzzer when we took off? Is anything wrong?"

Jan shook his head. "Stall warning; always goes off if I pull up too quickly or takes off overloaded. Sometimes it stays on until I burn off some fuel to get lighter. I thinks I'll sommer disconnect it if I remembers. It upsets the passengers."

The Cessna was still bucking quite badly as they approached the underside of the cloud layer.

"So, are you going to tell me what the dondor is going on? That poluka with the pony tail isn't sommer going to stand in front of my plane for fuckall."

Phil thought he owed Jan some sort of explanation. After all, if it wasn't for the pilot, he would still be stuck on the ground with probably another search taking place.

"I work for the US government. It's to do with finance."

"I hopes you're not with the IRS. I hate those okes. They took half my farm away. My wife took the other half. At the divorce, she called me an ignorant buffoon. I doesn't even knows what that means."

Jan belched loudly and then leant over in his seat to fart. "Daar sy, that's better out than in."

"No, I work for the FBI financial intelligence. The guy back there tried to stop me. He gave me a gun, then informed on me."

Jan whistled. "So where is this here gun now?"

"It is hidden inside my tape recorder. A normal search wouldn't find it."

"Lucky for us. You would be in a African jail by's now. Those places aint so lekker. No glass in the windows. You sleeps on straw mats and you have twenty okes in one room all kaking in the same bucket. I don't knows what happens if they run out of graze. Maybe they shoots a few of em."

The aircraft started shaking, lifting and dropping a metre at a time. Phil gripped tighter to the underside of his seat.

"What is happening?" Phil called above the engine noise.

"It is the time of day. There is hot air rising from the ground. The cloud acts as like a buffer. Once we gets above, then we only have to worry about the Charlie Bravos."

Phil didn't want to ask what a Charlie Bravo was, but he did anyway.

"Oh." Jan rolled his eyes.

"It's a thunderstorm that goes from the ground to ups high. You get em this time of year. Sometimes they sommer move around in groups."

"Are they dangerous?"

"Not so much for an airliner. They fly's over the top. We has to go around. The smaller ones we can fly over cos I as turbo. If I gets too high we will sommer pass out. No oxygen. If I get inside a groot one, it could sommer breaks the wings off."

Phil decided to polish his glasses. He hadn't seen any parachutes when the plane had been searched. They entered the cloud and everything outside the windows turned grey. Phil stared panic stricken through the windscreen and the side window. He couldn't see a thing. The muscles in his ass clenched together while he waited for the airplane to collide with some unseen object. Sunlight lighted up the cabin, then disappeared again. Moments later, they broke through the cloud completely. Phil exhaled and relaxed. The light above the cloud was brilliant. Sun reflected from huge balls of cotton wool. It was like a fantasy world of fluffy white castles. Here and there were gaps to the ground far below. Phil could just make out a gravel road and the flash of sunlight from a tin roof before the view was obscured.

Jan pushed the controls forwards slightly and reduced the engine RPM. The noise in the cabin was less and the shaking had stopped.

"We is nearly at our right height. I like to fly in and out of these clouds, but can't do it too much or we is never going anywheres."

Phil had to agree it was a really neat view, and stopped gripping the underside of the seat.

The pilot reached back and handed Phil another beer. He cracked one open for himself and, after a gulp, wedged the can into a makeshift holder. Phil wondered how many miles the Cessna flew to the beer. The two fuel gauges on the dash still showed three-quarter full.

"How long can you fly on full tanks?" he asked Jan.

"About six hours, but you're not supposed to use the reserve or you sommer falls down. We should use half of one tank for Malenga."

Phil was starting to feel more relaxed. From here on in it should be a joyride.

Chapter 40

In frustration, Simon Pointer punched Freda in the mouth, splitting her lip. Her TNT white jeans were splashed with blood and tears.

"I told you to steal the phone, not the fucking camera," he raged.

He was surrounded by morons. Mr. Philip Jones Jr. was probably telling that motherfucker Watson everything on his special fucking phone at this very minute. His job at the embassy was fucked up. Watson would crucify him. More important was the fact that Jones was on his way to Malenga. Komenda had also fucked up, or Jones had ditched the shooter on the way to the airport. Everything had turned into crap. Simon checked his watch. He would have to blow this country with a speed. His benefactor did not like failure or any loose ends floating around. Simon had personally seen what happened to dudes in the failure or loose ends category.

Ignoring the weeping girl, he walked out of the shabby room into the alley. The banks were closed. He would have to transfer his account from outside the country.

The alley was full of people, mostly women carrying containers of water on their heads and babies on their backs. It was also full of rotting garbage two metres high down one side. The Toyota he could sell at the northern border. He knew one customs official who would buy it.

A tall beggar wrapped in a blanket and limping with a stick blocked his path.

"Give me small money for food," he pleaded.

Simon impatiently pushed him to one side and continued on his way. In the next instant Simon saw a hand with a bird tattooed on the palm close over his mouth. He felt a sharp pain in his chest and stared down at one foot of slender, pointed steel that appeared sticking out the front of him. It quickly disappeared and the hand uncovered his mouth. Simon stood for a moment before collapsing into the heap of garbage.

A woman screamed.

He looked down at the front of his blood-soaked shirt. Lying in the garbage with a faltering heart, Simon's last thought was, *I'll never get this godamn shirt clean again.*

Chapter 41

The refuelling was finally finished. Ken paid the grounds man for his services and gave him some extra money.

"That's for last year's Christmas," he explained.

If he didn't give a reason for the extra money, the man would expect the same amount next time. Ken could be financially embarrassed again by then.

He was busy checking the old girl's engine oil when the olive green Land rover arrived. A captain and six soldiers walked along the jetty towards him.

"Oh Lord, here we go," Ken muttered under his breath.

"Mr. Marshal," the officer called.

"Yes, that's me. What do you want here?"

The captain arrived at the float plane, accompanied by the soldiers.

"I have been given some orders regarding your aeroplane."

Ken's moustache started brisling. "What sort of orders?" He demanded. "This aircraft is private property."

"As you must have heard, this area is under marshal law. That means the commandant of Malenga District has the official power of the government to take what measures he sees fit."

"And what, may I ask, are those measures?" Ken asked indignantly while he closed the side cover.

He could see it would be useless to argue with this man.

"The commandant is worried that this aircraft could fall into the hands of the rebels. To prevent that, we are placing four guards here on a twenty-four hour basis. Also, I have been ordered to immobilise it by removing a part from the engine."

Ken exploded. "I don't want some fool tinkering with my plane. This aircraft is my livelihood. I have a paying guest arriving this evening."

"Mr. Marshal, we both have no choice in the matter. I am following orders. This man…" He pointed to a soldier in coveralls. "…Is a trained mechanic from the base. He will remove an item that can easily be refitted."

The captain nodded to the mechanic, who opened the engine side cover.

"You should be pleased, Mr. Marshal, that we are placing guards to look after your property. I am sure you would not want it destroyed."

The captain gave Ken a meaningful look. "And besides, do not place too much hope on your guest arriving."

"What do you mean?"

"There is a large storm coming in from the south-east. I think your tourist will turn round and fly back to Mabarta."

Ken was puzzled. "How do you know he's flying? He could be coming by road."

The officer shrugged. "Just a guess. Most tourists fly in."

The mechanic handed the captain the rotor arm from the distributor and closed the side cover.

"Thank you for your cooperation." He smiled and jerked his head towards the shore.

Ken opened the side cover and checked the mechanic had replaced the distributor cap properly. He didn't want any dampness getting in there. The captain drove off in the Land rover, leaving four men near the land end of the jetty.

Ken looked over to the south-east. The sky was as black as ink and he could feel the wind rising. A large storm was gathering. He hoped Jones hadn't decided to fly. That storm was moving right into the flight path from Mabarta.

Chapter 42

Jan pushed forward slightly again on the controls.

"Now we is at our correct attitude. We has to stay at this height until we's gets to Malenga."

"How come? What's to stop you going up or down?" Phil asked through a mouthful of chicken roll.

"Our flight plan says we is to fly this high. That's to stop us from crashing into some other oke. Another plane can fly above or below depending his flight plan sees."

Phil nodded. "So it's impossible to collide?"

"Not unless we have to go up or down in an emergency like, then I as to tell them at Mabarta tower."

"So it's just a case of flying straight now in the right direction."

"Ja, but it's not so easy. If we have a strong crosswind, the plane can be pointed the right way, but also moving sideways. If we have a strong headwind, it will take longer to get there, so you can't calculate your arrival on speed and time."

Phil's confidence regressed back to zero after this enlightenment.

"So what's to stop us from getting lost? You have GPS, right?"

"Ja I has, but its sommer getting fixed. On a short flight like this one we can't be too far outs. If I sees the river ever so often I knows we is going to the lake."

Phil had fallen into the trap of asking too many questions again. Jan gave him another can of beer, which he accepted. Being drunk was an improvement on being scared shitless.

Phil decided this would be the first and last time he flew 'Central African Mystery Tours'.

Chapter 43

Sunday had worked in the contract manager's garden at the construction camp for the past two years. Having suffered in the past from TB, he appeared younger than he actually was because of his size. It was frustrating being seventeen and being treated like a fourteen-year-old. Nobody took him seriously. Even his mother hugged him like a child when he returned home every day to the small village near the golf club. Secretly, he enjoyed those moments of affection his mother bestowed on him.

Even Mr. Galleria patted him on the head like the little white dog every time they won the best garden of the camp competition. The contracts manager displayed the little tin cup with pride of place on top of his television. Sunday received an extra month's pay every six months because of winning the competition. The project manager's wife had tried to lure him to work in her garden. She only wanted to win the cup. The extra money would have been useful, but Sunday did not want to desert the garden he had created over the years. He and the little white dog were also close companions. It was a lonely business working every day from dawn to dusk in someone's garden.

Sunday looked up at the sky. He would have to leave soon, because of the curfew. It was a long walk back to the village on the other side of the town. There was great excitement in the air. Soldiers were everywhere. He could even hear gunfire now and again in the distance.

Last year at the army camp the soldiers had laughed at him when he had gone there to enlist.

"Come back in ten years' time."

Sunday had cried all night inconsolably in his mother's arms.

Today was special. His boss had a very important visitor. The commandant of the army himself was here. Maybe he could speak to him before he could drive away in his shiny green staff car.

Two of his personal guards waited for him outside with sub machine guns over their shoulders. They wore red berets with the winged, silver paratroops insignia, which flashed in the afternoon sun. As he weeded the flowerbed, he stole the odd admiring glance at these two impressive soldiers while they waited for their commander. One glanced at his watch, then spoke to the other. They threw down their cigarettes, then something very strange happened. The one who had spoken rolled something in Sunday's direction while the other un-slung his submachine gun.

Inside the house, the commandant was admiring Galleria's cup while they discussed the local situation. He held it in his left hand. An outline of a bird reflected from the polished surface. He glanced at his watch, then stood with his back to the wall. There was a clatter of automatic fire from outside. Galleria dived to the floor with his drink in his hand. A split second later, the windows blew inwards, showering the room with splintered glass and wood. The tin cup was thrown down as the commandant drew his pistol. His boot crumpled the cup flat as he ran outside. The contracts manager lay amongst the shattered glass until he was called from outside. With his ears ringing from the explosion, he disentangled himself from the debris and stumbled into the garden. There was a jagged, smoking hole in the manicured lawn and what looked like bundle of red rags lying in the flowerbed.

"Dai porko. What has happened," he gasped.

The commandant pointed with his pistol.

"Your garden boy tried to throw a grenade through the window. Luckily my men shot him before he could do so."

Galleria stared in disbelief. "But Sunday is not a rebel."

The commandant lifted his hands. "How can you tell the difference between a rebel and an ordinary person?"

Galleria stared at him. *This must be a trick question.*

"I do not know," he yelled.

"Exactly. We have the same problem until they attack. I think you and I together made too good a target for this one. We have heard rumours of rebels working inside this camp. I am not pleased."

The commandant raised his voice. "I was nearly killed inside your camp. All none expatriates must be removed immediately for the safety of your people. Do you not agree?"

The contracts manager was still dazed from the explosion. "Yes. I suppose so."

Three security vans pulled up outside the house.

"Remove all non-expats from the camp," the commandant ordered.

The vans sped away and turned in different directions. Galleria stared at the heap in the flowerbed that had once been Sunday, and vomited. The commandant helped him back inside.

"Do not worry. My men will remove that mess from your nice garden."

He nodded to the two soldiers, who rolled the broken body into a plastic sheet and dumped it into the rear hatch of the car. Unbeknown to him, one of Sunday's dreams was about to come true. He was about to ride in a military staff car.

Chapter 44

Jan fumbled at the flap of his bush shirt top pocket and pulled out a small curved pipe. Phil didn't object. The smell of stale farts inside the Cessna's cabin was starting to accumulate. The beer Jan had been feeding him gave him a sedated outlook of his present predicament, which was a definite plus. The negative effect was a full bladder. Phil turned round and examined the cabin behind him.

"Where's the washroom?"

All he could see were two pairs of empty seats and the baggage compartment. Jan's bushy eyebrows kitted together.

"Where's the what?"

"The washroom. The toilet. Where's the toilet?"

Jan's eyebrows rose in surprise, then he started laughing. "You is joking, right?"

Phil realised with horror he was drinking beer inside a plane with no toilet. Jan eventually stopped laughing.

"Some twins have a tube you sommer piss down. It sounds like a suction pipe. If you have a groot peel its best not to put it in too far or it could get stuck."

Jan started laughing again. Phil clenched his teeth together in discomfort. He didn't find any of this remotely funny.

"So how do you pee up here?"

"Peeing is easy. I use a condom then ties a knot in it. Kaking is a problem."

Jan rummaged around with one hand in a plastic shopping bag and pulled out a packet of condoms. "What flavour does yous prefer?"

Phil took the packet and struggled into the back seats. He wouldn't be able to pee with Jan watching. As it was, it was difficult to get started. It felt unnatural, as if he was pissing in his pants. Once started, it was difficult to stop. He filled one and half condoms. Jan was doing the same with one hand.

"I once had a woman passenger with the same problem. She managed somehow. Never saw her on the return trip. I doesn't knows why."

Phil struggled back into the co-pilot's seat. He felt much better. He realised that was the second occasion he had peed into a condom that day.

"Grab hold of the stick on your sides while I cut some biltong."

Phil was horrified. "I can't fly a plane."

"It's easy. Just hold it straight and level."

Phil took hold of the controls with ridged hands and arms. Jan let go of the controls on his side and started tying a double knot in all the full condoms.

"Don't want these donnerser things leaking."

He placed them back into the plastic bag and tied the handles together.

"Now, whatever you do, don't step on this ear bag with those big feet of yours."

The Cessna had drifted over to the right and the wing on Phil's side was starting to dip. He was powerless to do anything about it. His hands and arms were frozen.

Jan pulled it back on course with one hand, then released the controls again.

"You has to relax. You can't fly a plane sitting like a statue."

Jan busied himself cutting some dried meat into strips with a penknife. Jan offered Phil a piece with the same hand he'd used to fill his condom.

"This ears what you Yanks call jerky. Have some; it's lekker."

Phil politely refused. He was starting to sweat and his arms ached. The Cessna was drifting off to the right again. He turned the control and over corrected. The plane was now turning left. Jan pulled it straight again.

"Now laster, you has been climbing." He pointed to the altimeter. "See, now we is too high." He pushed the stick forward slightly and waited.

"Now we are right." He pulled back slightly. "Daar sy.

You see, this pointer is not moving anymore. So to fly level keeps one eye on this. To fly straight keeps one eye on this." He pointed to a compass just above the centre of the windscreen.

"That is our heading. If we turn, it sommer moves round. The other one is this."

He pointed to a large, round, green gauge with some horizontal lines moving slowly up and down. "This ear shows the wings are level. So keep one eye ear, as well."

"That's three eyes you mentioned. I only have two."

Jan shook his head. "You don't sommer keep staring at em. You glance like from one to the other. Ear, try again."

Jan released the controls and sat back, cutting some more biltong. Phil hadn't time to look out of the windscreen. His eyes were constantly moving from one instrument to the other while he moved the controls ever so slightly.

"Daar sy. Now pretend the plane is balanced on top on a pointed tower and you is to stop it falling off."

He couldn't think of anything less relaxing, but he understood what Jan meant.

There was some slight turbulence. Phil felt as if he was walking a tightrope while somebody was shaking it. The Cessna swung to and fro while Phil over corrected, but it was starting to settle down into something like level and straight. The stress of concentration was very tiring, but Phil also felt excited. A noise distracted him. It sounded like a hog foraging for food in a farmyard. Phil glanced across at Jan. His head was propped against the side window and his mouth hung open.

Holy shit! I'm flying a godamn airplane.

Chapter 45

Three floors underground and eleven floors below the apartment level, the control room was staffed by eight of the senior sons. Nabusano observed a faint blip on the outer edge of the radar screen. The system was old, and had been built for detail rather than range. Even a flock of birds could be tracked flying over the surface of the lake. The blip was appearing in the top right edge of the huge circular screen. Malenga, shown as an inlet on the mainland shoreline, lay approximately one quarter of the way from the top of the screen and slightly over to the right. Forty years ago, the system had been assembled on the island, but would still surpass any modern installation in Africa.

"This aircraft contains an agent of the west," he explained.

"He seeks to destroy us."

Nabusano scrutinised each face in turn. These were the most loyal of the followers. They were old enough to have witnessed the power. The younger ones living in Malenga had been contaminated, and could no longer be fully trusted. They had never been exposed to the fear and wonder that the power instilled.

Nabusano's bony finger tapped on the consol in front of him to emphasise his words.

"If the aircraft survives the storm that is building in its path, and if it appears to be able to land safely, you will inform your brother, the commandant. Do you understand?"

"Yes, father," they all answered

"Continue to track any craft that leaves the shore, and have them intercepted for searching. Your brothers..." He paused for a moment. "Have failed to find the white man, Parker."

The control room staff glanced at each other with a flicker of fear in their eyes.

"Keep me informed."

The wheelchair hummed as it turned from the consol and travelled towards the lift. He stopped and turned the chair.

"I presume the equipment is working perfectly?"

"Yes, father," they all answered again.

Every hour that passed, Parker was becoming stronger, as he himself was becoming weaker. Soon the Englishman would become too powerful to be confronted by any human force. The plan to exploit Parker's weakness would not fail. Of that he was sure.

Chapter 46

Roberto was roughly pushed to one side as the Medusacor men entered the house. The girls had been terrified by the explosion inside the camp.

"What is going on? You cannot enter my house by force. I will complain to the company."

The senior of the four men turned to face Roberto. "A rebel has been killed inside the camp. All none expatriates are to be removed. This is an order from your manager."

Sara and Monica put up some resistance, but were manhandled outside and bundled into one of the waiting vans. Roberto tried to intervene, but was pushed away from the door. The largest of the men remained behind and blocked the exit with his yardstick in his hand. Roberto could see this man was only too eager to use it by the way he kept striking the bird tattoo on the palm of his left hand. The van drove away with Sara and Monica enclosed in the back.

The tall guard pointed his nightstick at Roberto. "Tell your friend, Parker, to give up, or you will never see these women again."

He turned and left Roberto staring after him in amazement.

Chapter 47

Ken fastened an extra nylon rope from each wingtip back down to the jetty. The wind from the south-east was steadily increasing. *Don't want the old girl flipping over when that lot arrives.*

The gently-lapping surface of the lake was gradually being transformed into waves. He examined the skyline again. If the wind didn't change direction, it looked as if the centre of the storm would pass by towards the east. Even so, the approaching storm was one of the ugliest Ken had ever seen. He walked towards the four soldiers, who had made a makeshift shelter with Ken's wooden ramp. They had wedged it up against a large tree with the surface facing the wind. Crouching behind in their waterproof capes, they were all busy smoking. Ken smiled and waved as he walked past.

"With any luck, they will be stuck by bloody lightning," he muttered.

Halfway to the cabin, he scanned the hillside for any sign of the Medusacor man with the radio. He also must be sheltering amongst the trees from the gusting wind. Ken lifted the trapdoor on the veranda.

"Bill," he called. "Come inside, old chap, we need to talk. I will leave Patch on the veranda. He will bark if anyone comes."

They both entered the cabin after Ken had pointed to the south-eastern sky. An indignant Patch was ordered outside.

"There are four bloody soldiers guarding the plane at this end of the jetty, and that storm is coming. I think they are more interested in sheltering than anything else, but they would certainly see anyone walking towards the plane. I can't see that bugger on the hill, but I'm sure he's there. Also, they brought a mechanic here who removed the rotor arm from the old girl."

Bill ran his hand through his hair. "Shit, so we can't fly?"

Ken smiled. "Yes, we can. That mechanic doesn't know his ass from his elbow. If he had opened the other side cover, he would have seen another ignition system for the engine. Piston engine planes have two of everything in case one packs up."

Bill thought a moment. "So, if I get rid of the soldiers and that man on the hill, we can fly."

Ken nodded. "Yes, depending on the storm." He checked his watch. "Could take three or four hours for the worst to pass. After taking off, I will fly west-south-west to Sid's place."

"Who's Sid"?

"He runs a game lodge on the other side of the lake. We work together. I sometimes bring him a tourist or fly his guests on tours."

Bill nodded. "Yes, that sounds good. At least I will be in a different country."

"But you won't be safe there. Nabusano has a helicopter and two bloody cruisers that look like coastguard cutters. It's best you head inland by road from Sid's place."

Bill shook his head. "I can't do that. Nabusano has shown his hand and at the moment he's winning."

Bill sat down and rubbed the palm of his hand over his mouth. "If I don't come up with a plan, I will have to give him what he wants."

"For godsake, why?"

"Roberto just phoned. Madusacor has taken Sara and Monica from the camp. I think Nabusano will kill them, unless I give him the ball."

Ken sat down heavily in the other chair. "Good Lord. What are you going to do?"

"I will go and pick up Roberto from the camp, or he could also become a hostage. Then we will fly out of here and hopefully come up with some sort of plan to rescue the girls. That's all I can think of at the moment."

Ken stood up and returned with two glasses and a bottle of whisky. "How are you going to get to the camp and back? They will be expecting you."

"I will use the motorbike and take the footpaths along the coast. The storm and the coming darkness will give me some sort of cover."

Ken took a sip of his drink. "Don't forget you will have to cross the water front. There are no footpaths there."

"Yes, I know, but the way things stand, there are not many options."

Ken cleared his throat. "I hope you realise that once Nabusano has what he wants, he will still kill everyone."

Bill just nodded as he stared into his glass.

Chapter 48

Phil noticed that a small square screen in the centre of all the instruments had changed colour. Jan had never mentioned it, so it couldn't be all that important. He was pretty sure most of the screen had been green before. Now it was orange, and a red patch was spreading rapidly down from the top.

The inside of the cabin was becoming dim. Daylight was starting to fade, giving the impression it was evening. He checked his watch. It was twenty-past-something. He quickly glanced over at Jan's watch. It was stopped at five to eleven. Phil had been so preoccupied with checking the gauges that he had never actually looked through the windscreen since Jan had fallen asleep. The whole western horizon ahead was in darkness. He found a clock among the instruments, which showed ten to five. Something was wrong. The sun set in the west at seven. Columns of high, grey billowing clouds boxed in the tiny airplane on all sides. Could it be he had descended into the cloud layer? No, the altitude was correct.

Large raindrops splashed onto the windscreen like hundreds of birds pecking on the glass. He hunted in a panic for a switch marked 'wiper', but couldn't find one. Some of the drops had ice in them.

"Jan! Jan! Wake up. Where's the wiper switch at?"

Phil kicked the pilot's foot. He was unable to loosen a hand from the control column. Jan grunted and started stirring.

"Vot maak jy? Vot fault?"

"I can't find the godamn wiper switch."

"You don't need wipers on a single. The fan blows alus off." Jan squinted out of the side window, then looked around with large eyes. "Yessus, vot the fuck is going on? Where the fuck is we?"

311

He stared at the small screen, which was now all red, and grabbed the controls, pulling them back sharply. The stall warning buzzer sounded at the same time that Jan pushed the throttle fully foreword.

"Straps yourself in. We is in for a rough ride," he shouted.

The buzzer stopped as the Cessna climbed at a steep angle.

"Is this a Charley Bravo?" Phil asked anxiously.

"Nay, it's more likes an army of em. We is to try to go's over." He pointed at the small red screen. "I doesn't know which way to turn. The whole blixamer screen is red."

"Shouldn't we inform Mabarta tower we are climbing?"

"Doesn't matter; only a complete palooka would sommer fly in this."

With that reassuring thought, Phil gripped the bottom of his seat as the turbulence started.

Jan adjusted the fuel mixture to rich, for more power.

"Now I must keep an eye on the temperatures, or she could sommer overheat."

He tapped the gauges marked 'engine oil temperature' and 'manifold temperature'. "This rain and ice should keep her fairly cool. It must be coming from high ups to be ice. I only hopes we can climb over it."

The whole aircraft vibrated with the increase in RPM and noise as it climbed steeply into the black clouds.

"Can't we kinda turn around?"

Jan shook his head. "No. It looks like this storm is heading back towards Mabarta. If we goes that way, we could be in it longer."

"What about going around the edge?"

Jan looked out of both side windows. "I doesn't know how groot this thing is. We are in it now. If you sees it soon enough on the storm warning." He pointed to the small red screen. "Then it's possible to go's round. It's too late now. All we can do is climb and keep our poopholes closed."

Jan wrestled with the controls as a series of updrafts tried to flick up the left wing. The long pointer on the altimeter steadily revolved while the short one doggedly followed at a much slower rate. Phil jerked against his shoulder straps as the Cessna suddenly fell for a couple of seconds. He pulled all the straps tighter and started polishing his glasses. Joe Lozano would be laughing if he could see him now. A huge jolt from below sent his glasses flying out of his hands. They came to rest on the floor between his feet. Phil couldn't reach them unless he loosened his straps. There was no way he was going to do that.

A faint beeping noise could be heard above the din of the engine.

"Oh shit. What's that?" he yelled.

Jan gave him a sideways glance. "I thinks it's your phone."

Phil stared at him for a moment before comprehending what he had said. He had placed Watson's phone in the shoulder bag. It was rather bulky and heavy to carry in his pocket. He rummaged around inside the bag while the beeping continued. A jerk caused him to bang his forehead on the side of the pilot's seat, making him slightly dizzy. The phone eventually in his hand, he raised it to his ear and promptly smacked himself on the side of the head.

"Shit." It was like waving a house brick around inside the cabin.

"Hello," Phil shouted, with one finger stuck into his other ear. "Yes, Mr. Watson. I'm two thirds the way to Malenga… No. I couldn't phone you. I was so busy trying to escape from Pointer. He tried to have me arrested at the airport because of the gun… What? Say again… Heck, are you sure? And the guy at the registrar of companies? Holy shit."

There was now a long pause while Phil listened.

"Tell the ambassador it's not my fault. I'm not killing them… No, we can't turn back. We are in the middle of a storm." Phil nodded in frustration. "Yes. I understand, but the pilot says we cannot turn back." Pause. "No, he's not an imbecile. He's got me this far."

Jan glared across at Phil. "Tell die blicksem to foot sack."

A series of jolts caused Phil to smack himself a few times with the phone. "Hello. Hello," he shouted, then checked the screen. "Shit. I've switched it off."

The plane was now acting like a shuttlecock in a game of badminton. Phil placed the phone back in the bag before it could knock anyone unconscious. He leant over and shouted in Jan's ear while steadying himself on the side of the pilot's seatback.

"That guy with the ponytail who tried to stop us."

Jan nodded. "Ja?"

"He's dead. Somebody killed him."

"Good riddance. He nearly killed us."

"Also, another man I saw in Mabarta this morning."

"Ja."

"He is also dead."

Jan raised his eyebrows. "Doesn't sound lekker for anybody you meets."

"Watson says to turn back. The ambassador will meet us at the airport. Says to throw the gun out the window."

Jan shook his head. "I can't turn back. We will be lucky to make Malenga strip. If I turn in this crosswind, she will flip over and go into a spiral dive."

"Watson says the same people who killed those men may try to kill us at Malenga."

"Tell die blicksemar Watson to sommer come and fly this ear fucking plane. I is too busy to thinks just now. Let's see if we makes it out of this here storm first."

The driving rain streamed off the windscreen in rivulets. At least there was no more ice mixed with it. Phil hoped that was a good sign. Lightning crisscrossed the dark sky all around them.

Still climbing, they entered black columns of cloud, which looked like smoke from the Gulf War oil well fires. The only illumination in the clouds around them was the dull, constantly flickering glow of the tropical storm.

Chapter 49

Sara and Monica huddled together inside the back of the speeding Madusaco van. At the end of the camp road, the vehicle had turned right, not left towards the town. This was the road to Mabarta. They glanced at each other apprehensively. Where on earth were these men taking them?

There was a roadblock ahead. The driver spoke on the radio and they were waved through without stopping. After another two kilometres, they turned right, towards the lake. This was the gravel road to the crocodile farm. The girls remembered what James had said about Nabusano's crocodile farm and the disappearing people. Apprehension turned into fear. They started screaming to be released. The guard in the rear of the panel van slapped them both hard across the face until they were quiet. Their shouts of protest were reduced to sobs. Much to their relief, the van passed through the farm and stopped at the shore of the lake. A sleek-looking cruiser was moored at the farm wharf, waiting for them.

Under different circumstances, a trip on this millionaire's boat would have been anticipated with great excitement. The vessel had an air of luxury and speed about it, but the black-uniformed crew also gave the boat an atmosphere of power and efficiency.

A second security van pulled up behind them before the rear doors were unlocked. They were not taking any chances. The tall guard from the other vehicle handcuffed the women's hands behind their backs before they were led away towards the cruiser. The man who had slapped them laughed while forming his hands into the jaws of a crocodile. He followed the women in great amusement as he snapped his hands open and closed. The tall guard turned and smashed his fist into the other's face,

315

knocking him backwards to the ground. He spat on the prone figure and took a step forward. The surprised Medusaco men took a step backwards.

"You people of the mainland have brains like chickens. That is because you worship the false gods." He glared at the group of guards. "Nothing of this will be spoken of or you will be punished by the anger of my father."

The men glanced at one another and shuffled their feet.

"Go now to the water front. The white man, Parker, may attempt to journey to the construction camp. It is an easy place to kill him."

He turned, dismissing them, and pushed the women forward. The crew of the cruiser seemed reluctant to set foot on shore. Two of them quickly cast off the mooring lines after the girls had stepped on board. The tall man removed his cap and shirt and threw them back on land as if they were contaminated. A crew member handed him the same type of black shirt. The only difference was the cap badge and shoulder flash being a bolt of lightning instead of the golden crown of Medusaco.

Down below, the girls sat in a sumptuous lounge behind the wheelhouse. The sound of running feet could be heard overhead as ropes were stowed in lockers and the crew took up their sailing positions.

Further aft, the throaty roar of two powerful diesel engines began to vibrate the craft.

The sky was dark and a strong wind blew from the lake to the shore. Flecks of white foam lifted from the crest of the normally-small lapping waves. Two men pushed off from the wharf with long boat hooks, and braced themselves for the expected acceleration of the vessel. The helmsman glanced at the tall man standing next to him, who nodded. He was obviously the captain of the boat when he was not masquerading as a security guard. The cruiser reversed slowly away from its mooring, then suddenly lurched forward. The bows swung round to point to the centre of the vast expanse of water, and gradually lifted as the throttles were opened.

"Radio control that we are returning to base. Both guests are on board."

Another of the crew nodded and started speaking into a hand mike.

The father would be pleased at the success of the mission so far. Failure was not permitted.

He surveyed the darkening sky and the surface of the agitated lake. Spray blew back from either side of the bows as the craft thudded continuously into the oncoming waves. He knew from experience that the waters could become very angry this time of the year.

Chapter 50

Bill opened the back door a crack and peeped outside. Patch ran around in circles, wagging his tail, but thankfully did not bark.

The light was fading rapidly due to the approaching storm. Tree branches waved to and fro in the rising wind, as if warning him to stay inside. Bill checked his watch. Six o'clock. It was usually dark by seven every night there on the equator. The overcast sky would bring that time forward. He pulled the ball away from his skin to see how dark it was for a normal person.

"Hmm, fairly dim, but not dark," he said to Patch, who cocked his head to one side.

He released his shirt, allowing the ball to touch his skin again. The pupils of his eyes expanded and the view down the hill gradually brightened. A peal of thunder rolled overhead and large raindrops started to thump on the veranda roof. That was what he had been waiting for. *Less chance of being seen in conditions of heavy rain.*

One disadvantage to seeing in the dark was being unable to differentiate between light and darkness. He closed the door as Ken came up behind him. "Okay, I'm going. You drive up to the golf club. I'll meet you there on our return. Be prepared to fly out at a moment's notice. Is the plane ready?"

"Yes. I even put a box of provisions inside and a couple of blankets just in case we have to ruddy well camp out somewhere."

Bill slipped into his leather jacket and patted his pockets and shirt. "Passport, money and the ball. I'm all set."

"My passport's in the old girl and the key is in my pocket, so I'm ready."

"Okay, when you get halfway up the hill, stop and kick your tyres. That will distract anybody long enough for me to slip out into the bush. Slam your door as a signal."

Ken smiled. "I have to bloody well slam it anyway, to shut the bugger. What I'm worried about are those ruddy soldiers."

Bill puffed out his cheeks and gave Ken a despairing look. "One thing at a time, old friend. I'm sure I can handle them. Now's the time if you want to pull out. Just say the word."

Ken stared at him for a moment. "Actually, that's really fucking tempting." He shook his head. "But I think not. Come on, Patch, we are going to the club for a drinky-poo." He opened the door and walked outside. "See you later, alligator."

Ken climbed into the Stout, followed by Patch, who leapt over him to land in the co-pilot's seat. The engine struggled to start, so Ken freewheeled down the hill a short distance and let the clutch out in third gear. After a couple of jerks, the Stout fired up, followed by black smoke.

The soldiers at the jetty stood up for a better view, then crouched back down under their makeshift shelter after losing interest in the old white man and his dog. Their primary concern now was to keep dry without leaving their post.

Bill picked up the motorcycle helmet and waited by the back door, listening to the Stout's progress up the hill. The engine slowed to a tick over and then, a moment later, the door slammed. Bill zipped up the front of his jacket and turned up the collar. *Time to get wet again.* He ducked outside and quietly closed the door behind him.

Running bent over double, he reached the bush in about three seconds, then listened intently. The Stout's door banged again, then the engine noise rose in volume as it laboured up the remainder of the hill.

Squalls of rain advanced over the hillside in waves. To Bill's acute sense of hearing, the drops pelting down on the leaves sounded like the drumming of hailstones on a tin roof.

The Madusacor man would have positioned himself where he could observe the cabin and the track. Bill rubbed some mud over his face and slowly raised his head above the bush in front of him. There was a prominent rise of ground surmounted by a clump of trees about three quarters of the way up the slope. He examined the trees for a full minute before he noticed a head turned towards the direction of the track. At least the diversion had worked. Bill cut across the hillside while watching the head. As it turned back to observe the cabin, he froze in a crouched position, then continued slowly traversing the hill. At a point midway between the cabin and the track, Bill started climbing. He was now out of the guard's field of vision, unless the man turned his head back towards the track.

The main problem now was that the Honda lay halfway up the hill between the guard and the cabin. There was no way Bill could lift it out of the thorn bush without being seen. He now had two choices. Wait until it was completely dark or eliminate the guard. Even if he didn't see the bike, he would certainly hear it start up.

> The man on the hill pulled the peak of his cap down to shield his eyes from the driving rain. Someone shouted and waved further down the slope. It was the white man Parker. The one they were all looking for.

He snatched up his rifle and ran towards Parker who stood with his hands raised. When he reached for his radio it was plucked from his fingers and flew into the white man's hand.

"I will take that, thank you."

His mouth fell open and his eyes widened in disbelief. He suddenly realised he had made a terrible mistake. Parker was not harmless and was not surrendering.

Another unexplainable thing happened. The barrel of his rifle flipped up and struck him hard between the eyes, causing him to stagger backwards. The last thing he saw was the Lee Enfield spinning round like a drum major's baton. The butt caught him a hefty blow to the side of the head that sent him cart wheeling down the hill. He came to rest in an unconscious heap up against a tree.

"One down, and two hundred to go," Bill murmured.

He focussed on the rifle, and gradually the barrel bent like a banana. In the thorn bush to the left, Bill visualised the motorcycle and attempted to lift it out. To his surprise, the Honda appeared above the bushes and floated over to him. *That's something new. As long as I have a clear picture of the thing and know exactly where it is, it's still possible to move it.*

He started the bike and rode up through the trees towards the golf club road.

The soldiers down at the jetty heard a motorcycle start high on the hillside, then returned to their conversation. They had not been briefed on anything concerning a motorcycle, so did not place any significance on the fading sound of the Honda.

Chapter 51

James and his family had arrived home safely. It was nearly curfew time. The heavy rain drummed on the tin roof and the wind rattled the corrugated sheets.

He sat in his favourite chair in front of the fire, sipping a mug of African tea. Lots of milk and sugar. His wife had lit the fire before going to bed.

James suspected the gossiping must have worn her out. The children had also gone to bed, frightened by the thunder. It would be cold again tonight. The rains had brought a sudden drop in temperature with them, especially at night.

James sat unmoving, his mind a turmoil. He had spent his life teaching the African people to disregard myth and superstition, and to rather adopt the Western civilization's system of technology and science. Now, an intelligent European, a geologist and technician, had shown him that there was some truth to the old legends. He himself had not believed until he had seen the little finger missing. Roberto had believed for a while until his culture had overridden the truth. A white man could not accept the whole truth without undisputable proof.

James knew in his heart it was true. It was the same man on both mats.

Chapter 52

The Cessna climbed through the turbulence with zero visibility. There was less engine noise than before, because of a loss of power due to the thinner atmosphere. A sudden shower of hailstones bounced of the windscreen, startling Phil as he clung to the seat.

"Hailstones in Africa?" he questioned Jan.

"Ja, it's cold up here. The groot ones can reach the ground, especially in Johannesburg, cos it's also high ups. There, they bliksem the cars and breaks the house windows ever so often at a certain time of year."

"Are you from Johannesburg?"

"Ghot no. Die plek is full of sout peels. Ek is from the Karoo. Only good for sheep, goats and Ostrich. I was a sheep farmer. Then the price of Mutton fell down and them polucas at the bank foreclosed on me. My wife up and left. Said I was a failure. I only comes out with my first plane, which I managed to pays off eventually."

Phil kept the conversation going. It took his mind off the present situation. "What about children?" he ventured.

"Ja is one masie, but she married a sout peel so I doesn't speak much to hers now anymore."

"But your friend Mister Marshal's a sout peel, err Englishman, isn't he?"

"Ja, but he's my sout peel. All us Afrikaaners have one sout peel that belongs to us. If somebody messes with my sout peel, I'll sommer bliksem them."

"Oh, I see," said Phil, completely mystified.

The storm warning screen had developed some patches of orange in both top corners instead of being totally red.

"Are we going to make it?" Phil shouted, pointing to the display.

"Ja, looks that way. Not possible climb much higher or we needs oxygen. This plane not pressurised. Just now we both falls asleep and no wakes up. This climb used up a lot of time and fuel, but necessary."

Jan pushed forward slightly on the controls, causing the aircraft to level out. Speed and visibility began to increase, but the rain still pelted the windscreen, only to be blown off in rivulets by the propeller.

Phil suddenly remembered the wad of papers in his back pocket, and pulled them out. They were all the photocopies of the registration certificates on his list. Shuffling though them, he saw that the owner's name was the same on every one, and not changed since the original registration. *It would have to be a family where the companies were inherited from father to son. Only one surname. No first names. Defiantly a close-knit family and one of the richest in the world. Not mega rich like Bill Gates with his fifty or sixty billion, but rich nevertheless. Why all the secrecy? It's not a crime to be rich. Is it possible this family wants to remain obscure so badly they are willing to kill?* It didn't seem likely, but two men were dead and he had the feeling of becoming a candidate for assassination. There was some secret this family wanted to remain hidden at all costs.

Could be Collins was right. He may be flying into a nest of terrorists.

"How far to Malenga?" Phil asked.

"We should be right on tops of Malenga now. Possible a bits north or south. When we goes down, I needs to see if we is over water or land. If we is over water, I needs to go north. If we is over land, I needs to go south to find the shoreline. We needs to get down quick 'cos the light is nearly klaar. Die oke at the strip has a genset and a few lights, but notink lekker to sees good. If there is any cows, we is in biar kak. I will calls him now to tell 'im we is landing."

"You think we should land or turn back?" He didn't like the idea of crashing into a cow.

"We is 'ear now. You paid to go to Malenga and now you is 'ear." Jan shook his head and started to descend.

"The man on the phone said it's too dangerous. I'm starting to think he is right."

"Die poluka who says I is a imbecile can voetsek," Jan growled. He picked up the hand mike. "Malenga, Malenga. Malenga strip come in." He released the talk button and heard the crackle of static.

"He knows what he's talking about; he's CIA."

"Malenga, Malenga, come in."

"Malenga receiving. Go ahead."

"This is Alpha Victor Delta Zulu from Mabarta. I hopes to be landing in twenty to thirty minutes. What is the conditions down there? Over."

"Alpha Victor Delta Zulu, we have low cloud and rain. The wind is from the south and the light is fading. Land as soon as possible. Over."

"Roger, will do. Over and out."

Jan turned to Phil with a smile on his face. "Daar sy. No problem. I doesn't care if die oke is YMCA. Tonight I'll be lekker drunk with my pet sout peel, Kenny Marshal."

Chapter 53

The handcuffs had been removed. There was nowhere for Sara and Monica to go, except over the side to a watery grave. Left to themselves, they had found cold water in the bar refrigerator. The cabin was fitted out with polished wood and leather chairs. Thick carpets lined the floor. The raised keel at the bows slapped into the waves in quick succession, sending buffeting shocks through the entire structure of the powerful vessel. A door opened from the wheelhouse and the tall man ducked his head while descending the four steps into the lounge.

"I see you ladies have made yourselves at home."

His spray-wet face smiled, but his eyes remained hard and unfeeling.

"Where are you taking us?" Sara asked.

Monica was too frightened to speak. He walked over to the bar and gently rested his finger tips on its surface. His face relaxed as he felt the vibrations from the engines below.

"Machinery in motion is a truly wonderful thing."

"Where are you taking us?" Sara repeated.

He snapped out of his trance and glared at her anxious face. "Not many of your half of our tribe has the opportunity to set foot on Nabusano Island. You are honoured guests of the father until Parker brings him the new power of the river god."

He strode over to the girls and pulled each of their lips back from their teeth while they tried to resist.

"You two are good breeding stock."

He walked back to the bar and poured himself a drink.

"Tomorrow, if the father permits, I may personally take you two on a guided tour of the island. Having lived all your lives in and around Malenga, I'm sure you will be very impressed."

The captain topped up his glass with cognac and caressed the top of the bar again. "I have come to the time of my life when I am allowed to take a wife."

He glanced at the girls before continuing. "One of you could be privileged to fill that position. Either way, neither of you will ever return to the mainland."

The captain finished his drink, inclined his head, then returned to the wheelhouse.

"What are we going to do?" Monica sobbed.

"There's nothing we can do. Our lives are in Bill's hands."

"Even if he brings them what they want, we will never be released. You heard what that man said?"

"I know,' Sara agreed. "We just have to hope for the best. Bill and Roberto will do everything in their power to help us."

"But what can they do against men such as these?" Monica cried.

"I do not know, but they will think of something."

Chapter 54

Bill rode carefully, traversing the hillside in between the bush and the trees on his way to the track. He accelerated up the hill and joined the golf club road. It wasn't long before he found a footpath on the other side.

All he had to do now was follow the maze of footpaths in the general direction of the town. After crossing the water front, he would find other footpaths towards the camp.

The bike came to a skidding stop. How the hell was he going to cross the water front? It would take too long to find a way round the inland side of the town. The bush was very dense to the north of Malenga. The only people moving around town at this hour would be Madusacor.

He accelerated and swung the Honda round to retrace his route.

The guard on the hill was about his size.

Chapter 55

Ken sat at the golf club bar, nursing his second whisky. *Wouldn't do to get plastered at this stage of the game.*

The club had been virtually empty, except for two of Ken's old cronies, who had left complaining about the curfew. None of the contractors had been in, due to being confined to the camp. Ken poured an unfinished beer into a clean ashtray and set it down at his feet for Patch. Stubby tail wagging, Patch eagerly lapped up the beer. "Well, at least one of us can get pissed."

Ken knew from experience it was prudent to leave Patch outside after one of his binges, or he would fill the cabin with foul-smelling gas.

"No flying for you tonight," Ken whispered. "Not good form for both of us to risk our necks."

Alex, the old barman, was busy checking the day's takings. Ken had paid his hefty bar tab and given the barman a fair-sized tip. It wasn't often he had a pocket full of money, but when he did, he made sure Alex was taken care of. Hard times were probably just around the corner.

"Aren't you going home, Mister Ken?" Alex asked while glancing at the bar clock.

Ken shook his head. "No, not yet. My house is just over the road so I'm not worried about any curfew."

He couldn't tell Alex he was waiting for Bill and Roberto. If something went wrong and they didn't arrive, he could always sleep on one of the benches. *Wouldn't be the first time.*

He slid off the bar stool and walked around the club, trying to kill time before the next whisky. Colonial faces stared down at him from the endless rows of photographs hanging on the walls. Most of them were holding some sort of cup or trophy with a half-suppressed, smug smile on their lips. One creaking door led him into a library full of musty old books. Ken hadn't been in there for years. *I'm not much of a reader; more of a dreamer,* he told himself. 'Escapist' was nearer the truth, and other things like 'alcoholic', which he didn't want to admit.

The place was dark, so Ken tried the brass Victorian light switch on the wall. To his surprise, a couple of globes under grimy shades came on. He removed one book at random and flipped it open, which started him sneezing. A few fish moths scurried for cover over the edge of the yellow page. The last date stamp was nineteen fifty-six.

"Hmm, not much demand for you," he murmured. *Moby Dick must be out of fashion.*

It was the same for *Teach Yourself Ballroom Dancing* and *How to Improve Your Cricket.*

Local History caught his eye on the shelf below. *Maybe Bill will be interested in this one.*

Ken tucked it under his arm and brushed off his hands while moving to the door. He felt like some archaeologist examining an Egyptian tomb. He also felt very old and depressed. *The next whisky will certainly have to be a double.*

Chapter 56

As far as Bill could see though the visor, the long Waterfront Road looked deserted. He hoped nobody would notice the slightly-bent barrel of the rifle slung over his back. It was very difficult to bend something straight again.

Bill took a deep breath and moved slowly forwards in second gear. After the first block of buildings, he caught sight of someone waving frantically from the entrance of the next side street. He hesitated, then rode over to the figure to find three Madusacor men with Kalashnikovs at the ready. One of them signalled for him to cut the engine of the bike by passing his finger across his throat. The same man hissed a sentence of local language containing the name 'Parker', and made a shooing motion with his hands. Bill nodded and pushed the motorcycle down the side street, away from the Waterfront Road. Halfway between Waterfront and High Street, Bill stopped to catch his breath. He remounted the bike and rested his elbows on the tank.

A bicycle would have been better in this situation. If he made any noise, the Madusacor men would be all over him. He needed the motorbike to reach the camp so he couldn't ditch it. Bill continued pushing until he came to High Street. There was a slight down gradient in the right direction.

After that, he had no idea what he was going to do. *One thing at a time*, he told himself. *One thing at a time.* He sat on the Honda again to rest, and pulled the ball away from his skin.

Semi-darkness.

The light was fading fast and the town was quiet, as if it was holding its breath, waiting for something to happen. Flying ants surrounded the street lights that were still working, in clouds of beating wings. The first heavy rain of the year had prompted them to take flight. Normally, groups of women would now be standing below with outstretched white bed sheets to catch them. By all accounts, the abdomens were supposed to taste alright after frying.

Bill ran alongside the bike with tired legs, and jumped on, wobbling all over the road. The Honda continued for a while and then started to slow.

"Keep going, keep going," he urged.

This section was virtually flat, and he was losing momentum from steering round the pot holes.

"Keep going," he cursed.

The bike did keep going, and was actually picking up more speed. Bill looked round, expecting to see someone pushing.

"You stupid fucker," he hissed inside the helmet.

The ball. I can move with the ball. I don't even need to start the bloody engine.

The only negative factor was that he was actually pushing the Honda along with the handlebars and his knees clamped to either side of the tank. He concentrated more on the bike, and the pressure on his wrists and knees disappeared.

A roadblock caused him to slow down, and he pretended to push the bike along with his legs. The guards observed him pass, though, with slightly puzzled expressions on their faces. They must have suspected something was wrong with what they were seeing, but couldn't quite put their fingers on it.

Bill was nearing the edge of town. He observed, every now and then, a Madusacor man standing in the odd doorway. They would have been invisible in the darkness to a normal person. Ahead lay another down gradient before a hill leading out of town. Bill switched on the ignition and clicked the Honda into gear.

The noise would not cause any reaction from Madusacor because he was far away from the water front ambush. The engine started and he switched on the lights to give the impression of normality. Bill accelerated up the hill, then slowed down, searching for a foot path.

Chapter 57

The ice cubes in Ken's glass made a soft ringing sound as he swirled them round and round to mix the drink. It was still raining outside, but it looked like the storm would blow itself out. Ken studied his own reflection in the mirror behind the rows of bottles, then switched his attention to Alex.

"How long have you worked here at the club, old man?"

Alex smiled. "That's an easy one to answer." He held the glass he was polishing up to the light. "All my life. I have been here all my life."

Ken raised his eyebrows. "Really, I didn't know that; how come?"

"My father was the chief barman here. I started to help washing glasses, then became full time. In the old days there were six of us working here. Counting me and the other glass washer," he added. "Those days, we were very busy every night. On weekends there were tournaments and dancing in the big room next door." Alex polished the same spot on the bar with a faraway look in his eyes, then turned to Ken. "Now it's only me left, and the grounds man."

Ken cleared his throat. "Have a drink on me and tell me about the good old days."

Alex poured himself a large glass of sherry, then the faraway look returned to his face. "Yes, in those days this place was full of white people. We called everybody 'mister' or 'madam'. If you could remember their names, they tipped you better. Like a personal touch to the service. Black people never came here. There was no sign that said 'no blacks'. It was just understood that this was a white man's watering hole. The blacks had their own places in town, which was closer to home and cheaper." Alex shrugged. "So why come here just to make trouble?"

Ken made a crooked face. "Yes, I suppose so."

The barman lowered his voice. "After the whites had gone, some blacks made a point of coming here, but they soon lost interest. They found out there was nothing they wanted here. Too quiet and boring."

Ken swirled what was left of his ice cubes around in his glass. "Pretty bloody well boring now, if you ask me." He tipped his head back with the last of his drink. "So how many people actually come here? I only see those two who just left, and the odd contractor."

Alex sipped his sherry and narrowed his eyes. "There's Gwasa every Saturday morning to check the books and order new stock."

Ken raised his eyebrows, waiting for Alex to continue. The barman raised a hand to his chin, trying to think of more names.

"Good lord, is that all?" Ken asked.

Alex shook his head and leant forwards. "All the Nabusano's come here early Sunday morning to play golf from six until ten. It's the sons from the town, not from the island."

Ken pointed to his glass for a refill. "Too ruddy early for me. That's why I never see them."

"It's not the same group every week. They keep on changing like on a roster. Never came last Sunday."

The barman turned to fix Ken's drink.

"Sounds a hell of a lot. How many are there?"

Alex turned with the new drink and squinted. "I would say thirty to forty."

Ken's head snapped up. "What! Thirty to forty. You must be bloody joking?" He shook his head and smiled. "Thirty to forty. That's not possible, old man. You must be mistaken."

The barman shook his head. "No, I'm sure, and that's not counting the ones who stopped coming."

Ken's eyebrows knitted together. "What do you mean the ones who stopped coming?" he demanded.

Alex cast a nervous glance around the empty bar. "Keep your voice down. People who talk about them disappear."

"What do you mean 'the ones who stopped coming'?" Ken asked in a whisper.

The barman leant forward. "The older ones. They just stop coming. Younger ones replace them."

Ken smiled and pointed to his glass for ice. "You are mistaken. How can you possibly know that they are all sons of Nabusano?" He raised his eyebrows and spread his hands. "They could be friends of the family, or just businessmen from Mabarta."

Ken lifted his glass to his lips, quite confident he had solved the puzzle. Alex poured himself another sherry. He looked quite annoyed. Ken had never seen him in a bad mood before.

"I know I am right," he stated. "I can remember black faces very well, not like white people, who all look the same."

Ken coughed into his glass, then shook his head. "That doesn't make them all the same ruddy family. They could be bloody well anybody."

"No, they all have the same mark."

Ken massaged his forehead. "Mark. What mark?"

"The mark of Nabusano. It is a bird on the left hand." He pointed to his palm. "Here."

Ken was slightly more interested. "What does this bird look like?" He asked smugly. "Is it like this?" He held out his arms and turned his head to one side.

Alex shook his head. "No it is nothing like that."

"Hmm, so we can rule out most of the eagles. It doesn't have two heads pointing different ways. That would be a Russian eagle?"

"No, it is more like a vulture and it has wings like this." The barman raised both his arms as if surrendering, and looked up slightly to the one side.

"That's a bloody good impression of Al Johnson about to sing *Mammy*," Ken chuckled.

"The strange thing about this vulture is that it is sitting in a fire."

"Good lord!" Ken exclaimed. "That's a phoenix. You have just described a phoenix."

"What is a phoenix?"

"A mythical bird rising from the ashes. It's a symbol of being born again; a new beginning; a second chance."

Ken could see Alex had no idea what a phoenix was, so he must be telling the truth.

"When did you first notice this bird tattoo?"

"Oh." Alex scratched the top of his head. "About forty years ago."

Ken stroked his moustache. "Bloody thing must mean something?"

Chapter 58

Gusts of wind from the lake buffeted Bill from side to side as he snaked along the winding tracks. He was more exposed to the elements up on the shoreline than in the shelter of High Street. One path ran parallel to the edge of the lake, so Bill accelerated to make up for lost time.

Topping a slight rise, the track before him suddenly disappeared. Muddy water boiled and frothed below as it cut through the Earth in its frantic attempt to reach the lake. Bill had no time to react in any way. He gritted his teeth and waited for the inevitable impact with the opposite side of the ravine. Instead, he flew over the gap and landed some distance along the path on the other side. Bill allowed the Honda to slow down and stop. The engine ticked over for a while until he stopped it. He released the trapped air from his lungs and breathed deeply.

A cigarette was required. He removed the helmet and dried his hands on his shirt while rummaging around for his packet and lighter inside the leather jacket. The rifle strap was in the way, so he tossed the useless weapon into the bush. The Madusacor jacket, he pulled over his head like a tent, and managed to light up a bent cigarette.

What the hell happened? A professional dirt bike rider could have jumped the gap with some sort of ramp to take off, but not Bill, with no ramp. He realised he didn't need paths or motorbikes or aeroplanes. He could fly himself anywhere he wanted to go. Nabusano must have known it was only a matter of time before he discovered all these things. *That's why he's holding the girls; otherwise I can leave any time I want with the ball, never to be seen again.*

A drop of rain or sweat extinguished the cigarette, which he flicked away in disgust. The foul taste lingered in his mouth even after he had spat and wiped his lips with the back of his hand. Precious time was passing. They could decide to use Roberto as a hostage instead of bait at any moment.

Bill refastened the Madusacor jacket and replaced the helmet. He pulled the ball away from his skin. There was a slight glow over the next hill, which could only be the camp security lights.

"Right, let's see what we can do," he said.

The Honda lifted vertically one and a half metres, then gradually accelerated in a straight line towards the camp. Bill glanced down at the milometer, then cursed himself. It was showing zero because the wheels were not turning.

The bike lifted and lowered over the rough terrain to keep the same distance from the ground.

Bill didn't want to fly any higher until he gained more confidence. The concentration was tiring. A white shape suddenly loomed in front of him, and in a split second he raised the Honda to pass over the bonnet of a parked security van.

Shit. He had been too preoccupied with flying the bike to notice the danger premonition.

The radio clipped onto his belt exploded in a babble of voices.

A motorcycle had just jumped over the camp to Quarry Road.

Chapter 59

Marco's head jerked up from a map of the area spread out over the office table. Two followers from the island were standing next to him. His suspicions about the motorcycle had proven to be correct. He no longer could afford to be an observer in this conflict between the father and Parker. He was the one now being observed.

Marco picked up the hand mike and pressed the button on the side. "Shoot the person on the motorcycle. It is probably the white man, Parker, going to the camp. Alert the camp guards to shoot on sight."

The two brothers hurriedly left the office. Whoever killed Parker and retrieved the power would certainly gain the father's favour. Marco felt relaxed now that the followers had left, and lay back in his office chair. He pivoted from side to side, deep in thought. A moment later, he picked up his cell phone and called the guard on the hill. There was no reply.

Chapter 60

Jan started his descent in a spiral pattern for three reasons. Firstly, because, by his reckoning, they were more or less over Malenga, and secondly, he was twice as high as normal. The usual method would be to start descending about one hundred kilometres from the destination. The last reason was that he had to get down as soon as possible, because of the onset of darkness.

Phil wasn't feeling too comfortable with the progressive change of pressure and continuous circling.

"I has to get down quicks," Jan explained.

The engine misfired and stopped. Jan scowled and started tapping on the glass of some gauges. The only noise was the rushing of air on the outside of the cabin.

"Why did you stop the engine?"

Jan glared at Phil. "Now why the donner would I stops the bliksemar engine?"

Phil sat with staring eyes and open mouth while he absorbed the implications of this question. The Cessna slowly fell out of is spiral turn and started to dive. Phil had lost the ability to polish his glasses. All the in-flight safety information he had ever read flashed before his eyes. None of it was of any apparent help, except 'brace for impact'.

Jan switched the ignition off, then on again, while listening. There was a soft, high-pitched whine coming from somewhere. Jan slapped his forehead with the palm of his hand. "Hgot, I forgets to switch over to the other tank." He grinned at Phil while turning a small lever on the floor. "That there storm sommer finished the one tank and I doesn't see it."

Jan tapped on the gauge marked 'fuel pressure' and the whining noise stopped. "Daars sy, now we is lekker."

He pressed the start button, which resulted in the propeller turning slowly. "Hgot, die bliksemar batteray is still pap. Now we is in biar kak."

Grey clouds rushed passed the aircraft as they continued to dive.

"I can't sommer ask you to gets out and starts the engine, so's I has to think of somtink very quicklies."

Jan grinned at Phil like a lunatic and moved a switch marked 'pitch'. He then pushed forward on the controls, which resulted in a vertical dive while he watched the air speed indicator. The Cessna accelerated and started to shake violently.

Phil was convinced the pilot had totally lost his mind and was trying to put them both out of their misery. If he had been able to move, he would have pulled back on the controls to end this mad, suicidal dive.

The speed and the shaking increased to a point where Phil was sure the airplane was starting to dismantle itself.

"Now we as this ear one chance to starts with the wind elping."

Jan pressed the start button again. This time the propeller turned faster and the engine roared into life.

"Daar sy, Daar sy," he shouted and started laughing while pulling back on the control column.

They broke through the last of the cloud, revealing an expanse of grey, uninviting water rushing up to meet them.

Chapter 61

The motorcycle's wheels cut through the top branches of the bush surrounding the camp. Bill's plan was to approach the back corner of the camp just behind Roberto's house. The floodlights faced inwards, illuminating the camp itself and not the bush outside the fence. Anyone watching from inside would only see an impenetrable darkness beyond the perimeter. A security van was already parked at the front of Roberto's house, with four guards standing close by.

Bill stopped behind the tallest bush he could find, allowing the bike to settle to the ground. A few small twigs snapped under the weight. To Bill's acute hearing, they sounded like gunshots. He glanced round in a panic, but found no indication of alarm. The conversation of the guards two hundred metres away continued in a normal fashion.

Bill removed his helmet and called Roberto on Sara's cell phone. He waited impatiently for him to answer. Distant thunder rumbled and the rain pattering on the shinny surface of the helmet showed no sign of abating.

"Sara, where are you?" Roberto gasped.

"It's not Sara, it's Bill; remember you gave me her phone."

"Oh yes," came a disappointed voice. "Where are you?"

"I'm outside the fence behind your house with the motorbike. Put a raincoat on and grab your passport, then go out the back door. We are flying out of here tonight with Ken."

"But what about the guards? I can see them outside."

"They are all at the front at the moment. Place something to cast a shadow on the curtains that looks like you, but be quick."

After a moment, one of the Medusacor men pointed at a window, then the conversation started up again.

The back door opened and something yellow stepped out.

"Oh my god," Bill hissed between clenched teeth. "I don't believe this."

Roberto was wearing one of the company waterproof suits and was now stumbling through the vegetable garden towards the fence. Bill stood up and ran to meet him. Roberto grinned foolishly through the diamond mesh when he saw Bill approaching. "Where is the hole?" he asked.

"You're not going through. You're going over the top."

Roberto stared up at the fence. "I cannot climb this. There is a barbed wire on the top."

"Step back. I'm going to lift you over it. Why the hell did you put that thing on? You look like a lollypop man. They can see you a mile away."

Roberto looked down at his suit the same time he started lifting. He held his arms out, trying to balance, thinking he may fall over. Near the top of the fence, panic over took him. He felt that he would drift upwards forever, like a child's gas-filled balloon. From Bill's side of the fence, Roberto looked like a spaceman, a yellow one, whose lifeline had snapped or come loose.

A shout came from one of the guards, who had walked around the side of the house. For a moment, he couldn't believe what he was seeing. A yellow figure franticly waved its arms and legs around while suspended above the fence by some unseen rope. He raised his rifle and fired. Roberto felt something smack into the waterproof jacket just below his armpit. While the guard worked the bolt action, Bill dropped Roberto quickly down on the outside of the fence. The second shot passed over his body as he fell facedown into the long grass. Confused shouts came from the camp as a volley of shots erupted from near the corner of the house. Bill ran to one side, away from the field of fire, and dropped to the ground. They couldn't see him, but he was in danger of been hit by a stray bullet.

"Crawl, crawl," Bill shouted in Roberto's direction.

The yellow suit galvanised into mechanical motion and rapidly cut through the bush, away from the fence. Some of the bullets buzzed overhead like angry bees after clipping the diamond mesh. One of them snatched at the plastic hood and threw it over the back of Roberto's neck. This prompted the suit to accelerate. The group of Medusacor men now rushed forwards to narrow the gap between them and their target. Bill had other ideas. All the men lifted and fell flat on their faces in a confused pile.

"Run, run," Bill shouted as he ran back to the Honda.

A second security vehicle arrived around the side of the house and charged towards the fence in an attempt to break through. The headlights lit up the departing yellow figure running through the bush, which resulted in more shots being fired. One follower jumped from the vehicle, which was now bogged down in Roberto's vegetable patch, and opened fire with a Kalashnikov. There was no specific target to be seen in the darkness beyond the fence, so he empted the magazine in the general direction of the last sighting.

In the following silence, Roberto rose from the ground and scurried head first away from the camp.

Chapter 62

Phil was pushed down heavily into the Cessna's seat as the plane started to pull out of its dive. The small waves on the gloomy surface gave a first impression of being far below, but Phil could now see that was not the case. He could not determine whether they would make it or not, because he had never been in that situation before. If he had been flying Central African Mystery Tours on a regular basis, he would probably have some idea if he was going to live or die. Jan must know.

He turned and looked at the pilot. The only thing he could read from his tormenter's expression was grim determination as he pulled back on the controls. *Oh well, let's see what will happen.* He wondered if Stuka dive bombers went through this experience every day. Certainly, a Kamikaze pilot would have a better idea of the outcome.

"Come now, come now," Jan shouted at no one in particular.

Was this a good sign? Quite frankly, he didn't care anymore. He was just an observer.

"Come now, you bliksem."

'In the event of the aircraft landing on water'. Yes, definitely an *event of major proportions.* He stopped gripping one of his legs and felt around under the seat.

Nope, no life jacket. Not to worry; Jan would probably give him a condom to blow up just before impact.

"Daar sy, daar sy, you bliksem."

The view through the windscreen now showed some land in the top part of it. This was a definite improvement to all being water. Birds floating around on the surface of the lake took off and scattered in panic. Phil wondered if they were storks or herons. He could check in *Birds of Central Africa*.

"Daar sy, daar sy."

'Daar sy' sounded better than 'daar sy, you bliksem', or was he just fooling himself?

The horizon with the dark strip of land was now halfway down the windscreen. Phil felt as if he was in a power boat or had been transported into some diabolical computer game. Grey water rushed by on both sides as they charged towards the shore. The Cessna's nose lifted and Jan started pushing forwards on the controls. Phil's body weight gradually decreased.

"Daar sy, I told you I would gets you down quicklies."

Jan smiled as if nothing had happened, so Phil decided to smile, too. He couldn't reorganise his brain to formulate any words.

"You has gone all quiet like. Most of my passengers go all quiet like before I gets where we is going. I doesn't know whys."

Chapter 63

Roberto was easy to find. He sounded like a cross between a broken-down old steam engine and a bull elephant crashing through the bush. Bill pulled alongside him and tapped him on the shoulder. "Get on the back."

Roberto sank to his knees while holding onto the seat.

"Are you alright?"

"Yes, just need to breathe," he gasped.

His face reminded Bill of one of those commercial art pictures of a sad child with large round eyes, except for the open mouth.

A flare suddenly illuminated the area. Bill's pupils contracted into small dots. More shots rang out. Bullets clipped off some of the foliage in the small tree next to them.

"Get on the bike. You can rest on the back. These 303 bullets can travel for miles."

Bill glanced up at the flare, which then flew sideways towards the camp. It fell in front of the group of guards at the fence, blinding them. One was busy cutting the diamond mesh.

"Start the engine," Roberto cried from the pillion seat.

"No need; we are on ball power."

The Honda lifted and sped off, dodging the taller clumps of bush. A second flare lit up the sky, followed by a fusillade of shots. Roberto clung tightly round Bill's waist as the motorcycle zigzagged away from the camp.

Chapter 64

Marco arrived at the golf club road followed by two pickup trucks full of men. They faced outwards on both sides, sitting on a central bench seat with rifles at the ready.

He listened to the reports coming in from the camp. Parker had collected the Italian and was now on his way back. The followers were organising an impenetrable barrier of men right through the town from north to south. Marco did not know how Parker planned to pass, but there was more to him than met the eye.

Strange, unexplainable things had already occurred. Rumours of Parker being a magician, the incident at the police station, Mugyenzi's sudden insanity, flares that fell down sideways, and a motorcycle that made no sound, but most of all, the father's fear of this man.

He would confront Parker himself, as a test. If Parker failed and was killed or captured, then he would gain the favour of the father. If Parker escaped from the trap that he was setting, then it could only be a miracle, which would mean Parker was the chosen one, and not the father.

The small convoy turned down the track to Ken's place, then reversed back into the trees to form a line. It was reported that Marshal and the dog were not in the cabin. He sent a man to alert the soldiers, who took up positions near the jetty.

Marco nervously lit a cigarette and waited.

Chapter 65

The Cessna raced towards the dark silhouette of the shore. Flares could be seen, falling one after the other, farther inland.

"Vot the donner? That's the construction camp. It's not Guy Fawkes. It must be Santa Barbara or summit. The Ities are mal when it comes to summit likes that. They sommer mark explosions all over the place."

Phil was not really interested. He just wanted to vacate the aircraft as soon as fucking possible.

More birds flew away in panic. Phil watched them beat the surface of the water with their wings in an effort to take off.

A motorcycle passed by in the opposite direction, with two people on it. Phil continued to stare out of the side window for a few seconds, then glanced at Jan. The pilot's expression hadn't changed.

"We wills be over land soon, and at the strip in five minutes."

Phil turned back to the window, wondering what else he would see. Jesus could walk on water so why not a motorcycle? He had been praying a lot during the last three hours. Could be they would fly over a man on horseback, or a hotdog stand. He clearly remembered the person on the back was wearing a yellow suit.

Chapter 66

Bill could not resist the occasional glance into the rear-view mirror. No one would be following them out here above the surface of the lake. Nevertheless, he instinctively stole the odd glace into the droplet-covered glass.

An aircraft had roared past, just above and to the right of them, causing the Honda to swerve violently away to the left. In the split second of the encounter, Bill had caught sight of an expressionless face at the side window, peering down at him.

He leant over and turned the bike to the right in an attempt to ride parallel to the unseen coastline. The instruments in front of him were useless. What he needed was an airspeed indicator, and a compass.

Bill glanced at his watch and estimated their speed so he would have some idea when to turn right again. The golf club lights should be seen from quite a distance offshore. According to his watch, the sun had set and the land was in darkness. The wind and spray now blew from the left, so at least they were moving in the right direction. Was the sudden appearance of the aeroplane anything to do with Nabusano? He didn't think so. There had been no feeling of danger. In fact, the face at the window had given Bill a feeling of benevolence. Like a chance encounter with a friend.

Chapter 67

The controllers glanced at each other nervously in the glow from the radar screen. Their green faces did not speak. Every sound inside the control room was recorded.

The aircraft was now nearly at the airstrip and its progress had been reported to the commandant.

One follower at the camp had confirmed that a low-flying plane had just passed overhead in the direction of the strip.

What worried the brothers was a small blip moving west. Only a water ski could make that type of signature. No one in the Malenga area owned a water ski. That sort of recreation was forbidden by the tribal elders on strict instructions from the father.

The other option was a malfunction. According to the radar, the aircraft had descended in an uncontrollable dive. No distress call had been made by the pilot. This gave the impression of a series of malfunctions made by the aging equipment.

The controller picked up the telephone in front of him. After a moment's hesitation, he gently replaced it in its cradle.

Chapter 68

Jan leant forward and peered through the windscreen into the darkness. Eventually, he saw two rows of small, twinkling lights some distance ahead.

"Daar sy, we is ere now." He moved the throttle forwards and pulled a lever to half flaps. "You is sulking cos the engine stopped?"

He then flicked a switch, followed by a whirring noise and two bumps as the undercarriage locked into place. Phil flinched as he felt the thumps, but remained silent.

"One time on takeoff, I bliksemed into some rocks what the grader had left at the end of a strip. Knocked the wheels sommer right off. Those folk all went quiet like, but I gets them where they is going. I stops the engine and we belly lands on grass. Never thanked me. Then there was the oke whose brief case falls out the back door. He went all quiet like."

Jan scratched the side of his beard. "Or the oke when I falls asleep; same thing."

Phil started to massage his temples.

"Another time, the one oke gets out and sommer walks straight into the propeller. That was nasty."

Phil lifted his hand and signalled Jan to stop talking.

"Look at it this ways. Things can't get any worse. We is ere now." He pushed forward on the controls and moved the lever to full flaps. "Prepares for landing and thank yous for flying Central African Mystery Tours." Jan grinned at Phil. "And has a nice evenings."

The two rows of twinkling lights were now just ahead of them. Jan switch on his landing lights and slowed down as they sank closer to the ground.

"Vot the? There is summit wrong here. The strip is in the wrong bliksemar place. I wills fly over first to kyk vot the donner is going on."

Phil removed his glasses and started polishing them with a fixed expression.

"We can checks for cows at the same time."

Jan increased the engine RPM and pulled back slightly on the control column. The aircraft entered the two rows of lights and illuminated the ground with its landing lights.

"Hgot! There is only bush downs there. Die oke is fucking mal."

The pilot grabbed the hand mic and started shouting, "Malenga, Malenga. *Vot* the *donner* is going on?"

A flare suddenly burst in the sky, lighting up the whole area. Both the Cessna's occupants squinted against the glare.

"There's the donnerser strip over there." Jan pointed to the right, where Phil could see a small white building surrounded by green trucks. Orange streaks of light started coming from the nearest truck and passed by in front of the aircraft.

"Kak! We is being shot at."

The pilot instantly started doing many things at the same time with switches and levers. Phil struck his forehead on the side window as the Cessna did a sharp left turn at full power. He could not see the trucks anymore, because his window was now facing the sky. The streaks of orange moved relentlessly towards them until they contacted the wing on Phil's side. A spectacular ball of fire erupted from the empty fuel tank, lighting up his horrified face.

"We are hit, we are hit," Phil screamed at Jan.

"Ek weet," Jan shouted back. "I is doing my best."

The fire consumed the fuel vapour, then suddenly blew itself out. Shreds of burnt aluminium sheet lashed around in the turbulence on the underside of the wing. Numerous small, red, twinkling lights on the ground could be seen through Jan's side window.

"There's a whole bliksemar army down there shooting at us, and I is not insured for an act of war."

A second flare lit up the sky as the aircraft pulled out of its sharp turn.

"With any luck, that there flare will blind em. All my lights is off."

Tufts of carpet and dust suddenly filled the cabin, while holes appeared in the roof material above them. Jan sucked in air through his teeth and clamped one hand on his thigh. The face of the radio fell off, followed by foul-smelling fumes emerging from inside the instrument panel.

"Where's the extinguisher?" asked Phil.

Jan shook his head. "Spray a beer in there, then sommer gives me one."

Phil opened a beer, then shook it with his thumb over the hole. He sprayed beer into the aperture made by the missing face of the radio.

The flare burnt out some distance behind them.

"Where are we going?" asked Phil.

"Back over the lake where there is no okes shooting at us."

"Where can we land?"

"I doesn't knows yet. I only knows we can't land heres. Let's see if this here plane can still fly's. It feels like I is pulling an elephant behinds us."

Phil offered Jan a tin of beer, which he took with a blood-soaked hand.

"You've been shot. Where is the first aid kit?"

The pilot shook his head again. "Tie summit round my leg. Find a belt or a tie."

"Watson was right. We should have turned back."

"How the donner was I supposed to know a whole bliksemar army is trying to kills you?"

Chapter 69

The commandant dropped his half-finished cigarette onto the radio shack's floor, then ground it out with his boot. There had been no distress call from the damaged plane so, the pilot was either dead or the radio was out of action. Even if the pilot had alerted the whole world he was being fired upon, the rebels would be blamed. The commandant sat in front of the radio set and composed the message he was going to send to Mabarta HQ.

Rebels have taken over the airstrip, killing the airstrip attendant. A small plane trying to land has been fired upon and damaged. The rebels have been beaten off, with no casualties on either side.

He nodded at the two soldiers who came in with a stretcher to remove the body slumped in the corner.

The control room on the island would continue to track the aircraft.

Why it had not crashed to the ground in flames, he did not understand. In any event, it was badly damaged and would probably crash into the lake.

To follow in the military helicopter would be an option. It was busy searching for Parker, but could land there at a moment's notice. The second thing he did not understand was why Parker and this ball were so important.

He would telephone the father for instructions.

Chapter 70

Bill checked his watch for the third time before deciding to turn. He clearly saw the land through the rain, but was unable to see any lights. Roberto would have a better chance of seeing lights when they neared the shore.

Bill's acute hearing had registered a crescendo of automatic fire from the general direction of the camp. He hoped the guards had not shot the contractors in a reprisal for Roberto's escape. In a state of emergency, anything was possible.

Riding just above the surface of the lake was very exhilarating, but also tiring. There was only the noise of the wind and rain. Under different circumstances, he would be enjoying himself. He presumed he would be able to fly around like superman.

Something that Erectus *would never have been capable of, because of his limited intelligence.*

The bike raised high in the air and stopped.

"Can you see any lights?" asked Bill.

"Yes, over to the left." Roberto pointed. "It looks like the golf club inlet."

Bill urged the Honda forward on its new coarse and increased speed. The sooner they joined Ken and left that place, the better. He could then try to think of a plan to rescue the girls.

Chapter 71

The cruiser's engines slowed to an idle and her bows gradually lowered into the water as she lost momentum. The island ahead formed a massive black silhouette against the night sky. To the left, the profile was broken by square ramparts and a large dome.

Small course corrections were given to the helmsman while the captain concentrated on the GPS. Any mistake on entering the island's harbour would send the craft to the bottom. A network of underwater walls and obstacles lurked just below the surface. There was only one way in and one way out of this dark, foreboding place.

The island's appearance was one of solitude and inactivity. In reality, that was far from the case. Nothing there was what it appeared to be.

Nabusano watched the cruiser cautiously enter the harbour from his apartment balcony. The most important issue now was that the two females would not be allowed to escape or be rescued. Escape was impossible. Rescue attempts, under normal circumstances, were also impossible, but Parker held the power. If the white man escaped the mainland, he would still have to deliver the power here to him personally. *An example will be made of this false prophet, witnessed by all the followers.* After that, everything else, including the followers, would become irrelevant. Now was the time to eliminate any loose ends.

He smiled. "Vengeance will be mine."

Chapter 72

Ken checked his watch for the fourth time during the last half hour, then turned to squint up at the bar clock.

"Are you expecting anyone?"

"Oh no no, of course not. Well, not really," he added.

Alex stopped polishing the glass he was cleaning for a second and wondered why Mr. Marshal was lying. "If you say so."

Ken jumped as his phone rang. "I'm expecting a phone call." He forced a smile. "That's what I was waiting for... Hello... Who is this? Jan? Jan who? Oh yes. How are you, old chap? What! Slow down, say again... You is been shot at? How the bloody hell should I know? I'm at the blooming golf club... Yes... Yes... Good lord! The nearest strip is at Sid's place... Yes, I know there are no lights. Sid could make a plan with cars or fires... Yes, but the next one is Mabarta."

Ken dropped his voice. "Listen, I could be flying there myself in half an hour." He placed a hand to his forehead and shouted, "I said I could be flying there myself in half an hour."

Ken looked up and forced another smile. "Yes, make for Sid's place. I will phone him."

He began pushing buttons on his cell phone. "It's an emergency. Someone's tried to shoot down The Flying Dutchman."

Alex had no idea what Ken was talking about.

"The flying what?"

Ken waved a hand at him. "A friend of mine. He's in the bloody shit."

Patch started barking like crazy at the glass doors facing the golf course. A moment later, they burst open. Bill ran inside, chased by a man in a yellow suit. Patch ran forwards and clamped his jaws on a yellow trouser leg. Wet and breathless, Bill reached the bar, followed by Roberto dragging Patch across the polished wooden floor.

"Let's go, let's go," Bill shouted.

"Let go, let go," Roberto shouted, shaking his leg.

Ken downed the last of his whisky and shoved his phone into his pocket.

"No time to lose. Let's go," Bill repeated.

All three ran out of the front door, followed by Patch, who was pulled along at every step.

Alex slowly restarted polishing the glass he had been holding since Ken's phone call. He shook his head in wonder.

I will never understand white people.

Outside in the car park, Patch reluctantly released his grip. He didn't like being dragged across the gravel surface, and the yellow suit showed no signs of stopping.

When they reached Ken's pick-up, Patch jumped into the passenger side and growled at everyone except his master.

"What's the plan?" asked Ken, gasping. "How are you going to get rid of those bloody soldiers?"

"Soldiers! What soldiers?" Roberto asked.

"Leave that to me. Let's just get there first. How deep is the water near the end of the jetty?" Bill asked Ken.

"Oh, about five foot. Why?"

"I don't want to drown anyone unless I have to. Get in and drive. We will get in the back."

The Stout's warm engine started first time, and she pulled out of the car park, spinning on the gravel. As they approached the turn off from the golf club road, the danger feeling mounted.

Bill shouted through the open window, "Switch off and freewheel down the hill, then stop when I tell you. I need to see the situation down there."

Ken killed the engine and the lights and trundled slowly down the hill. "I can't see bugger all," he hissed back at Bill.

Bill leant through the window with one hand on the steering wheel until they were halfway down.

"Stop," he whispered.

The four soldiers near the jetty were lying in firing positions. Somebody had warned them. Somebody else was here waiting for them to arrive.

"You two make your way to the water and start wading to the jetty. There are not only the soldiers here."

Ken and Roberto didn't seem too enthusiastic.

"Trust me; it's the only way."

Bill waited for what seemed hours until he saw the two heads safely reach the end of the jetty. Ken lifted Patch from the water and placed him on the deck.

"Right, now for the ones I can see," he whispered.

*   *   *

Marco, standing next to his X5, caught sight of some movement, through his night vision binoculars, where the soldiers were lying. Terrified shouts broke the stillness of the night. He took a step backwards, further into the trees, as he saw something like four huge bats rise into the air. They flew some distance over to the left, then dropped into the lake, causing four splashes in quick succession. It was the soldiers. Their capes looked like inside-out umbrellas as they hit the water.

"Right now for the ones I can't see."

Bill switched on the pick-up's lights and released the handbrake. The Stout slowly increased speed down the hill, steering itself in the deep ruts of the track. Firing erupted from the tree line, riddling the old vehicle with holes. Shattered glass and bits of plastic flew in all directions. Bill trotted down the track on the grass, in the centre of the two wheel ruts, keeping a safe distance behind. Ken's pick-up overturned and came to rest on its side with its two uppermost wheels spinning in the air. Bill noticed Ken standing on the jetty staring towards his wrecked Stout. Judging from his body language, he wasn't very pleased. Roberto was struggling out of the water onto the decking like a landed fish.

Marco apprehensively nodded to his driver, who spoke on the radio. The guards hurriedly boarded their vehicles, which then charged down the hill towards the overturned Stout. His driver started the X5's engine, but Marco raised his hand. He was not about to commit himself in any way until he understood what had happened to the soldiers.

Before the two Madusacor vehicles reached the overturned pick-up, they started lifting. Marco's driver cried out and pointed in fear. The brake lights came on as both drivers tried to stop in mid air. Rifles hit the ground and two men jumped from the rising vehicles and fell heavily to Earth. The others clung to the hand rails, screaming. They sounded like a wailing siren as they passed over the Stout, forty feet above the ground. Marco's driver turned and ran away in panic. The two vehicles floated some distance over the lake, then fell like stones. They smacked into the water with terrific splashes, spilling out the occupants in all directions when they rebounded from the surface. Marco was frozen for a moment, then lifted his night glasses to his eyes. The two vehicles began sinking, surrounded by floundering men.

A white man ran past the overturned pick-up, towards the jetty. Another man, in a yellow suit, was untying the ropes of the aeroplane while the propeller started turning. A few shots rang out, kicking up splashes of water close to the yellow figure. The engine roared to life as the running man reached the aircraft and jumped onto one of the floats. Before entering the cabin, he turned and looked directly back at Marco as if he was a few feet away. The other quickly lowered his glasses and slid round to the other side of the tree he was standing next to.

It was Parker. Marco recognised him from the photographs he had on file of all the expatriates who stayed at the camp.

Some of the senior brothers had told him of the father's power. Stories of a diamond-studded ball that had risen from the temple's altar and was made to spin.

He had now seen for himself that Parker was lifting vehicles complete with men, two at a time. Who knew what else he was capable of?

The engine noise from the float plane increased in volume, then gradually started to fade as it moved away from the jetty. Marco breathed deeply for a moment, before peering from behind the tree with his glasses. The plane was now accelerating out into the darkness. It started skipping on the surface of the water, then lifted into the air.

He slid behind the wheel of the X5 in a state of shock. This was a turn of events that he never really expected. After all, he had been educated and trained in America. Parker had swept his men to one side like ants from a table top.

The babble of voices and shouts from the lake interfered with his concentration.

He started the engine and drove slowly down the hill. There were two patches of illumination under water, which marked the location of the vehicles. Some of his men sat on the shore, rocking back and forth like mentally retarded children. Others were standing on the roof of the sunken vehicles, waiting for rescue. None of them approached him for fresh orders or a ride back to town. *Parker could have killed them all. They had been trying to kill him. This man is defiantly the true prophet. A mixture of compassion and power.*

Marco drove up the track to the golf club. He was badly in need of a double brandy and a quiet place to think.

Chapter 73

Mugyenzi rolled his bulk around in the perspiration-soaked bed, trying to get out. He had no idea of the time, or even what day it was. Eventually, he succeeded in sitting upright and held his head to stop it exploding. After five minutes of groaning, he managed to get his brain working again and switched on the bedside light.

Mugyenzi squinted at his gold watch. Eight o'clock and it was dark. One whole day had passed since the last time he had been conscious. There were about twenty missed calls on his cell phone. Most of them were from the charge office. Even Gwasa had tried to call him. That reminded him of the events at the police station, and he started shivering. *Maybe the whole thing was a bad dream. More like a hideous nightmare. Yes, that's it. None of it can be true.*

A folder lay on the bedside table, which Mugyenzi could not remember. Curious, he opened it and saw it was the report about the four thugs being killed in his office. The shivering restarted and he was sweating at the same time.

A foul smell of sweat and urine surrounded him and the bed. Or was it the smell of fear?

In desperation, he forced himself to stand up. *No time to waste.* He must leave Malenga as soon as possible. Actually, he was surprised he was still alive. He was the only one who could blow the whistle on the state of emergency sham. *A cold shower?* Yes, he must wash the stink from his body and dress in his best uniform. What better way to leave town than being the commanding officer of the police force?

He swept some of the empty beer bottles under the bed with his foot so that he could cross the room and switch on the lights.

The refrigerator was missing, along with many of his more valuable items, like the CD player. His cry of rage stopped abruptly as he started to remember something about the previous night.

Outside in the yard, all the missing things were packed on the back of his 4x4. He passed a hand over his greasy face and forced himself to think. Anyone could see he was making a run for it. *I am not leaving these things for some swine to steal. A lot of hard work has gone in to acquiring this stuff.* No matter; he would switch on his blue light and siren, and drive straight through the roadblocks. No one had the power to stop him.

With that reassuring thought, Mugyenzi re-entered the house and turned on the shower.

Chapter 74

The silver float plane climbed on full power and broke through the low cloud into a moonlit sky.

"The conditions are good for night flying," Ken remarked. "Did you really have to do that to my bloody car? It looked like a complete bloody wreck."

"I'm afraid so. There was no other way, but at least we are all still alive and on our way out of here."

"My friend, Jan, was not so ruddy well lucky. They tried to shoot him down over the strip. He's wounded and the plane is damaged. I told him to make for Sid's' place."

"Why did they fire on his plane? He's got nothing to do with any of this. Doesn't make sense. Must have been the plane that flew over Roberto and me when we were on the bike. There was a passenger who saw us from the right side window."

"Good lord! The American bird watcher," exclaimed Ken. "I had forgotten about him."

Bill shook his head. "He has to have something to do with Nabusano; that's the only explanation."

Ken turned round to face Roberto. "Find a bottle of whisky in that box behind you. I am ruddy freezing. Flipping well wet through. Need some central heating."

Roberto found the bottle, which they passed around. Ken took a heavy swig of the life-sustaining liquid.

"That's better. I nearly feel bloody human again. I will phone Sid and then try to contact Jan. He must be ahead of us. That's if he hasn't gone down."

Roberto tapped Bill on his shoulder. "Have you any a dry cigarettes? Mine are a sodden mess."

Bill handed Roberto his crumpled packet, and they both lit up with Roberto's Zippo. While Ken was talking on his phone, the bottle was passed around again.

"Well that's Sid organised. I will phone Jan now. His ruddy radio is shot up, and everybody would hear what's said on the radio anyway."

Roberto tapped Bill on the shoulder again. "What about Nabusano's helicopter? Even the military have one. Will they not try to a shoot us down?"

Bill shook his head. "No, he won't order them to do that. He would run the risk of losing the ball in the lake. Also, he knows I can force a helicopter down into the water."

The cloud below began breaking up into patches. Moonlight reflected from the lake's small waves, forming a dazzling display of tranquillity.

"In different circumstances, I would be enjoying this," Bill remarked. "I feel really tied. It's either the whisky or lifting those Madusacor cars around."

"Yes, if I had a not seen that with my own waking eyes, I would not have-a believed it."

Ken finished his second phone call. "Jan says he doesn't know how long his bloody kite can fly. Also sounds like he is struggling to speak, and he's not sure of the strip's location. We will have to guide him there and pick them up if he ditches along the way. Should be just ahead of us, but he has no lights. Damn difficult to see him."

He signalled for the whisky bottle again. "What's the idea of the yellow suit? Nearly got us shot with that ruddy thing on. You look like a pregnant canary."

Roberto snatched the bottle back from Ken. "Okay, okay. I know it was a mistake, alright?"

Patch, sitting next to Roberto, barked and started sniffing his backside.

"Cazzo! What is that-a horrible smell?"

A second later, a foul stench reached Bill and Ken. They both gagged while desperately opening the side windows. Cold air rushed into the cabin and the noise was deafening.

"Stone the crows, what the hell was that?" asked Bill, gasping.

Ken cleared his throat. "I'm afraid that was my fault," he shouted.

"Then there's something really wrong with your insides," Bill shouted back.

"Is a dead species of-a rodent has died in your anus," Roberto added.

"No, no; not me. It's Patch. I gave him some beer at the club. Didn't plan on him bloody well coming with us."

Eventually, the smell cleared and they managed to close the windows. Roberto lit another cigarette while apprehensively watching Patch.

"You could have sold that dog to Sadam Hussein to fire at Israel in a Scud missile," Bill remarked.

"I said it was my fault," Ken snapped. "Pass the whisky. I need to rinse my mouth."

They all took another swig from the bottle. Bill started sniffing. "I can smell something else," he exclaimed. "Smells like fuel. Put that cigarette out, Roberto."

Ken checked his gauges and shone a torch light out of the side window to illuminate the underside of the wing.

"Nothing wrong on this ruddy side. Check your side, Bill." He handed the flashlight to Bill.

"What am I looking for?" he asked.

"Anything that looks like a vapour trail. We could have a bullet hole in one of the tanks."

"But then the smell would be left behind. Not inside the cabin."

"You're right. Must be ahead of us. I can smell it now."

They both turned to face each other, realising where the fumes must be coming from. Ken switched on his landing lights, and Bill pointed.

"There's something ahead of us on my side. Turn left to get out of these fumes, and go higher."

The float plane swung over to the left and lifted.

"I can't see a ruddy thing, but it sounds like a good idea."

It was another five minutes before Ken could make out an object ahead, followed by a vapour trail.

"Golly gosh, that kite's in really bad shape. She could go down at any moment."

"Why do you say that?" asked Bill.

"Jan's nearly got full left rudder on just to keep her flying straight. There must be one hell of a drag on his starboard wing."

"But the fuel is coming from the left wing."

"Yes I can see that, but she is flying like a crab and the air speed is very low."

Ken reduced speed as they approached the crippled aircraft.

"Can't see much damage from this side. I will fly over the top of her and check out the other side."

The float plane swung to the right and passed over Cessna. Bullet exit holes could be seen here and there along the top of the left wing and the roof of the cabin.

"Good lord," exclaimed Ken, pointing to the right wing. "I can't believe this kite is still flying."

Roberto leant forward to get a better view.

"Dio can, I am very much pleased I am not in that plane," he said grimly.

The half of the wing near the fuselage was just a backend mess of flapping metal. Some of the framework could be seen through the openings.

"His bloody fuel tank has been on fire. That wing should have melted off. Don't understand why he didn't go down in a ruddy ball of flame."

"We have to be thankful he didn't. Do you think they will make it?"

Ken shook his head. "If that wing doesn't fall off, they will run out of fuel before landing."

Bill closed his eyes and massaged his forehead with both sets of fingers. "Maybe I can help them if that happens."

He was feeling very tired. More and more life or death situations seemed to be surrounding him. Being responsible for other people's lives was a heavy cross to bear. The water below now looked dark and formidable.

Chapter 75

Mugyenzi examined his reflection in the mirror. He looked quite impressive in his best uniform. Some of the polished buttons had been difficult to fasten. The swagger stick tucked under his arm completed the picture. The only letdown was the worried expression on his face. After a number of failed attempts to change it, he gave up and turned off the lights.

With his automatic in his right-hand, he held his breath and slowly opened the door into the yard. The loaded vehicle shone in the moonlight, inviting him to depart.

He stepped outside, and all the frogs stopped croaking.

In the following silence, Mugyenzi felt hundreds of eyes watching from every dark corner. A rapid thumping pulsed in his ears. One frog close to him started croaking again, prompting him to move towards the Colt. He cursed under his breath. *I am being controlled by frogs.*

After fumbling with the keys in his left hand, he eased his bulk behind the wheel and breathed a sigh of relief. The fuel gauge indicating a full tank was very comforting. *More than enough to reach Mabarta, where everything follows a normal course of events. Not like this crazy town, full of devils and assassins.*

He started the engine and drove up to the sheet metal gates waiting for the boy to open them. Nothing happened. In anger, he lifted a fist to strike the horn, then stopped himself. The boy wasn't there. It was nearly the middle of the night. He would have to open them himself.

The two halves that opened had sliding bolts at the bottom, which operated up and down. He would have to kneel down on the ground to open them. Also, he would have to get out of the car.

He didn't want to do either of these things, so he pushed the gate gently with the bulbar. The bolts held, so he pushed harder. Both gates fell down with a huge crash, so he drove over the top of them out on to the road.

"Stupid gates," he hissed between his teeth.

The street was deserted. Mugyenzi switched on the flashing blue light to make sure no one was tempted to open fire on the pickup. The roadblocks he had seen being hastily erected on his way home the previous night were still manned, but not in use. Madusacor men stood around talking, or sitting on whatever they could find. For whatever reason they had been put in place, they were now obsolete. This suited Mugyenzi very well, and he sailed right through the whole town without stopping.

Five kilometres out of town, on the Mabarta road, there was a permanent roadblock at the bridge. This was used by the police and the customs people, mainly to check on what the trucks were transporting. If he could pass this one, he was virtually home and dry. His heart sank as he approached the lights of the bridge. Soldiers wearing red berets were manning this one. He cocked the automatic and placed it into the door cavity. If they blocked his path, he would shoot some of the swine and make a run for it.

The soldier in front of the boom waved his torch up and down for him to stop. Mugyenzi cursed and switched his siren on and off. Seeing this was not going to work, he stopped and wound down his window.

"What are you fools doing at my roadblock?" he demanded.

"We have orders to stop everyone. You are no exception. Where are you going?"

The soldier shone his light over Mugyenzi's household effects and gave him an enquiring look.

"I am moving some things for a friend of mine. It is none of your business," the OC managed to say, in a controlled voice. "Now let me pass before I lose my temper," he shouted.

The soldier seemed to be distracted. He was focussing on another soldier in the guardhouse, who was holding a radio to his ear. This man nodded and the boom was lifted.

"About time," Mugyenzi snarled, and drove onto the bridge.

The insect-surrounded lights on the bridge flashed by in quick succession as he accelerated towards the roadblock at the other end. There, the boom was already raised and the soldiers stood in line. The sergeant saluted as he drove passed. *That's better. Some respect at last.*

He studied the rear-view mirror with suspicion and noticed the soldiers were now staggering around, patting each other on the backs.

"What the...?" Mugyenzi pondered on what they were doing.

"Swine; they are laughing. They are laughing at me."

He ground his teeth and gripped the steering wheel in anger.

We will see who is still laughing after I have reported to Mabarta.

The refrigerator banged the rear of the cab as the pickup hit a large pothole. He took a few deep breaths and concentrated on his driving. After another thirty kilometres, there was a bad stretch where the road was full of potholes. If he was not careful, he would damage his possessions.

Some distance ahead, an owl stood in the middle of the lane, mesmerised by the oncoming headlights. Mugyenzi accelerated, with a grim smile on his lips. There was a small thud from the front bumper as he passed over the spot.

"Stupid bird."

Chapter 76

Roberto leant forwards and tapped Ken on the shoulder. "How far to the other side?"

Ken twisted his moustache between his finger and thumb. "At this rate, it will take another good half hour. We are about two thirds of the way to Sid's place." He glanced across at Bill, who was fast asleep. "Poor blighter has worn himself out, by the looks of it."

"Will Sid have-a everything ready for the other plane to a land?"

"So he says. There are some hunters staying there who are giving him a hand lighting fires. The local police are also involved."

"How can we land with no lights?"

"Not a problem, old chap. I land a good way out on the lake, then taxi to shore. Only thing I can hit is a bloody boat. They are supposed to have lights."

The way Ken said 'supposed' didn't reassure Roberto very much. He felt cold and wet, but at least the infamous plastic suit retained some of his body heat. Could have been worse. He could have put on the one with the reflective strips. That would have really put the fan in the shit.

Roberto felt around the suit with his fingers and found three bullet holes. One was high up on his inside leg. He felt his scrotum contract, lifting his balls high into his groin. Roberto's knees started dancing up and down, forcing his heels to tap on the cabin floor. He lit another one of Bill's cigarettes.

Chapter 77

The bad stretch of road appeared ahead in the Colt's main beams. Mugyenzi cursed while slowing down, and changed into third gear.

From the left, something streaked towards him with a fiery tail. It impacted on the vehicle's body with a deafening explosion. Hundreds of items erupted into the air, engulfed in a sheet of flame. A refrigerator somersaulted spectacularly into the night sky, spilling out its contents.

Mugyenzi fought to control the stricken vehicle. There was a figure standing in the middle of the road with what seemed to be a pipe on his shoulder.

A round, dark object silhouetted by flame shot out from the pipe, straight towards him. Mugjenzi realised what was happening, and screamed in defiance. The RPG deflected off the road just in front of the Colt and exploded under the engine, flipping it back into the cab. In the last second of his life, Mugjenzi saw the engine with a rotating fan land on top of him. The fiery, twisted hunk of metal, which moments before had been a vehicle, slid down the road, leaving a trail of burning fuel. It eventually stopped in the ditch.

Red-capped soldiers emerged from the darkness to recover anything of value scattered on the road. The commander flicked his cigarette into the burning cab, then shuffled his boot through some CDs scattered in the grass.

He shook his head in disgust. *Mugyenzi's taste in music was appalling.*

Chapter 78

Phil had not been able to stop all the bleeding from the pilot's leg. With a compress made from shirts bound tightly on the entrance and exit wound, the flow had reduced considerably. Of course, there was no first aid kit, like there was no fire extinguisher or life jackets.

"I doesn't normally fly's over water," was Jan's lame excuse.

Phil knew the reason there was no parachutes. All his passengers would bale out.

The special cell phone rang. Why were they flying in the opposite direction to Mabarta, was the first question asked by Watson. After Phil had given him a quick summery of the events that had taken place, there was a moment of silence.

"You realise there's no time to help you? It sounds like you are going to run out of gas."

"Yep, looks that way," Phil grimly admitted.

"This Nabusano bunch is as sure as hell hiding something. Your only chance is the float plane that's with you. He's there, and he can land on water. I will follow your progress with the signal from the cell. Good luck. I really mean that, okay."

"Yeah, thanks."

*　　　*　　　*

Watson slowly laid down his phone and rubbed his eyes. *Everything has turned into crap.* He had suspected some sort of attempt on Jones' life after the two murders in Mabarta, but not by the army. This paper chase had uncovered something really mind blowing. He would have to inform Collins and his boss at Langley as to what had happened. They would be asking heaps of questions he didn't have the answers to.

Who the heck is this Nabusano family and what are they doing?

* * *

The escorting float plane gave Phil some reassurance. *Like a guardian angel watching over us. So close, yet so far.* Waiting for something to happen, was more like it.

Phil searched the cabin for anything that would float, and repeatedly opened the bag of piss-filled condoms. The only thing he could think of was his suitcase at the back.

"Phil," Jan called out in a weak voice. "Put your feet on the pedals, but doesn't summer move em. Hold the stick like what you did befores. I is feeling all funny like."

No sooner had Phil done this than Jan passed out against the side window.

"You can't do this to me," Phil shouted. "You can't do this to me."

Chapter 79

High on the hill above the town, John Gwasa closed his bedroom window and shivered. He had been standing naked in the cool night air, deep in thought. An hour before, he had noticed flares illuminating the horizon, and then heard distant gunfire. Something had happened at the camp or airstrip location, but he had no idea what. Maybe they had found Parker, but why had they been shooting into the air?

Pointer and Mugjenzi were not answering their phones. John hated both of them, but was starting to feel isolated. The three of them worked on more or less the same level in Nabusano's organisation. Useful until not required. John had known this since he had been blackmailed by Pointer into working for the evil old man. Over the last few years, he had gradually organised an escape plan. Was now the right time, or should he wait? His parents and sister in Mabarta were still vulnerable to Nabusano's' retribution.

He decided to phone his father and, on the second attempt, managed to get through. His father told him that they had just heard on the radio of a rebel attack on Malenga airstrip. They were about to phone him to make sure he was alright. He spoke to his mother and sister, then was handed back to his father. John tried to make some small talk.

"Anything happen in Mabarta lately?"

"Yes, we had two murders. One of them a white man."

John swallowed a lump in his throat. "A white man, you say; do you know his name?"

"Not sure; he worked at the American embassy. Could have been Printer."

The lump was starting to form in John's throat again. "Was the name Simon Pointer?"

"Yes, that sounds like it. Did you know him?"

"Listen, father. I want you to do something for me without question. Can you do that?"

"I suppose so, but why?"

"That's a question already." He paused. "I think my boss had that man killed, and I think you all could be in danger. You must go somewhere else until I phone you, and don't tell anyone where you are going."

"But I have things to do tomorrow. People will wonder where we are."

"Father." John spoke very slowly. "If you do not do as I say, you could all be killed."

"Are you sure?"

"No, I'm not sure," John shouted. "Are you willing to take that chance?"

"Alright," his father shouted back. "We will do it, but I want an explanation later."

The phone went dead. He had angered his father, but it was the only way.

John walked over to the bed and lay down. The moonlight filtering through the window had a calming effect.

He could hear the hum of the ceiling fan slowly turning above him. Everything pointed to him escaping Nabusano's clutches tonight, but he was not sure.

John remembered the first meeting with Pointer four years ago in his Mabarta office. The white man had sauntered in and sat down, placing his feet on John's desk. He had handed him a video camera and lit a cigar.

"Take a look at that, my man," Pointer had smiled.

John had pressed play and looked through the viewer to see a hotel room. There were two men on the bed, and one was him. He had stared for a moment, unable to move, then switched off the machine.

"Oh, why switch off so soon? It gets a whole heap better further on."

"What do you want?" he had demanded.

"You. I want you to work for a guy in Malenga, or I show this to your father."

"Why me?"

"Because everyone knows you are a good guy, helping the poor and all that crap, and as a lawyer you are good, and you have upset a lot of important folks here abouts, and you will keep your trap shut because of this."

The man had waved the camera at him and then blown smoke into his face. "So, you won the grand prize and have got the job. Terminate your business here, or should I say, affairs."

"What is it this man in Malenga wants me to do?"

"He has someone lined up for next year's presidential election and we are going to make sure this guy wins. Money no object. Simple as that. Are you in or out?"

John had reluctantly agreed, thinking that after one year he would be released from his bargain. It was not to be. He had sold his soul to the Devil. Four years of working with criminals, thugs and murderers had taken their toll. Being forced to do the opposite of what he wanted to do; John was now a broken man. The truth would destroy his father. Homosexuality was not acceptable in most African cultures. He would become an outcast from the people he loved - his own family.

A tapping on the window made him jump. John could see a brilliant white smile and the flash of gold chain on the other side of the glass. He went over to the window and slid it open.

"What are you going here tonight? There is a curfew. I did not expect you."

"I am not allowed in the construction camp and have nowhere to stay."

The boy smiled again and touched John gently on his cheek. "I prefer to sleep with you. The white man in the camp does not love like you do. Also he snores and farts all night."

John could not help a faint smile.

"Come in quickly; the security guard will see you."

The boy sprang through the window and landed lightly on the thick carpet, placing his arms around John. He hurriedly closed the window behind his visitor.

"Guards do not worry me. I move like a ghost. A child of the night. Besides, the guard is not there. I would have seen him."

"Not there; he is always there. Maybe you just did not see him?"

"I did not see him because he is not there. No matter, we are together again. That is all that is important."

John allowed himself to be led over to the bed.

"I am not in the mood tonight," he protested. "I have many things on my mind."

"Lie down. I will make all your troubles vanish like smoke."

The boy massaged John's head and temples in an expert manner that was very soothing. This continued for an hour until the boy snuggled up to him and fell asleep. John's mind was still a turmoil of indecision. He gently pulled himself away from the sleeping form and entered the bathroom to splash his face with cool water.

John stood in the darkness at the bathroom door, thinking. He suddenly heard a click, which made him flinch. It had come from the bedroom door. The handle was now slowly turning. John rubbed his eyes. Maybe the moonlight was playing a trick on him.

No, the handle was now in the vertical position and the door slowly opened. His hart hammering in his chest, he stepped back into the bathroom and pulled the door nearly closed. Four figures swiftly entered the room, the foremost one carrying a bottle and a cloth. This was placed over the nose and mouth of the sleeping boy, who struggled for a few seconds. The cloth was then taped to the boy's face, who was then wrapped up into the bed sheet and whisked out of the room. John could smell a hospital smell, which he identified as chloroform, and then the foul smell of a strong cigarette.

A figure emerged from the shadows and moved to the window, which it opened. Then came the sound of vehicles arriving in the courtyard below. After a few seconds, one of them drove off.

The figure flicked his cigarette out of the window, then left. John held onto the bathroom door for support, trying to control his breathing. The last vehicle pulled out of the courtyard and stopped. After the gate had banged closed, it also drove off down the hill.

John felt his way to the toilet, sat down and urinated. He had just witnessed his own abduction.

Chapter 80

Ken cursed, then banked the float plane to the right, increasing the distance between the two aircraft.

"What are you doing?" Roberto asked.

"Something has changed. That kite is drifting all over the ruddy sky."

Ken picked up his phone and dialled Jan's number. It was a while before the call was answered.

"Jan, what the hell are you playing at... Oh... Bloody hell... Okay, do the best you can, old chap."

Ken turned back to Roberto. "See if you can wake Bill. I think we are going to need him soon. Jan is unconscious and the bird watcher is flying the plane."

"Dio porco!"

"Yes, exactly. Dio fucking porco."

After some shaking, Bill eventually woke up, and the whisky bottle was passed around while he was updated on the situation.

"Alright, in theory, if I can lift and move two Madusacor vehicles, then maybe I can do the same with Jan's plane. Fly to the left of him so I can see the plane better. It will help my concentration."

Ken banked to the left, flying over the top of the Cessna, and took up station on its portside. Bill could see Jan's head resting on the side window. The fuel vapour trail was less in volume. Probably because the tank was nearly empty.

"Ken, can that plane glide if the engine stops?"

"You must be bloody well joking. With that damaged wing, she will fall like a stone."

Bill thought for a moment. "Okay, so here's the plan. If the engine stops I will try to keep her flying next to our plane. If there is a change in speed or height, then this plane will have to do the same. If she goes down, I will do what I can to lessen the impact."

Ken turned round with raised eyebrows and glanced at Roberto, who was biting his bottom lip. "Alright, let's just ruddy well hope for the best."

"How close are we a now to the other side?" asked Roberto.

Ken reached forward and switched off the dim cabin light, then peered through the windscreen.

"I can just make out a darker patch on the horizon. Can you see anything, Bill?"

"Yeah, looks like land to me."

Bill pulled the ball away from his skin by grabbing the front of his shirt. "I can see a light over to the left," he pointed.

"That must be Sid's fire," exclaimed Ken. "The start of the strip is right on the shore."

Bill released the ball, staring in the same direction. "Yes, there's a plume of smoke above where I saw the light."

Ken picked up his cell phone to tell the bird watcher to try to turn left. The Cessna's propeller faltered and kicked to a standstill.

"Bloody hell! Here we go," shouted Ken as he pushed forwards on the control column.

Bill took a deep breath. "Don't disturb me. I will need my full concentration. Fly towards the light."

Both planes lost height rapidly, then the Cessna's decent started to slow. Ken turned gradually to the left and throttled back to nearly a stall so he could stay alongside the stricken aircraft. Bill signalled with his left hand for Ken to carry on flying while he stared out of the side window.

"Golly gosh. That kite is staying with us. It's working. Well done, Bill, old chap."

Both Ken and Roberto raised a cheer, until they suddenly realised not to disturb Bill's concentration. They fell quiet and

Ken signalled to Roberto for the whisky bottle. *Time for a quick celebration.*

The sight of a plane flying alongside, with a stationary propeller, was mesmerising and a little disturbing for Bill's companions. Ken tore his eyes away and peered forwards. Even after the sudden loss of altitude, he could see the flickering light ahead him now.

"Good old Sid," he whispered to himself, quite surprised his friend had done something right for a change. He turned to Roberto and pointed, giving him the thumbs up sign. Roberto smiled and nodded, then lit up the last of the crumpled, dry cigarettes.

Chapter 81

John eventually managed to control his breathing. The time of indecision had passed. Now was the time to initiate his escape. There was no other choice, except death. If the soldiers discovered their mistake, they would quickly return.

He dressed in warm dark clothing and opened the wall safe behind the bedroom picture. Two years of careful covert planning was now to be activated.

John pulled a black rucksack, of the type used as airplane hand luggage, from the confines of the safe. Inside were sealed plastic bags full of hundred dollar bills. He removed three special keys from his car key ring and slipped them into his pocket. What better place to hide keys than on a key ring, among other keys?

John paused at the open window and listened intently. One of the soldiers could have remained, or the security guard may have returned. This gave him time to reflect on his planed route through the town, down to the water front. In this respect, information gained from his night visitor had been invaluable. A tear formed in the corner of each eye as he wondered about the boy's fate. He slipped his arms through the shoulder straps of the backpack, and then, with a clenched, fist thumped the windowsill in frustration. The boy being in the wrong place at the wrong time had saved his life, but there was no way of saving him.

Taking a deep breath, John ducked out of the window and slid rapidly down the drainpipe to the ground below. Moving silently through the shadows, he reached the side gate of the perimeter wall and carefully unlocked it with one of the keys. John breathed a sigh of relief as he quietly closed the gate and turned the key in the lock again.

On the other side of the door was a different world. The dark alley between the next property and his had accumulated some rubbish on either side. Listening intently while waiting for his eyes to adjust to the darkness, he heard the sound of unseen rats foraging and squeaking among the litter. He flung the key at the nearest of the sounds. *Won't need that again,* he told himself. *One key down and two to go.*

John moved off at a quick walking pace, which speeded up into a jog once he could see better. The heavy flashlight in his hand would only be used as a last resort. He picked up the pace so the soft padding noise of his feet on the ground blended with the thumping of his heartbeat. After crossing Main Street at the bottom of the hill, his progress would be slowed by many unseen obstacles in the poorer part of town. The first task would be to cross Main Street unobserved. He turned west for two blocks along a back road, then another alley running south. At last, the open drain the boy had told him about lay before him.

This carried water right through the town down to the lake. The fast-flowing rain runoff had swept most of the rubbish away. John slid down the sloping concrete embankment and waded through the cold water quite easily, towards the first of many culverts. Bending double, he slowly walked through the square structure beneath the road. As he approached the Main Street culvert, he heard the sound of voices from above. The entrance was in darkness, but the other side was lit by a street light. He would have to check where the men were positioned before passing through.

John inched his way up the left side of the embankment and peered over the wall. About ten Madusacor men stood around a roadblock made from oil drums placed across the road. The voices were much clearer at the top.

"So I went to see the witch doctor and he gave me some white powder," one of them said. "Now I can fuck three times without stopping," the same voice continued.

The others murmured their approval at the speaker's interesting statement.

John could see they were not interested in observing the waterway. In fact, they did not seem interested in anything except passing the time away.

"So what does it taste like?" the youngest of the group asked.

"Ha, ha," the speaker laughed. "You do not swallow it; you sprinkle it on your hard member. Everyone knows that."

Laughter erupted from the group. They had all been wondering what it tasted like.

John ducked down and froze like a frightened rabbit. One laughing man was walking directly towards him. A figure appeared above him, unzipped and started peeing. Some of the warm, sweet urine splashed on John's lips. After some shaking, he heard the zipper again, then a strong beam of light shone up and down the waterway.

"The water is still flowing fast," called out the figure from above, and then he was gone. While John lay frozen, a vehicle arrived and stopped.

"Dismantle the roadblock and go back to your normal duties," instructed the driver. "Parker has escaped."

John peeped over the wall and recognised Marco's car. He slid down the embankment on his belly, then splashed his face with water. What Marco had said explained the curfew situation in Malenga. Calling off the manhunt may help his own escape. As far as the commandant was concerned, he was already dead. Unless they had discovered their mistake or he was recognised.

On the other side of the culvert, he checked his watch in the glow of the street light, then hurried through the illuminated patch of water into the welcoming darkness.

Chapter 82

Both aircraft struggled towards the flickering light on the other side of the lake. Ken wondered how the American bird watcher was coping mentally with his present situation. *He must be scared shitless.* The plane was virtually flying itself thanks to Bill, but the bird watcher wouldn't know that. Ken thought about phoning the American and explaining the situation, then discarded the idea. How would one explain what Bill was doing by telephone? What would happen if Jones let go of the controls? Best to leave things as they were. At least they were still flying and moving in the right direction.

A row of smaller lights could now be seen behind the fire on the shore. Ken turned and pointed. "That's the strip," he said to Roberto. "I will fly to the left of it so Bill can see to land Jan's kite."

Roberto smiled and nodded. Sounded like a good plan to him. Everything seemed to be working out fine. He thought about Sara. *If only it could be so easy to rescue her.*

The float plane descended as Ken lined up for a dummy landing to the left of the strip. He could see the lights behind the fire, comprised of six cars parked at intervals with their dipped headlights shining across the strip. *Good old Sid; you're a ruddy star.*

Ken glanced across at the silhouette of the Cessna and realised something was missing.

"Oh lord! The wheels. Jones hasn't put the bloody undercarriage down." He frantically pushed buttons on his cell phone and lifted it to his ear. "Answer, answer you idiot."

Both planes passed through the smoke of the fire. In a few seconds it would be too late to land. Ken sat with the phone glued to his ear. The other phone was ringing, but Jones was not answering. It was entirely up to Bill if he landed the Cessna or not. Bill pointed upwards with his left hand, signalling Ken to abort the landing. After a few seconds, he pointed to the right and then upwards again.

He turned to Ken. "Quick, what does the undercarriage control look like?"

Ken pointed to a switch on his panel. "Like that, but with a green light to the right of it."

Bill focussed his attention back to the window and pointed down. The other plane had fallen far below them. He managed to stop it hitting the ground, and gradually brought it back alongside. Ken turned right, following the pointing finger. They were now heading back towards the lake to try a second approach. He turned to Roberto.

"Bill should have belly landed her. How the devil is he going to put the ruddy wheels down? That blighter is still not answering the bloody phone. Maybe the ruddy undercarriage doesn't even work anymore."

*   *   *

Phil could not feel his arms or legs. They had been fixed in the same position on the controls from the time Jan had passed out. After the engine had stopped, his brain had also shut down into a dormant state.

Unexplainably, the inevitable crash had not happened. Could be he had already crashed and was reliving the experience in an out of body state. Beyond the stationary propeller, he had seen the fires of Hell below. The Devil was playing a cat and mouse game with his soul. Yes, that was exactly what was happening. Falling into Hell and then living again. The only noise was the hissing of rushing air and the relentless buzzing of a cell phone. Every now and then he noticed the silver float plane though Jan's side window. Shining in the moonlight like an angel trying to rescue him. More like the angel of death tormenting his lost soul.

The click of a switch on the pilot's side made him flinch. This was followed by a soft humming sound, then a gentle *bump, bump*. A green light flickered on. For a moment, Phil struggled to understand what was happening, and then it all became clear. *The ghost of the dead pilot is flying the plane. Jan will eventually turn into an animated skeleton and start laughing and farting.*

That would be the finishing touch to his own personal purgatory. To spend eternity being flown through an endless night by the Flying Dutchman.

On the ground, Sid was confused. The wiry little Londoner scratched the top of his bald head. He looked up at the African policeman standing next to him.

"What the fuck are those fuckers fucking doing?"

The tall sergeant shrugged. He was also confused. Not because the two planes had gone round for a second attempt, but because there was something wrong with the sound.

Part of his job of being a village chief of police was to stamp the passports of people landing and taking off from the small strip. This extra work was not very demanding, because on average one plane every two weeks came and went. Sid normally phoned him in the morning of the day a plane was due, so that he could perform the duties of an immigration officer. Some of the tourists gave him a few dollars on arrival, but never on departing. After a few days at Sid's Safari Lodge they left looking extremely bored.

Clement inserted his little finger in his ear and waggled it around. He did the same for the other side. The two planes had sounded like one as they had flown over the strip. He had never heard two planes flying together, so didn't really know what two planes sounded like. These two sounded like one.

The landing lights of Ken Marshal's plane were approaching again from the lake. The one that was to land was in darkness until it passed over the blazing fire.

Clement noticed the propeller was not turning. That's why two planes sounded like one. He nodded in satisfaction. His policeman's brain had found the answer.

The damaged aircraft touched down and bounced a few times back into the air, while the float plane passed overhead and banked to the right. He waved his flashlight as a signal for his two nephews to start the cars they had requisitioned from the village. They were part time policemen, so the whole force was out tonight. He may need some help in loading the injured pilot into the back of his police van. Now was the time for his plan of action, and he was the official in charge.

Sid was already driving down the strip, chasing the bouncing plane, blowing his horn. Clement didn't like the idea of civilians being involved in this rescue, so quickly jumped into his own car and switched on the siren. The headlights dimmed while the siren made a scratchy burble noise and faded. After switching everything off, the engine still refused to crank. The nurse from the clinic, sitting next to him, gave him a hard look.

"You do not expect me to push this lump of scrap do you?"

Clement ripped open his door and waved his flashlight frantically at the nephews. They were busy trying to start their cars with the headlights on. The flashlight in his hand dimmed and went out.

*   *   *

Sid sped after the Cessna, followed by two four by fours containing a group of hunters from the lodge. He glanced into his rear-view mirror and addressed the fire extinguisher sitting next to him. "Those fuckers fucking well can't complain about being fucking bored after this fucking lot."

The plane in front had stopped bouncing, but showed no sign of slowing down.

"This fucking pilot is a fucking nutter. Put the fucking brakes on, you stupid fucker."

Now the plane was gradually tuning left. Sid noticed the rudder was in a full left position.

Stone the fucking crows. This fucker's going into the fucking bush.

*   *   *

Clement fired two shots into the air to attract his constables, who abandoned their cars and came running towards the police Nissan.

"Has there been a change of plan, uncle?" the first one asked breathlessly.

Clement shook his head. "We are on duty; call me 'sir'. Now you and your brother push my car."

"Has there been a change of plan, uncle?" the second one asked on arrival.

"Yes, push my car now. The plane is already landed."

The Nissan started with a jerk, then accelerated away, pulling the nephews off their feet and leaving them behind. Clement was anxious to reach the plane before the civilians, or he would never hear the end of it from Sid.

*   *   *

Bill lost sight of the Cessna as the float plane flew over the strip. He had seen it safely reach the ground, and had kept it running straight for a while. Now they circled round to see what the final outcome was. Car lights were focussed on a point some distance from the strip.

"She is on her nose in the bush," called Ken. "Not such a bad prang as long as they were belted up," he added.

Roberto could now see a white fuselage illuminated by headlights, standing vertical in the bushes. He turned to pat Bill on the back, but saw he was asleep.

"No ruddy chance of a fire. She is bone dry. Pass the whisky. Time to bloody celebrate, old chap."

Roberto took a swig from the bottle and handed it over to Ken. He was pleased the plane had landed, but any idea of celebration was far from his mind whilst Sara was a prisoner of a madman.

The float plane turned north, searching for the lights of the lodge.

*   *   *

Sid reached the crashed plane first and pulled open the left door. The pilot hung over the controls, suspended by his safety harness. He struggled with the release, but failed. Someone behind him handed him a knife Rambo would have been proud of. It made short work of the straps, but Sid was unable to budge the dead weight of the unconscious body. The owner of the knife lifted Sid out of the way, passing him back to the man behind, who passed him on to the next man.

"Hang on, hang on, mate. I ant a fucking fire bucket."

The man at the door grunted while lifting Jan from the cabin, then passed him to his companions. Sid looked at his four guests really well for the first time. All four were big men with broad backs and bullet-shaped heads. *No wonder these South Africans keep winning the fucking rugby world cup. They are all built like brick shit houses.* He made a mental note not to take too much money off these four at his pool table.

In the light from the cars, the pilot's leg could be seen, drenched in blood. Sid looked round for Brenda, the nurse.

"Typical fucking policeman; never a fucking round when you fucking need em."

Clement's police pick-up arrived in a cloud of dust, and the plump nurse jumped out in a business-like manner.

"Where the fuck has you been, then? Giving out fucking parking tickets?"

The sergeant scowled, but said nothing. With the help of the hunters, Brenda bound Jan's leg tightly, then loaded him in the back of Clement's Nissan onto an old mattress.

"That there's a bullet wound," one of the hunters remarked.

"Yes," Brenda replied. "The flesh is torn. I will have to stitch it. Hold this bag while I fix a drip."

At the mention of bullet wound, Clement took a more commanding interest in the situation and decided to examine the aircraft. Even in the poor light, he could see the right wing was badly damaged. The rest of the plane had bullet holes everywhere.

"Sid," Clement called. "Do you think you did a good rescue job?"

Sid stuck out his small chest. "Of course I fucking did. Left you, Bill, and Ben, the flower pot man, fucking standing."

"Then who is this other man still sitting in the plane?"

Chapter 83

The last culvert before the lake lay just ahead. John had slipped and fallen into the cold rain water twice before reaching this point. It did not matter, because, before arriving at his objective, he would have to swim for a while. The water was now starting to increase in depth. According to the boy's information, the drain kept the same gradient all the way to the lake, so why was the water getting deeper?

He peered into the gloom ahead. Some tree branches had blocked the entrance of the last culvert, causing all the smaller rubbish to be trapped upstream. John cursed under his breath. There would have been less chance of detection going through the culvert to the lake and then swimming to his destination. Now he would have to revert back to the streets, and only then swim the final leg of his journey.

John climbed the embankment and entered an alley running uphill and east for two blocks. This would place him more or less due north of his objective.

In the old days, Malenga had once been the industrial centre of the country. Now the small factories and warehouses had long since fallen into disuse and lay neglected. Most of the viable businesses were now in Mabarta. Road transport and the railways had taken over from the steamers, which used to sail to all corners of the lake. The only vessel to put into Malenga large enough to be called a ship, was the ferry. She ran from north to south on a weekly basis, carrying two rows of railway wagons parked down her length. A large, long pier protruding far into deep water made loading and unloading possible. Passengers slept on deck during the overnight voyage, lulled to sleep by the throbbing of heavy diesel engines below.

John could see the moonlight reflecting form the crowns of railway lines that ran towards the pier. An expanse of broken rusty tin roofs and factory yards lay between him and the lake. He set off down the side street at a fast walking pace, trying to shelter in the more impenetrable shadows.

At the bottom of the hill lay the last tarred road, which separated the residential area from the industrial area. A streetlight bent double by some careless truck driver looked like a jointed reading lamp. It examined the broken pavement with its blind, baleful eye.

Piles of sand, washed down from the side roads, lay in mounds at every intersection. There were no dark alleys here in the docklands. Only dirt secondary roads, badly eroded by the rain. The whole place radiated an uneasy atmosphere. He turned the next corner and walked straight into a security guard.

"Who are you? What are you doing here?"

A blinding light shone in his face.

"Hey, don't I know you?"

John shielded his eyes with his hand and tried the oldest trick in the book. "What is that?" He pointed, causing the guard to swing round.

"What?"

The lens shattered as the heavy flashlight struck the man's head. He staggered, but did not collapse. John brought the weapon down harder this time. Batteries flew in all directions as the guard fell to the ground. Standing over the prone figure, he listened and glanced around. Thankfully, the guard had been alone.

John's heart hammered inside his chest and the muscles at the back of his thighs started twitching uncontrollably. He placed two fingers on the man's neck, as he had seen many times on television. John exhaled. The guard was still alive. What to do now, was the question in John's mind. He examined the man's face, but did not recognise him. There were many Madusacor men in town, but only one John Gwasa. The most logical thing to do would be to kill the guard and continue on his way. John knew he could not do this.

He removed the man's boot laces and tied his hands behind his back, then rolled him into the ditch. With any luck, he would not be discovered until morning. At that time, John should be far from this place, but would never be safe anywhere in the world unless presumed dead. His only hope lay with this man not identifying his attacker.

A car engine could be heard in the distance. Headlights slowly lifted and fell as the vehicle passed over the mounds of sand on the boundary road. John removed the guard's radio and flashlight, then hid behind a broken wall. The car turned round at the intersection and stopped. It was Marco's BMW. After a few minutes, a man stepped out and lit a cigarette. Marco seemed to be examining the night sky for a while, then re-entered the car. The engine started and the X5 slowly retraced its route back down the boundary road.

What was Marco doing? He could check on his men by radio. He seemed to be driving around aimlessly, totally uninterested in the rest of the world.

John checked his watch, then set off towards the water front. He wanted to be well clear of the mainland before first light.

Chapter 84

The sons had not failed against Parker. They had failed against the power.

Marco's report had arrived late. He had lost his faith. Both aircraft were now on the other side of the lake. Parker must have somehow kept the stricken plane flying. It was not the commander's fault. He had succeeded in the other matters. Pointer, Mugjenzi and Gwasa were dead.

Nabusano smiled in satisfaction. *Two more days will pass and then immortality will be mine. Many years of waiting in torment are about to end.*

He would reshape the world at the time of renewal, but not by squandering the force of the power. He had learned from his mistakes. The power must not be consumed unnecessarily.

Light from blazing torches reflected off the diamond-encrusted ball on the temple altar. It also shone from the oiled skins of the guardians who attended the temple day and night. Electricity would have been an insult to the river god in this scared place. The guardians were the biggest and strongest of the followers, who never saw the light of day. They stood guard with traditional weapons of war in this vast underground cavern.

This is where it will end for Parker and the followers.

A mass bloodletting followed by the cleansing waters of the lake.

Chapter 85

Sid stared at Clement for a moment, then ran back to the plane.

"Cor blimey, I never fucking seen im. E looks like part of the fucking seat."

They opened the door to expose a tall Negro clutching the controls. He was not slumped forwards like Jan, but sitting straight up in the seat. The belt clasp was easy to release, but to release his hands from the controls was another matter. Each finger had to be pried from the control column one by one before the big South Africans could lift him out.

"E's dead and gone into fucking rigafucking mortis."

Brenda shone a light into his eyes. "No, he is in shock."

She turned to the hunters. "Put him in Sid's car. I must take the pilot to the lodge now before he dies."

"Here, ang about, I doesn't want somebody dying and a fucking zombie at my place."

Brenda pushed Sid out of the way. "Your place is nearer than the clinic and there is no power in the village tonight."

Clement's nephews arrived, covered in dust.

"Looks like Bill and Ben as been playing in the fucking flower pots again."

"Stop insulting my officers."

"What officers? It's Rag Tag and fucking Bobtail. Andy Pandy could av done a better fucking job."

Brenda lost her temper and pushed in between the two men. "Stop fighting like children while someone is dying. We must go now, sergeant."

Clement scowled at Sid, then took control of the situation. "You two put that fire out, then take the cars back to the village." He pointed to the hunters. "Bring the luggage from the plane."

He pointed at Sid and just scowled again, then got into his car. The siren started working as he drove off into the darkness.

Clement turned to Brenda. "Who are Bill and Ben and this Andy Pandy?"

"How should I know?"

*   *   *

Sid looked at the man sitting on the ground, and scratched the top of his head. "Ear, give us a hand with this fucking geyser. E don't bend anywhere."

He held his car door open while the South Africans lifted the rigid man inside.

"Good job e ant standing up or we would av to tie im on the fucking roof."

Sid contemplated the Negro next to him, who was also sitting in the driving position.

One of the hunters climbed into the back.

"Should av ad a car with two fucking steering wheels, then we wouldn't look so fucking stupid."

Sid wondered if the man would ever come out of shock. Maybe he could sell him as a crash dummy.

*   *   *

Ken pointed at a group of tiny twinkling lights below. "That's the lodge."

He turned right to fly out over the lake.

"Do you see any boats down there?" asked Roberto.

"Shouldn't be any out at this time of night, but I will check."

400

The float plane dropped rapidly, then turned in a circle to line up with the lodge.

"Here we go, landing lights on, tally ho."

Roberto felt inside the empty pack of cigarettes with his finger for the third time. Finding it still empty, he crumpled the packet and dropped it to the floor.

"Will be bloody nice to drink a whisky and soda with ice. Also, a dry pair of ruddy under pants wouldn't be amiss."

Ken wiggled around in his seat, unable to improve the situation. Roberto decided that the first thing he was going to do after a cigarette was take off the yellow suit. He did not like being the focus of attention, especially when being shot at.

The moonlit surface of the lake rushed passed them below. Ken engaged full flaps and throttled back into a slight nose-up position. The pontoons kissed the water a few times, then settled into full contact, leaving a twin trail of wake behind them.

Chapter 86

John was nearing his objective. The putrid smell of fish and lake water was strong in the air. Around the next corner, only a dirt road crowded with wooden stalls separated him from the defensive stone wall of the lake. He walked quickly over the road and down the steps built into the side of the wall. His trainers disappeared into the black, squelching mud of the shoreline as he struggled towards the water while holding onto small boats for support.

John had not calculated on the slow progress through the mud. Swimming, he had practiced every day in the pool at the house. Eventually, he reached the small lapping waves and it became easier to walk on the bottom. The air was fresher one hundred metres from the wall, and he was able to swim.

His swimming time had been reduced by the detour, but had left him extremely exposed in the industrial part of town.

Small waves splashed him in the face in quick succession. John turned the back of his head into the path of the oncoming waves, while swimming left. The dark silhouette of the ferry pier loomed before him. A row of lights ran down its centre, terminating at its end. The wall and the water below were in darkness. Light also shone from the guard house windows, where the pier joined the mainland.

John focussed on the halfway point, and slowly swam in that direction.

A large trawler with a rusty superstructure lay on the bottom, near the pier wall. She had suffered an engine room fire many years ago. Bold black letters stood out along her white side: 'DONATED BY DANIDA'.

John had often wondered what the Danish tax payers would think if they saw this sorry sight.

He swam breast stroke to the trawler, and made his way around the bow.

A small, nondescript grey-painted craft was moored between the pier and the trawler by a heavy padlock and chain. It was only visible from above. On one of John's visits to the town at the south end of the lake, he had left specific instructions with the boatyard owner. He would only find out now if those instructions had been fully carried out.

John knew the boat had been delivered because every Sunday the pier was part of his jogging route. He would stop and pretend to catch his breath above the trawler while examining the small craft below. No one had complained about the craft being there, because no one else wanted to moor alongside the pier. There was no access up the side of the vertical wall. Most of the vessel was obscured by an old, canvas-covered frame, which gave it a box-like shape. The outboard motor had been removed after delivery by the boatyard people. This practice was normal for overnight mooring, to prevent it from being stolen. It also gave the impression John wanted. *One of inoperable disuse.*

He pulled himself over the stern and rolled inside the makeshift awning. With key number two, he unlocked the door of the small cabin and entered the confined darkness. Closing the door behind him, he switched on his flashlight to illuminate the contents. Most of the space was taken up by a row of jerry cans, full of petrol. Two new car batteries stood to one side, next to a tool box. On the other side was a gas stove with its cylinder. A few shelves on the front bulkhead contained tins of food and bottled water, a compass and a map of the lake.

John smiled in satisfaction. The substantial amount of money he had given the boatyard owner had been well spent.

Switching off the light, he quietly stacked the jerry cans in the stern. Returning to the cabin and closing the door, he now found he had room to move around. From deck to deck head was only one point two metres, so standing up was not possible. John opened a cover in the centre of the floor to reveal a squat-looking engine connected up to an electric water pump and a propeller shaft running aft. He checked the oil, then dipped the fuel tank. Finding the levels good, he closed the cover and opened the tool box. Removing a screw driver, he switched off the flashlight and went outside.

To the left of the offset cabin door, he could feel a panel held in position by four screws. These he removed, and inserted key number three into an ignition switch. Above the switch were a square shaft sticking out and a throttle control alongside the switch. Returning to the cabin, John emerged with a small steering wheel, which he fitted to the shaft. Also in the tool box was a forth key, with which he now unlocked the mooring chain and carefully fed it into the water. A few pushes on the wall and the trawler turned the boat in the right direction.

All ready to go, John held his breath and turned the ignition key.

Nothing happened. Fighting the rising panic, which threatened to overcome his mind, he forced himself to think. *What have I forgotten? No power equals no battery. Of course.* He had forgotten to connect the battery.

Back inside the cabin, John found two cables on the floor, which he connected to one of the batteries.

On the next attempt, he heard the muffled cranking of the engine from beneath the deck. The engine had not run since testing at the boatyard six months ago, so the float chamber would be empty. After cranking for a third time John felt a vibration and heard the gurgling sound of the exhaust rising from underwater. The boat started to move forward and inched its way towards the end of the pier.

*　　　*　　　*

A college friend in America had shown John his old Ford car. He had been impressed by the quietness of the low compression engine, and also the raw power of the V8 side valve. In the forties and fifties, the flathead, as it was called, was tuned up for budget drag racing. The only problem being the fuel consumption, which was of no concern to John. A few extra cans of petrol did not make any difference.

*   *   *

At the end of the pier, the boat emerged into an area of soft illumination. John held his breath. It would take two or three minutes for the craft to pass again into darkness. To a casual onlooker, it may appear that the boat was drifting, unless they realised it was drifting into the wind.

Once again in darkness, he loosened the clamping bolts of the canopy and pushed it overboard. Now the small craft took on a totally different appearance. She was extremely low in the water and the cabin surfaces were made up of angled, flat pieces of wood. John had copied the stealth design of American aircraft.

Now he increased the throttle to one third ahead, careful not to allow the bow to lift. He would not know if he had succeeded in outwitting the radar station on the island for another hour.

John set a course for the other side of the lake, where he would become just one more fishing boat. The steering was such that it could not move by itself. He shivered in the cold wind, then retired to the cabin to light the gas stove and make a cup of coffee.

*   *   *

The controller on the island peered at his screen. There was a slight disturbance just offshore of Malenga. The signature had no substance. He had seen this before, caused by birds flying just above the surface of the lake.

He rubbed his eyes, then turned his attention to a different part of the screen.

405

Chapter 87

The lodge comprised of a large, thatched roof building, which was the bar-come-restaurant. A line of small, thatched round rooms called *rondawels* were placed along the shore of the lake. Each had its own shower. Other additions were a kitchen built on to the back of the main building and a generator room some distance away. The focal point was a wooden water tower with a large, plastic polytank on the top, overlooking the staff quarters. Almost everything was made from local materials, which gave the lodge a rustic appearance. More important to Sid was the fact it had cost next to nothing to build. The bar and the pool table were the best money makers. There was nothing else to do.

Two South Africans lifted Phil out of Sid's car and placed him on a chair. He was easier to carry on a chair. Sid followed behind, muttering, "I'm going to av to put up a fucking sign, 'no fucking zombies'.

He stopped on the veranda and listened. Mixed with the soft *put, put* sound of the generator was the whirring noise of a plane engine. Turning to face the lake, Sid could see two lights far out on the water. He rubbed his hands together, smiling.

"Good old Ken, more paying fucking customers."

Inside, there was a hive of activity around the pool table. A drip was hanging from the overhead light while Brenda was stitching Jan's leg.

"'Ear, 'ang about! That fucking table cost me an arm and a fucking leg just to get it 'ear."

Sid was panicking about a bloodstain, or even worse. Somebody dying on the table could put a jinx on his game, resulting in a financial disaster.

He stroked the rabbit's foot hanging round his neck nervously. Brenda had finished stitching the front of Jan's leg and was now placing sanitary pads on both sides. Sid picked up the empty packets.

"Stone the crows, 'e's been shot, 'e's not having a fucking period."

"Bleeding is bleeding," replied Brenda shortly.

The pads were held in position while she bound them tightly in place. An empty beer crate with a cushion was used to elevate the injured leg.

"That is the best I can do for him. We will have to wait and see what happens. If there is an infection, he will need to be taken to a hospital."

"'Ear, what about the other fucking bloke?"

Brenda placed her hands on her hips and tilted her head from side to side. "Try to get him to swallow some sugar. He should come out of it eventually."

"Eventually, eventufuckingally ant good enough."

"Suit yourself. I am going to find an empty room to sleep in. Call me if any change."

Clement looked from the pilot to the passenger and back again. He was not sure who the pilot was. One thing for sure was that neither would be answering any questions tonight.

Chapter 88

The small craft slowly but surely left the dark shoreline behind. John was tempted to increase speed, but decided it was not worth the risk. He checked his watch. If they had seen him on the radar, he would have been intercepted by a cruiser or the helicopter by now. At this speed, it would take him the whole night and half the next day to be near the other side. Then he would turn south and head for the nearest large town, where he could purchase a car. John's problem was that he knew too much about the organisation. He had seen inside the island's vault. With access to the information and evidence that was stored there, one could virtually manipulate world politics. Only after Nabusano's death would he feel safe.

John checked the compass heading and made a small course correction. Sometime tomorrow afternoon he should see land, then follow the coastline south. To sail south-south-west from his present position was out of the question. It would mean passing close to Nabusano Island.

The shivering started again, so John retired to the warm cabin. He removed his wet cloths and wrapped himself in a blanket. A tin of tomato soup was opened and poured into the small pan on the gas stove. The V8 side valve quietly hummed beneath the floor. It looked as if his escape plan was succeeding, but it was defiantly going to be a long night.

Chapter 89

Ken steered towards the light at the end of Sid's floating jetty. The propeller fluttered to a stop and they drifted the last fifty metres to a spot one third of the way from the end. Ken kept away from the end, because of the cloud of lake flies that surrounded the light. The planks below the light were thick with their dead bodies, and the pungent smell was really nasty.

Ken climbed out of the cabin onto the plane's pontoon, and threw a line to Sid.

"How is Jan?" called Ken. "Is he alright?"

"Cor blimey, it's like emergency ward fucking ten in there. If e don't improve by morning you may av to fly im to a fucking ospital."

Patch jumped onto the jetty and ran ashore to disappear among the palm trees. A shiny yellow figure climbed out of the cabin, followed by Bill. Sid rubbed his hands together and put on his best PR smile, which made him look like a leering gargoyle.

"So oow is the giant plastic fucking garden gnome then?"

Roberto stared at the little Londoner for a second, then pulled off the waterproof suit and jumped up and down on it. Sid took a step back while the jetty rose and fell on its floating oil drums. Sid gave Ken an enquiring look.

"He's Italian," explained Ken.

"Oh, alright then, and the other one?"

"He's English."

"Oh, good, good." Sid was pleased he didn't have two raving continentals arriving.

"This is Roberto and Bill."

Sid shook Bill's hand while he watched Roberto kicking the yellow suit into the lake.

"Thanks for the lights at the strip, old man. Is the other chap all right?"

"Why didn't you tell me there were two fucking blokes on the fucking plane? I looked a right fucking Charlie in front of inspector fucking Clement. 'E's waiting for you inside with a lot of fucking stupid questions."

"So is the other chap alright?" repeated Ken impatiently. "He's an America bird watcher booked with me for a week," he added.

"Well 'e 'ant no American any more, e's a fucking zombie and 'e's your fucking responsibility."

"What do you mean?" demanded Ken.

"E don't move or bend anywhere. E don't even fucking blink, and it looks like e even pissed is pants."

Ken rubbed his eyes with his fingertips and turned to the others.

"Let's go inside; I need a bloody drink."

Sid stood to one side, allowing his guests to go first. He didn't want the crazy Italian behind him.

Inside, the focus of attention had moved away from the pool table to the bar. The four big South Africans sat on bar stools with their forearms resting on the counter. They played dice while sipping their drinks and speaking Afrikaans to each other. Clement sat alone, drinking his second beer with two passports on the table in front of him. He waved at Ken when he saw him enter.

"Don't tell him anything strange," whispered Bill, who was walking behind.

Ken stopped at the pool table to check on Jan. His skin was a light grey colour, except for his red, blotchy nose. The pads and the bandage seemed to be holding back the flow of blood.

"Bring all your passports over here," called Clement.

Ken collected Bill and Roberto's passports, then sat down in front of the sergeant.

"Arr, Mr. Marshal. So nice to see you again. Who are your two passengers and why are you flying at night with no flight plan?"

Ken cleared his throat. "These two chaps are working for the Italians at Malenga. Jan, over there..." He pointed at the pool table. "... Phoned me that he was in trouble, so I guided him over here."

Clement stopped writing and gave Ken a hard look. "So, are they on holiday and just fancied a joyride to do some sightseeing in the middle of the night?"

Ken coughed and looked round frantically for some help. "Yes, that's about the size of it."

"Do you know the other two?"

"Yes, that is Jan, the pilot. He flies from Mabarta, and that, I suppose, is his passenger."

He pointed at the Negro sitting by himself, then stared at the seated figure. "Good lord, he looks like he's driving a car."

"Yes, we found him like that, holding the controls."

Ken had visions of having to look after a six-foot-four black man for the rest of his life. It took him all his time just to look after himself and Patch.

"Do you know what happened to the other plane?"

"As far as I know, somebody tried to bloody well shoot her down. You can see the damage for yourself."

Clement checked his watch, then finished his beer. He picked up all the passports and stood up. "I will interview everyone tomorrow. All this is most irregular."

Ken breathed a sigh of relief. He was also dying for a drink. His heart sank when the policeman pulled him to one side.

"Tell me something, Mr. Marshall. You are an intelligent man, not like Sid over there." He nodded towards Sid, who was serving behind the bar.

Ken cleared his throat, waiting for a difficult question. "Yes, if you say so."

"Who is Bill, and Ben, the flower pot men, and who is Andy Pandy?"

Ken stared for a moment, wondering what all these characters had to do with the investigation. "Err; they are people from old English children's television shows."

Clement wrinkled his brow, trying to understand. "So are they bad people?"

"Oh no. Quite friendly, in fact." Ken bent his knees and stood straight again, with a silly grin on his face. "A lob a lob," he said. Then he lifted his hands and feet up and down. "Andy Pandy."

Clement's face was blank.

"You know, like Muffin the mule."

Clement's face darkened. "Now I understand. We arrested two men from the next village for doing that to goats."

The policeman strode away and shook his fist at Sid on the way out. Ken rushed over to the bar and slapped his hand on the counter. "Usual, ruddy quick."

Sid poured him a double with ice and soda.

"What's up with inspector fucking Clueso then?"

Ken downed half the drink in one gulp, then rubbed the palm of his hand over his face.

"I think that Cement thinks that Muffin the mule is an unnatural sexual act involving donkeys and Bill and Ben and Andy Pandy."

Sid scratched the top of his head.

"I dunno where he got that fucking idea. Mind you, I've often wondered about Noddy and Big Ears. I'm sure there was some fucking hanky panky going on there."

Ken moved away from Sid, with a headache starting to materialise. He wasn't sure whether it was because of talking to Clement and Sid, or the fact that it was the middle of the night.

Roberto stood at the bar, engulfed in his own private smoke screen. Bill slapped a hundred dollar note on the bar, which turned Sid into a smiling gargoyle again.

"Thought you lot would try to pay with that fucking funny money from the other side."

"Drinks on me tonight. Well done everybody," Bill announced.

A small cheer came from the hunters. He inclined his head for Ken and Roberto to follow him to the pool table.

"I want to try something. If it works, it may help me free the girls."

"But how!" Roberto exclaimed.

"I am busy thinking of a way, but no guarantees."

Bill took the ball from his shirt and held it against Jan's leg.

"Oh yes, the healing properties. But how will that-a help us against Nabusano?"

"Depends how quick it works. May give me enough time to do what I need to do while being shot at."

"But if you are a shot in the head or heart you would die."

"Yes, I think you are right."

Ken's headache wasn't getting any better. Jan moaned and licked his lips.

"Good lord, I don't ruddy well believe it. You could go through a whole bloody hospital and fix up everybody."

Sid pushed between Ken and Roberto in a ferret-like manner.

"Wot's that then?" he asked, pointing at the silver ball.

Bill dropped it back into his shirt and smiled. "It's a good luck charm."

Sid stroked the rabbit's foot hanging round his neck. Bill noticed Sid's arms were covered with brightly-coloured tattoos.

Jan moaned again and opened his eyes.

"Stone the fucking crows. 'E's goner be alright."

The injured pilot lifted his head and peered around through half-closed eyes. Sid thrust his face into Jan's field of vision.

"'Ow the fuck are you, mate?"

"I thinks I is still sick. This bed looks likes a pool table."

Ken smiled. "That's because it is one, old chap."

"How is my aeroplane?"

"Core blimey, fucker's fucking fucked."

Jan wrinkled his bushy eyebrows and looked at Ken. "Wot's 'e say?"

"He says that your kite is really broken, old man."

"Where's e from? I doesn't understand 'im."

"He is from England."

"Then why doesn't he speak the queen's English like wot I does?"

Ken could feel his headache getting worse. "Because he is from East London."

Jan thought for a moment. "I 'as family from East London and they doesn't talk like 'im."

"The east part of London in England, not East London in South Africa," shouted Ken. He wondered if Jan being conscious was actually a good thing.

Bill walked over to the staring American sitting stiffly in the chair. It was the same face he had glimpsed at the plane's window while riding over the lake. The feeling of benevolence was not there anymore. It was as though he was trying to read the blank page of a book. He didn't know if the ball could fix a mental problem, but it was worth a try.

Bill placed the ball on the back of the man's neck, out of sight of Sid's prying eyes. The arms slowly relaxed and gradually lowered to hang limply by the sitting figure's sides. Nobody had noticed, so Bill dropped the ball back into his shirt and walked over to the bar for another beer. Ken was there, helping himself to a drink.

"Bloody tiring job, being a ruddy interpreter for those two buffoons."

"What's the name of the Yank? I think he is coming out of it."

"Golly gosh, I hope so. Sid is trying to bloody well lumber me with responsibility for him. His name is Philip Jones, if I remember correctly."

Brenda walked in and was surprised that Jan was conscious. She took down the drip, because it was empty and she didn't have any more.

"I will be sleeping in number four if I am needed in an emergency," she announced to everybody.

"Promises, promises," Sid called out.

She walked back out through the kitchen, slamming the door behind her. The South Africans nodded at Bill as they left the bar. He was feeling tired and glanced at his watch, wondering how good the plump nurse was at doing minor operations. Bill was forming a plan of action that involved paying Brenda a visit before morning.

"Brings me a drink," Jan shouted at Sid.

Sid ran back behind the bar and opened a bottle of red wine.

"This 'el replace some of that fucking blood e as lost."

Ken raised his eyebrows. "That's not what Jan calls a drink," he murmured.

Two minutes later, a shout came from the pool table. "Gives me a spook and diesel, not bliksemar faljarpee."

Sid returned, breathless, back to the bar. "Wot's e fucking say?"

Ken sighed and rubbed his forehead. "He says bring a brandy and coke, not tractor fuel."

"Give him a packet of biltong," Bill added.

"That should keep him ruddy quiet for a while," agreed Ken.

Sid dashed off back to the pool table, feeling fairly confident of success this time.

Bill walked behind the bar and helped himself to three packets of biltong, handing one to Roberto and Ken. He split the remaining wine between himself and Roberto.

"Can't see the kitchen opening till dawn."

"Hope you like fish," remarked Ken. "That's all you get here until somebody bloody shoots something. Sid's a real skin flint."

"We a need some changing of dry cloths. I am-a ready for a shower and my bed now," said Roberto through a mouthful of biltong.

Ken pointed to a shelf displaying some safari suits for sale. "That's the best we can do if we all don't mind looking the bloody same."

"Suits me." Bill smiled, while checking them for size and placing some more dollars on the counter.

Sid arrived back at the bar and scooped up the money. "Ear, im over there is fucking moving." He pointed to the American, who was polishing a pair of glasses.

"Maybe if I puts 'im behind the fucking bar 'e can polish all my glasses."

"Best to sort out the luggage and get him to a ruddy room for the night."

Sid rubbed his hands together, smiling. If he also charged Brenda, then the lodge was full. Jan would sleep on the pool table, but he would have to pay room rate.

"Who is paying for this fucking lot then?"

He eyed Bill, who had been splashing hundred dollar notes around.

"Don't worry, write everything down and I will pay every morning we stay here."

Sid handed out five keys with numbered tags, then got Jan to point to his bags.

"So these fucking others must belong to the Yank then?" He lifted a plastic bag up in front of Phil. "Is this yours?" he asked, shouting.

Phil stopped polishing his glasses and stared at the bag.

"Is this yours?" Sid shouted again.

The American smiled, then started laughing. "No, it 'ant," he laughed. "It's the pilot's. It's the godamn pilot's."

"Cor blimy, 'e's gone fucking bonkers."

"No," said Ken. "He's coming out of it. He's coming out of it. That's what is ruddy well happening."

Sid opened the bag and sniffed inside while lifting out a full condom. He dropped the condom back into the bag. "Piss. This bag is full of piss," cried Sid in disgust.

Phil stopped laughing abruptly and moved his legs around. "I think I need the washroom."

Sid snatched one of the keys from Bill, then picked up the American's bags. "Follow me, sir; I will show you to your fucking room."

Phil stood up and followed the little Londoner out of the front door on to the veranda. The pair reminded Bill of Frankenstein and Igor.

"Well that's a bloody improvement. We only have to worry about Sara and Monica now."

They finished their drinks in an atmosphere of gloom, then checked on Jan, who was snoring and grunting.

"Is this-a normal?" asked Roberto.

"I'm afraid so," answered Ken, shaking his head.

"His ruddy kite is-a right off. Don't know what we can do about that?"

"First thing's first," remarked Bill. "What I want to know is why they shot him down? Mr. Jones holds the key to that question."

They walked out on to the veranda, carrying their safari suits, and found Patch curled up in one of the chairs.

"Come on, boy, time for bed. I am ruddy well exhausted."

Patch jumped out of the chair, wagging his tail.

Ken's float plane rocked gently on the lapping waves alongside the jetty. Oil drums softly bumped and thudded into each other under the deck. The moonlit scene gave an air of peace and tranquillity, hiding the events that were taking place elsewhere in the world.

Chapter 90

Keith Watson had switched off his phone over an hour ago. Jones, by some miracle, had reached the other side of the lake, but was not picking up. Whether he was alive or dead, he didn't know. The constant calls from the states were making it impossible for him to think. As every hour passed, a more senior member of government called, wanting to know what the heck was going on. By morning, he expected the secretary of defence to call. After that, who knew? The president.

Everything depended now on what the satellites could see. This Nabusano Island had become the focus of attention. Were these people terrorists or just a bunch of loonies? There was a good chance that some sort of local mafia was based on the island and the whole thing was just a storm in a tea cup. The government in Mabarta was still sticking to their rebel story. Keith knew for a fact it was a load of hogwash.

Who had fired on Phil's plane, and why? A bunch of drunken soldiers? Anything was possible in Africa. Pointer was no loss to the department, but he been an American citizen. A British citizen was missing in the area. How did he fit into the puzzle? According to the Brits, this guy was just an expat contractor with no criminal history.

He turned over in bed and tried to sleep. Nothing could be done without more information.

Chapter 91

The second time John jumped in the water from the stern of the boat, he took a screwdriver with him. A knife would have been better, but there wasn't one in the tool box. He felt around in the darkness and pushed the blade in between the strands of Water Hyacinth wrapped around the propeller.

The craft had run into a floating patch of the weed, transforming the propeller into a ball of vegetation. With the loss of forward motion, John's first thought had been that the propeller had fallen off. Eventually, he had noticed the boat was surrounded by a green, tangled raft of Water Hyacinth.

He had instructed the boatyard to fit the propeller shaft directly to the engine. Less moving parts equaled less to go wrong. This resulted in having no reverse. Reversing the prop would have probably dislodged the stands of weed and backed him out of his predicament.

After cleaning the propeller, he pushed and pulled with a paddle until facing the way he had entered. He restarted the engine and carefully steered the boat out of the obstruction.

The eastern horizon was now a shade of grey. A new day was dawning. John would feel very naked without the cover of darkness. He comforted himself with the thought of being a tiny speck on the great expanse of water.

Chapter 92

Bill awoke with a start and checked his watch. He felt much better after last night's shower and a few hours sleep. Most of the others would not be up and about for a good three hours yet. Bill showered again and then dressed in the new safari suit. The brown material reminded him of his time in the army.

"The only thing missing is the badges," he said to himself in the cracked mirror.

Five minutes later, he was tapping on the door of number four.

"Just a moment."

The door opened to reveal Brenda, who was still half asleep. "What is wrong?"

"Sorry to wake you. I want to talk to you."

She looked around at the sky, then placed her hands on her hips. "It is still night. What do you want?"

"I want you to do something for me. It's worth a thousand dollars."

"I do not do that kind of thing, and besides, I am married with children."

"Have you ever done an appendix operation?"

She cocked her head to one side. "Two or three times; we are far from any hospital. What do you want?"

"I want you to do an appendix operation on me now."

"You do not look sick. Come in; I will check."

Bill removed his shirt and Brenda pointed to the bed. He lay down while she moved the reading light to shine on his abdomen. She pressed just above his right groin, then stared at his skin where there was a faint scar.

"Is this a joke? She demanded. "Your appendix is already out."

"I don't want you to take something out. I want you to put something in."

* * *

Roberto knocked on Bill's door. There was no answer, so he walked to the bar to see if there was any breakfast. He knew it would be too early to try knocking on Ken's door.

Sid had sent the cook to the village to buy more eggs and bread, so breakfast was out for the time being. Together, they helped Jan off the pool table and then to the toilet and back. They then sat him on a cane chair with another one for his leg to rest on. He would not hear of going to his room.

"There wills be no oke to brings me a drink," he explained.

Sid spent the next half hour sponging and brushing the surface of his pool table, while muttering some F words.

He then knocked a few balls around to see if it was still working alright.

Breakfast was a set affair comprising of porridge, fish and eggs any way you wanted them. The South Africans wolfed down their food, then started packing their vehicles with cooler boxes and rifles. Brenda arrived, carrying her medical bag, and checked on Jan's leg. She gave him some antibiotic tablets and said she would come back again tomorrow. Bill entered, walking stiffly, and sat down next to Roberto. Brenda gave him an apprehensive glance, then scurried off to catch a lift back to the village with the hunters. No one noticed she was clutching the crucifix that hung around her neck.

* * *

Marco asked the guard again. "Are you sure it was John Gwasa who attacked you?"

"Yes, sir." The man nodded his bandaged head.

Marco did not understand. Why would the lawyer of the father attack one of his men?

Another report was circulating the town, which worried him. The OC had been killed by rebels on the Mabarta road and the airstrip attendant was also dead.

Marco knew the rebel story was a lie to cover up the manhunt for Parker so who had killed these people?

If they had been killed to make the rebel story more convincing, then his older brother, the commander, would have to be involved. If they had been killed to eliminate some loose ends in the father's organisation, then the airstrip attendant did not fit. Gwasa could fit in the loose end theory along with the OC. Either way, the commander would have to be involved. He would have a meeting with his brother to determine the facts.

The state of emergency had been lifted. Some of the followers were still in town, waiting to go back to the island. It was better that he informed the father about Gwasa rather than someone else. He picked up his phone and dialled the father's number.

*   *   *

Brenda arrived at the clinic and sat down in her office chair. She looked around at the familiar surroundings, but still felt a weakness in her knees.

What had she done? She did not understand. At first, she thought the man a drug smuggler, but he said no.

"My task is to help the down trodden of the world," he explained. Sincerity had shone from his eyes.

After the local anaesthetic, he instructed her to cut along the scar of the appendix operation and insert a silver ball as deep as possible. The operation had been normal and straight forward until the ball was in position. Then the bleeding stopped and the mussel and tissue started to pull together by itself. The incision already healed before Brenda had time to do any stitching. She forced herself to stay long enough to tape a dressing over the wound before she packed her things, then hurriedly left the room.

Now Brenda counted out the thousand dollars on the table in front of her. Before the operation, she planned to spend half of it on herself. Now she would spend it all on the clinic. The man was either a saint or Jesus reborn. The possibility of him being a devil or demon, she refused to believe.

*   *   *

Patch licked Ken's face, bringing him back to the land of the living.

"Hallo, old boy. I expect you need to go out?"

He opened the door and Patch ran off in the direction of the palm trees. After splashing some water on his face and rinsing his mouth, Ken realised he was hungry. The safari suit was a bit on the big side.

"Now I look like ruddy Andy Pandy," he said to himself.

He removed the belt from his old trousers and treaded it through the top of the shorts. *Need to buy a toothbrush from the village. If I bought one from Sid it would probably be second hand.*

Ken combed his hair with his fingers, then stepped out into the sunlight. His *rondawel* was at the end. A brisk, five-minute walk along the shore brought him to the main building just in time for a late breakfast.

*   *   *

Phil opened his eyes and stared at the slowly-revolving ceiling fan. For some reason, it reminded him of an airplane propeller. The wooden beams above supported a thatched roof. A small lizard ran along the side of one of the poles and snatched an insect in its jaws.

423

Where was he? This was not his mother's back bedroom in Washington.

Women's voices passed by outside in a sing song language he did not understand. He sat up in bed and examined his surroundings. The room was round with one small wall protruding inside. There was a wooden door and two small windows opposite to each other. He placed his feet on the painted concrete floor and stood up. Behind the wall, he found a shower with one tap. A suitcase lay on a small table and a shoulder bag rested on top of the only chair. They looked familiar, but he had the feeling something was missing.

He decided to investigate the contents. A tag was tied on the suitcase with a name and a Washington address. Philip Jones; yes, that was him, but what was he doing here?

The suitcase contained the usual change of clothes. In the shoulder bag, he found his toilet gear, a book, a tape recorder, a pair of binoculars and a large cell phone. The phone was flashing recharge and missed calls. He put it on charge and decided to take a shower. It was pointless answering the missed calls until he knew where he was.

Phil towelled himself off and dressed in clean shirt and jeans. They were a perfect fit, so the case had to be his. Not everyone was six foot four. The tape recorder, he wondered about. Nothing had been taped. He turned it over and, without thinking, pressed two small, square buttons on either side. The bottom opened to reveal a pistol. Phil stared at the nine millimetre for a full minute, trying to remember how it fitted into his life.

He was a policeman. FBI, to be more exact. Memories of Watson and Pointer developed in his mind.

He closed the tape recorder, then noticed some discarded clothes on the floor. The shirt pocket contained a driving license and a credit card. Some dollars were found in the jeans, which told him nothing. A wad of papers had been stuffed into a back pocket. Phil tried to read the faint Photostats, but the print was not clear. On top of the bedside cabinet was a reading light and a pair of glasses. He gave them a quick polish and put them on.

Chapter 93

Nabusano sat in darkness, watching the antics of Charlie Chaplin on the screen in front of him. The little man had always been his favourite. That was why he sent the letter telling him to sell just before the stock market crashed. The only other anonymous letter he sent was to Henry Ford, explaining the merits of a production line. His stock value in Ford Motors rose dramatically in the years that followed.

The power eventually failed, and he was unable to foretell coming events like the World Trade Centre. He had known the outcome of the Second World War before it even started. The bank that he established in Switzerland near the German boarder was full of Nazi gold. What a pity the account holders all hanged at Nuremburg.

He managed a slight smile as the policemen chasing Chaplin fell over each other.

He could have given Adolph Hitler the atomic bomb, but it was in his own interests that the dictator should fail. The descendent of slaves who the commandant had failed to kill only knew the tip of the iceberg. Stock in the Japanese market was enormous. Who else could have known that the obliterated nation would turn into a powerhouse of industry?

Gwasa was still alive. The most trusted son on the mainland had failed twice. It was time to take control himself. First, he needed a souvenir from the two prostitutes locked below.

Chapter 94

After breakfast Bill, Roberto and Ken moved out onto the veranda to discuss the situation. Bill assumed the next move would come from Nabusano in the form of a deadline. His own next move would be to find out from Jones why Nabusano wanted him dead. There had to be a connection, which could affect his plans. Bill asked the others if they had any ideas or knew anything about their adversary. Roberto chain smoked in a cloud of despair while Ken sipped thoughtfully on a whisky and soda.

"Anything at all?" he asked again.

Ken set down his glass and twisted the end of his moustache. "While I was waiting in the club for you chaps, Alex, the barman, told me something quite interesting."

"Go on," urged Bill.

"Well, he said that all the sons of Nabusano have a tattoo of a ruddy phoenix on the palm of their left hand."

"How can that a help us?" asked Roberto sullenly.

"The more we know, the better," stated Bill.

"Anyway, Alex said this tattoo story started about forty years ago."

"Hmm, what was Nabusano doing at that time?"

"He was a looking for the ball."

"Yes, even before that. This tattoo must be some sort of symbol for a new beginning. If Nabusano gets his hands on the ball, it would certainly give him a fresh start in life."

"If you do not give him the ball, he will-a kill the girls."

"Yes, and even if I give him the ball, I'm afraid he will still kill them, and anyone else he can get his hands on. What I have to do is trick him somehow into thinking I am giving him the ball, and then use the ball to rescue the girls."

"It sounds like the only ruddy way. Even with that ball thingy, you are somewhat bloody well out numbered."

"I have the feeling not all the sons are still giving Nabusano their full support. It would be a different story on the island. They will be more fanatical, but also more superstitious. That could work in my favour if I play my cards right."

"Sounds like you want to ruddy well take over from the old man."

"Why not rescue the girls and then do some good in the world?"

Clement's Nissan arrived in the car park.

"Oh lord, here we go again," mumbled Ken.

Bill pulled out a hundred dollar note. "Give him this for his trouble. I am going to visit the Yank and find out what I can."

*   *   *

A flash of sunlight attracted the attention of the keeper at the crocodile farm. On closer examination, he noticed a gold chain hanging from the tooth of a crocodile.

Chapter 95

Marco drove past the sentries at the gates and parked next to the commander's car, which was outside his office. The camp was filling up again with army trucks. A soldier escorted Marco into his brother's office, then saluted and left.

"What are you doing here?"

The commander sounded tied.

"I came to visit you. We are of the same mother, are we not?"

"Yes, but I am sure that is not the reason."

Marco sat down in front of the large desk. He glanced uncomfortably up at the smiling president's face hanging on the wall.

"What does this mean?"

He held up his left palm, facing his brother.

"The new beginning of the father."

"Do you think that we are included in this new beginning?"

The commander remained silent waiting for his brother to continue.

"You know what happens to people who fail the father?"

"How does that concern us?"

"We both failed to stop Parker from escaping. I also failed to stop the Italian leaving the camp. There are no rebels. You failed to destroy that plane you were shooting at."

His brother shrugged and lit a cigarette.

"Did you know that John Gwasa attacked one of my men last night?"

The commander's expression did not change, but Marco saw a flicker of concern in the other's eyes. His brother started to repeatedly flick nonexistent ash from the end of his cigarette.

"I see that you did not. Another failure, brother?"

"It is none of your concern what the father bids me to do. What are you implying?"

Marco took a deep breath. "I have seen with my own eyes how Parker is using the power. I am sure if he wanted to, he could destroy your little army here single handed. He let my men live when he could have killed them. If he were not the true prophet, why would the river god allow him to use the power?"

His brother stood and gazed out of the window. "Are you suggesting we should disregard the father and follow this white man who we do not even know?"

"The father is weak and Parker is strong; which one of them are the gods favouring?"

"I think you should leave and take this talk of treason with you," said the commander quietly. He looked Marco in the eye. "You know I could have you arrested and sent to the island?"

"Yes, but you will not. You know I speak the truth."

Chapter 96

The constant flashing of the camera irritated Nabusano's yellow eyes. He smiled in satisfaction at the high-pitched screams of the women as the small toe of each was snipped off by the surgeon. The toes were then slipped into a small plastic bag and sealed.

"Why all the fuss?" he asked them. "I could have started with the big toes, or an ear or two."

Both he and the wheelchair hummed as he left the noisy chamber. The package was completed with the Polaroid photographs and a cell phone. 'Attention Mr. Parker' he wrote in bold letters with a permanent marker.

"Make a small parachute and drop it at the lodge, where you will see the white man's silver float plane."

The helicopter pilot took the package and stood to attention, waiting for any further instructions.

"Do not confront Parker or he will destroy you. I have use for your helicopter concerning another matter."

The pilot nodded and strode to the elevator. Nabusano did not want to undermine his men's confidence, but he also did not want them to do something stupid. Any irresponsible action against Parker would result in a defeat, and would further undermine his control of the followers.

Rumours of Marco's humiliation at the hands of Parker had reached the island, carried by the retuning followers.

It was time for him to make an example of any follower who had failed. That reminded him of Gwasa. He would first exterminate the lover of men himself.

Chapter 97

Bill knocked on Phil's door and found him reading some papers. He had brought him a bottle of coke and a packet of biltong.

"Thanks. Is this place called Malenga? I can't remember how I got here."

"No, we are on the other side of the lake from Malenga. You were going to land at Malenga, then your plane was shot at from the ground ,so you landed here."

Phil rubbed his forehead, trying to think. "I seem to remember a nightmare involving a small plane that ended up flying itself."

He shook his head and smiled foolishly while drinking the coke and eating the biltong.

Bill picked up a book from the table, then moved the chair near the bed and sat down facing the American.

"I think the same people who tried to kill you are trying to kill me. I know why they are trying to kill me, but I don't know why they are trying to kill you."

He lifted the book up in his hand. "I don't believe you are a bird watcher."

"Which people? Who are you talking about?"

"Does the name Nabusano mean anything to you?"

Phil looked down at the papers on the bed. "Yeah, I was supposed to check him out from a distance. What is your involvement in all this, and who are you?"

Bill stuck out his hand. "Bill Parker. I'm an expatriate contractor. I was working at Malenga."

"Phil Jones. I still don't know if I should tell you who I really am. What is going on over there?"

"To make a long story short, I found something that Nabusano wants. He called a state of emergency so he could hunt me down and kill me. I suppose that gave him a good opportunity to kill you, too."

"I thought the president is the only one who could call a state of emergency?"

"Normally, yes. Over there, the president does what Nabusano tells him."

Phil digested this information. "So what the heck did you find?"

"I'm not going to tell you. It's a bit mind blowing and I'm not sure you need to know about it as yet. Your mind is still a bit blown already. Are you remembering things all the time?"

"Yeah. If I see something, like those papers or a name tag, then I remember. I woke up this morning not knowing anything."

Bill glanced around the room. "Don't you have a computer? That could tell you a lot."

"Yeah. I used to have one, but it ant here."

Bill thought for a moment. "It could still be in the plane. They took the things out last night in the dark. If I can hire a car, we can go and have a look."

"Yep. Sounds like a good idea."

"I will make you a deal. If you tell me who you really are, then I will tell you all about Nabusano."

"Okay. My cover is blown anyways with the bad guys. I'm FBI. We latched onto Nabusano because he has stock in America, which he was trying to hide. That's all I know, except that he likes to kill people."

Bill told Phil everything he knew about Nabusano, with the exception of the legends. He himself didn't know for sure if that part was true.

"Real strange guy. A religious cult with access to heaps of money sure is dangerous. What the heck is he hiding on that damn island of his?"

Bill shook his head. "I don't know. Maybe something; maybe nothing."

"The people I work for won't accept maybe maybe. We went into Iraqi on false rumours. A little old island 'ant going to stop us."

"One thing I know for sure is that he kidnapped two women and is holding them hostage until I give him what he wants. You people stay out of there. I need a crack at getting them out first."

Phil gave Bill a sideways glance. How could one man think he could succeed over an island full of armed men?

"Is there any proof of this kidnapping?"

"A friend of mine was there when the security company took them away."

"That's no proof. They could be anywhere. Besides, it is his word against theirs. Have they been reported missing?"

"Yes, just now. You still don't get the picture. The security company, the police and even the army work for Nabusano."

Phil was starting to think that Bill was one of those conspiracy theory wackos.

"Come and meet my friends. They can back me up on what I've told you."

The tall American stood up and stretched his arms, just missing the ceiling fan.

"I need some exercise; my arms and legs feel stiff."

"They are not as stiff as last night," remarked Bill.

"What do you mean?"

"You were frozen in a driving position when they pulled you out of the plane crash."

They walked outside and made their way along the shore.

"I still can't get a handle on this plane ride."

Bill threw a pebble, which skipped across the water. "Just as well, I think."

Chapter 98

Watson's boss at Langley examined the photographs on his desk with his number two.

"These first shots of the island are from one of the older satellites," the senior man explained.

"We should be getting the real interesting stuff soon, when one of the high tech babies passes over."

"What does the report say?"

The chief ran his finger down the report's first page.

"Nothing here to worry the secretary of defence as yet. This recluse guy has sure spent a whole heap of money out there."

He pointed at one of the photographs. "See here, this fort or temple or whatever, is this guy's house. There's a whopping great dome on the roof and a chopper landing pad. That chopper has some of the guys worried. She is built on the lines of some of the latest attack helicopters. That's a bit weird, because they can't ID it. Nobody knows where it comes from."

"Could be the guy built it himself," the other joked.

The chief smiled and shook his head. "Could be a Russian import. One of their prototypes that they never got around to producing. Look at this."

He pointed to a different picture. "Agriculture, like a collective farm, all under irrigation. It's like the guy's aiming to be self-sufficient."

The other man tapped the photo with his finger. "That's too much land under the plough. He must be selling produce on the mainland. What are these other small buildings under the trees? They are spaced out around the edge of the whole island."

"The report says possible housing for the people who work the land. Their second choice is defensive pill boxes."

Both men laughed.

"What's their third choice? Internet cafes?"

"No, they don't have a third choice. Take a look at this guy's harbour. It's unbelievable. Like a miniature sea port. Massive concrete works like two arms sticking out into the water. Railway lines, a crane and a diesel loco."

"What do they say about that?"

"They just say it's way over the top. Too much infrastructure for the barge and trawler this guy has."

"What about this lighter area underwater? It looks like a long reef or something."

"Man-made. Dumping ground for unwanted material."

"And these two boats; what are they?"

"They say something like small coastguard cutters. Millionaire's dreams come true. This guy sure is a nutter to have two. The whole picture points to a guy with money he doesn't know what to do with."

"How much is this guy worth?"

"According to Collins at financial intelligence, seven billion dollars, plus what he has at Malenga."

The other whistled. "That explains a lot of this crap we are looking at."

"Sure does."

"So what's all the panic about?"

"This guy was not on the level about the bucks he has here. Collins sent an agent to check him out, and we don't know if he is dead or alive. Watson reckons this Nabusano guy tried to shoot his ass off to stop him from landing at Malenga. The president in Mabarta won't let us onto the island. Refused point blank. So all in all, we are a mite concerned."

"So, what's the plan on this one?"

"We are organising a couple of black hawks in East Africa to go check the place out. Better safe than sorry. We will be in and out before their president has time to scratch his ass."

The number two smiled. "It sure will scare the crap out of these guys when they see a couple of black hawks landing in their backyard."

Chapter 99

"What is that?" Nabusano pointed to the disturbance on the screen.

"We think it is birds."

Gwasa had attacked a guard at the water front, so he would have been making his way to a boat.

"Play back last night's recording at high speed."

They all turned to a large, flat monitor on the wall and saw the disturbance materialise near the end of the ferry pier. It then moved south and turned south-west. Just before dawn, it stopped for an hour, then continued.

"What is the speed of these birds?"

The controller did a quick calculation, then stared at Nabusano without speaking. There was the loud crack of a small calibre pistol in the confined space of the control room. The controller was still staring, but now there was a small hole in the middle of his forehead.

"Is there anyone else who thinks it is birds?"

They all shook their heads without saying anything.

"Good, so we are agreed it is not birds." He pointed to the dead man sitting in chair. "Push him to one side, but leave him here as a reminder of failure. What are we going to do now?"

"Dispatch a cruiser to investigate," volunteered one of the followers.

"Yes." The old man smiled. "You are now in charge. See that it is done."

A red button was pressed, causing a klaxon to start blaring down at the harbour. Twenty men galvanised into action like the crew of a fire station. An armour-plated door slid open in the side of the wall next to the cruiser, allowing the men to run directly to their battle stations.

By the time Nabusano reached his apartment's balcony, the cruiser had passed the underwater obstructions and was now racing off at full speed.

The anomaly had crossed over the halfway point of the lake, so technically it was now in a different country. An unseen border passing over water was of no concern.

Because the Americans were now aware of him, there was no need to hold back. He would return to the anonymous shadows after the renewal and recreate a new empire in a changed world.

The controllers had calculated that the interception would take place well away from land. There was no need to involve the helicopter. It had the more important task of delivering the package.

Chapter 100

Bill introduced Phil to his two friends, who were still sitting on the veranda. A bearded man with a bandaged leg waved at him from inside. Phil raised his hand half-heartedly.

"Who is that? That guy gives me the willies."

"That's Jan, your pilot, old man. I can understand you not ruddy remembering flying with him," chuckled Ken.

Phil started polishing his glasses with a worried expression on his face. "I remember the airplane being shot at now. Also remember heaps of stuff that don't make sense. There were two bikers riding over the lake."

Bill winked at Roberto and put his finger to his lips.

Sid came over and asked what they wanted to drink.

"What's on for lunch?" asked Bill.

"A real bit of nice fucking fish. My cook is an expert with the tilapia from the lake."

"So he should be," murmured Ken.

Sid scowled at Ken, then smiled, rubbing his hands together. "So what'll it be, gents? Fried, grilled, boiled or fucking steamed. With or without rice, or with or without chips."

"Fish and chips for all, I think."

Everyone nodded.

"Can we hire your car? Phil thinks he left his laptop in the plane."

"Sure, sure; not a problem. Hundred dollars a day and that's a fucking bargain."

"We only need the bloody thing for a couple of ruddy hours."

"Sorry mate; daily rate."

Bill gave Sid the money and he came rushing back with the keys.

"We are all on the same side. Can I tell Ken and Roberto who you really are?" Bill enquired.

"Yeah, don't make any diffs anymore. I am not even at Malenga."

As soon as Roberto found out Phil was FBI, he launched into a heavy discussion about the kidnapping of the girls and demanded what Phil was going to do about it.

"First off, the family can only report them missing after forty-eight hours. Then the local cops can call us in to assist, if they want. The only thing you witnessed was the security company removing them from the camp. They were acting under instruction from your boss. So where's the kidnapping?"

"They told me we would not a see them again unless Bill cooperated."

"Yes, but you need proof before anything can be done."

"Are you a calling me a liar?"

"No, I'm just explaining the legal side of things."

Bill placed his hand on Roberto's shoulder. "Even if they organised a raid on the island, it would end in a bloodbath. At least one of the girls would be killed, and the swat team or whatever would be massacred."

Phil raised his eyebrows at Bill's words.

"You see, they have no idea what they would be getting into. I have the only chance, by tricking Nabusano."

He turned to face Phil. "It's not just a group of men waving AK47s around. They have had years to prepare for something like this, and I would say any sort of assault would fail. The more men involved would mean the higher the casualties."

Phil shook his head. "They are isolated there. They would not be able to call on the army from the mainland to help them."

"They are better than the army on the mainland. Years of fanatical training and no shortage of money. We have no idea what Nabusano has out there, or even the number of men he has."

They ate their lunch in silence, then climbed into Sid's car. Ken drove, because he knew the way to the strip.

The fifteen-minute drive along the sand road south was pretty uneventful. At the strip, they found one of Clement's nephews standing guard.

"That's good," remarked Ken.

"With no guard, you can kiss your ruddy laptop goodbye."

As they walked towards the plane, the policeman stopped them.

"What do you want here? I have orders to stop anyone going near the aeroplane."

Ken shook his head and forced a smile. "Good afternoon, officer. This man…" He pointed at Phil. "… is a passenger from this plane, and he is looking for something that belongs to him."

"I have orders to stop anyone going near the plane."

"Be a good chap and let us pass."

Ken stepped forward and was roughly pushed back with the man's Lee Enfield.

"Bloody hell, you nearly broke my ruddy arm. Phone Clement and bloody well ask him."

The policeman stood in sullen silence.

"I will phone him," exclaimed Ken.

While Ken was busy with the phone, Roberto lit a cigarette. Phil was staring at the wrecked aircraft standing on its nose, while polishing his glasses. Bill cocked his head to one side. He thought he could hear something far off in the distance, over the lake.

"Clement, this family member of yours nearly ruddy broke my arm. Mr. Jones thinks his computer is still on the plane and your bloody man is stopping us from having a quick look."

He handed the phone to the young policeman, who stood to attention.

"Yes uncle… Yes, sir."

He then gave the phone back to Ken.

"What did he say?"

"He said to let you pass and not to use unnecessary force."

"I should think so. Now be a good chap and step out of the way."

"Anyone hear anything?" asked Bill.

They all shook their heads. Roberto climbed up the inside of the fuselage and checked under the seats. He emerged again, carrying a laptop bag.

"This is-a yours?"

He held the bag in front of Phil, who looked a bit dazed. "Yeah, thanks buddy."

"Come on, let's get out of here. Something is coming."

Bill walked quickly back to the car and started the engine.

"Golly gosh, I think we should do as he says. When Bill say's something is coming, it's usually something bloody nasty."

The sun shone into their eyes as they drove north, back towards the lodge. Phil glanced out of the rear window and noticed a flash of sunlight reflect off something above the airstrip.

"There's a darn big white chopper turning over the strip."

"Oh lord, now we are ruddy well in for it."

"I don't think so. They wouldn't know who is in this car from the air," said Bill.

"What are you guys worried about? It's only a chopper."

"It is a Nabusano's helicopter."

"So what can a civilian aircraft do, anyways?"

No one said anything as the heavy beating of rotor blades grew louder and vibrated the air inside the car. Bill gritted his teeth, keeping the vehicle's speed down to a normal level. A fleeting dark shadow passed over them as they craned their necks in an attempt to look up. The belly of the nose-down helicopter was clearly visible before being obscured by flying dust.

"Holy shit," exclaimed Phil. "Did you see that?"

"If you were referring to all those ruddy air-to-ground missiles under the wings, yes, I think we all saw that."

Bill slowed the car, waiting for the dust to clear. "What were you saying about a civilian chopper?" he asked.

"But that's illegal; those guys are breaking the law."

"What a law are you speaking about?"

"Clement's the only ruddy law here. Excuse me for a certain lack of confidence. He is more interested in bloody Bill and Ben, the flower pot men."

"That cop at the strip must have seen those rockets."

Bill shook his head. "He wouldn't know what he was looking at. What's Clement going to do? Wave his truncheon at them?"

The small bushes flew past on either side as Bill accelerated again.

"Well, I'm as sure as hell goners report them to the cops."

"Dio porco, what can you a do here? You have not your badge."

Bill pointed ahead. "They are hovering over the lodge."

"I hope they don't zap my old girl," murmured Ken.

"Now they are leaving. They have done whatever they came here to do. Could be Nabusano's ultimatum. He won't leave things as they are."

The car arrived at the lodge, where Sid and some of his workers milled around in confusion. Two of them pointed to the lake deep in conversation. When he saw Bill, he came running over, carrying a package.

"You lot should av bin ear. There was this great big fucking helicopter ear what dropped a fucking parcel for you. See ear, it has your fucking name on it."

Sid lifted the package to his ear and shook it.

"Hope it's not a bomb," remarked Bill.

Sid quickly handed the box to Bill and walked rapidly away.

"Come, let's go to my room. I think this concerns all of us."

Bill placed the package on the table while the others gathered round, and started to open it. He removed a cell phone and a collection of photos marked with numbers.

"He wants me to look at these in sequence."

Bill placed them on the table one by one.

"Holy shit," exclaimed Phil.

"Good lord," whispered Ken.

Roberto started moaning, with tears in his eyes. "Is this-a proof good enough," he shouted at Phil.

Bill looked in the bottom of the box with a grim expression, then spoke to Ken. "Take Roberto to his room and look after him. I need to speak to Phil. At least we know they were still alive when they took these pictures."

Ken placed his arm round Roberto's shoulders. "Come along, old chap. I think we both need a drink."

After the door closed behind them, Bill lifted out the plastic bag. "Would a couple of toes interest you?"

Phil sat down in shocked silence and polished his glasses.

"The last time I received one of Nabusano's surprise packages, it contained the head of my foreman. This one is not so surprising. It could have been a lot worse."

Bill placed everything back in the box, except the phone. "I will have to wait for instructions now. Keep your people off the island. That's all I ask. Go and phone them now, and find out what is happening. Take this box with you. I don't want it. One of my girlfriend's toes is in there."

Phil took the box and returned to his *rondawel*. He would contact Watson, then fill in any missing pieces of his life with the laptop.

*   *   *

Bill lay down on the bed, feeling sure that Nabusano would not call him soon. More like waiting for the maximum effect of the package. Did he really know Nabusano, or was he just guessing? The old man had made the mistake of not knowing his adversary. Maybe he was doing the same?

He closed his eyes and concentrated on Nabusano's past. Soon, he had left the *rondawel* and was in a different time and place.

Chapter 101

John empted a jerry can of petrol into the fuel tank and threw the empty container over the side.

He checked his watch and squinted at the late afternoon sun. In another hour and a half the light would be fading and the darkness would bring him some sort of comfort. *Fool's paradise*, he thought to himself. The all-seeing eye of the radar covered the whole lake.

On one of his visits to the underground vault, he had inadvertently stepped out of the lift on the wrong floor.

The huge, round disc of the radar screen had dominated the control room.

In the beginning, he had contemplated an escape overland, but had later decided over water would be easier. Under normal circumstances, a small craft on the lake would not be challenged unless it ventured too close to the island. The stealth design was just an extra precaution. Over the last few days, the situation had changed dramatically. He wondered how Parker had escaped.

Everywhere was watched by the eyes of informers on a day-to-day basis. John had been forbidden to fly anywhere, except to the island on the helicopter when summoned by the father. When going to the town at the south end of the lake on Nabusano business, he had noticed a man on the ferry watching him. The only contact with the boatyard owner had been the passing of a large brown envelope under the table at a restaurant. After delivery of the boat, a second envelope had been passed to the son of the owner at a restaurant in Malenga. John had pretended to be interested in the young man.

He breathed the fresh air of the lake deeply and felt free for the first time in years. There were no eyes watching him from behind a corner or a newspaper out here.

As far as he could see in any direction, there was absolutely nothing and nobody.

*   *   *

"The helicopter has completed its mission and will be back in one hour."

"Good. What news of the cruiser?"

"She will make contact just before sundown."

"Make sure the destruction of the anomaly is filmed. I would like to enjoy the spectacle at my leisure."

The uniformed officer nodded and left the apartment.

Parker was now waiting for a telephone call. *He and his companions will be worrying about the females.*

"I wonder if he has involved the descendant of slaves?" he asked himself.

The Americans will be over confident, like the Germans before them. It would be pleasant to destroy his enemies in open combat, as in the days of old. A test of the island's fortifications would be most welcome before everything was obliterated after the renewal.

Chapter 102

Phil could not believe what Watson was telling him.

"But according to this guy, Parker, any sort of raid will fail with massive casualties."

"Who the heck is Parker?"

"He's a contractor from Malenga."

"So has he been there?"

"No, but he seems very sure of himself. I have seen their helicopter, and I sure wouldn't like to tangle with that."

"So lemi get this straight. A Limey contractor who has never been there says 'pull the plug'?"

"Yep, and there are hostages on the island."

"How many, and who are they?"

"Two women. I have seen the proof."

"I bet they are friends of this Parker?"

"It just so happens they are. What difference does that make?"

Watson sighed and paused for a moment. "I'm goner tell you what my boss is goner tell me. Ever heard of collateral damage?"

Phil swallowed a few times. *The CIA sure has a different set of rules to the FBI.* It was a whole new ballgame. He had been taught to preserve life at all costs.

"Look, the end result is more important than a couple of lives. They have to eliminate this guy off their list of possible threats. From what we know up to now, he is some sort of murdering sonofabitch with a whole heap of money. I'm not the one who authorised this action. As far as I'm concerned, it's too early to make a decision like that. The best I can do is to tell them what this Parker guy says. I will also put Collins in the picture. Could be he can talk some sense into them."

$$*\qquad*\qquad*$$

Phil tapped on Bill's door and partly opened it. The Englishman appeared to be sound asleep. He decided not to disturb him with the bad news, and closed the door again. The bottom line was that the black hawks were already in the air and Watson was unable to stop them.

Chapter 103

Bill became aware of lush vegetation dripping with raindrops after a heavy shower. Gradually, the sound of running water entered his mind. A fast-flowing stream cascaded over steps of rock, forming large pools before continuing on its meandering course. A group of African women washed clothes and chatted to each other, in a sing song language, on the side of one pool. Further upstream, others filled clay pots with water, and helped each other to place them on their heads. Children carried smaller pots, depending on their size. The water-carrying procession disappeared into the foliage along a well-used path.

Eventually, Bill began to understand what was being said. First of all, it was the odd word, then whole sentences started to make sense. A fisherman expertly cast his net in the largest pool, and smiled when one of the women waved at him. The whole scene of domestic chores in an organised manner gave an impression of peace and tranquillity. He tried to estimate what point in time this was, and failed. The women's talk was ageless.

They would continue talking about the same things till eternity. The only clue was the clay pots. This was a time before metal buckets and plastic containers.

Bill thought about Nabusano and was drawn to the path like a floating balloon. Some distance ahead, a large column of blue smoke rose into the air. The path split into smaller ones as he approached a village comprising of about seventy circular huts. Sticks had been knocked into the ground and covered with mud. The roofs were made of reeds over more sticks and branches. In the centre stood a large rectangular hut surrounded by a stockade. The smoke rose from a patch of land on the other side of the village. Men were busy cutting the undergrowth away and stacking it onto smouldering fires. Four old men sat on stools near the large hut. The oldest of the four seemed to be the focus of attention, and held a staff in his right-hand. Two of the others listened, while one picked up a coconut from a pile and threw it on the ground. He waved his arms around, holding a rattle, and started shouting and dancing. The white-painted face of the agitated man reminded Bill of a skull. Some sort of political debate involving coconuts was in progress.

He passed through the stockade's wall of logs like a ghost, and floated up the hill in the direction of the fires. A tall, athletic man with a baton in his hand stood alongside two small boys. Could this be Nabusano as a young man? No. He moved on past the man and stopped near the elder of the two boys, who watched their father supervise the clearing of the land.

"Father, why is the chief's brother angry?"

"Because the chief is without sons, and favours me as his successor, and not the son of his brother." He patted both his sons on the head and smiled. "I have fathered the best two sons of the village. We are not like his brother's family, who is weak in body and dull of mind."

"Why is he angry about the nuts?"

"Because it was not his idea. I was sent to the kingdom in the south to trade skins for iron cutters from the city of Abomey. There I saw many wonders, and decided to bring back the fruit of the palm tree. After the nuts are in the ground, I can journey back to the iron works with more skins to trade for the cutters."

The younger of the two boys picked up a coconut and shook, it wondering what was inside.

"Within is food and drink. Oil can also be made from the fruit. In the times of no water from the sky and a season of poor hunting, our people can eat the fruits and live. The chief is well pleased. You, the children of the village, will prosper."

"How do we plant the nut in the ground, father?"

The man took the coconut in his hands and dropped it on some level ground.

"Whichever way it comes to rest on the Earth, that is how it must be planted, half into the ground."

"When will it start growing?"

"The same time a woman is with child before the birth, then it will sprout. After seven seasons, the trees will give us more fruits to plant and eat."

The father crouched and gathered his sons within his arms so that all three of their heads came together.

"We, the N'gou family of the Bariba, are destined to do great things upon this Earth. Remember, wherever we may be, even after death, we will always be together."

The tall man stood and looked down upon the village with a troubled expression. He addressed the elder of the two sons.

"Go hide yourself and listen to the poison words that are being spoken, so that I may know our enemy. We must not underestimate the chief's brother. Because he is the juju man and speaks for the Supreme Being, he is of great danger to us."

The boy ran off down the hill, and Bill's mind was drawn to follow. Bill now knew for sure that this young boy was definitely Nabusano, and that something was going to happen that would shape his mind forever.

Chapter 104

Watson's boss scratched the stubble on his chin and forced himself to drink more coffee. "Your not goner believe this. That man Collins sent there has reported in and has told Watson that we have to put a hold on everything. Reckons we will get our asses kicked."

"So where is this guy?"

"He's sitting on the other side of the lake in a different country. Never even made it to Malenga, and get this... He gets his info from a Limey, who also has never been on the godamn island."

The two men laughed and shook their heads.

"They say there are two women hostages being held there. The FBI guy says he has seen proof of that. Photographs and toes cut off. Not a pretty picture."

"You're not going to stop the operating because of them, are you?"

"Nope, but I think the choppers should land on the roof and work their way down the inside of the building. Give less time for these mothers to kill anyone before we secure the place."

"Yep, makes sense. Presuming the hostages are inside."

"Yeah, well how the hell should I know? Come on down to opps. I want to explain this hostage thing to green leader. Good excuse for going in, anyways."

The two men boarded an elevator by using a pass card, and descended into the heart of the building. An armed guard stood at the entrance of the operations room and nodded as they passed. Four men wearing headphones sat in front of large screens like air traffic controllers. Another man was standing while talking on the phone. He waved frantically at the two men who had just entered, and covered the mouthpiece.

"Who is it? What's all the panic?"

"Henderson, the secretary of defence himself. Wants to speak to you like now."

"Hallo, Mr. Secretary. How can I help you? Err, just a moment, sir." He covered the mouthpiece. "Where are they now?"

The seated man in front of him pointed at two blips on the screen.

"They are starting to fly over the lake as we speak… Yes, sir, of course they are still flying. Why shouldn't they be…? Yes, sir… Right away, sir. Turn them around. Turn them around now," he shouted.

"Green leader, green leader, come in."

Watson's boss grabbed the microphone. "Abort, abort. Do you read, over?"

The seated man nodded and held out his hand for the microphone. "Affirmative, abort mission over."

Everyone in the room watched as the two blips stopped and then retraced their path. The chief picked up the microphone again. "Get your asses outer there pronto."

It was only when the blips were back overland and heading east that Watson's boss relinquished the microphone and picked up the telephone again. "They are outer there, sir; we haven't lost any of them. Yes, sir… Yes, sir… Will do, sir."

He put the phone down and stared at the screen. "Any one of you fuckers got a cigarette?"

"What the heck's going on?" the number two asked.

"Situation has changed like big time. The latest satellite info is just in at the intelligence office. It was so radical that they phoned Henderson first. They haven't even finished the report yet."

"What do they know so far?"

"All we know for sure is that they now have a third choice on those pill boxes and it's not internet cafes."

"So what are they?"

"Half of them are radar-controlled ground-to-air missile sites. That nutter over there can take out anything flying anywhere near him at the push of a button."

"Holy shit, what happens now?"

"We wipe the egg off our faces and attend an emergency meeting with all the big brass at the intelligence office. They say it will take a few hours to know what they are looking at, and even then some of it will be guesswork."

*   *   *

Nabusano flipped the covers over the line of red buttons in front of him. What a pity they had turned back and spoilt everything. The lover of men would not escape so easily.

Chapter 105

Bill followed Nabusano through the village to the back of the chief's hut. The stockade was no barrier for the boy, who nimbly climbed over the top and dropped silently on the other side. Bill experienced the uncomfortable feeling again of passing through the wall of logs. Next to the hut was a small structure on stilts, used for storing grain. Nabusano crept inside and made a small hole so he could see as well as hear what was happening at the meeting place. All the elders were now attending. They were seated on the ground, surrounding the council members.

Near the stockade, on the other side of the chief's compound, he could see his mother helping to build their new house. Never before had anyone been allowed to build within the stockade of the chief.

The juju man stole the occasional hateful glance in his mother's direction as he continued speaking. "N'gou did not bring back the iron for which he was sent. He disobeyed this very council."

The chief thumped his staff on the ground. "There were not enough skins to trade for the nuts and the iron. N'gou made a decision; something your son is incapable of."

"The journeys to the south are placing our tribe in danger. I do not trust the Fon. They came from the east and have built the great kingdom of Dan Homey. Many tribes have been swallowed up and enslaved by their King Agadja."

The chief nodded. "All these things I know. We do not possess the red stone for the making of iron. N'gou and his men made certain they were not followed by the soldiers of Abomey."

"He has angered the spirits of the forest by burning the trees. These nuts are from a place where the land meets salt-tasting water. They are not welcome here by the spirits. Even the Supreme

Being is angered and will not protect us from King Agadja's evil. He deals with the white-skinned men and exchanges people for weapons of war. I have heard of thunder sticks that can strike down a man from a distance."

The juju man paused and noted the worried expressions on the faces of the elders.

"Ten thousand people every season are taken from the city of Abomey to Porto Novo and Ouidah. There, where the great water meets the land, they are never seen again."

The chief looked down at his feet. "I, too, have heard it said from our hunters who have met travellers in the forest. Our hunters know not to bring strangers here, because of this. After I have joined my ancestors, N'gou will lead the tribe to prosper with his new ideas. We, the Bariba, will become strong and trade the oil from the new trees for our own thunder sticks. Are you saying we should do nothing and hide ourselves forever within the forest?"

"That is better than the death and destruction that N'gou will bring upon us."

The juju man sat down. He knew he could not win against his brother, but he had sown the seeds of doubt within the elder's minds.

"Where is your son? I have not seen him since N'gou returned."

"I will not permit him to be involved in the burning of trees. It is blasphemy against the spirits of the forest. I have sent him north to sacrifice a goat on the tallest mountain there. It is all I can do to try to appease the gods."

Nabusano was puzzled. He had seen the son of the chief's brother travelling south, carrying a sack and a skin of water. There had been no sign of any goat.

A young girl ran into the village, causing a commotion. "There are strangers in the forest," she cried, pointing to the south.

"What number of men approaches? the chief demanded.

She held up all her fingers four times, then ran off to her hut.

A council member blew a horn to summon all the men to the compound. Soon one hundred men of different ages, armed with bows and spears, were gathered before the chief.

"We will see what the strangers want."

N'gou told his two sons to hide until they knew the visitors intentions, so Nabusano returned to the grain store with his brother. The newcomers entered the compound and formed a line facing the chief and his men. They were all dressed in the same white skirt and leather sandals. Their leader stepped forward from the centre of the line. He wore a headdress and a shiny metal plate covering his body, and now smiled at the men gathered in the compound.

"Which one of you is chief, and what tribe are you? I wish to thank you for the welcome you have shown us."

The old man with the staff stepped forward. "I am chief of this village. We are Bariba, and strangers are not welcome here. State your business and then return from where you came."

"I am not a stranger here. I am a captain in the service of your King Agadja. He bids that you give me twenty of your best males for trade with the men of white skin."

"I do not follow the bidding of your king. My king is to the north in the town of Nikki. He does not deal in the trading of people."

"The kingdom of Dan Homey is bounded by the great water in the south and the mountains of the north. You are all subjects of Agadja and will do his bidding or suffer the consequences."

The men on either side of the chief lifted their weapons.

"Do you not see that the number of your soldiers is less than half of that of my warriors? Return from where you came or die."

The captain held out his hand and one of his men placed a wooden club with a metal handle in it. The club he held the wrong way round and lifted the handle to point at the chief.

"Are those your last words?"

"Yes, leave here or die."

"Then let them be your last words forever."

There was a flash and puff of smoke near the captain's face, followed by a clap of thunder. A flame shot out from the end of the metal rod, surrounded by a large cloud of black smoke. The chief was flung backwards by the impact of the lead ball, which passed through him and brought down two of the elders standing behind him. The warriors stood rooted to the spot in wonder and surprise. N'gou, who had seen the thunder sticks before, charged towards the captain with his spear. He knew it would take time for the captain to prepare the stick for firing again. Halfway to the captain, N'gou threw his spear and drew his knife. The captain smiled and sidestepped the onrushing spear, which stuck in the ground behind him. Just before N'gou reached him, the captain pulled out a pistol and fired at point blank range. He side stepped again as N'gou fell dead to the ground. Nabusano sank his teeth into his wrist to stop himself from crying out.

"You see, it is of no use to resist. This is a waste of a brave warrior. Who is now your chief?"

The juju man stepped forward.

"Tell your men to lay down their weapons or be killed."

The chief's brother signalled the warriors to do the captain's bidding, then walked bravely up to him.

"You have done well," said the captain in a low voice.

"Where is my son?" whispered the chief's brother.

"Do not worry; he is hiding in the forest. No one from the village saw him guide us here."

The soldiers tied all the warriors' hands behind their backs and lined them up for inspection.

"Choose the men with the animal tooth hanging from their necks. They are of the same family as N'gou. It is better for me if they are gone."

Before Nabusano could stop him, his brother jumped from the grain store and raced over to his father's body. Nabusano wept as he watched his brother try to wake his dead father. The captain pulled the boy away, who then attacked him like a wild animal.

"I see there are two warriors among the cowards of this village," laughed the captain.

He knocked the boy unconscious with his fist.

"He is one of the sons of N'gou. Take him with you. I will deal with his brother and his mother," whispered the juju man.

The captain picked out the men he wanted, who were then fastened together with a long chain.

"How did you find us?" called the chief's brother. "The only well-trodden path is to the river and back."

The captain smiled at this prearranged question, and pointed at the column of smoke rising into the sky. "It was the smoke that led us here. Without the smoke, we would never have found you."

The soldiers filed out of the village, taking their prisoners with them. Long slender sticks were used to lash the reluctant ones. Nabusano's brother was tied to the end of the procession. The juju man cut the bonds of the remaining men and summoned a meeting.

"It has come to pass as I foretold. The chief did not heed my warnings. N'gou now lies dead, struck down by his own evil. We must cleanse our village of the N'gou poison."

He took a burning brand and set the half-built hut on fire while the others cheered. Nabusano left the grain store and retraced his path over the stockade. He must hurry to the old house and warn his mother and two sisters. Bill followed the fleeting figure of the boy as it dashed in between the huts of the village. Women stood in their doorways, wondering what had happened inside the compound. They had seen some of the men folk pass by in chains, and the wives of these men were crying and wailing in anguish. Women who lost their husbands would become the property of the other men of the village. If no one wanted them, they would be cast out to fend for themselves. Nabusano breathlessly told his mother what had happened with tears in his eyes.

"There is no time to grieve over your father. We must flee for our lives."

She handed the boy his bow and arrows and a skin of water.

"Take your sisters and run like a deer to the east, where the sun rises. Wait for me near the great, flat rock at the foot of the mountain. I cannot move at your speed, for I am with child."

She kissed them all on the forehead, then pushed Nabusano away. "Go now, for the sake of your sisters. I will follow."

His older sister reached the foliage of the forest first, closely followed by Nabusano, pulling the youngest along by her hand. They turned east and quickly made their way up the hill. Their mother had reached the forest, but was some distance behind. Her breath came in short gasps as she laboured up the hill. Nabusano stopped to look down upon the village.

The men inside the compound were now throwing coconuts into the flames of the blazing hut, and dancing around in a frenzy. Some of them were called to one side by the juju man. He pointed in the direction of the N'gou hut with the chief's staff. Nabusano told his sisters to continue while he waited for his mother. A group of men ran to the N'gou hut and found it empty. Nabusano's heart sank as some of the women pointed to the forest. A line of men spread out and entered the trees. Soon there was a shout of triumph. He watched helplessly while his mother was dragged towards the compound. Another shout was raised as the men entered with their victim. The chief's brother raised his hands for silence.

"The Supreme Being needs a sacrifice to appease him," he shouted.

Nabusano's mother stood in defiance before the juju man, not showing any sign of fear.

"Your husband brought this curse upon the tribe. You are part of his evil and must pay for his sins."

She spat into the old man's face. "You are the evil one here," she said.

He struck her on the head with the staff, knocking her unconscious, and pointed to N'gou's body.

"Throw them both in the fire. We must be rid of the evil."

Nabusano watched in horror as both his parents were tossed into the blazing hut, raising a shower of sparks.

The chief's brother raised his hands to the sky. "The gods have spoken," he shouted.

Nabusano suddenly became aware of another presence nearby. He was not the only one watching the scene below. Stealthily, he merged with the undergrowth and moved to his left. He came upon a crouched figure peering over the top of the bushes. It was the son of the juju man, and he was smiling. Nabusano fought to control himself. His body was shaking with rage. The juju man's son was physically a man who could easily overpower any young boy.

He fitted an arrow to his bow and pulled back the string with all his strength. The first arrow pierced the crouching figure's throat, causing the man to stand up. He tried to call out to his father below, but just made a gurgling sound. In quick succession, the next two arrows embedded into his stomach, forcing him to sit down in surprise. Nabusano emerged from the foliage and slowly approached his prey. An expression of understanding and fear showed on his victim's face while he tried to push himself backwards through the undergrowth. The fourth arrow entered an eye socket and lodged in the brain.

Chapter 106

The setting sun sank behind the silhouette of land on the western horizon. John turned south to run parallel with the coastline for the rest of the night. He relieved himself over the side of the slow-moving boat, and washed his hands in the water.

Far to the north, a dow loaded with sacks of charcoal glided past in the opposite direction. John presumed it was on course to Malenga. They did not show any sign of seeing the low-lying craft. Dows had been sailing the lake for hundreds of years. They used an outboard motor to run against the prevailing wind, then sailed back again.

John was bored. There was nothing to do except drink mugs of coffee. The second night was going to be even longer than the first.

He fiddled with the radio he had taken from the Madusacor guard. Motorola P0 40. He remembered buying some of these a couple of years ago. They were normal issue to security companies and construction workers. It had a range of about twenty kilometres, if he remembered correctly.

He shook some drops of water out of it, and turned it on. The knob to the right was a channel selector, so he slowly switched from one to the other, not expecting to hear anything. To his surprise, there was a voice on one channel.

Who could be out here on the lake using a hand-held radio? He looked to the shore. There was nothing on the other side except a game lodge.

He turned up the volume. The voices did not sound like hunters. They had a more military sound to them.

"Are the engines on full RPM?"

"Yes, sir. It would be advisable to slow down slightly. It is not advisable to run full ahead for extended periods, over."

"Are you telling me that your engines are no good?"

"No, sir. I am just explaining the situation, over."

"The situation is we have to kill John Gwasa or face the consequences. I am the captain of this vessel. Full ahead both. Over and out."

John stared at the radio in his hands in disbelief. His cover was blown and a cruiser was closing in. There could even be two of them.

He pushed the throttle fully open and turned west. The steering wheel nearly came off in his hands with the sudden acceleration. It was now a case of trying to out run his pursuers.

*   *   *

Nabusano studied the green screen with his yellow eyes. "There has been a change. What is happening?"

"The boat has increased speed and is now visible."

"I do not care if it is visible. Will it be intercepted before it reaches the land? Once on land Gwasa, could escape in the darkness."

"At the new speed, he will reach land the same time as the cruiser."

Nabusano shook his head in frustration. "Send back the helicopter. I need to be sure."

Chapter 107

Bill was woken by someone tapping on his door. He swung his legs off the bed and held his head in his hands. Visions of fire and death still clouded his mind.

"Come in," he managed to croak.

Phil entered the room and switched on the light.

"I came around earlier, but you were out of it."

"Yeah, I was into something else."

Phil raised his eyebrows, not understanding. "Has that phone rung as yet?"

"No, but it should be ringing fairly soon, I think. Any news from your side of things? What's that CIA man, Watson, up to?"

Phil sat down on the chair near the bed. "His boss sent two black hawks to the island, but turned them around at the last minute."

"Don't tell me they've started to listen to me." Bill smiled.

"Not really. I think finding out the island is surrounded by ground to air missile sites sorter changed their minds. You, me and Watson are in a bit better position now by the fact that we can say 'told you so'."

"It was only a lucky guess on my part. I didn't know for sure. What do you know about West Africa? I worked in Ghana once, but I don't know much about the history of that area."

"What do you want a handle on stuff like that for?"

"Trying to get to know my enemy a bit better. Nabusano came from around there. Could be important when I get to meet him face to face."

"We did all that stuff at school. Tracing back your roots. Heaps of stuff on the slave trade. I have a photographic memory, so I'm like a walking encyclopaedia on slave trade history."

"Where's a town called Abomey?"

"That's in Benin. Two countries east of Ghana. Capital there is Porta Novo. Lots of slaves came from there and a town called Ouidah. There is a monument on the beach called 'the gate of no return'. Abomey was the capital in the old days, in the time of the kings' before the French took over."

"Ever heard of a king called Agadja?"

"Yep; he was around when the slave trade was at its height. Exchanging slaves for cannon and muskets. There was always a slave trade going on, even before the Europeans arrived. It was them who created the demand for so many."

"When was this Agadja around?"

Phil thought for a moment while polishing his glasses. That was the time my ancestor left there as a slave. I would say about seventeen-twenty. Why?"

"Just trying to figure out somebody's birthday. That's all."

Bill did a quick calculation in his head. Nabusano was over two hundred and eighty years old.

Chapter 108

The secretary of defence had stopped smoking a good ten years ago. He now asked someone for a cigarette. "Better dig up an ashtray from somewheres," he remarked, blowing out a plume of smoke. "Explain this here again. You sorter lost me a while back."

The head of the intelligence room pointed to the image on the screen and cleared his throat. This was the first time since the gulf war he had so much brass waiting for him to speak. "Half these small structures are ground to air missile sites. We came to that conclusion because of their radar signatures. They are unmanned automatic systems, controlled from a central point. Possibly from the main structure over here." He pointed to the square-shaped fort. "On the roof of this building, we have a helicopter landing pad and a large dome. Looks like a mosque of some sort. Inside this dome is a very large, revolving radar antenna of the type an airport would use, or an aircraft carrier."

A murmur of voices erupted from the audience. Henderson raised his arm.

"Godamn it, how long has all this hardware been there?"

"We don't know, sir, but judging by the trees growing against the walls of the missile bunkers, our best guess is more than fifty years."

A clamour of voices now filled the room.

"You gotta be kidding," an air force colonel shouted. "That kinda stuff hasn't been around that long."

The man at the screen waited for the uproar to subside. "Let me make myself perfectly clear on one point before I continue. We at intelligence are giving you the information that we conclude from the facts to the best of our ability. We are not in the business of making up stories or wild guessing."

"Okay, we get your drift. Do the best you can," said Henderson.

"At the four corners of the roof on the main structure we, have these smaller domes. We think they house very heavy, rapid-firing anti aircraft guns of the type fitted to the latest warships. They are installed at the corners so they can be deployed as anti-personnel weapons covering a three-hundred-and-sixty-degree radius around the structure."

The secretary of defence asked someone for another cigarette.

"We don't know what's inside this building because the roof is made of twenty-foot thick reinforced concrete."

"That's a mite like those flack towers the krauts had near Berlin," an army colonel suggested.

"Even the Russians had to go around them," Henderson added.

"Okay, let's go to the harbour. These two piers are hollow. At the ends, they have the same type of weapon as on the roof of the main structure. They lift up and down hydraulically. The rest of the space is used for barracks and fuel storage."

"How many men are you talking about?"

"We estimate two hundred. We don't know how many are in the main building."

"Holy Moses," said Watson's boss.

"Offshore from the harbour is an underwater barrier. At the end of it is a shipwreck."

"What sort of ship is that?" a navy man asked.

"Size of an ocean going tug, and she is broken in half. The only ship on record that went missing anywhere on the lake was a German gunboat called the Derflinger. Looks like she was blown up in nineteen-fifteen."

"Bit before my time," the navy man said.

"We were very worried about the underwater barrier until we found the answer a couple of hours ago."

"I think there is a lot more to worry about than a pile of stones," remarked Henderson dryly.

"No sir, this barrier is made of blasted rock and there are thousands of tons sitting there. The rock had to come from somewhere. There is no quarry on the island."

"Then from the mainland. They have that barge thing."

"We did a calculation on capacity of the barge, the sailing turn around and the quantity involved. It would have taken them a hundred and five years. Some of the rock is on top of the shipwreck, which has only been down there ninety years."

"So where did it come from?"

"You see the railroad on top of the piers? It runs all the way around the back of the harbour from pier to pier, so they need a shunting line, otherwise it gets hooked up with a gridlock.

"There's a set of switches and a shunt line
at the start of the right-hand pier."

"Yes, now take a look at this close up." He pressed the remote in his hand and the picture changed to show the buffers at the end of the track. "This shot explains everything."

"I can't see jack shit wrong with that."

"Notice the track just in front of the stopper is shiny."

"Holy shit, so that's not the end of it."

"No, sir, there must be an artificial rock face."

"Open fucking sesame. What the hell is inside?"

"We don't know, sir, but we can give you our best guess."

Henderson shook his head. "Guess away. I haven't got a clue."

The remote button was pressed again, showing a concrete structure next to the right-hand pier.

"See here, this is a water pumping station. It's way too big for irrigation. Here's an inferred shot of the return pipes. It's capable of cooling something really big."

"Like what?"

"Like a nuclear reactor."

The ash fell off Henderson's cigarette onto his trousers.

Chapter 109

John kept glancing over his shoulder, expecting to see a probing search light. The cruisers had small radar antennas turning round and round. He did not think they would need light to find him. More than one radar would now be watching every move he made. John needed a new escape plan. The old one had become obsolete. Hopefully the speed of the boat had caught them by surprise and they had miscalculated. If not, he would have to abandon ship before they destroyed it.

John entered the cabin and strapped on his rucksack. It would keep him afloat as well as provide him with money. The trick now was to get off the boat before they could observe the craft visually.

He scanned the dark horizon ahead for any sign of life. A few goat herding policemen would be no match for Nabusano. You do not politely ask a group of uniformed men armed with submachine guns for their passports. The lodge should be more or less dead ahead. Maybe they would think twice before shooting at Europeans.

$$* \qquad * \qquad *$$

In the control room, everyone watched the drama unfolding on the radar screen. Even the unseeing eyes of the dead controller seemed to be riveted to the life or death situation. Nabusano grunted when an assistant gave him his eight-hour intravenous injection. The last thing he wanted was to fall asleep at the crucial moment.

Chapter 110

Bill held up his hand while Phil was talking. "Some danger is coming. It could be Nabusano's helicopter with another package. I think I better warn the others."

"What the heck are you talking about? How can you know some danger is coming?"

Bill stood up and walked to the door. "Let's just say it's like a sixth sense. Are you staying or coming with me?"

Phil followed Bill out into the night and listened. All he could hear were crickets and frogs. The Englishman had been right about the chopper at the airstrip, so he decided to give him the benefit of the doubt.

On the veranda, Bill beckoned the others to come outside. Sid was busy chatting away to a contented Jan near the pool table. He sat with his bandaged leg on another chair, eating biltong with a brandy and coke in his hand. Sid was talking non-stop, oblivious to the fact that the other was not listening. Ken and Roberto finished their drinks and walked outside.

"What's up, doc?" asked Ken.

"I have that special feeling again. Let's stand out of the light, somewhere high up, so we can see over the lake."

"Wait up," the American requested. "I have some binoculars in my room."

Roberto lit a cigarette with a worried look. "I am hoping very much it is not another package."

"Me too. Nabusano hasn't phoned yet, so I don't think so."

"Any plan to get the flipping girls out yet, old man?"

"I am busy working on something. The Yanks tried a crazy stunt until they got a fright. Found out the island's defended with ground to air missiles and back tracked very fast out of there."

470

"You think they-a tried to save the girls?"

"I think they would have done if given the chance."

He turned to Roberto. "Don't pin too much hope on the Yanks. They will have their own agenda by now, like saving the world from the bad guys. Our girl friends won't rate too high in their councils of war."

Phil approached in the gloom, waving around a flashlight. Roberto gave him a distasteful glance and turned away.

Bill pointed to the right. "Come on, follow me. We can climb that small hill over there."

The others looked in the direction indicated, but couldn't see anything. Phil only noticed something strange after Bill kept calling out where to step over something.

"Hey! It's like you can see in the dark."

Nobody answered.

Chapter 111

The light on the shore was quite distinct now, and was near a group of smaller lights.

John glanced behind, but could not see anything. They would not be showing any navigation lights tonight.

He climbed over the top of the cabin and listened. Most of the boat's engine noise was left behind from this forward position.

At first he wasn't sure. Then the beating of rotor blades steadily became more distinct. John scrambled back to the rear of the cabin and turned the steering slightly to the right. Then he pulled off the steering wheel and threw it over the side. Taking a deep breath, he tipped over backwards into the water and bounced a couple of times. The boat sped off, leaving him behind in the darkness. Five seconds later, the helicopter roared overhead, flying after the departing craft. John was about to witness his own death for a second time.

A bright light suddenly illuminated the rear of the boat. Something lowered itself from under the nose of the helicopter. John had never seen this thing before on previous flights. Noise and flame erupted from the front of the chopper as a steady stream of tracer bullets linked the two craft together. The effect on the boat was dramatic. Pieces of wood flew in all directions, then the jerry cans in the stern exploded into a ball of liquid fire. A second explosion in the cabin converted the craft into flaming debris, which rained down over a wide radius. There was nothing left of the boat, except floating flames on top of the water. Smoke was blown in all directions by the hovering helicopter.

John swam hurriedly away from the area of flickering light and swirling smoke.

*　　　　*　　　　*

The watchers on shore stared in the direction Bill had pointed out.

"I can't see a darn thing," said Phil, with the binoculars pressed to his eyes.

A searchlight flicked on in the distance.

"There." Everyone except Bill pointed at the same time.

Then there was a ball of fire and an explosion, all with no sound except for a surprised exclamation from the watchers. After a second, a double detonation reached their ears.

"What the heck is going on?" asked Phil of no one in particular.

"It's like ruddy World War Three out there. Those blighters are really playing for keeps."

Bill asked Phil for his binoculars and scrutinised the horizon. "It's Nabusano's helicopter. They have just blown something up in the water. Must have been a boat. Now they are hovering over the spot, looking for something, or someone. I wonder who it is."

"You mean 'was'; no one's goner survive a thing like that," surmised Phil.

"Who ever it was, or is, is in the same boat we are in; candidates for assassination. So it might be worth my while going out there to have a look round."

"But what about that chopper, old chap? I wouldn't go anywhere near that bloody thing."

"Can't stay there forever. Going to need fuel sometime or other."

*　　　　*　　　　*

Nabusano pressed a button and the scene replayed frame by frame.

"Gwasa must be inside the cabin. There are no controls on the outside," the officer stated.

"That is no proof that he is dead. I need to see the body. When the cruiser arrives, it must search for the body."

"Yes, father."

He contented himself by replaying the destruction of the boat a number of times at normal speed. The explosion gave him a taste for his old feeling of power. Secrecy did not matter anymore, so why stop? What else could he blow up while he was in the mood?

*   *   *

A cruiser arrived below the helicopter and switched on all her searchlights. Bill watched as two divers jumped over the side. The helicopter lifted, then turned towards the land.

"The chopper is coming in our direction," said Bill.

"Porca Madonna, can they-a see us in the dark?"

"They can if that bird has infrared sights," answered Phil.

"Nabusano won't take a chance on attacking me. I can make scrap out of that machine anytime I want."

Phil turned to Bill in the darkness. "What the heck are you talking about? You're talking like some kinder wacko."

"Nabusano thinks I have some sort of power, so he will keep away from me, that's all." Bill cursed himself for the slip of the tongue. Phil wasn't ready to know the whole truth, especially after his latest experience.

The helicopter turned and roared off towards the airstrip.

"You sure have a knack of knowing what'll happen."

Ken took out his cell phone. "I'm going to phone Clement. All this shit is his ruddy business, not ours."

*   *   *

Eventually, John was halfway between the cruiser and the shore, but was exhausted.

He had removed his shoes after entering the lake, otherwise he would not have made it this far.

John took off the small rucksack while treading water, and strapped it to his chest. This allowed him to rest his weight on the bag and swim breast stroke at the same time.

The cruiser was moving again, turning slowly in ever-widening circles. It was only a matter of time before they found him. John prayed for a miracle.

Chapter 112

Clement parked his police Nissan at the beginning of the strip and pressed the horn. He hoped this was not the shit of a cow story. Mr. Marshal had been talking about explosions and helicopters. Clement checked his watch and wondered how many whiskies the white man had drunk. He ran his finger over the bonnet and examined the dust on it in front of the headlight. *Waste of time washing and polishing the car this afternoon.*

His nephew eventually reached the vehicle, panting for breath.

"Mr. Marshal phoned me about a helicopter coming this way. Have you seen anything?"

"Yes, it is the same one that flew over before. It has landed at the other end."

The young policeman pointed into the gloom.

"Landed, why did you not phone me? These tourists think they can do anything they like."

"I have no credit in my phone uncle, err sergeant, sir."

Clement stared into the impenetrable darkness.

"What are they doing? Did you not ask them? They could be stealing something from the crashed plane."

"I saw them put something into the plane while I was hiding."

"Hiding, what were you hiding for? We are the law here. We do not hide from anyone."

"There are a lot of men who do not look very friendly."

Clement shook his head. "Have I not told you before, as long as you do not use excessive force, you are entitled to demand an answer to your questions?"

The sergeant drew his pistol and pulled back his shoulders. "I will find out what is happening. You stay here and guard the car. I do not want to frighten them with a show of force."

Clement marched down the strip with a determined expression. One of his officers hiding from tourists was totally unacceptable. No wonder Sid did not show any respect. He was a little concerned that these people were doing something in the dark, but he needed to show his nephew an example of law and order. Clement's pace slowed as he neared the end of the strip. The grey shape of the helicopter standing there was enormous. He wondered if he had made a mistake, but it was too late now to change his mind. Black-suited figures were walking towards the helicopter from the direction of the crashed plane.

"Police, stay where you are or I will open fire," he shouted in a commanding voice.

One second later all hell broke loose. The six figures in front of him ran towards the helicopter, firing sub machine guns in his direction. Clement's cap was removed by one of the hundreds of bullets flying all around him. He hit the ground covering his head with his hands. Dust and stones kicked up from the strip, showering him with dirt while ricocheting bullets passed by like angry bees. There was a lull in the shooting as they boarded their aircraft.

"You are all under arrest," he shouted again.

This prompted more firing, so he decided to keep quiet. Rotor blades started turning while the whining of the gas turbine engine increased in volume. The helicopter lifted and headed down the landing strip. Clement stood up and fired two shots after the departing shape. He picked up his cap and dusted himself off with it. Suddenly night turned into day and a huge force lifted him from behind. Clement was reminded of the time when he was a young boy. He had fallen from a fast-moving, overloaded truck when the rope he was holding had broken. Now he was experiencing the same sensation, except for the fire.

Flames surrounded him while he flew through the air like Evil Knievel without a motorcycle. From this elevated position, he saw another explosion further down the strip. At least they had not escaped. He had shot them down with his pistol.

The ground rushed up to meet him, so he curled himself up into a ball. After the bouncing, rolling and sliding stopped, Clement slowly got to his feet and looked around. Where the crashed aeroplane used to be, there was just burning bush. He had lost his cap, pistol and cell phone. The back of his uniform was smouldering and there was a whistling noise inside his head. He turned and limped down the airstrip towards the other fire and met his nephew.

"Were there any survivors?"

"Survivors from what?"

The young policeman was preoccupied with the top of Clement's head, which was smoking.

"From the helicopter."

"But the helicopter did not crash."

Clement struggled to raise his arm and pointed to the second fire. "Then what is burning inside that hole over there?"

"That is our police car."

Clement stared at the flaming hole in the ground.

"Uncle, can I ask you a question?"

"Yes."

"Do you think we used excessive force?"

*   *   *

The watchers on top of the hill saw the two explosions at the airstrip.

"Clement has started a bloody war over there. He's not answering his ruddy phone. I hope he's alright."

"Borrow Sid's car again and check on Clement. Wasn't a good idea to get him involved. I think he is a little out gunned." Bill gave Roberto the phone they had received inside the package.

"I'm going to do a spot of swimming, so hang onto this in case we get a phone call."

They all made their way down to the lodge again. Bill slipped off his clothes and waded into the water. The mud on the bottom pushed in between his toes. The lights offshore seemed to be slowly moving round in circles.

Chapter 113

Sid marked off another brandy and coke on the slate behind the bar, then trotted over to his captive audience.

"As I was saying, when I was just a cheeky abastard apprentice, the fitter I was working with made a right fuck up with this 'ere fucking job. So 'e says to me, all nonchalant like, 'did you spot my deliberate mistake?'."

Sid burst out laughing. "Did you spot my deliberate fucking mistake? It took us two days of hard fucking work to fix the fucker."

Jan farted and continued eating biltong with a glazed expression on his face.

"Then there was this ear other fucking time, when this bull shitting fucking supervisor tries to tell us that 'e was the only fucker in the tank core to sink a U-boat."

Sid laughed again. "Can you fucking imagine, a tank sinking a fucking U-boat? So the fitter I work with said 'that's nowt. We sank a U-boat when I was an anti-aircraft gunner on the Queen Mary'. Everyone listened 'cause everyone knew 'e was on the fucking Queen Mary in the war. So 'e says 'we was waiting to form convoy off America' so 'e was painting the side of the fucking ship like when this 'ere periscope pops up out of the water. So's quick as a flash 'e paints over the fucking glass with blue paint and this 'ere U-boat keeps fucking surfacing. Then 'e says 'we waited till 'e got to three hundred feet and shot the fucker down'."

Sid burst out laughing again and took a swig of beer. "That there fucking supervisor never spoke to any fucker for two days."

Jan held up the empty packet of biltong and farted again.

*   *   *

Ken found Clement and his nephew limping towards him on the airstrip road.

"Golly gosh, you look a bit worse for wear, old chap. Where is your car?"

Clement pointed back to the strip and painfully eased himself into Sid's car. He had to push Patch out of the way, who kept barking at him. There was a smell of burnt cloth and barbeque in the air.

"Take me to the clinic," he croaked.

"What the ruddy hell happened? We saw two bloody explosions."

The constable in the back leant forward. "It was a case of excessive force."

Clement smacked the boy in the face with the back of his hand. "I want you people out of my country," he whispered.

Chapter 114

The president of the United States listened to the secretary of defence on the phone.

"Can't you sort this thing out? I have a televised meeting with the French president tomorrow."

"No sir, come back immediately."

Henderson heard an exasperated sigh on the other end of the phone.

"What on earth could be more important than tomorrow's meeting? We have even rehearsed our speeches together. The voters of both our countries are expecting to get their monies worth out of this."

"I can't say too much on the phone, sir, but I can give you a couple of comparisons."

"What sort of comparisons?"

"Like North Korea or Iran having the bomb."

"What, have they?"

"No, sir, they were just comparisons."

"Then what the hell are you talking about?"

"Let's just say you are the only one who can authorise a nuclear strike."

"I know that. Are you making a comparison again?"

"No, sir. It may come to that."

"Who in the hell do we want to obliterate?"

"Let's just say, come back now or you could run the risk of losing some of your voters—permanently."

Chapter 115

Bill poked his head up above the surface. The lights were much closer now. He was able to move very fast underwater, propelled forward like a torpedo. Every so often he had to come up for air, like a seal or a dolphin. This mode of travel was very satisfying. He was flying like an underwater superman. The only problem was that the water rushing past his skin was causing him to experience an erection. Next time he must remember to leave his shorts on. He could give someone a hell of a fright like this.

*   *   *

John placed some floating weed on top of his head as the beam of a searchlight flicked over him. The next time around, they would surely see him, unless he could dive to the bottom and hang onto something.

*   *   *

Phil stood in his room, holding the special phone to his ear. It wasn't long before he was polishing his glasses.

"An underground nuclear reactor. That's unbelievable."

"Yeah, and they think it's been there a long time judging by the age of the pumping station," added Watson.

"That don't mean to say he has the bomb. Could be he's just making electricity."

"Too big for what he needs. You could supply a whole darn city with what that thing is capable of."

"How do they know how big it is?"

"All depends on the size and number of cooling water return pipes. There are pipes coming out from underground feeding water back into the lake all around the island. At the moment, the thing is just ticking over for their own power production."

"How do they know how long it's been working?"

"There was a Russian guy working for the fisheries people who put in a report about the unnatural level of radiation in the lake's water. Nothing dangerous, but higher than normal."

"When was that?"

"Eleven years ago. He was deported on a rape charge and nobody followed up on it."

"So the reactor has been working eleven years?"

"A mite longer than that. To raise the level of the whole lake, to what the Russian was saying, which was just a fraction above normal, would take years."

"How many years?"

"At full capacity they, reckon a minimum of seventy years, which can't be right. That would put these guys ahead of the Manhattan Project. There must have been a radiation leak at some time or other."

"How long before somebody can make a bomb?"

"With unlimited resources, it's possible in a couple of years to enrich enough uranium for a bomb."

"So Nabusano has had plenty of time?"

"Yep, this is why there are crapping themselves in Washington. The president is flying back from France."

"But without a rocket there's no real danger to the rest of the world."

"We don't know what else is inside that hill. They are still busy with the information from the satellites. They won't be satisfied until they do an inspection."

"Parker says to hold on."

"Don't matter what he says. They would need a reason to hold on. Not much they can do anyways. Even cruise missiles would be taken out before they arrived on target. If that reactor or the cooling system was damaged, we would end up with an African Chernobyl. Could be they might risk that, because the whole darn thing is underground. Easier to contain."

"What are their immediate plans?"

"We have a carrier in the Indian ocean. They are going to send a UAV to do some snooping around."

"Don't you think the ground to air missiles will take that out?"

"Less chance. It will be a Global Hawk, which has some stealth design and flies at four hundred miles an hour. Also, no risk to a pilot. The only risk is the thirty-five million bucks it cost to make."

John saw the cruiser heading straight for him, and took a deep breath. The sailor on the bow saw the searchlight reveal a splash, and shouted. It wasn't easy swimming to the bottom with the sack of money strapped to his chest. Bullets zapped into the water, leaving trails of bubbles behind them. They slowed down and eventually sank, landing harmlessly on the bottom. The surface was brightly lighted above him, except for the dark shape of the cruiser. *A killing machine waiting for its prey.*

Two divers splashed into the water and started swimming towards him. John struggled to find something to hang onto, and only managed to kick up clouds of sediment as he grasped at the muddy bottom. It was useless to resist. The miracle he had prayed for was not going to happen. He gave up and allowed himself to slowly rise to the surface.

A man appeared between himself and the dark shadow above. His head was surrounded by a glowing halo of light like the pictures of Jesus he had seen in the bible. The only difference being that this angel had a hard on and was smiling at him. If this was heaven, then John didn't mind going there.

The stranger grabbed his wrist and pulled him along at great speed, away from the lights and the swimming divers. John started to struggle, because his lungs were about to explode. The angel took him into his arms, then covered his mouth with his own and blew some air into his chest. They sped off again into the darkness.

*   *   *

Ken entered the lodge and nodded at Roberto, who sat on a bar stool holding Nabusano's phone.

"Any ruddy news yet?" He pointed at the phone, then poured himself a drink.

"No; I do not know why he has not a phoned yet. The waiting is-a killing me."

"That's probably why the blighter is doing it, old chap. Clement's not a happy chappy right now. He's lucky to be alive. Tried to take on that chopper with a bloody pistol."

"What happened?"

"That first explosion was Jan's plane." He glanced over at Jan and saw that he had fallen asleep. Sid was still busy talking to him.

"Don't tell him till tomorrow. They must have placed some sort of incendiary device in it. Clement got half-barbequed in the process. The second explosion was Clements' car. He's not very chuffed about that. Wants us all out of here ruddy well post haste. I've just dropped him off at the clinic to get patched up."

Ken glanced around the bar. "Where's Bill, still swimming?"

"Yes, not here. The FBI went to talk to the CIA in his room."

"What's for dinner tonight? Not bloody fish again."

"The South Africans came back with a Wart Hog. They are in the kitchen a-skinning it."

Ken smiled and brushed his moustache with his fingers. "Can't beat a bit of pork with apple sauce. No chance of the ruddy sauce, I would suppose."

He finished his drink. "Come; let's see how Bill is doing. See if his clothes are still there, at any rate."

Ken paused on the veranda to call Patch, while Roberto fetched a towel. He thought he could hear the distant rattle of gunfire and the lights on the water were disturbingly closer now. Fearing the worst, they walked down to the shore.

Chapter 116

Nabusano snarled at the follower who brought the news of Gwasa's escape. Only Parker could have accomplished it. The power had beaten the followers at every turn.

Word of Parker's invincibility was spreading among the followers. He could see it in their eyes. The superstition instilled in them was now working against him.

He waved at one of the attendants.

"Make ready the temple for a ceremony involving all the followers and all the sons. Tomorrow, everyone must be in attendance to witness the renewal, which will take place as the sun goes down. Go now and spread the word of the prophet."

Chapter 117

Patch started barking into the darkness. A figure pulled another through the water towards the shore.

Ken pointed. "Good lord, Bill has rescued somebody."

Roberto rushed into the lake to give Bill a hand with his coughing companion.

"It is a John Gwasa," Roberto exclaimed. "I wonder why they wanted to kill him?"

Ken eyed Bill as he turned to dry himself off. "Are you feeling alright, old chap? You look a bit swollen in the lower region."

"Yes, my mistake. It's the water passing by that does it. I will remember next time."

"For a ruddy minute I thought you and John Gwasa were a bit more than just good friends."

Bill blushed in the darkness and quickly put his clothes on. He knew Ken would always have this idea at the back of his mind. *Probably hasn't seen an erection in years.*

Once John started to breath all right, they helped him towards the lodge.

"What's in the bag, old man?" Ken asked him.

"This bag contains all my savings. I can give it all to my saviour."

He smiled at Bill, who was walking ahead.

"Oh lord, love at first sight," mumbled Ken. "Bill," he shouted. "This bloke is not bloody well sleeping in my room tonight."

"Don't worry. Number four is still empty. I think Phil will be very interested in John."

"Good lord, are you match making?"

"No, he is the only one here who has been to the island, numbskull."

The phone in Roberto's pocket started ringing. He took it out and stared at it, then quickly handed it to Bill.

"Bill Parker here; what do you want?"

"You will bring the power to me before sunset tomorrow. Mr. Marshall will be allowed to land five kilometres to the south of the island. You will transfer to one of my cruisers, where the power will be locked in a metal box. You will personally hand the box over to me in front of the followers. Then I will release the women into your custody and you will be free to leave. Failure to comply will result in the amputation of many body parts, depending on how angry I am at the time. Do you understand, Mr. Parker?"

"Yes, I understand perfectly. I will do as you ask. Let me speak to the women…" The phone cut off in mid-sentence.

"What did he say?" demanded Roberto.

Bill placed the phone into his pocket. "The handing over will be tomorrow evening. He has some sort of ceremony organised at sundown. Ken is to drop me south of the island. Can you do that for me?"

"Yes, least I can do, old chap. Sounds like a one way bloody ticket for you."

"I have a surprise up my sleeve. All depends on how the followers will react. There are definitely no guarantees as to the outcome."

Roberto took hold of Bill's arm. "I will be going with you. I cannot let you risk your a life alone."

"That's not a good idea. I will have my hands full trying to save myself and the girls."

"This is a final. If Sara dies, then the life for me is also ended."

Bill shook his head and started walking again. "Let's find some food. I am starving and really tired now, after all that swimming."

The aroma of roasted pork became stronger as they neared the lodge. Ken smacked his lips in anticipation.

"Things are looking up a bit on the food side, no thanks to Sid, by the way."

They entered the lodge and found Phil already eating at an empty table.

"I have brought you a present," said Bill as he sat down.

"This is John Gwasa. He is Nabusano's lawyer; he knows a lot about the island."

Phil's excitement showed by the fact that he nearly choked on some of the food in his mouth.

"I don't know how much information you will get out of him tonight. He looks a bit like a drowned rat at the moment," Bill added.

Sid came over from behind the bar. "Who the fuck is this then?"

"New guest. His boat had a bit of a ruddy problem," said Ken.

Sid rubbed his hands together, smiling. "No fucking problemo."

He glanced at Roberto apprehensively. "He can stay in number four, then I'm fucking full again."

"Four dinners," Bill ordered. "Where did you get all those tattoos done on your arms?"

Sid stuck out his small chest, showing off his arms. "I used to have a tattoo parlour in the dock area. One of my fucking mates did these for me."

"Do you still have all your gear?"

"Course I fucking 'as. You don't throw fucking gear away like that. Its part of my artistic life you're talking about."

Ken pulled a funny face, but said nothing.

"I could have a big job for you tomorrow."

Sid walked away whistling, thinking about the money he was going to make.

After diner, Phil took John away with him, eager to extract what information he could. The tape recorder would be put to good use. John left his bag with Bill for safe keeping. Ken and

Roberto retired to the bar, while Bill made his way back to his room. The money in John's bag amounted to about four million dollars. He could smooth over a few ruffled feathers with that kind of money. He was thinking about Clement's car and Jan's aeroplane.

If his plan worked tomorrow, he would pay the money back to John. If the plan failed, then he wouldn't be around anymore.

Chapter 118

Bill lay down on the bed and switched off the bedside lamp. He thought about Nabusano again, wanting to know more about him. In his present state of tiredness, he drifted off immediately into semi-conciseness.

*　　　*　　　*

Lush green forest blotted out the bare walls of his room. A feeling of humidity washed over him. Sounds of chattering monkeys and bird calls entered his mind. A large expanse of flat rock lay before him. Nabusano stepped out of the forest with his two sisters.

"We will wait here as our mother instructed," he told them.

The feeling of satisfaction and triumph at the killing of the juju man's son was starting to wear off. The reality of his parents' death was taking over. He would never be able to explain to his sisters what had actually happened.

They waited near the flat rock for three days. He occasionally refilled the skin with water from a spring close by, while his big sister gathered berries from the bushes. The little one played and chatted for a time, then gradually fell into silence. If they stayed here any longer, then they would die. The family of N'gou must survive. He owed that to his father.

Nabusano stood on top of the rock the next morning and watched the sun rise. His mother had said go east. That's what he would do—keep travelling east until they could start a new life.

The progress was slow. They took turns carrying the little one when she was tired. Big sister complained that there was not enough time to collect berries. As the days passed, they were becoming weaker. Nabusano spent restless nights calling out for his father. *M'ba, m'ba. Father, father.*

One day, the sisters rested while he went out hunting. He killed an animal the size of a cat with a long, bushy tail. On his return, he found big sister lying unconscious upon the ground. The telltale mark of a snake bite was plain to see on her arm. It took two days for her to die.

They passed a place where there were fewer trees. A group of black men rode by on horses, wearing round-shaped hats and carrying spears. Nabusano hid in fear of being taken as slaves. *Better to die in freedom than to live as a slave.*

The forests reappeared as they journeyed east, and they came upon a great river flowing south.

"Look, little sister. Look at the big water," he called out.

There was no response from the infant on his back. He buried her where she could see the great river passing by below.

He was now the only one left. Whether his brother was dead or alive, he did not know.

The strength of the great river prevented him from crossing, so he floated south on a log. Sometime or other, the log would approach the opposite side and allow him to continue east. Nabusano caught the odd fish with his hand and ate them raw, like an animal. Where the river widened, its anger turned to quietness, and the crocodiles swam ever closer. He broke branches from the floating log and threw them at the inquisitive reptiles. One stretch of fast-flowing water pushed the log to the other side, where it stuck fast among some rocks. Nabusano waded ashore and stretched his legs. After a day and night on the log, his limbs were cramped and a fever burned inside him. The late morning sun shone down on him, showing him the way.

He passed through a land of mountains and mist where huge, hairy man-like things beat on their chests in a show of defiance. Eventually, he reached the shore of a great expanse of water, and thought the land had ended. Nabusano tasted the water. It was not the same water the juju man had spoken of.

This barrier marked the end of his journey. He would start a new life here at the end of the world.

Men passed by on the water, standing on flat logs of wood. They tended nets strung out between sticks knocked into the bed of the lake. The fever had returned, making it difficult to walk. Wood smoke drifted through the air. He staggered into a village and collapsed.

*   *   *

Bill now knew the horror Nabusano had gone through as a boy. The killing of his wife later on in life by the hunters must have been the last straw.

That event had finally turned Nabusano into a monster.

Chapter 119

The president examined the information laid out in front of him.

"None of this makes any sense. Everything points to the fact that this cult, or whatever these people are, built a reactor in their own backyard a heck of a long time ago. For what reason, god only knows. Where did they get the technology?"

All the experts gathered in the room glanced at one another, but remained silent.

"We don't know, sir," Henderson said with a grim expression.

"They don't have any rockets, do they?"

"Well…" Henderson looked towards the head of the intelligence room for support. "We are not sure."

"Will someone explain what 'not sure' means?"

"Well, on top of this hill, we found twelve round patches of heat three or four yards in diameter."

"Go on," said the president in the following silence.

"We think they are metal doors painted the same colour as the rock."

"Ventilation," ventured the president.

"No, sir, they are not open." Henderson took a deep breath before continuing. "We think they could be doors for ICBMs."

The president stared at Henderson in disbelief, while all the other people in the room pulled on their earlobes or rubbed their foreheads.

"What do we intend doing about this?" he asked in a croak.

Henderson fiddled with his pen and licked his dry lips. "First off, we mustn't let the media get a handle on this."

"I think that is pretty obvious."

"Second, we have been discussing our options. Any sort of aerial assault by smart bombs or cruise missiles is out, because of the ground to air missile batteries. They would have to be taken out at night by attack helicopters at low altitude first. The problem with this is that the main radar station can see all the way down to the water. We can't go under the radar like we did in the gulf war."

"How do you know that?"

"We tried a few hours ago with a UAV flying just above the surface of the lake. Didn't last five minutes before they took it out."

"That's a mite like an act of war. What about a landing force in rubber boats?"

A marine colonel cleared his throat. "Huge loss of life, sir. They have concrete bunkers all over the place, even on the opposite side of the island. Another thing is, if he has ICBMs, a ground assault would probably end up with him pressing the button."

"So are you folks saying we just have to sit with our fingers up our asses?"

Henderson squirmed around in his chair. "There is one other option, Mr. President, but it's mite over the top."

"And what is that?"

"We could take out the whole island instantly. They would never know what hit them."

The president chewed on a fingernail. "If you drew a straight line from us to the target, and just swung it a tiny bit to the left and carried on further, what do you have there?"

Everyone in the room glanced at each other.

"China, sir."

"And if we fired one from the other direction, what is right in the flight path?"

"China, sir."

"What do you think the Chinese will say when I try to explain to them 'don't worry; this bomb is not for you or North Korea. It's for a small island in the middle of Africa'? I don't think starting a global nuclear war could be described as 'a mite over the top'."

"With all due respect, sir, I was thinking of a ballistic missile from a submarine off the east coast of Africa. We could remove all but one warhead from a Trident."

The president chewed his fingernail again. "Have we a boomer in position?"

"No, sir. It will take twenty-four hours."

"And this reactor; it would go into meltdown?"

"Yes, sir. If the cooling system is damaged."

"Understand that this would be a very last resort. We are in the business of sending aid to Africa, not radioactive fallout. Asses the collateral damage on the last option."

Chapter 120

Bill awoke the next morning feeling refreshed. He would spend the day preparing for the evening's confrontation with Nabusano.

After breakfast, Ken was busy checking out the old girl. He pushed a few wine bottle corks in to some of the bullet holes.

"That should stop a bit of the ruddy whistling noise," he said to himself.

Phil resumed his questioning of John Gwasa about the island and the Nabusano organisation in general. He passed on the main points to Watson, who then passed them on to his boss. The CIA was very interested in the contents of the island's vault, and the network of agents controlled by Nabusano. They were like sleepers who were just called upon to do certain tasks every now and then. This ranged from blackmail to the odd assassination. There was also a network of informers who passed on anything interesting of a classified nature.

As far as the CIA was concerned, the island's vault was the mother load of information.

Bill hired Sid's car and went in search of Clement, who he found at home, nursing his wounds. His attitude of hostility changed to amazement when Bill handed him enough money to buy a new 4x4.

After that, Bill visited the local garage and bought a tin of silver spray paint. Mission accomplished, he returned to the lodge to ask Ken about the replacement value of Jan's Cessna.

"Tell him about the new plane before you tell him the other one is destroyed."

"Yes, I think that would be the safest bloody way of doing it. I will go and talk to the big ape now."

"I'm going to be busy with Sid in my room for a few hours."
Ken eyed him suspiciously.

"I want him to do a special tattoo for me. Could help me tonight."

They both walked back along the jetty to the lodge. While Bill was talking to Sid about the tattoo, Ken was talking to Jan.

"What, withs a new batteray?" he asked Ken.

"Yes, with a new battery, old man."

Bill went back to his room with the can of spray paint and waited for Sid to arrive with all his tattooing gear and drawings. This idea may not save his life on the island, but anything was better than nothing.

Sid walked in and started to show Bill a whole book full of illustrations.

"No, this is what I want." He sketched something on a large piece of paper.

"Looks like your mind is already fucking made up."

"Yes; can you do it or not?"

"Course I fucking can. How big do you want it and what colours do you want?"

Chapter 121

The twin engine King Air roared over Malenga strip and then circled round to land. From the open door of the staff car, the commander watched it taxi to the parking area. He sighed and flicked his cigarette away, then swung his legs inside, closing the door. Two smartly-dressed men alighted from the plane and waited impatiently for him to drive over.

"Good morning, brothers, how was your flight?" he asked sarcastically from the open window.

The two loosened the knot of their ties and climbed into the car behind the commander. He promptly lit another cigarette and blew smoke in their direction. They wound down the rear windows and sullenly stared back at him.

"I hope you are not going to tell me to stop smoking in my own car? You are not in Mabarta now, telling the president what to do. I am the one in charge down here."

"What do you know of this meeting the father has called?"

"It is not a meeting. It is a ceremony. The time has come for the renewal. Everyone has been instructed to attend."

The two in the back seat glanced at each other with worried looks on their faces.

"Something has changed. The father is not acting rationally. The Americans are pushing for permission to inspect the island."

"That will not happen. The father controls the island, not your president."

"We have reports that the helicopter destroyed a police car on the other side of the lake. He is drawing attention to the followers. Gwasa has disappeared with much information inside his head.

For the renewal, the father needs the new power. Has he found it yet?"

"A white man called Parker has it. He will bring it to the father tonight."

They drove in silence for a while.

"We are wondering what will happen after the renewal. The Americans will not go away."

"What do they want?"

"They are interested as to what is inside the hill on the island. Even we do not know that. Only a few of the island followers have access to that section."

The commander shrugged. "Maybe Parker can make them go away."

"What are you talking about?"

"Speak to Marco. He has seen Parker using the power. It is of no concern of mine."

The car stopped in front of the hotel, but the two in the back did not get out.

"It is easy for one man to start a new beginning, but what about the rest of us?"

The commander shrugged again and turned to face his brothers.

"I do not know what will happen. I am a soldier who follows orders. I do not fear death."

Chapter 122

Sid started humming as he set out his gear next to Bill, who was lying face down on the bed.

"Will be real fucking nice to get my teeth into a big job for a change. Most of the female tourists ask for these stupid little fucking butterflies."

"I want something very dramatic, in bright colours."

"Don't worry, my old cock. I know exactly what you want. They don't call me artistic fucking Sid for fuck all. What fucking colour do you want the eye?"

"Red, I think, or orange."

"Red eye is always better than a fucking brown eye, I always says."

He moved the bedside lamp to shine on Bill's back.

"First, I will do the outline, then the detail, and finish off with all the fucking colours you want. Should be a real corker, if I says so myself."

Bill relaxed and listened to the *tick, tick* of the ceiling fan overhead. He could feel Sid's fingers on his back as he measured and marked with a felt-tipped pen. A few minutes later, he heard the buzz of the styles and felt a pricking on his skin. He isolated his mind from the discomfort and gradually drifted out of the present back into the past.

*   *   *

A landscape of mist slowly materialised. It was too early for the morning sun to dissolve the dense patches of fog. It filtered through from above, struggling to reach the surface of the water below. Bill felt as if he was floating aimlessly around within a solitude of half light.

A grey shadow moved within the fog He was not alone. Something large passed by, causing the mist to swirl and eddy in its wake. The grey shadow moved towards a patch of sunlight.

A steamer with a tall funnel sailed out from the fog bank. The white-uniformed men on deck shielded their eyes against the dazzling sun. Bill could hear the throb of her engine and voices speaking in German as the men went about their duties. The odd word and sentence formed itself into English. A cook threw a bucket of swill over the side, then disappeared into the superstructure. Blue smoke rose from the tall black funnel into the sky. He presumed they were burning wood, because coal would have given off a large plume of black smoke.

The difference between this ship and a pleasure boat was the large, menacing, grey-painted gun positioned on her forecastle, and the battle flag fluttering from her stern. A canvas awning shielded the officers and men on her open bridge from the elements. Her bow stood vertical in the water, which was common in most ships of that era. From what Bill could remember, this whole vessel had been made in sections, transported overland, and then welded together at the lake.

Bill floated past the forward-facing ventilators and heard the *swish, swish* of the steam engine below. On the bridge, two officers pondered over a large chart spread out over a table. The topic of the conversation was about the course they were now sailing. Normally, they patrolled the western side of the lake and cut across to the east to replenish bunkers at the north or the south. Because they were short of fuel, they were now sailing across the centre of the lake. An island lay in their path, and they were unsure about the depth of the surrounding water. The captain decided to avoid the island and pass by to the north.

"*Links zehn Grad,*" he barked at the helmsman.

The war in Europe was not going well. It was becoming more and more difficult to persuade the tribesmen to cut wood for fuel. One town commandant had resorted to hanging some of the more uncooperative citizens. This kind of action did not fit in with the captain's code of ethics, but without fuel they were dead in the water. The whole function of the ship was to transport the Krupp's quick-firing 105 mm gun from one place to another.

At the moment, the enemy was powerless to stop the Derflinger and the other two steamers from sailing up and down the lake. There was a rumour that the British were transporting two motor boats overland, pulled by traction engines, but he did not see how this could threaten his command. He looked down at the gold braid on his sleeve, and noticed how threadbare his uniform had become due to the constant washing.

The lookout's bell started ringing from the crow's nest on the foremast.

"There is a sail on the horizon, off the *steuerbord* bow," reported the first officer.

The captain lifted his binoculars while contemplating his options. To chase this nondescript sailboat and burn up precious fuel, or continue on his present course?

He saw the expectation in the eyes of the men on the bridge and made a decision. "Make for the sailboat. Maybe she is carrying something of use to us."

The helmsman swung the wheel over and the first officer pulled backwards and forwards on the engine room telegraph.

"We will have to use her for firewood," the first officer smiled.

Two cups and saucers on the chart table started to rattle and then eased off into a steady humming noise. *The chase was on.*

*   *   *

Bill slowly became aware he had returned to his room. The humming noise continued as Sid worked on his back.

"All fucking right; the outline is finished. Take a gander to see if you is fucking 'appy."

Bill stood in front of the large mirror on the wall and looked through a hand mirror, which Sid had given him. "Yeah. That's looking good up to now."

"Wait till its coloured, then it'll knock your fucking block off. I'm fucking fucked, so I'm 'aving a break. See you after lunch."

Bill checked in the mirror again. *Yes, this might just do the trick.*

Chapter 123

Malenga, for all intents and purposes, was back to normal. The followers had returned to the island, and there was no sign of the hastily-erected roadblocks.

A collection of quality cars was now parked at the crocodile farm. The first batch of sons had already left for the island on one of the cruisers.

Marco's phone had been busy the whole day, because a number of the brothers had been nervously asking him discreet questions about the ceremony and Parker. He didn't know anything concerning the ceremony, but told them what he had seen on the night of Parker's escape.

Some of the brothers contemplated not going to the island. They also knew what happened to people who refused a direct instruction from the father. The captain of the cruiser would no doubt inform the father which sons were missing from the boarding list.

Marco asked the hotel receptionist in which room the brothers from Mabarta were staying. While he waited, a group of Americas arrived, accompanied by an African.

They carried a collection of fishing rods. The American who signed Watson in the register asked the receptionist about the direction of the wind, while studying a tourist map of the lake. Marco and Watson glanced at each other before going their separate ways.

Chapter 124

After lunch, Bill waved at Sid, then walked back to his *rondawel*. Patch ran ahead of him for a while, then decided to examine the line of palm trees again.

Bill sat outside his door, gazing out over the lake, wondering if his life was about to end. He was unable to see into the immediate future; probably because one small thing could affect it one way or the other. His life was balancing on a knife's edge. Nothing could be certain at this point in time. Something told him there was more at stake with this approaching life or death struggle. More like good versus evil on a momentous scale, affecting millions of lives.

Bill suddenly remembered about the can of silver spray paint in his room. He dashed inside to fetch it, along with a sheet of scrap paper. After placing an object from his pocket on the paper, he shook the can and sprayed it silver. Bill carefully carried the item into his room and placed everything inside a drawer, out of sight.

Sid arrived five minutes later, walking quickly along the path with his head down, humming to himself. He stopped and sniffed the air. "I can smell fucking paint."

Bill checked his watch. "Let's get started. I'm flying with Ken later on for a spot of night fishing. Do you want the thousand dollars or not?"

Sid's face distorted into a smile. "Course I fucking does. Get yourself on the fucking bed, mate."

After Bill's shirt was removed, Sid exclaimed in surprise. For a sickening moment, Bill thought the ball had pushed all the ink out of his skin.

"Stone the fucking crows. You 'av special fucking skin, my old cock. This 'ear tattoo looks like a few days' old. It's all nice and fucking healed already."

Bill breathed a sigh of relief. "Okay. Let's get started."

"Alright, alright. Hold your fucking horses, mate. I'm not a fucking machine, ya know."

The styles started buzzing, and every so often Sid rubbed the coloured ink into the tiny wounds.

Bill closed his eyes and tried to concentrate on Nabusano in more recent times. The gunboat on the lake forced its way back into his mind. It seemed as if the vision had to run its course before he could switch over to anything else. He relaxed and resigned himself to whatever the ball wanted him to see.

*   *   *

The sail near the horizon became more distinct as the Derflinger closed the gap.

"She is an Arab dow and she is making for the island ahead," announced the captain.

He lowered his binoculars. "Place a shot over her bow when we are in range. I want to reduce speed as soon as possible."

"*Jar, Kapitan.*"

The first officer rang the brass bell on the bridge. "*Alarm,*" he shouted.

Men ran in all directions for the next minute, taking up their action stations. The gun layer wound a handle at the side of the deck gun, causing the end of the long barrel to lift into the air for maximum range. Its crew slipped a shell into the breach, then snapped it closed in readiness for firing. The captain glanced at the pocket watch he was holding, and nodded.

"*Sehr gut;* now let us see if we can still shoot straight."

The gun fired and the Derflinger faltered for a split second before resuming her forward motion. A cloud of cordite smoke drifted back over her bridge. Everyone peered ahead to see where the shell would land. A fountain of water erupted two hundred metres in front of the sail boat.

"I think they have got the message. They would be real *dumbkoffs* not to *halten*."

The captain viewed the approaching island with some concern, and ordered the helm starboard twenty. This could be a trick to run them aground.

"Prepare to take soundings. We draw more *wasser* than the dow."

The gunboat reduced speed while a team of men dropped a lead-weighted line at the bow, then ran towards the stern to keep the line vertical.

"They have spilled the wind from their sail," reported the first officer.

"*Sehr gut*." The captain produced a bottle of snaps and two glasses. "Have a drink while we close on the enemy. This is like the old days of the pirates, *ja*."

"I think the term 'surface raider' is more used nowadays, *Kapitan*."

"*Alarm*," the port lookout called. "The dow is not stopping. They have only changed course."

"*Got in Himmel*! What are those *dumbkoffs* doing?"

The snaps were abandoned on the chart table as both officers strode to the bridge rail and raised their binoculars.

"They are making directly for the island. In a moment, they will be behind that point."

The captain grabbed a speaking trumpet. "*Feuer* at will," he shouted down to the foredeck.

Three shells pumped out of the gun in quick succession while its crew worked like a well-oiled machine. The dow sailed through a maelstrom of erupting water and flying shrapnel until it passed behind the headland.

"They will not get far. The sail is torn and they cannot disappear," commented the first officer.

"Give that point a wide berth and approach the island in the same direction as the dow. Continue taking soundings until otherwise ordered," snapped the captain.

The Derflinger steamed slowly away from the island until she could round the headland some distance from shore. *What are these people doing,* the captain asked himself again. *They must know that they cannot escape.*

Was it possible that British spies were on board? The last thing he wanted was to run aground. Then he would have to radio one of the other steamers for assistance.

The gunboat steamed back towards the island and approached a small bay. Both officers were amazed to see a fort-like structure built of large blocks of stone.

"*Stopt die Maschine.*"

The dow lay beached on the shore, half full of water, alongside a second one.

"Who are these people? There is no flag flying from tower. They build like Egyptians and dress like Africans."

The second officer noted the island's number on the chart, then paged through a reference book.

"This island used to be *Britisch.* It is reported as being sold to some African thirty years ago."

"Who in *Gott's* name would want to live here? Instruct the engineer to bring the chief stoker to the bridge. Our stokers used to be fishermen before joining us."

The captain's fingers drummed impatiently on top of the bridge rail.

"Tell them not to touch anything. Last time the engineer came up here, there was grease everywhere."

After five minutes, the two men from the engine room arrived on the bridge, blinking in the midday sun.

"Ask your man what island this is and who the people are that live here."

The engineer turned to the African and started speaking in Swahili while pointing to the island.

"He is asking where we are. You forget we work in the *Maschinenraum* and cannot see where we are going."

"Here." The captain's finger thumped on the chart. "More or less in the middle of the lake."

The stoker stared at the chart, then walked out onto the portside end of the bridge and shielded his eyes. He raised his hands to his head and started wailing.

"What in *Gott's* name is wrong with him? Has he gone mad?" the captain asked the engineer.

A lengthy conversation ensued between the engineer and the stoker, involving numerous arm waving and wailing. The engineer walked back to the captain, shaking his head.

"He says that we must leave here immediately. This island is taboo. The headman here kills all people that are not of his tribe. He says we must leave now or prepare to accept death."

"I take orders from Colonel Von Lettow Vorbeck, not some witchdoctor."

"He says the man here is not a witchdoctor; he says he is a powerful wizard who has killed many by magic."

The engineer made a crooked face, waiting for the captain to speak.

"Only a primitive savage would believe this kind of mumbo jumbo. Take your man away before I lose my temper."

After the engineer had left the bridge, the two officers scrutinised the island more carefully. The first officer brought his father's brass telescope from his cabin and rested it on the hand rail.

"Those blocks the tower is made of have been cut from the front of the hill. I do not see how they could have lifted them or even have moved them," he said.

"There is a wooden frame on top of the tower. It must be a lifting device."

"I do not see a wheel on the end of it. There is a man standing there, looking back at us."

"Something is wrong here. He is the only one interested in us. If we do not instil fear wherever we go, at least we attract plenty of curiosity. He seems to be waiting for us to do something."

"What are your orders, *Kapitan?*"

"I will not risk a shore party. They could have rifles. I think we should destroy the dows, then bring back a troop of Askaris and land them on the other side. There are not many trees for fuel, but we could keep some stock here for emergencies. That tower could be of some use to us as a defensive position."

"This island is neutral, *Kapitan.*"

The captain turned towards the first officer. "*Wolfgang, mein Freund.* The German Imperial Navy controls everything in and around this lake. Eventually, we will lose our mainland bases to the Belgians and Britisch with their Indian soldiers. Even the South Africans are fighting against us. What better plan than to have a base on an island protected by the Derflinger?"

"What about supplies?"

The captain shrugged. "Zeppelins, they could be more purposely used supplying us than wasting their time bombing London."

Wolfgang thought about the captain's ideas, and decided to mention them in his next letter to his father. It would not be the first time he had been used to suggest an idea to the high command.

"Take charge of the gun and destroy those boats. It will be good shooting practice, if nothing else."

While the first officer climbed down to the foredeck, the captain trained his glasses on the tower. There was no sign of any heavy guns anywhere, yet the man standing on the top made him feel uncomfortable. He swung over to the top of the hill, and only saw bare rock. No surprise attack from that direction.

Wolfgang was now giving orders down at the gun, so the captain trained his glasses on the dows. The first shot exploded out of his field of vision. It had landed four hundred metres to the right.

"*Was tun sie hier?* That shooting is terrible."

"*Links, links,*" the first officer shouted. "*Feuer!*"

The second shot landed in more or less the same place as the first. Wolfgang and the gun crew stared in disbelief. After swinging the gun to the left, the shell could not possibly land in the same place.

"There is something wrong with the weapon, *Kapitan,*" the first officer shouted, then looked up the inside of the barrel.

"It cannot be bent, or it would give the same error every shot. *Schwenken nach links* and *feuer* again."

This time, the captain observed the man on the tower when the gun fired. He held something in his right-hand and swung his left arm over to the left, as if pushing something away. The shell exploded in the same place as before. He wiped the sweat from his eyes while the crew waited for his orders.

"*Wolfgang,* return to the *Ruderhaus,*" he called out.

The young first officer arrived breathless on the bridge and clicked his heels.

"The bad shooting is not your fault or the fault of the gun. Tell them to shoot again and watch the man on the tower."

"Tell them to shoot where, *Kapitan?*"

"It will not matter where we shoot; the shell will land over there." The captain pointed to the smoking hole on the shore. "Shoot at the tower if you want, then tell me if I am mad or not."

Wolfgang shouted down to the foredeck, and the gun swung twenty degrees to the left. Both officers trained their glasses on the tower, waiting for the gun to fire. The captain wondered what the crew's reaction would be if the shell landed in the same place. His own mind was struggling to accept what was happening. The gun fired, sending a shudder through the whole ship, and the man on the tower lifted his arm, turning to the shore.

"You see what he is doing, Wolfgang. He is pushing *unser* shell away."

"But *das* is impossible, *Kapitan.*"

Mud and stones exploded into the air close to the other craters. No one spoke as the smoke slowly drifted away. The crew looked at each other in confusion, not understanding what had happened.

"*Wir* are like a wolf with no teeth against this man," whispered the captain. "*Wir haben ihn* to kill. Sharp shooters to the bridge now," he snapped.

Four men arrived at the wheel house, carrying rifles. The captain pointed towards the tower. "Shoot me that man standing on the top. Fire together so I can see where the bullets strike."

The four sharpshooters rested their elbows on the rail and took careful aim through the Mausers telescopic sights. They fired in a ragged volley similar to a firing squad. The man on the tower moved his forearms in a downward motion, and the captain saw puffs of dust spit from the tower wall twenty metres below the target.

"*Sie* is pushing the bullets down. *Ich* will use his own magic against him. Aim twenty metres over his head and *feuer* again."

The riflemen glanced at each other with bewildered expressions. They had never been ordered to fire into thin air before. The bolt actions thrust another round into the breaches and they took aim again.

"This witchdoctor will not outfox *mich*. Have *das* gun target *zu den* dows in readiness."

The first officer shouted to the gun crew, then pointed his telescope at the tower. A second volley fired from the Mausers. The man on the tower repeated his arm movements, then was thrown backwards as a bullet struck him in the shoulder.

"*Ja*, now fire at the dows," shouted the captain.

The one hundred and five millimetre pumped a shell in the direction of the boats beached on the shore. One of them exploded, showering the area with falling pieces of wood and debris. A cheer sounded from the gun crew below.

"*Kapitan*, that man on the tower is standing up again," called the first officer, peering through his telescope. "I cannot see anything wrong with him. There is no one assisting him."

"*Scheibe*, I should have fired on the tower instead of the boats. He will not give me that chance again." He turned to the sharpshooters. "*Feuer* at will. Kill *diesen Mann*."

Suddenly the Derflinger heeled over to starboard, nearly capsizing. Anything not fastened down rolled or slid along the deck. Only the men who had managed to grab hold of something remained standing. Cries of surprise or pain sounded throughout the ship. A cloud of steam rose from the galley window. Wolfgang's telescope and the bottle of snaps disappeared off the end of the bridge, which nearly touched the water. The ship recovered and rolled back again, rocking from side to side.

"*Voll* ahead, *hart rechts*," shouted the captain.

He turned to the first officer with fear in his eyes. "We cannot shoot at anything rolling like this. The witchdoctor has beaten us. Let us get out of here."

The gunboat slowly started to move forward, turning to the right with a slight starboard list. All the loose material on board was now at the right side of the ship, upsetting her trim. Two African stokers jumped over the side and swam away.

"*Kapitan*," shouted Wolfgang. "Something is happening on the roof of the tower."

Clouds of smoke billowed around the wooden frame. The captain ran to the portside and raised his binoculars. A strange droning noise like a continuous belch could be clearly heard. The smoke increased in volume, then a grey torpedo-shaped object accelerated along the top of the inclined frame and leapt into the air. Two rockets fell away from under the stubby wings as the missile flew in a straight line, away from the tower. A pod mounted on top of the rear of the flying machine trailed a long, flickering, orange flame.

"*Gott im Himmel, Was ist das?*" whispered the captain.

"It must be some sort of weapon. It will not hit us. It is flying too steep and off to the one side."

The captain thought Wolfgang was trying to convince himself that there was no danger. If the witchdoctor could nearly push the ship over, this flying thing would be easy for him to move.

He looked back at the tower and saw the man standing there again. The engine turned faster and faster, churning the water behind the stern as the Derflinger swung away from the island.

"Did you see any windows or cabin on that flying *Maschine*?"

"*Nein, Kapitan*; there is no pilot or a propeller. I do not know how it can even *fliegen*."

"Then it is a *Bombe*, a flying *Bombe*." He pointed at the grey shape climbing into the sky. "Shoot at that thing. *Schiessen* it down. Our *Leben* depend on it."

There was a chance the sharpshooters could hit the target, because the ship had now stopped rolling. They kept on firing until it disappeared into a low cloud. The captain shook his head. They had come here full of confidence, and were now running like rabbits.

He snatched a rifle and took aim at the figure on the tower. Holding his breath, he started to gently squeezed the trigger. *I will not lose my ship without a fight,* he told himself.

The Mauser's cross hairs centred on the chest of the witchdoctor. If the man was concentrating on something else, like the flying machine, then it may be possible to kill him.

Before the captain could pull the trigger, the picture started to shimmer, then turned completely black. Was this more of the witchdoctor's magic?

He looked over the sites and saw that the funnel of the turning ship had blocked his view.

The deck crew of the Derflinger peered apprehensively up into the sky, searching for the source of the droning noise high above them. Suddenly there was an ominous silence.

"*Hart links*," shouted the captain in an attempt to avoid the falling bomb.

The helmsman spun the wheel until it stopped hard over.

Wolfgang could see his own fear reflected in the face of the captain, who suddenly smiled at him. "If that thing hits us, it will solve the problem of what to *schreiben in das* log book."

The young officer smiled back, then a dark object flashed passed the front of the bridge. There followed a blinding white glare, and then oblivion.

Chapter 125

Bill awoke with a shout, causing Sid to leap back from the bed.

"Stone the fucking crows, you frightened the fucking shit out of me."

Sweat dripped from Bill's brow and he was shaking.

"What the fucking hell is wrong with you? I thought you were busy fucking snuffing it."

"I was snuffing it, with twenty other men out on the lake."

"Yer what?"

"Don't worry; it was just a bad dream."

"I don't want any of your fucking dreams." Sid smiled and rubbed the side of his face. "I always 'as the same fucking dream, trying to get my leg over with this gorgeous dolly bird. Stupid bitch keeps crossing her legs. One of these nights, I'll get my end away, just you wait and see."

Bill swung his legs off the bed and lit a cigarette with a shaking hand. "Are you nearly finished?"

"Nearly; just a bit more fucking orange and yellow flame at the bottom of the bastard, then she will be a real smasher."

Bill forced himself to breathe deeply and slowly while trying to recover from the effects of the vision. He could still feel the searing heat of the explosion on every part of his body, and examined the skin on his arms, expecting them to be blistered.

"Are you feeling all right? You look fucking terrible. If you are allergic to the fucking ink you should have said so."

"I'm fine. Just need a minute to finish my smoke." He poured himself some water from the plastic bottle on the bedside table.

Nabusano was using the full power of the first ball in nineteen-fifteen. If that ball was still working, he would not be so interested in the second one, except to maybe corner the market. From what

Bill had heard, Nabusano had aged dramatically over the last ten years. That in itself pointed to the fact that the first ball's power was all but spent. Bill remembered what the Germans had said about the moving of the blocks of stone on the island. Nabusano must have thought the power of the river god was never ending. He stubbed out the cigarette and lay back down on the bed. Sid started humming, feeling very pleased with himself.

"This is the best fucking tattoo I 'as ever done. It's usual to make a small fuck up now and then, but with this 'un everything I do turns out fucking magic."

Bill wondered if the tattoo was going to be enough to impress the followers. It certainly would not impress Nabusano. He would have to get his act together if he was to succeed in overthrowing him. One card seemed to be missing, and he didn't know what it was.

Chapter 126

The number of vehicles parked at the crocodile farm doubled as the second lot of brothers arrived. They viewed the afternoon sun with apprehension, as if measuring their life expectancies.

The only one who didn't seem worried was the commandant, who casually smoked a cigarette. He gave the impression of a bored schoolboy who had done the school a favour by turning up for class. The officer holding a clipboard ticked off his name as he stepped onto the deck of the cruiser. His eyes hardened when his sidearm was removed and the officer told him to extinguish his cigarette. Both the brothers from Mabarta smirked in satisfaction at his discomfort as they entered the cabin with the others. Marco and the commandant were the only two who preferred to remain on deck. He opened one side of his jacket, revealing his empty holster to the soldier.

"They do not trust us to carry weapons."

"You know as well as I that only traditional weapons are allowed inside the temple."

"Yes, but we are not there yet."

They both noticed a mini bus taxi arrive at the farm with some tourists. Marco nodded towards the men, who seemed more interested in the departing cruiser and the parked cars than the crocodiles.

"The Americans have arrived. If we survive what the father has in store for us, we still have to survive whatever they are planning."

Chapter 127

Bill admired the finished tattoo through the two mirrors. "Yes, that's exactly what I wanted. How did you blend one colour into the other like that? It's as good as an oil painting."

Sid shook his head. "I don't rightly know, old cock. One must have fucking mixed with the other somehow. Now that it's finished, it looks a bit fucking disturbing like. Menacing, I would fucking call it. You could frighten little fucking kids away with a thing like that."

Bill flexed the muscles in his back, giving the impression the wings and flames were moving. Sid hurriedly packed up his gear wanting, to leave his masterpiece behind. He watched Bill count out a thousand dollars on the table top, which he scooped up and pocketed with a grin.

"Pleasure doing business with you, my old cock. How long will you people be staying here?"

"One way or the other, I will be out of here tomorrow."

Sid looked disappointed. His income would revert back to normal after Bill had left. The South Africans had wised up to Sid on the pool table, so maybe he would have to think of a different game to play. He left the *rondawel*, whistling his way along the path back to the bar.

Bill showered and dressed in his original clothes, which had been washed and ironed. He picked up John's bag of money and slipped the silver-painted item into his shirt. *Right, now for a council of war before we leave for the island.*

Ken and Roberto were in the bar, sipping their first drinks of the day. Both of them looked as if they were waiting to be executed. Bill hoped that this would not turn out to be the case, and gave them a reassuring smile.

"Take your drinks to Phil's room. We need to talk."

He grabbed himself a bottle of beer and led the way.

*   *   *

Phil sat with John at the table, with the tape recorder between them. He pressed the stop button when Bill knocked and entered.

"We need to pool any information each of us may have, for me to rescue the girls and save my own skin at the same time."

Bill handed John his black bag and the three newcomers sat on the bed. Roberto lit up a cigarette, causing Phil to open the window.

"I have spent some of your money, John. Hopefully I can pay back tomorrow."

John sat smiling at Bill, and whispered, "No problem."

Ken covered his eyes with his hand. "Oh lord."

"Roberto, are you still sure you want to go with me?"

"Yes. I cannot a sit here when my women is in the danger. It is not the Italian way of doing things."

Bill shook his head. "I can see you're not going to change your mind. Ken, you are going to drop me five kilometres to the south of the island?"

"Yes, not a problem, old man. Do you want me to wait for you?"

"No. If things go wrong, Nabusano may decide to kill you. I have told Sid we are going night fishing, so you can't come back here. Is there anywhere you can wait, out of danger?"

"The closest place to the island is a town south of here. I could wait there for you to phone."

"Okay. John, you know the island. Where would Nabusano hold a ceremony or a meeting of some sort?"

"There is only one place, and that would be in the temple."

"Where is that?"

"The temple is below the tower, at the bottom level."

"Shit, so there are no windows or any way of getting out of there in a hurry?"

John shook his head. "No. There is also a big sliding door, which closes the entrance. You would be trapped like a rat. Do not go, or you will die."

"That's the best advice so far. This godamn wacko will kill you," said Phil.

Roberto jumped to his feet. "How can you-a say that? It is your job to save the girls, and you are not even going."

Bill held up his hands. "Calm down. The last thing we need is to be fighting among ourselves. I have to go, because I have what he wants."

"I would go if I could see any chance of success. This is my investigation anyways."

Bill passed a hand over his face and took a swig of beer. "I think it is time I showed Phil what Nabusano wants and what my plan is."

Ken cleared his throat. "Do you think that is wise? He represents a foreign government. They could lock you up and start doing all sorts of ruddy experiments."

"If I take over from Nabusano, I will need a man like Phil to sort out all that information in the vault. The Americans may leave me alone to do my own thing if we have one of their own on the inside. I'm sure I can twist a few arms with the kind of information that's sitting in that vault."

John nodded. "That is true. Even some of the old records would be very embarrassing to many of the world's governments. Nabusano has been doing that for years, and lately I have been a part of it. How can you possibly take over from him?"

"The thing that made him powerful in the first place has lost its power. I found a second one and intend to use it for good, and not evil, like Nabusano. Some of his followers have seen me using this power. In the past, they have been ruled by fear. There must be a certain amount of discontent in their ranks. To take over from him at this ceremony is the only chance I have of saving the hostages and my own skin."

Phil started to get the feeling he was listening to a madman. "What the heck are you talking about?"

Ken and Roberto glanced at each other. "I think a ruddy demo is required, old chap."

Bill pulled a silver ball from inside his shirt. "I found this in the quarry." He slipped it back into his shirt. "If it touches my skin, I can control its power."

Phil looked at everyone's face and only saw confusion on John's features. Roberto seemed to be enjoying the situation. The tape recorder in front of Phil lifted into the air. Both men at the table stood up so quickly that the chairs flew backwards with a crash. Roberto started laughing at Phil's staring eyes.

"Welcome to the real world, Mr. FBI. Who do you think was a flying your plane with no pilot and no fuel?"

"This gotter be some kind of trick."

The tape recorder settled back down on the table, then John's money bag started floating round the room. Phil and John backed away from it when it came close to them. Ken cleared his throat with a worried expression on his face.

"Surely Nabusano will not let you arrive on the island with that thing in your possession, old man?"

The money bag landed back on the floor next to John, who jumped out of the way.

"No. His instructions are that it be locked into a steel box when I board the cruiser."

"Then you are bloody well done for. How can you get the fucking followers on your side without the bloody ball?"

"Watch."

Bill removed the ball from his shirt and gave it to Ken. The tape recorder lifted again from the table.

"Good lord; did I do that?"

"No. Set the ball down."

Ken dropped the ball next to him on the bed, and the tape recorder still hovered in the air. The two fallen chairs stood themselves up and the money bag started floating again. Now both Ken and Roberto looked surprised.

"How the flipping hell are you doing that without the ruddy ball?"

Bill smiled. "Because that ball is a fake. The real one is still with me."

Roberto picked up the ball from the bed. "Yes. This is not the real one. It is a too light and not as shiny as the other."

John shook his head. "You will not be able to smuggle anything into the temple. There will be x-ray and body search, even the rectum."

Roberto was not too impressed with this latest information.

"It is well hidden, and the ball does not show on x-ray. I'm sure Nabusano would not insult the river god by trying to x-ray the first ball."

Phil polished his glasses. "I don't believe what is going on here, but at least you have some sort of plan that could work. Moving stuff around like that would sure scare the hell out of anybody. Watson is never going to believe this."

"Just tell him I have something Nabusano wants, and nothing more. I need you as a go between with some sort of credibility. What do you know from your side?"

"Watson is in Malenga. He says all the sons have left for the island. He also says that they think there is a nuclear reactor on the island and possible ICBMs. This Nabusano guy is the world's biggest nightmare."

"He is also unstable and full of hate, but he won't do anything until after this ceremony. Tell Watson to give me a chance. If I succeed, I will allow weapons inspectors onto the island. They can dismantle and take away anything that can threaten the rest of the world. I saw Nabusano using a V1 in 1915, so Christ knows what he has there now."

"What!"

Bill stroked his eyebrows, regretting his last remark. "I have visions. Sometimes I can see the past, and what the future may be."

"So what's going to happen here? Is this wacko going to blow up the world?"

Bill shook his head. "I don't know. There is too much uncertainty to foresee the outcome."

"Oh, well that's just great. Watson can't tell them to hold off on an uncertainty."

"I know, but it's the best I can do. I'm risking my own life on this, too."

"Yeah, I know, but that won't mean jack shit to the brass in Washington. You gotta get rid of this guy and get Watson onto the island ASAP so he can tell them not to vaporise the place."

Bill glanced at his watch, then turned to Ken. "The sooner I'm there, the better. This looks like a race between me and the Yanks. Nabusano must have miscalculated on today's technology being able to see what he has there. He must have thought he would find the second ball years before now. That stuff was built for a reason, and I think the finale is tonight. He is going to go out with a bang and start over somewhere else."

"What about all his followers and those sons of his?" asked Phil, still polishing his glasses.

Bill shrugged. "The final sacrifice."

Phil offered his hand to Bill, who shook it. "I would go with you guys if I thought I could help, but I don't see what I could do. I would just be one more liability."

Roberto saw genuine concern in Phil's eyes, and offered his own hand. "Thanks," he said with a smile.

Bill checked his watch again. "Okay, let's get the show on the road."

"Into the valley of death," murmured Ken as he stood up.

"What's the flying time to the island?" asked Bill.

Ken rolled the point of his moustache between his finger and thumb. "Oh, about one hour."

"So, we can be out of here at five, one hour there, arriving one hour before sunset, and then one hour after that; only time will tell."

He was going to say 'dead or alive', but thought better of it.

They all filed down to the jetty in an air of gloom, while the afternoon sun seemed to mock them. Ken busied himself checking the fuel tanks for condensation, then moved the flaps up and down. He glanced at Bill, who nodded, so he pressed the starter button and the engine roared into life.

Sid and the hunters appeared on the veranda with drinks in their hands. Jan limped out of the bar door with a sweeping brush tucked under his arm. Bill waved and stepped on to the pontoon, leaving John and Phil on the jetty casting off the mooring ropes. A strong feeling of danger started to overpower his senses. Bill could not understand this. Nabusano island was one hour's flying time away. What factor was now causing him to feel in imminent danger? He raised his hand as a signal to wait while he tried to sort things out in his mind.

"John," he called out above the engine noise. "Step onto the aeroplane."

This he did, not understanding what Bill wanted. Bill shook his head, then pointed for him to go back.

"What are you doing?" shouted Roberto.

"Something is wrong here. I have a strong danger feeling."

"I can understand that. I also have a feeling of a danger. We are going to Nabusano Island."

"No, it's something else that's wrong. Phil, come here."

Phil pulled the drifting plane closer and stepped over the one-metre gap. "What do you want?" he asked.

Bill rubbed his forehead with his fingertips. "For some reason, I need you to come with us," he shouted. "It will mean the difference between success and failure."

"I don't understand."

"I don't understand either. There is a connection between you and Nabusano. What was your ancestor's family name?"

"N'gou. I think that's how it's pronounced."

"And he was taken from Benin when still a small boy?"

"Yep. So what has that to do with anything?"

"Get in the plane. I will take you to meet a relative of yours."

The group on the veranda watched the float plane taxi away from the jetty and take off. There seemed to have been some confusion as to who was going and who was staying. Only the African with boat problems was left behind. Sid thought it a bit unusual for Ken not to have asked some of the South Africans if they had wanted to go. After all, there were still two empty seats.

Sid shook his head, then followed the others inside. First of all, he would tell Jan a funny story while thinking of some way of earning more money from the hunters.

"Did I tell you what my fucking foreman said to me when I was just a cheeky abastard apprentice?"

There was no reaction from Jan, except for a loud burp.

"Well, 'e says to me 'shape yourself, my lad, why don't you start shaping yourself?'. So I fucking stands like this." Sid put one hand on his hip and lifted the other one with the hand pointing downwards. "How's this for a tea pot?"

Jan struggled to his feet and hobbled off to his room. He farted before reaching the door. Sid's captive audience was not so captive anymore, so he turned his attention to the hunters at the bar.

"I know! How about a game of table tennis? You younger blokes should be able to beat me easy and win some of your money back, eh."

The men at the bar shrugged while Sid rubbed his hands together. He wasn't going to tell them he used to be a YMCA champion, and quickly set up the table. After five minutes of searching in a cardboard box, Sid glared at everyone.

"Some bastard 'as stole the fucking ball," he exclaimed.

Chapter 128

Watson and his group drove back to the hotel. The crocodile farm keeper had been quite talkative after being slipped a few dollars as a tip. This was surprising considering the value of the heavy gold chain around his neck.

He had told them that all the sons had parked their cars and boarded one of their father's boats, which made two trips. Judging by the return time, they must have sailed to the island. He kept smiling and fingering the golden links of the chain. What seemed to have amused him the most was the sons' expressions while they had waited to board. Normally, there would only be two or three of them who would strut around giving him instructions like 'wash my car'. This time, they had stood around in groups, whispering among themselves like children waiting to see the headmaster.

When Watson mentioned Nabusano, he stopped looking so pleased with himself and also stopped talking. What the keeper had said confirmed what Phil had told him about some sort of ceremony and the mood of the sons.

Could be Parker's plan had some merit, after all. He checked his watch. This was going to be a closely run race.

His boss had promised that he would phone him when the missile was in the air so he could high tail it out of there. They would drive east, away from the path of the prevailing wind.

Chapter 129

The float plane reached its cruising height just above the low cloud, and Ken steered a course for the island. They were now flying into the jaws of the enemy, and possible obliteration by the Americans.

Phil phoned Watson and told him that he was on his way to the island. Judging by Phil's raised eyebrows and the eventual ending of the call by Phil, the information had not gone down too well.

"Tell me again why the heck I am going with you? Watson thinks I'm an asshole."

"Maybe he's right. You could always fly back to the mainland with Ken. The ball has never been wrong. For some reason, I am going to need you there."

Bill told Phil about Nabusano's life as a boy and the killing of his parents.

"Holy shit, to live with trauma like that for two hundred and eighty years would drive anyone crazy. If I hadn't seen those things floating around with my own eyes, I wouldn't believe any of this crap you are telling me."

"What put you on to Nabusano in the first place?"

"I was just following a paper chase of hidden money. I never expected for it to turn into something like this. A lot of what you just told me explains a whole heap of things I could not understand about the case. If you take over from this guy, what are you going to do with all the money involved?"

Bill scratched the top of his head. "I haven't really thought about it. Everything would be in the name of Nabusano, I presume?"

Phil nodded.

"There are plenty of Nabusano's on the island. If they back me, then they won't object to me calling the shots. That is the system they are used to, anyway. I won't change the way of doing things too much, just the direction. You could probably look at it like a secret trust fund where there would be unlimited funds to correct the wrongs of the world. I would start with the third world countries first, promoting the right type of people to be in charge."

"I hope you don't plan on changing democratically-elected governments? That would be wrong."

"No, I wouldn't go that far. A bit of help in the right direction is what I am thinking of. Where there is a president doing a good job, then I would create industry and employment to make sure the people vote for him again."

"You would be meddling in the natural order of things whatever you did."

Bill started to feel frustrated. He would never have believed it would be so difficult to help people.

He raised his voice. "I would help people in any way I could. In many places, the natural order of things is wrong."

There followed an awkward silence between the two men. Phil new Bill's heart was in the right place, but that he had not thought through all the implications. In a position of power, a man could quite easily become a tyrant. There could be a situation where one wacko was replacing the other wacko.

Bill broke the silence. "Look, the first order of things is to remove the danger. We can talk about a committee of some sort to advise on any action to be taken. Retired UN members or something like that. Just so long as things are not bogged down and nothing happens. Are you with me or not?"

"Sure, I'm with you. I just wanted you to know you can't rampage around the world like some vigilante."

The idea appealed to Bill. He smiled at Phil. "Why not?" he asked. "I could become like one of your American super heroes." He thought for a moment. "Ball Man; how does that sound?

Phil smiled back and shook his head. "Like you say, first thing's first. Let's see what happens. I owe you my life, anyways."

Ken cleared his throat. "If I can interrupt you two planning the world's future for a ruddy moment? Nabusano Island, dead ahead."

The word 'dead' had inadvertently popped up into Ken's vocabulary again, which, under normal circumstances, would go unnoticed.

They were approaching the island from the same direction as the Derflinger had ninety years before.

"I don't see any buildings," said Phil.

"The harbour and the fort are over the other side of that point," explained Bill.

Thankfully, nobody asked him how he knew this, otherwise he would have to tell them all about the Derflinger vision.

"According to Watson, there are supposed to be missile sites and bunkers all over the place. I can't see jack shit down there," continued Phil.

Ken tilted the left wing down slightly so they could see better through the side windows. Most of the island looked like farmland, with small groups of trees here and there.

"There is a small building under every one of those clumps of ruddy trees. That's the usual place to build a farm house, for the shade from the sun. I suppose it would be dead easy to paint bigger windows around the gun slots of pillboxes. Wouldn't know the bloody difference unless you were standing next to the ruddy things."

Bill pointed. "The trees near the shore have been planted in a staggered zigzag pattern about a hundred metres apart. That would be the ideal firing positions for pillboxes. The ones further inland are more random. They would be the missile sites."

A dome-shaped hill of bare rock came into view on the other side of the point.

"That's where the ICBMs and the reactor are supposed to be hidden," said Phil.

Something gold glinted in the setting sun, then the tower and the harbour came into view.

"That golden dome has the radar antenna inside."

They all started to feel like a group of tourists with Phil as the tour guide.

Bill examined the silver-painted table tennis ball and hoped it would fool the captain of the cruiser. His instructions would be to lock a silver ball in the box. The size was correct. Only the weight and the degree of shininess were wrong.

"Turn south and land after five kilometres. Nabusano said there will be a cruiser waiting for us."

Phil felt much safer flying with Ken. There had been no surprises up to now, like the pilot falling asleep or running out of fuel. He could imagine many pairs of eyes watching the progress of the tiny float plane with keen interest.

Absentmindedly, he removed his glasses and started polishing. How had he managed to get himself into a mess like this? He was now going to put himself into a hostage situation where the chances of survival were very slim. There was still the option of flying back with Ken.

"Anyone for a drop of Dutch courage?"

Ken fished around under his seat and pulled out a bottle of whisky. Nobody refused, and the bottle circulated the cabin twice before being returned to its place under the seat. Roberto sat at the back in his own private smoking area.

"Nabusano boat, dead ahead."

"Stop saying 'dead' all the time," shouted Roberto.

"Sorry, didn't know I was." Ken pushed forwards on the throttle and lowered the flaps. The plane lost altitude in a long, gradual left turn and landed on the water.

"Leave all the talking to me," said Bill. "I am going to do a couple of tricks with the ball to prove it's not a fake."

He opened the door and stood on the float in the wind from the propeller, while the cruiser slowly came towards them. A line of black-uniformed men with submachine guns stood along the side, facing the float plane.

Ken swallowed. "They look like Nazi storm troopers, except with black faces," he mumbled.

"Are you Mr. Parker?" an amplified voice asked from a speaker.

"Yes," shouted Bill. "I am coming on board."

He showed the ball between his finger and thumb, then lifted himself up off the float. The line of men took a step backwards. Some of them opened their mouths. Bill smiled confidently while floating across towards the cruiser. The line of men gradually opened in the middle to form a gap for Bill to step on board. At first, the men shuffled their feet as if straightening a line on the parade ground. As he came closer, they walked to the bow and the stern and stood there in two groups, as far away from him as possible. The captain came out from the wheel house and cursed at his men for breaking ranks. Bill floated over to the captain and hovered one metre above the deck.

"Permission to come aboard?"

The captain was about to say something, then just nodded. He had expected to take a prisoner, not to have someone take over his command. Bill floated down onto the deck and smiled.

"Thank you. I have two companions that are coming with me."

The officer frowned, feeling more confident now that the white man was standing on his feet. "My orders only concern you and the power to be taken to the island. No one else."

"Okay," Bill shouted. "I will sink your boat and then come back another day."

The crew glanced at each other nervously, but the captain stood his ground and narrowed his eyes. Bill shrugged, then waved goodbye to the men standing at the bow and the stern. The cruiser started to settle deeper in the water. At first, the crew could not believe what was happening, and then they started to hold onto anything close at hand. The captain's face shone with perspiration. As the cruiser sank lower, the hull started to groan and creak. She was not designed for the pressure that now pushed on her sides. The officer held up his hand and walked back inside the wheel house. He spoke on the radio for two minutes, then returned.

"The father says you can bring as many companions as you want."

"Thank you."

The cruiser bobbed up from the water, causing everyone to fall down, except Bill. One man fired his weapon into the air as he fell over.

"You must instruct your men to keep the safety catch on. We could have had a nasty accident here."

The captain got to his feet and glared at him. Bill waved at the float plane for Roberto and Phil to climb onto the pontoon. They then floated across to the cruiser with unhappy expressions on their faces, and landed on the deck. The officer snapped his fingers and a crew member appeared from the wheel house, carrying a steel box.

"You are to place the power inside this box."

Bill pointed to the float plane. "Only after that aircraft is well away from here."

He waved at Ken and gave him the thumbs up sign. Ken waved back. The engine roared up to full RPM and the silver plane took off. She skipped along the surface for a while, then lifted into the air, flying into the setting sun. Roberto and Phil suddenly had the feeling of being deserted. Bill checked his watch, then turned to the captain.

"Alright, bring this box of yours here."

The box appeared fairly heavy for its size, and was fitted with an internal lock. Inside, there was an indentation lined with green felt. Bill placed the ball inside, and pushed it into the cavity. The captain quickly closed the lid, and locked it with a key. He then threw the key over the side into the water and smiled.

"Now, Mr. Parker you are nothing without the power. I could easily have you and your friends killed at this very moment. For some reason, the father wants you and your friends alive."

"The god of the river only allows the new prophet to use the new power." Bill pointed to the box. "This power is useless to your so-called father. The days of the old power and the old prophet are over. Now is the time of the renewal."

The officer slapped Bill hard across the face. "Stop this talk. We will see who the true prophet is at the ceremony."

One of the crew carried the box inside the wheelhouse, and the three of them had their wrists fastened with cable ties. They were forced to sit on the deck in front of the wheelhouse, surrounded by armed men. The cruiser sped off to the island at full speed, with the bows lifting and slapping back into the water. Their hands were tied in front of them, so at least they could rub the spray from their faces with their forearms. Roberto thought about lighting a cigarette, but decided against it.

"Nice boat," commented Phil. "You must give me one of these to play with after you take over."

"Remind me to give this captain fellow a job cleaning toilets. Fanatics like him will not be easy to convince."

He nodded towards the crew. "The rank and file will be a pushover in comparison. They will follow like sheep once someone leads the way."

"I think this guy is one of Nabusano's most trusted, so you won't get any more worse than him."

"I hope not; the shit will hit the fan once his boss opens that box."

The island grew in size as they approached. Long shadows reached out along the ground from the structures behind the harbour. Last time Bill had seen the place, only the tower had been standing. Now it was twice as high and covered in reinforced concrete.

The cruiser slowed down and inched its way into the harbour. They stopped next to a steel door in the jetty wall, which slid open.

More armed men were inside the cool interior of the concrete structure.

Bill noticed the opening mechanism on the inside wall, operated by a pass card. Another officer slipped the card into his top pocket and led the way towards a lift. The card was used again inside the lift. Bill wondered if the same kind of security system was in use at the temple door. Probably all the senior men on the island carried the same kind of card. He decided it may come in useful to have one of these cards.

Just as the lift started to move, the overhead light blew out in a shower of sparks. On arrival at the top of the jetty, the last of the daylight flooded inside when the doors opened. Two lines of men waited for them, standing on either side of a railway line. They turned and marched after the group from the cruiser, led by the captain carrying the box.

"I have always liked a parade," said Roberto, trying to make light of the situation.

Even under tight security, Bill had made some sort of headway. A pass card was now safely tucked into the top of his socks. Nabusano had not calculated on him still being able to use the power.

Where the rail line ended at the rock face stood two bunkers with windows painted on the walls.

"That will be the entrance into the hill," whispered Phil.

They turned left at the end of the jetty and marched along the back of the harbour. Phil glanced at his watch. It was half-past-something. The sun lay behind the point to the west ,so it must be half-past-six.

Another group of men with an officer waited for them at the door to the tower. It looked like different officers controlled different sections. That would suggest different pass cards, making the card Bill had stolen useless for the temple door. He would have to try to switch cards when passing through the last door.

The men from the jetty and the cruiser, except the captain carrying the box, turned around and marched back. Bill forced himself not to smile. An expression of importance showed on the captain's face. Little did he know he was carrying a steel box containing a table tennis ball.

The new officer pressed his hand onto a screen and looked up into a camera mounted on the wall. A few seconds later, the door slid open. The whole system seemed to be designed to stop people from entering, rather than from leaving. On the inside wall, Bill noticed the pass card arrangement. He would not need a means of escape if everything went well at the ceremony.

"I wonder what the running cost is of all this," Bill said.

"I don't think these guys are on salary," commented Phil.

He was suddenly struck on the shoulder with a baton.

"No talking."

"Let them talk. They are dead men," said the captain.

The officer led the way to the lifts and pressed the button for down. Bill noticed that there were twelve floors up and five down. A large lift arrived, and they all filed inside. Button B5 was pressed and the doors closed. *Here we go*, thought Bill. He experienced an attack of nerves, like the best man at a wedding, and forced himself to keep calm.

They stepped out into a brightly lighted reception area, like an airport security setup. Cell phones were removed and placed on a shelf that was nearly full. Pockets empted and then patted down. The three of them stood in front of an x-ray screen one at a time, which a technician monitored. They were then led into a small room and ordered to strip down to socks and underpants. The cable ties were now cut, as escape was impossible. A white-coated man pulled on a surgical glove and waved Roberto forwards.

"This is not necessary after been x-rayed," said Bill.

"I am following the orders of the father."

Roberto was pushed over by the four guards in the room, then it was Phil's turn next. The guards seemed to be enjoying themselves. Roberto limped back to where Bill was standing.

"Are you alright; do you need a hand?"

Roberto forced a smiled. "No thanks, I have already had a one."

Bill did not want to play his cards to early, but he certainly was not going to submit to this humiliation.

"I am the new prophet. You will not lay a finger on me."

The four guards looked at each other, then walked over to grab Bill's arms from behind. It was then that they saw the tattoo on his back and hesitated. Bill flexed his muscles and, with the help of the ball, the tattoo seemed to come to life. The guards stepped back in confusion.

"What are you doing? Bring that man over here."

"He has the sign of the renewal. I will not touch him," said one of the men.

"Rubbish; the true prophet is waiting in the temple."

"I am the true prophet and you are starting to make me angry." Bill bared his teeth and rose a metre into the air while clenching his fists. The white-coated man backed away and ended up against the wall.

"Tell me why I should not tear the servants of the false prophet to pieces?"

"How can you do that? You have not got the power," the man stammered.

"I do not need a trinket to work the wonders of the river god. He has bestowed the power to the new prophet."

The man fell to his knees and the guards followed suit.

"Forgive us, we did not know. Have mercy on your followers."

Bill lifted the man from the floor, then floated across the room. He stopped with his face inches away from the man's.

"You will not speak of this to anyone, or I will make you my first sacrifice."

He pushed the man away, who landed on top of the others. Bill sank back down to the floor and smiled.

"Why did not you do that before our holes were a searched?"

"Because you two are not prophets; that's why."

He helped the men up from the floor and dusted them off as if he was a concerned friend.

"You will behave normally or die. The choice is yours."

They all nodded. Bill and his companions dressed. When they left the room, the officer outside noticed something wrong with the white-coated man's expression.

"Is everything in order?"

"Yes. Nothing was found."

He gave the man a searching look, then signalled his men to reform, ready to escort the prisoners. The captain turned to the white-coated man.

"Do not believe what the white man tells you. He is nothing without the father's power."

The group set off again, led by the officer and the captain. Fifty metres along a passageway, they arrived at another steel door where the officer placed his hand on a screen again. It slid open and the captain's side arm was removed, along with the officers'. He and the senior officer would be the only two allowed to enter with the prisoners.

Chapter 130

On the other side of the door, they passed into another world of flickering torchlight and huge blocks of stone. Uniformed guards were nowhere to be seen. They had been replaced by warriors armed with spears and bows and arrows. Dressed only in loincloths, the flames reflected from the oiled skin of their muscular bodies. White stripes painted on their cheeks signified that they were ready for battle.

Bill thought that he had been transported into a scene from *King Solomon's Mines*. There were no prizes for guessing who would play the part of the wicked witch.

He looked around for the pass card arrangement on the other side of the door, and was shocked to see one warrior pulling a lever.

They now stood on a ledge-like balcony, which seemed to be reserved for temple guards only. A long ramp led down from this, through the middle of what looked like a Greek theatre built of semi-circular steps. About five hundred people dressed in white stood in rows, looking down onto a raised platform at the other side of the huge cavern. Another ramp led up onto this, where a group of about forty men dressed in western clothing stood. Centre stage contained a massive stone altar with a waterfall behind it. A woman could be seen chained to each of the pillars on either side of the altar.

Roberto grabbed Bill's arm. "Look, Sara and Monica. They are still alive."

Bill gave him a reassuring smile. "Yes, but we are not out of the woods yet. I wonder where Nabusano is."

For him to wait on the stage for Bill to arrive would have been a loss of face. He must have some grand entrance planned.

Roberto pointed. "There is Marco and the commandant standing with those men to the one side."

"Yes, they must be the sons from the mainland. I wonder why they are separate from the other people."

"Those guys don't look too happy," commented Phil.

"Nobody down here looks too happy, if you ask me. This water must be coming from the lake." Bill pointed at the waterfall. "Where does it go to?"

"Gotter be pumped out from below. Could be pumps with long drive shafts so the motors stay above lake level. That way you don't lose your pumps if they break down."

"Makes sense, but they would lose the bottom two levels for a while."

"Why the heck are you interested in the plumbing?"

"Just thinking of another way out of here."

"They could be using submersibles, where the whole pump stays underwater. For that, they would need a service shaft to lift the pumps up and down."

"So if one was to follow the path of the water, it should lead to an exit shaft."

"Yep, I would say so."

They now walked up the ramp onto the platform lit by a line of torches along its edge, and stood between the sons from the mainland and the altar. Six priests wearing headdresses of feathers instructed people where to stand. Bill cast his eyes over the audience made up of men, women and children. This must be the whole population of the island, except for the men on duty. He wondered how they would witness the ceremony until he saw a camera fixed into the roof of the cavern. This seemed to be the only technology Nabusano would allow into the temple. Bill had been worried about getting the message across to the men on duty about him being in charge; the camera would solve that problem.

Drums started to beat on the balcony where the warriors were gathered, and a doorway in the front of the altar slowly slid open.

Bill nudged Phil. "Here we go. The man has his own special entrance."

He glanced up at the camera and saw a small red light glowing. It was probably activated by someone in the control room.

Horns started to blow as a throne slid forward from out of the altar. The figure sitting there, wrapped in the brown robe of a chief and holding a staff, took Bill and his companions completely by surprise. They thought it the corpse of a dead man until it moved.

"I have summoned you all here to witness the long overdue renewal. The phoenix will arise again from the ashes."

The thin, reedy voice echoed throughout the chamber. "The stealer of the power will now give to me what is rightfully mine."

This sentence ended in a fit of coughing. Nabusano signalled to the captain, who proudly stepped forward with the box. Bill was prodded forwards with a spear of one of the priests. Now would have been a good time for him to take over, except for two of the priest holding knives pressed to the throats of the girls. The captain handed Bill the box, who presented it to the seated figure. Nabusano's face cracked into a smile. The corner of his mouth split open in the process.

Bill shuddered at the thought of himself ending up like this in three hundred years' time.

He was then pulled backwards by the priest, away from the altar. Nabusano slotted the staff into a hole at the side of the throne and placed a charcoal-coloured ball into a recess on the left armrest.

That was the first ball, which Nabusano had seen shining in the waters of the river two hundred and fifty years ago.

The heavy box pressed on the bones of the prophet's legs as he lifted a cord from around his neck with a key fastened to it.

He unlocked the box and sat with a fixed grin on his skull-like face, savouring the moment. Then he pointed at the sons from the mainland.

"You, the blood of my blood, have failed me. You have been contaminated by the outside world. The penalty of failure is death."

He raised his arm and warriors rushed in from both sides of the platform with spears. Other temple guards on the balcony lifted their bows, ready to fire at the trapped men.

"The false prophet and his friends I will destroy myself with the new power."

Nabusano turned to face the audience. "You, the followers, I have no further use for. The renewal is for me to start a new beginning in a distant place."

Bill was pleased Nabusano had shown his true intensions, but things were now moving very fast. He would have to take some action very soon to save as many lives as possible.

Nabusano pressed a button on the arm of the throne. "The countdown for the retribution has now started."

Phil grabbed Bill's shoulder. "Holy shit, he has activated the rockets. Do something."

"The descendents of the slavers will be punished."

Nabusano opened the box and stared at the contents. He picked up the table tennis ball and glared at Bill with fiery eyes. A small automatic appeared in his hand as he turned to the captain standing near the altar.

"You fool; this is not the power," he screamed.

He pushed the box off his knees, and the ball bounced over the stone paving, making a *click, click* sound. With a snarl, he shot the captain between the eyes and raised his arm again. A volley of arrows flew towards the sons. Bill pushed most of the projectiles over to one side, but some of them fell among the warriors. The commandant had shielded Marco's body with his own and now lay dying in his brother's arms. The temple guards reloaded their bows. Bill tore off his shirt and raised himself into the air, while watching the priests holding the knives at the throats of the girls. They stared up at Bill and the blades were lowered. Bill flicked them away to land into the waterfall. Roberto ran forwards and lifted Sara's tied wrists from the hook she was suspended from. The temple guards hesitated from firing again at the confusion on the platform and the floating man. Bill raised his arms and turned slowly in the air. He noticed the red light of the camera still glowing.

"I am the true prophet." He pointed at Nabusano. "This evil old man planned to kill you all."

Nabusano glared back at him. "So the power is inside your body."

He smiled and lifted another cord from around his neck. It held a small silver whistle, which he placed between his cracked lips and started blowing. No sound could be heard, but the effect on Bill was dramatic. He fell heavily onto the stone paving and rolled around in agony.

"Cut open the white man," shouted Nabusano at the priests. "The power is trapped inside his body."

He continued to blow the whistle every few seconds. The priests and some of the warriors encircled Bill and moved slowly forwards, carrying knives and spears.

"Stop him blowing that a whistle," Roberto shouted at Phil as he unhooked Monica from the other pillar.

Phil charged towards Nabusano, but was confronted by the pistol aimed at his head.

"Prepare to die, descendent of slaves."

"I am of the family N'gou and not afraid of death. My ancestor was taken into slavery as a boy by King Agadja of the kingdom of Danhomey."

The hate in Nabusano's eyes turned into wonder, like a flame going out. "You are the descendant of my little brother?" he stammered, touching the charcoal-coloured ball next to him.

"Yes; he survived. We are from the same father."

Nabusano saw in the other's eyes that this was true. The pistol started to shake and the whistle fell from his quivering lips. Phil removed the weapon from the old man's hand and, accidentally knocked the dark-coloured ball from the armrest of the throne. It landed on a flagstone and shattered into a million pieces in a cloud of grey dust.

Bill recovered and rose again into the air. The attention of the priests and the temple guards were now focussed on Nabusano. He offered his claw-like hand to Phil as the last breath left his body.

"Get out of here now," he whispered.

"Tend to the wounded," Bill ordered the warriors.

He landed next to the senior officer. "How do we stop the countdown?" he asked.

"I do not know anything about a countdown. What are you talking about?"

"There are missiles inside the hill and Nabusano pressed a button on the throne to start the countdown."

"We must get to the control room. I do not know if it can be stopped from there."

A rumbling sound, then a gigantic crash, shook the temple. The doorway was now covered by a huge block of stone, crushing some of the guards underneath. Bill turned to one of the priests and pointed behind the throne. "Where does this passage lead?"

"To a small elevator. It is now the only way out."

"I must get to the control room. Get as many people out as you can."

The waterfall behind them started to increase in volume, until the noise of its roar vibrated throughout the chamber. Bill waved at his companions to enter the passage. He pushed one of the priests and the senior officer in first. The tunnel led to a waiting lift, into which they all managed to squeeze.

"Phil, get off on the next floor and find your phone. Tell Watson I am in charge and that Nabusano is dead. Don't tell him about the countdown or we are all goners. Take this priest with you in case you come across someone who doesn't know what has happened."

After dropping Phil and the priest, the officer pressed the button for the control room.

"Roberto, you and the girls carry on to the roof and take the helicopter to the crocodile farm. Tell the pilot to contact the control room if he refuses. Phil will phone Watson to come back out here with the chopper. We have to convince the Americans the danger has passed."

Bill and the officer jumped out of the lift and ran towards the control room. There they found the control room staff gathered around the monitor displaying the scene inside the temple. Most of them had families trapped inside the chamber.

"The rockets inside the hill," shouted Bill. "How do we stop the countdown?"

"The hill section is totally separate from us. It has its own control room."

"Shit, can we contact them from here?"

"Yes."

The controller turned a switch and a screen lit up, showing a technician. Bill grabbed a microphone. "The countdown, can you stop it?"

"No. Once the father pressed the button in the temple, there is no provision for stopping it. That is part of the system design."

"How long have we got before ignition?"

The technician glanced to one side. "Fifteen minutes and forty-five seconds."

"Are the doors open yet?"

"No. They open five minutes before launch."

"Wait a minute; if the doors don't open, the countdown will stop. The system will not fire a rocket at a closed door, will it?"

"No. It will detect that the door is not open."

"Turn off the power to the doors."

"We are in lockdown. The power for the doors comes from the substation in the blockhouse to the right of the harbour entrance."

"Is there anyone inside who can switch the power off?"

"No; access is denied during lockdown."

Bill turned to the officer standing next to him. "Have we anything that can destroy that blockhouse within ten minutes?"

"There is a high-velocity gun inside the harbour wall. If it fires at the same place, it will eventually breach the wall."

"Order it done now!"

Bill switched his attention to the situation in the temple. He could see on the monitor that the water was covering the floor in front of the platform. Some people were escaping through the altar, but that would soon be under water.

"The smoke from all those torches must go somewhere. Where does it go?"

One controller pressed a button. He pointed to the screen in front of him with the caption of temple ventilation.

"There is an extraction duct and a downdraft duct in the roof of the cavern. Both have heavy metal grills over them."

"It will take hours to drill and blast a way through that stone blocking the door. Also, the entrance will eventually be underwater. It will also take hours to block the water coming in from the lake. The only gate is probably the one that Nabusano opened. Have anything light weight that can float placed where those ducts pass through the floor above the temple. I will head the rescue operation myself."

The island had turned into a hive of activity, with groups of uniformed men running in all directions. A klaxon sounded off as the gun inside the end of the harbour wall slowly lifted. Both cruisers left the harbour in search of the place where the lake water was rushing into the temple. This would not be easy in the darkness.

The officer called out to Bill as he was running towards the lift. "The elevator house on the jetty is blocking the target for the gun."

"Fire; blast it out of the way. Do not waste a minute."

As Bill rode down to the floor above the temple, he heard the *thud, thud* of the jetty gun.

*   *   *

After four rounds, the structure halfway along the jetty had virtually disappeared in a cloud of smoke and flames. Now the shells were exploding in the same place on the thick blockhouse wall, gradually eating a way through. Showers of concrete fragments burst from the wall, exposing the embedded reinforcing bars. It would only be a matter of minutes before a shell could penetrate and explode inside, destroying the substation.

Chapter 131

"Mr. President, we are ready to fire the missile," announced Henderson.

"That FBI guy; what's his name?"

"Jones, sir."

"Can we trust what he told Watson? That this Englishman has taken over from this Nabusano guy."

"Sounds very unlikely. He could have been forced to say that under duress. How could three men take over from an army?"

"How the heck should I know? I'm asking you the godamn questions. It's my ass that's on the line now."

Henderson rubbed the middle of his forehead. *These politicians are all the same when it comes to the crunch. Indecisive, gutless assholes.* He was pleased he didn't have to call the shots on this one.

"There has been no evidence of a takeover, sir. The only thing that pans out is that the helicopter has left for the mainland. Could be it's not going to pick up Watson. Could be it's that wacko escaping before his ICBMs are flying."

"Why would he fire at us? He has all that stock on the American market. He would have to be a crazy son of a bitch to do that."

"Yes, sir."

The president glared at Henderson, realising that he was the only one carrying the can. He would go done in history as the guy who let some wacko destroy half the world, or the guy who nuked Africa.

"Something is happening down there, sir," called out one of the men observing a monitor.

"There has been a lot of activity over the past ten minutes."

"Like what?" asked the president, his voice raised.

"Men running around all over the place, and now some sort of fire fight on the pier."

"Who is shooting at who?"

"Don't know, sir. Looks like they are shooting at themselves."

A group of top brass surrounded the monitor, with Henderson and the president in the middle.

"Get that Jones guy on the phone," called the president. He turned to Henderson. "See, I was right not to fire."

"Holy shit," called another man on a second monitor. "The doors are starting to open. They are going to launch their ICBMs."

"Fire!" shouted the president. "Fire our missile."

Henderson shook his head. "By the time our missile gets there, those birds will be long gone."

"Fire anyway. It's not my fault we are too late. I order you to fire."

"The doors have stopped opening, sir. They are only a quarter open."

"What do you want me to do now, Mr. President?"

Chapter 132

Phil listened to Watson on the phone.

"You expect us to fly out there? That place could be nuked at any minute."

"With you here, they won't do that. Will they?"

There was a moment of silence before Watson answered, "I really don't know."

Phil polished his glasses. "So what do you suggest?"

"Do something to show that Parker is in control there."

"Like what? The substation that hooks up the power to the missile doors has been destroyed. What more can we do?"

"Switch off all the radar stations as a sign. Something like that. If you do that, I will haul ass over there."

Phil ended the call, deep in thought. Bill was not here in the control room. His own people in the states didn't trust him, and the controllers here sure wouldn't follow the instructions of an American. There was too much at stake. He would have to find Bill.

He boarded the elevator with the officer and pressed button 4B. The picture of the temple in the control room showed that the altar was now submerged and the water was still pouring in. He stepped out of the elevator into a hive of activity. One of the ventilation ducts lay to one side like a crumpled piece of tinfoil, exposing a three-metre, round hole in the floor. Bill was now busy concentrating on the other one, which started to tear away from the concrete ceiling. Phil peered down the first hole and saw two men with cutting torches working on the steel bars of the heavy grid five metres below. The sounds arising from the hole filled him with fear. Through the smoke and steam that glowed from the torch flames, he could hear a multitude of wailing and crying, like a scene from the very gates of hell.

Four men in coveralls pushed him to one side as they slid a heavy steel girder across the hole. From the centre, they hung a chain block, which they fastened to the middle of the grid. The men below held onto the chain with their left hands and continued cutting around the edge of the hole. Bill had finished ripping out the second pipe, which now lay in a crumpled heap with the other.

"Bill," Phil shouted. "Watson says to give them a sign that you are in charge, like switching off the radar stations. Only then will he come here. He thinks they still might nuke the island."

"I'm not turning off the radar. Just now the whole place is crawling with Americans telling me what to do. This is my island."

Phil stared at him in surprise. Could be Bill had turned into wacko number two already.

"They are afraid of the silos," Bill continued, and turned to the officer. "What kind of doors are on the hill?"

"They were built before my time, but I have seen them from the outside. They slide open sideways."

"Good, that means we can park something on the top to show the Americans we are not going to open them. What have we got?"

The officer shrugged. "We have tractors and trailers that work on the farms."

"Good, you and Phil organise that. I'm a bit busy at the moment."

The lift arrived, full of empty plastic containers, which took a couple of minutes to offload before Phil and his companion could ride up to ground level. The officer led the way to a garage containing a few military vehicles. They jumped into a jeep and sped off, followed by a truckload of men.

*   *   *

Out on the lake, the men on one cruiser noticed a small whirlpool in the beam of a searchlight. It lay close to the outside of the left harbour wall. A diver jumped over the side with a rope around his waist, which was slowly fed out from the craft. The pulling force on the rope gradually increased until the cruiser had to reverse engines to pull the diver clear. They repeated the exercise again with a pack of explosives fastened to the rope, which was played out to its full length. When the suction started to draw the cruiser towards the whirlpool, the pack was detonated. Water and stones rained down onto the vessel, causing some superficial damage. When they looked again after the explosion, a part of the lower section of the harbour wall had collapsed. The crew cheered, confident that the water inlet to the temple was now blocked.

*   *   *

The grid in the ventilation shaft broke loose and Bill lifted out the two men. He then lifted out the grid as the engineers moved the girder over to the other hole.

"Throw down the plastic containers," he ordered.

A floodlight was lowered at the same time, because most of the torches in the cavern had been extinguished. The roar of the falling water suddenly stopped, seemingly amplifying the cries of the people struggling in the water. Bill floated down into the temple, while the containers rain down all around him, landing in the water. A shower of sparks cascaded down from the other grid as the engineers began to cut the bars. The balcony packed with people still stood above the surface, but the majority of them splashed around, trying to stay afloat. Bill singled out the ones who looked as if they were drowning, and lifted them out of the water. He formed them into a group of about ten, then lifted them through the open shaft in the roof. This process he repeated every three minutes until the panic below had subsided. Most of the people now either stood on the balcony or floated around, clinging onto a plastic float. The ones who had drowned would be submerged. Bill could not bring the dead back to life. Their bodies would be recovered along with Nabusano after the pumps had removed the water.

Chapter 133

Henderson lit up a cigarette, not caring what the president thought. They sat as far from each other as possible in the intelligence room, drinking coffee. Neither of them could leave until the situation had been resolved one way or the other. He checked his watch and saw it was six in the evening. This sure had been a heck of a long day. John Collins walked into the room, holding a piece of paper.

"Hi John, how are you this evening?"

"Fine, sir; just fine. What did you want me to do?"

Henderson swung round in his chair. "I want you to phone that boy of yours, Phil Jones, and ask him if everything is okay out there. I want you to recognise his voice and then ask him what his national security number is. He is using one of Watson's phones. There's the number." He pointed to a slip of paper on the desk.

"Why the heck don't you phone him, sir?"

"Because I don't know him, and we are busy here trying to decide whether or not to push the button on a Trident."

Collins' jaw dropped open, then he noticed the president and smiled, lifting his hand in a greeting. The president forced a smile and nodded. Henderson pointed again at the phone number.

"There you go," he said.

Collins picked up the phone and dialled, then waited a few seconds.

"Hi, Phil; it's John Collins. How are things there?" He smiled and nodded, then covered the mouth piece. "Yes, that's Phil. So what's that noise I can hear? You're driving a what?" He covered the mouth piece. "He says he is driving a tractor. So is everything okay where you are?"

Collins frowned, then covered the mouth piece again. "He says the doors have no power, so the missiles can't fire. They are busy parking tractors on the top."

Henderson waved his hand around.

"So what's your national insurance number, son...? Yep, I'm feeling okay. I need it for something." Collins looked at the paper in his hand and nodded a few times. "Thanks, son. You want me to tell them what?" Collins put the phone down. "He says check your monitors and get Watson out there."

"Thanks, John. We will have to play golf together one day soon."

Collins took that as a dismissal. He raised his hand and smiled at the president, then left the room.

The president got up and walked quickly over to Henderson. "What's he say about tractors and monitors?"

"Dunno; let's take a peek and find out."

They went over to the monitor, where the chief of intelligence was sitting. Henderson rested a hand on his shoulder. "What's happening now?"

"Lot of engines moving around on infrared. They are moving up the hill and stopping on the top."

"Jones says they are parking tractors on the doors. Does it look that way to you?"

"Yes, that would explain everything."

"I'm going to phone Watson and tell him to get his ass out there."

He looked at the president, who nodded.

"I think the boomer can stand down, but stay in position."

The president nodded again, while Henderson called Watson. He put the phone down and lit the last cigarette in the packet.

"Well, that was running a mite close for a while there, but you ended up doing the right thing. Pity we can't tell the voters how well you did." He forced a smile and nodded. "Good night, Mr. President."

Henderson walked out of the room, leaving a grey-faced president staring at the palms of his hands.

Chapter 134

The helicopter landed back on the roof of the tower, and Watson and his group were escorted to the control room.

Bill swung round on a swivel chair to face them. "The hill complex is still in lockdown, so it could be morning before you get inside."

Phil polished his glasses. "The doors for the missiles are blocked. You can check that out right now if you want."

Watson nodded. "Yep, that sounds good."

Bill held up his hand. "Now here is the deal. You have access to anywhere you want to go, except the vault. The missiles in the hill you can dismantle and remove as scrap. Any bomb grade plutonium, you can take away. Any information in the vault relevant to your national security, Phil will hand over to you. The names and addresses of Nabusano's agents, I will give to you. You can use them or just leave them as sleepers if you want."

Watson nodded. "Okay, all that sounds good. What do you want?"

"All Nabusano funds will remain where they are. Nothing will be frozen or interfered with. You will only be allowed fifty of your people here at any one time. My people will assist your people if required. I am in total control of this island. Any attempt by any government to take control will be resisted. None of these points are negotiable. Are we clear on that?"

"Yep, loud and clear. What are you going to do with the people here?"

"They will have the choice of leaving or staying. I will start paying them a monthly allowance into a bank on the mainland to do with what they want. Any military installation here is purely a defensive deterrent. You could even set up an office here to keep an eye on things, if you want."

"Okay. Let's get everything in writing. I don't think there will be a problem with any of that. What do you want this island for?"

"I have some plans of a peaceful nature."

"What about the government in Mabarta?"

Bill smiled. "Leave that to me. I have two government representatives here now. I just saved their lives, so I don't expect any problems from that direction as yet."

"Okay. We will go up on the hill, then I will report back to my boss."

They shook hands, but eyed each other like a cat and dog in the same room. Watson and his group left to examine the doors on the hill.

"Phil, phone Ken to pick up John, to be here first thing in the morning. I want you to go to the vault with him and find something really mind blowing on the Republican Party. All any government thinks about is staying in power. I don't trust them an inch. Look for something like Water Gate."

Phil smiled. "My pleasure. I'm a democrat."

"I wouldn't look so smug if I was you. There's probably tons of stuff about what they have been involved in. Lucky for us, politics is a real dirty game to play."

"I reckon I'll phone Roberto to see if he made it home with the girls okay. What plans have you in mind for him?"

"He can come and work for me at ten times his salary, or stay with the construction company if he wants. Same goes for you, Ken and John. I will finish the dam and supply the Malenga area with free power. Companies will be falling over themselves to set up shop there. The surplus power, we will sell for running costs."

"John told me a whole heap of things about Nabusano and the local president. What are you going to do about that situation?"

"There are elections at the end of this year. We will be sponsoring our own candidate. No cloak and dagger stuff. I'm sure the best man will win. I just so happen to have the right man for the job. I'm sure he won't refuse."

"Is he a politician from Mabarta?"

"No, just a school teacher in Malenga who is trying to do the right thing."

Bill was starting to feel good about the situation. Everything seemed to be heading in the right direction. The renewal had actually happened, but not how Nabusano had envisaged.

He suddenly felt tired and rode up to the apartment on the top floor. One room was fitted out as a movie theatre with only one seat. He sat down with a double brandy in his hand, and pressed a button on the armrest. Charlie Chaplin appeared on the screen.

Epilogue

Early the next morning, Bill held a meeting with all the surviving sons. He outlined his plans for free power for the Malenga area, and told them that the businesses they controlled would become their own. The only stipulation from his side would be the control of the overseas stock and the Swiss bank accounts. John drew up an agreement, which all of them signed.

Nabusano's body would be cremated and the ashes cast over the waters at the source of the river.

Phil and John spent the rest of the morning inside the vault, poking around among the files and tapes stacked on rows of shelving. They eventually emerged with a file and two cassettes, which Phil transferred to a CD.

Watson and his team examined the reactor and the rockets inside the hill. They removed some key components from the missiles, disabling them. The reactor had just been ticking over for the past thirty years, producing electrical power for the island.

Bill invited Watson to a private viewing of the CD in the theatre room. Both of them were shocked by the revelations contained on the disk, and sat in silence for a while, turning over the implications in their minds.

Bill spoke first. "This assassination information is forty years old, but I'm sure you realise what the world reaction would be. Everybody loved that guy."

Watson nodded, finding it difficult to speak. "Sure." He cleared his throat. "What are you aiming to do?"

"Take a copy of this with you to show your masters. Tell them if I have any problems with them, I will download to CNN."

"Are you fucking joking? I'm not touching that disc with a six-foot pole. My life wouldn't be worth a nickel. I know some of those guys."

Bill shrugged. "Okay. Then just tell them what's on it. If something happens to me, someone here will download."

Watson nodded. He wondered how much his life was worth just now. "Can I tell them that last condition applies to me as well?"

"Yes; if it makes you feel better."

"Yep, it sure as hell does. Lock that fucking thing up again."

Bill slipped the disk into his pocket and they both walked out onto the balcony. He waved for an assistant to bring some drinks.

"What did you find inside the hill?"

"The reactor is no problem. It's too big for you, but like now, if you pull enough rods outer her, she is just like a small one."

"And the rockets. What's the situation with them?"

"All obsolete. Built years ago, with a few upgrades. The single warheads are primitive, gun-type fission. Thirteen kiloton."

"What sort of damage could they do?"

Watson swallowed his drink in one shot. "Could make a nasty hole in a city. One-mile radius obliterated. Five miles on fire."

"Wow, twelve of them could have made a hell of a mess worldwide, considering the fallout."

"Yeah, but not like modern multiple warhead ICBMs. You know what I don't understand?"

"What?"

"The targeting. None of it makes any sense. Four of them were aimed at England. All sea ports like Bristol, Liverpool, Southampton and London docks. Some aimed for South America. Lot of coastal cities in the southern states, and some European port cities."

"I don't want any media involvement in any of this."

"Don't worry on that score. All this is top secret. The chosen few ant likely to spill the beans."

The assistant refilled their glasses and backed away from the table. "Not a bad spot you have here. These guys treat you like the lord and master."

"I can't help it if they think I'm JC superstar."

Watson started laughing. "You know one target that crazy sonofabitch had lined up?"

"No."

"A stupid little fucking village in the north-east of Benin, for Christ's sake." Watson laughed again. "Can you fucking believe it?"

Bill sipped his drink, looking out over the lake. "Yes. I think I can."

*   *   *

The helicopter took off for Mabarta with Watson and his African assistant on board. He didn't seem to fit in with the others, and had spent his time walking around with big eyes.

Phil arrived on the balcony, looking as if he had turned back into a zombie. Bill pushed the bottle and the ice bucket over to him. "What's up with you?" he asked.

"I'm not sure if I want to go back in that vault again. There's a small room with an old cup in there. Looks about two thousand years old."

"Is there anything else like that down there?"

Phil polished his glasses. "In the corner is an old, carved, wooden box on something like a wooden stretcher."

Bill lit a cigarette. He hadn't quite kicked the habit.

"Does John know what they are?"

Phil poured himself a stiff drink. "No, he has never been in there before."

"Are you thinking what I'm thinking?"

"Yeah, must be something pretty valuable to somebody."

Bill thought for a while. "I think we should lock the door and throw the key away. Some things in Heaven and Earth are best left alone."

Phil gulped his drink down and poured himself another. He replaced his glasses and nodded.

*　　*　　*

One of Watson's team, being a medical man, was not involved with the rockets in the hill, so he took a guided tour of the island's medical facilities. The laboratory had been working on stem cell research for the past twenty years. He swirled the clear liquid around in a small bottle from the fridge and peered at it, holding it up to the light. The label on the bottle showed a code number, which he typed into the lab's computer. He stared at the screen for a good five minutes without moving. What he held in his hand was the cure for cancer.

Bill stood and looked out over the harbour. "When the repairs are finished on the substation, we should close the doors and pour concrete over them. The rockets are disabled, but the concrete will give some extra reassurance for those who need it."

Phil finished his drink. "Sounds good. Other people's fear is our biggest problem."

He joined Bill standing at the balcony wall. "I have decided to work for you. I couldn't handle going back to my old job after this."

Bill smiled. "Good. I want you to start gradually selling all our stock in the auto industry and the banks. Rather invest in gold shares and environmental protection projects like wind turbines and hydroelectricity."

"Why the change? The stocks you have are doing well."

The sun broke through the cloud and bathed the island in its glow. Bill breathed in the cool, fresh air from the lake and turned to face Phil. "Last night I dreamt. We are busy destroying the planet and heading for a point of no return. All men are motivated by profit and will not stop until it's too late."

"Why sell auto and bank shares?"

"The banks are giving out too much credit. There is going to be a worldwide recession."

John arrived on the balcony holding a piece of paper and approached Phil. "I found a list of people on the take in American government agencies. Do you know an FBI man named Lozano?"

Bill was not listening. He was thinking about the future.

About the Author

Harry Peterson was born in the north-east of Yorkshire at the end of the Second World War.

After a technical engineering education, he became bored with life in England due to repetitive work, so spent the next thirty-five years as an expatriate in Africa.